D1482336

Originally published in Slovenian as *Galjot* by Pomurska Založba, Murska Sobota, 1978
Copyright © 1978 by Drago Jančar
Translation copyright © 2011 by Michael Biggins

Library of Congress Cataloging-in-Publication Data

Jancar, Drago.
[Galjot. English]
The galley slave / by Drago Jancar ; translated by Michael Biggins. -- 1st ed.
    p. cm.
"Originally published in Slovene as Galjot by Pomurska Zalozba, Murska Sobota, 1978."
ISBN 978-1-56478-690-6 (cloth : alk. paper)
I. Biggins, Michael. II. Title.
PG1919.2.A54G313 2011
891.8'435--dc23
                        2011031305

Partially funded by the University of Illinois at Urbana-Champaign, as well as by grants from the National Endowment for the Arts, a federal agency, and the Illinois Arts Council, a state agency.

The Slovenian Literature Series is made possible by support from the Slovenian Book Agency.

In cooperation with the Slovene Writers' Association—Litterae Slovenicae Series and Vilenica Festival.

This project has been funded with support from the European Commission. This publication reflects the views only of the author, and the Commission cannot be held responsible for any use which may be made of the information contained therein.

This translation was supported by a grant from the Slovenian Book Agency.

www.dalkeyarchive.com

Cover: illustration by Nicholas Motte
Printed on permanent/durable acid-free paper and bound in the United States of America

The Galley Slave
Drago Jančar

Translated by
Michael Biggins

Dalkey Archive Press
Champaign / Dublin / London

1.

Dense layers of air. Slime creeping up the walls. An arrival from out of the swamp. Plague commissars afoot in the land. One strange introduction, one drunken beginning.

Dark spots of dampness were contorting on the wall. In the dead silence he could have sworn they were slinking together and apart, forming incomprehensible images in their monstrously slow motion. Down below it was wet through and through, the wall saturated to blackness with some slimy liquid that was pushing imperceptibly upward, toward the spots and their contortions. In between some whitish fluid collected into drops and then slowly slid back down into the swampy dirt floor. It was as though the chapel had grown out of the earth, as though all this damp, runny slime were saturating it and at the same time dragging it back down into the swampy ground. He reached his hand out toward the wall and felt the warm, supple slime on it. Goose bumps shot down his back and he flinched at the touch of this dead, living substance.

This sudden agitation dislodged him. His eyes were drawn from the walls to the gate and the dark opening behind it. He went up to it and for no reason took hold of its cold iron fixtures, and he shook the grate so that the door's lock gave a hollow clank. Inside there was a squawk, immediately stifled. He pressed his face up as close as he could and waited for his pupils in their anxious orbits to pierce through the darkness and make out the shapes inside. The walls were rough and covered in some kind of whitewash that had turned gray from the dampness. There were wet spots shifting around here, too. Toward the back he could make out at first a heap of rags and then a tall figure that rose up out of them. A young man with symmetrical but clumsily chiseled and etched features on his face was standing tied to some pillar right next to a stout and bare, black cross. An arrow was sticking out of his shoulder, its tip buried deep in the flesh, with black blood gushing out of the wound beneath it. It must have been red at one time, he thought, and the walls must have been white. The arrows stuck out of his chest, his legs, everywhere on his body—this immortal had been shot through and through. Behind his pale, white face there hung a ragged, tattered flag. ST SEBASTIAN stretched across its folds and its faded pink field. Only now did he notice a shorter fellow on the other side of the cross. This statue was slightly bent, leaning its back against the altar. A pilgrim or a beggar or something dressed in beggar's rags. One hand was pointing at a blistery boil on its thigh, and something ran out of this festering wound too, something thick and shiny, some kind of smear oozing out. Both of them looked upward, both of them had their gazes fixed firmly on the black ceiling of heaven.

In the silence he could hear only his own breathing. Only his breath and the drumming in the pipe of his throat and his oral cavity as it drew in and expelled the dense air. Those two in there were stone silent. The black cross stood motionlessly between them, facing him. He wrenched his whole body around and with abrupt yet still measured agility he dislodged himself once more from that knotty torpor.

After this he didn't look back at the chapel or the slime creeping over its walls. His wet boots waded through low grass. He could feel damp bunches of stalks lashing at his legs, their thousands of little suckers grabbing hold. It was hard going. The atmosphere was dense with humidity. Warm steam rose up from the ground and got under his skin. He felt something cool on his forehead and when he reached up, globs of a wet substance were sticking together there too. Sweat streamed out of his pores and his eyes misted from the strain. Painfully he pressed on through the dense layers of air. He walked across a grassy land bridge. To the left a swamp shifted its warm steam lazily amid its motionless high growths of reeds and darnels. From the right, dense undergrowth gaped at him and black and red sphericles shone between creeping, clinging vines. Fetid dead nettles pressed in on him with their dizzying smell. The sun stood high in the noonday sky. Its persistent glow shone through the dense mixture of air and fluid substances. He gasped and chased after the pockets of pure air amid the swollen element pressing in on him from all sides, preventing him from moving faster.

Eventually the underbrush broke and he pressed through the opening in among the trees and into the forest. The air was no better here. The lichenous mosses steamed just as much, but at least he could move more freely. The terrain sloped slightly up and he could sense more light up there among the tree crowns. He walked straight up the slope. When he reached the top, he walked face-first into a gauntlet of thorns; black, shiny berries dangled before his eyes. This was the edge. Alongside it ran a path, with green, level ground on both sides of it.

He sat down in the damp grass and threw his heavy bag on the ground. He wiped his wet forehead with his sleeve. He couldn't go on. The air was soft and unctuous. It pressed him to the ground. Now he knew: if he got up, he would have to slog through it like water.

A bell rang somewhere close by. The sound grew muffled and vanished in the sagging air. Then he caught the sound of many voices coming to him in waves, and before much time had passed, they were murmuring right behind him. Along a forest path a slow and undulous clump of people was moving through the misty, porous tissues down to the grassy flatland. As in a dream, first a brightly colored banner with bulbous little cherubs perched all red against its blue field bobbled past him overhead, and then the murmuring crowd in their holiday clothes gradually etched itself into the mist.

He got up, flung his bag and saddle over his shoulders, and followed the last of the herd. He tried to talk to a straggling old man, but the latter just kept mumbling to himself and lifting his eyes into the precipitation above him, toward the blurry sphere in the sky that stood in for the sun. He refused to be put off. He kept walking alongside the hunched old man, who kept falling farther and farther behind the rest of the procession. He'd have to get someplace eventually. This pilgrimage had to finish somewhere.

The wagon trail pushed back into the forest and then bit into a steep slope uphill. Now the ground beneath his feet turned muddy and slippery. Small, stinking puddles decanted their stale liquid into the holes left by their footsteps. The old man slipped several times. It looked as though he was about to fall and tumble back down the hill. He looked around bleary-eyed and then drilled into the stranger with his stare. The old man's fingers felt distrustfully over the fellow's face and clothes before coming to rest on the saddle. Then he said in a slow, tentative way, as though still considering whether to say anything at all, "Where's your horse?"

He threw his bag up over the saddle and took such tight hold of it with his right hand that it twisted his back. With his left he took the old man by the arm and slowly drew him toward the edge. He wanted to get into the trees, but the path was in a ravine and the slope was as slick as if oil had been poured over it. At first the old man tried to get away, but then he yielded to the other's firm grip. They proceeded slowly to a place where the path assumed a gentler slope. There they stopped and then headed into the trees, where it was easier for them to advance.

It was only then that the stranger answered.

"I left it down below, in the swamp. I think it has mud fever. I drove it through the puddles too hard while it was overheated."

"Well then you boil up some ash," the old man said, pleased to be able to speak expertly. "And some pine cones. And then you use oil to spread that onto the horse's legs every day."

The stranger kept looking ahead. He could see the sweaty, tottering animal with the dampness spraying off its hide, coming to a sudden halt among the grapevines and staring vacantly ahead, unable to move forward or back.

"It was oozing a lot of pus already," he said after a while. "There was nothing I could do."

The old man became taciturn again. His distrust had returned all at once, and he kept his eyes stubbornly fixed on the ground.

"We got lost in the swamp," the newcomer tried to explain. "I didn't find my way again until the chapel."

They walked on silently. The forest began to thin out and down below wooden huts with black straw hats began to appear. The procession wended its muddy way through a village. A few dim figures rushed out of the mist enshrouding the houses and joined up with the pilgrims. The stranger and the old man picked their way downhill slowly and carefully. Outside the first clump of houses the old man began to fidget and mutter, as though hoping to take his leave.

"I thought maybe I could get a little warm milk or wine," the stranger said.

The old man wavered. His footsteps were leading him elsewhere, but the stranger's voice held him back. He sized this man up once again with his bleary eyes, then came to a decision. Come on; he squinted and turned onto a narrow path between two wooden fences, heading into a hive of blackened hovels.

The village was virtually empty. A few hens scattered underfoot and a few pigs refused to budge. The stranger sensed some motion behind the window of one of the houses. When he looked back in that direction, he glimpsed a woman's face darting out of sight. A few paces on and the old man shoved aside a wooden cover to reveal a yard dominated by a great heap of manure sitting in the middle of a single, stagnant pool of stinking water. He pointed the stranger to a log outside a wooden hut, called out something, and went inside. Moments later a woman's wizened face framed in limp strands of gray hair appeared in the doorway. She nodded encouragingly.

He sat and waited. An impatient stream of words came from the house. Back among the other buildings something darted again, and then a plump little woman appeared right next to the fence. Did he recognize this face? Had those black eyes been sizing him up before? There was something razor sharp in their anxious pupils. She dug into him, her hips swaying.

Then from the doorway there was a sudden shout of "whore" or something like it, and the little woman whooshed back in among the other buildings and out of sight. The old man was standing on the threshold with a dish of milk in his hands. He splashed his way across the puddle and offered it to the stranger.

He gulped down the warm slop until large drops of sweat reappeared on his forehead.

"A lot of whoring and rutting going on," the old man said, as though he were answering a question.

"Indeed," the stranger said, eagerly accepting this opportunity for conversation. "The air is so strange here, humid and hot all at the same time."

"Heat and bad air," the old man whispered confidentially. "Makes people susceptible to especially vile and vicious demons."

"Is that why everyone's praying?" the stranger asked.

"Yes," the old man said. "All the signs are here. Sickness is on the way. Only Saint Roch can save us."

He wasn't going to waste any time. Muddled old men were always making crazy prophesies.

"A horse," the stranger said. "Where can I buy a horse?"

"Not here," the old man gasped conspiratorially. "All the horses here have died. The innkeeper. In the next village down this road."

The stranger heaved his load back onto his shoulders and waded across the stinking puddle. The air really is strange here, he thought. Down below, on the path between the two fences, he heard someone call to him. He turned around and saw the old man standing motionless, staring at him goggle-eyed.

"You won't get far!" he called out.

He stopped again mid-afternoon and asked for the way to the inn. A sturdy fellow with sleeves rolled up to his shoulders showed muscular arms that were sunburned up to the elbows and white as milk above that. With big strokes he lit into logs with his ax so hard that chips would go flying and the logs would fly in two with the first blow each time. He was friendly and good-natured. So was the slender woman with sharp features who appeared in the doorway of the barn, wiping her hands on her apron.

"Straight ahead," he called out. "You'll be there soon enough." He stepped inside and brought out a wooden bowl of fruit brandy. "In this heat," he said, "it helps you walk." He told the stranger that travelers often stopped at his house. Sometimes they would even stay the night. He could, too, if he wanted. The fellow was talkative and inquisitive. But the stranger did not feel like wasting words.

"I have to keep going," he said. "I need a horse."

Clumsily he tried to thank his host, but the latter waved it off. "Be careful, then. The innkeeper is a brute," he said and strained his face trying to wink.

The road began meandering through some grassy swamp again. But this time it was easier. His destination was close.

Even so, the atmosphere remained saturated with warmth and humidity.

It was night when he reached the inn. Some light shone out of its windows. He banged on the door. Something moved inside and then someone opened the door a crack. A scent mingling smoke, wine and bodies wafted out through the gap.

"A bed for the night," the stranger said. The door opened and a fellow with a twisted, ill-humored face let him in. The light in the room came from two or three candles placed on the tables and the flame of an oil lamp in the corner, fluttering in the draft. Several men were sitting around one of the tables with jugs of wine, speaking in subdued tones. Everyone turned to look when the stranger came in. The other tables were empty. He threw his bag and saddle onto a bench and collapsed onto a vacant seat in the corner. Wordlessly the innkeeper set a jug of wine before him and sat down across from him.

"You come a long distance?" he asked.

"Mhm," the stranger replied.

The innkeeper glanced toward the neighboring table, where the men were straining to pick up their words, and he leaned in still closer, over the jug.

"Don't worry, I'm not in the habit of asking a lot of questions," he said.

He got up and went to a door that led further into the house.

"Guest for the night," he called out.

"Need his horse fed?" a male voice yapped, and a head covered with a tangle of shiny red hair appeared in the doorway.

"No horse," the innkeeper said, nodding his head toward the stranger's gear.

He gulped down some porridge with large chunks of fatty meat swimming in it. Then he couldn't hold out any longer. His eyes squinted from the smoke and fatigue and he could feel all the heat, all the humidity, and the dizzying steam of this long day course through his whole body. He called the innkeeper, who slowly got up from the next table.

"I'll need a horse tomorrow," he said.

The innkeeper's eyes grew lively and interested.

"It won't be easy," he said and his eyes darted over the stranger's clothes and bag. "Horses aren't easy."

"We'll talk tomorrow," the stranger said and went upstairs following the red-haired fellow, who stopped at a door and handed him a candle.

"It's so you won't be scared," he said, smiling as the shadows flickered over his face.

The stranger shoved his bag under the bed and locked the door behind him. He put a dagger under the pillow and began to undress. His attention was caught by a printed icon that lay on a wooden bench next to the candle. It was a picture of that same vagabond he had already seen somewhere, but drawn bright red. His hand was pointing to a boil on his thigh, which was oozing a bright fluid. In the chapel, this morning, that's where I've seen him.

He lay down and with his eyes shut looked at this red specter of Saint Roch. In his nostrils he could smell the humidity and the dizzying steam rising up from the swamp.

The innkeeper was waiting for him with a big smile on his face. It was a warm morning and all the signs were that the sun would dispel at least some of the humid muck that had been poisoning the air. It hadn't cleared up yet, but it was already a bit easier to draw air into your lungs. The innkeeper's face no longer showed a trace of the previous day's ill humor. And yet he greeted the stranger with such a strange smile—did we sleep well?—that in spite of all this good cheer the newcomer still felt his chest squeezed by some anxiety.

That passed once they'd sat down to talk.

"I have a horse for you," the smiling innkeeper said. "But I'm afraid you won't need it."

The stranger looked at him, confused.

"No, don't look at me like that," the innkeeper chattered. "There's no need for you to be in any hurry. This morning we had a visit from Justice Albin, a real big shot around here, and he said they've got visitors in town."

He paused and set some wine down on the table. Even though there was no one else in the room now, he leaned confidentially toward his guest.

"The plague commissar," he whispered.

The stranger shrugged his shoulders. It looked like the big news made no impression on him whatever. Disappointed, the innkeeper leaned back against the wall.

"I see you have no idea what that means," he said. "The office of the deputy of the provincial duke has issued a decree on plague roadblocks and quarantines. Nothing has happened yet. There's no sickness. Just preventive measures. The thing is, no travelers can be out wandering the land.

Now it seemed as though the man understood what was at stake. "I can't move on?" he asked.

"Ah, at last," the innkeeper sighed in relief. "You've got it now. You can't move on."

He sat back up and observed his guest carefully. The stranger took a swallow of wine and seemed quite calm. Then he drummed his fingers on the table and this movement betrayed the fidgety sequence of thoughts uncoiling inside his skull.

"Well, actually, you could go," the innkeeper said soothingly after a while. "But they're stopping and searching every stranger who passes through, and thoroughly. Not everyone is partial to that."

He stood up and went to the door.

Wordlessly the stranger stared at the red drops of wine that slowly slid down the side of the jug and gathered in a bloody puddle on the table.

All morning he rode through the surrounding countryside. The innkeeper had sold him a good horse. He looked at the gentle green hillsides that the horse negotiated so easily. It was humid, but pleasant. Once the sun finally drives this steam off, this will be a fine, pleasant place.

At noon he ate quickly and withdrew to his room with a jug of wine. He looked at the small red icon and poured out a glass. He saw the old man in the red cloak standing by the fence between the black huts and calling after him, "You won't get far!"

Down below they could hear the loud, gnarled laughter from his room.

That evening he came downstairs, his eyes bloodshot, and sat down at a table alone again. By nightfall the inn was full—local people and traveling merchants. He heard them swear. If it's plague roadblocks, then no more fairs, no more loads to haul, no more pay. All they could do would be to sit at home and count their losses.

Clearly the innkeeper hadn't been lying.

Wine saw him through the following day, too.

On the day after that, the innkeeper came into his room. He sat down and looked at the stranger and was silent, and that's how he left, too—without a word.

That night he woke from his vinous sleep and thought he heard the lock clanking in the door. In the morning he decided to leave. He couldn't stay in this inn. One of these nights they were going to bury his wine-saturated corpse in the forest out back. One of these nights that shiny redheaded fellow was going to stab him while he lay in bed.

But the next morning was sunny. All the humidity and mist had been burned away. Out on the horizon the clouds pressed down to the ground and he could feel their hot embrace, but here it was bright and sunny.

As he was tying up his traveling bag, the door opened behind his back. He spun around and found the innkeeper standing there, leaning on the doorframe.

This time he said something.

"You're not well," he said. "I don't mean to pry, but you're not well. You shout in your sleep every night."

The stranger was silent. Then, smiling, the innkeeper added, "I really don't have any intention of holding you back, but it's my duty to tell you that pesthouses are being set up. Think about it."

He said this with his smile and then left his guest alone. This time something in the peculiar stranger had been touched. He sat down and buried his head in his hands. Doubts of some kind, questions of some kind, were building up inside him.

Slowly he untied his bag and headed downstairs. Two peasants were sitting in the tavern wordlessly with a jug of wine, filling their glasses. He pushed aside the jug that the innkeeper set in front of him and waited silently until the other two got up, paid, and left. He motioned to the innkeeper to come join him.

"I don't understand why you try so hard to keep me from my journey," he said quietly and calmly, "but you must have some reason for it. Are you waiting for just the right moment? Are you waiting to see if I'm traveling alone? If there might not be someone coming to join me? Are there very many bones buried in the forest behind your inn?"

The innkeeper smiled.

"There," he said, "it's possible to have a conversation with you after all. Until now all you've done is drink and gad about as if you were being hounded by some evil spirit. But now you've begun to think. As God is my witness," he said, "I've never been one to prey on lone travelers. I'm just warning you. It benefits me if you stay. It benefits you if you stay. A pesthouse is a vile place. And the grueling questions that the judges and investigators ask at roadblocks are even worse."

The stranger looked him straight in the eyes.

"I'll stay," he said.

The innkeeper nodded in satisfaction.

"But not in this inn, full as it is of your good intentions."

The innkeeper squirmed and started waving his arms in the air.

"This is the best inn," he thundered, "by far the best inn anywhere around. Everywhere else they'll just cheat you, worst of all they'll pry into your business. Not me. I welcome every guest."

The stranger kept his eyes fixed on the innkeeper.

"That's not the point," he said. "I want to find more settled lodgings. At least for as long as this idiocy lasts. I need a house, a place to live."

This brought the innkeeper to his feet. He paced uncertainly back and forth between the tables. Finally he came back to the stranger's and leaned on it with both arms.

"You'll stay?" he asked, perplexed.

"Yes," the stranger said.

"And you have enough money for a house?" the innkeeper said.

"Yes," the stranger said.

"And here I thought you were just some escaped galley slave," the innkeeper said.

That evening the deal was settled. The innkeeper came into his room with a definite offer. Nearby there was an empty house. He was not to ask why it was empty. He could move in. He would need to pay the innkeeper and Judge Joseph Albin in town, to avoid unnecessary prying. He could stay.

The next day he had a look at the thing. The house was abandoned, but in good shape. He would stay. That same day he went into town. He had a long discussion with the judge. He would stay.

The next evening he moved in.

And so he stayed. Suddenly, and under the influence of drink, he decided to confront his fate. Suddenly and simply he entered his story, with no end in sight.

He came at night and he came alone.

That's how this wretched thing begins.

2.

Pinpricks of some memory. The paws of a skeptical demon. Warnings from the Karolina of Styria. The new brotherhood. The just proceedings of Justice Lampretič. The dance of a swarm of flies under the skin, in the brainpan, the eye sockets, the arteries leading to the heart.

A bad conscience is a silent hangman or, in other words, something wasn't right with this man. Even when he first arrived, even at the very outset of this difficult, edifying tale. The fact that he was alone wasn't right, the fact that he came at night wasn't right, and the fact that the following night the lights kept shining and shining in his windows was worst of all. In these difficult times, with strange things happening in the air, the water, and on land, when the sin of the first man was taking possession, you might say, of every soul; when there was talk of witches conspiring day after day and night after night; when soothsayers and alchemists were pronouncing their formulas in secret; when secret brethren, Anabaptists, and other heretics were stirring people up and having intercourse on moonlit nights with wild, licentious women; when at one end of the land they had not yet forgotten "that bastard Primus and his fellows preaching that the

Virgin Mary was a whore," and at the other the law known as the Karolina of Styria had her forthright judge Lampretič and his colleagues condemning possessed women and men to torture, drowning, and the stake—in these difficult times, whose beginning and end we can't even determine with certainty, this kind of light in one's windows night after night was a clear enough sign of a bad conscience inside. It's quiet, it's mute, but it gnaws and gnaws, slowly and steadily. Such a conscience would dig in under people's skulls and weigh down on their chests in the night like an incubus. Everyone knew that each soul faced its own either/or, which learned men called predestination: either peace, honor, health, and goodwill here followed by glory there, or else tribulations, wicked thoughts, bad dreams, horrific illnesses, as well as thumbscrews, the rack, the torch, and whatever else the Karolina deemed fit here in word and deed, followed by endless torment there.

And if a person kept his lights shining at night, you could be sure something was not right with him.

But this wasn't enough to denounce a person. After all, a hard judiciary demanded hard proof. It's obvious that facts must be gathered about this person. And let no one be too concerned if later, elsewhere, other honest people come forward with entirely different kinds of information about this man—so different that at times we might doubt that they're talking about the same person whose edifying tale we intend to trace. For the moment let's believe them. These things were heard. These things were seen. And in the fullness of time, these things were known.

He wasn't from around here. He had never lived here before. He had come from the northern mountainous regions. This fact was ascertained and confirmed, based on his clumsy movements and his awkward speech, based on what he himself admitted later on. His name, Johan Ot, was a giveaway as to his origins, too. After he had migrated south, the whisperers confirmed, he had spent years wandering around Carniola. He had hired on as a hand with one after another landowner. He had learned the local language and made his money here and there. How he'd managed this was obvious enough to honest people—it certainly hadn't been through work. How much wealth and what sort of wealth remained a complete mystery. But wealth there was. He had a house, he had untended fields, he had a horse, and he had weapons. He lived alone. He renovated the house alone. He cooked alone. He rested alone. Did he sleep alone? Did he sleep at all? His eyes were always red and inflamed. A light was always shining. He had been seen walking around in the early morning hours, then again in the evening twilight. So he didn't sleep much, or at all. A person who doesn't sleep sits up through the wee hours, his dark thoughts spinning through the empty rooms or venturing out into the dead of night. A rat with its legs cut off hung over his doorway. A talisman meant to protect him. From whom? Or more likely, from what? Once he was seen catching bats, the birds of the night, another time he went wandering through the swamp, and still another he chased children away from his house, shrieking at them in a terrible voice. An individual who goes wandering, catching birds, and shrieking after children, who doesn't love those pure souls, is clearly burdened in his own, for whatever reason. He was accomplished in altogether too many things. He could ride, handle a gun, forge iron, do carpenter's work, and make shoes. He had books. So he read. But read what? In these difficult times, all kinds of books were making the rounds, teaching all kinds of knowledge. A person who read them could learn to think the wrong thoughts, or more likely fall prey to the demon of skepticism.

In truth, there was no shortage of facts. What's odd is that they didn't arrest him right away and poke him and jab him and pry a little.

No, all was not well with the arrival of Johan Ot. He was off to a bad start, a very bad start.

What was concealed in the memory of this spent person, what was simmering in the memory of a lunatic like this that caused him to rave through the night with those candles or whatever was casting that light, what was burbling and gurgling through his soul and body that caused his shadow to dance in his windows at night? To cause him all at once to seek out a home elsewhere and to flee or hide from someone or something? To do so many things to lead even the most patient soul to put pressure on him right away, right from the start? He'd already given them enough performances, already handed them enough facts on a silver platter to be of serious interest to Lampretič and his cohort. How easy it would have been for Lampretič and his cohort to come question him about that memory of his, or, in view of other evidence, simply put the squeeze on him and finish him off without a second thought. But Johan Ot hadn't come to this land to bring his unusual life to an end without further ado, just like that. No, the Karolina and all the other judgments are still ahead of him, as are the galley and plenty of other things that make our hair stand on end just thinking of them.

And, truth be told, this man was not to be trifled with. His past, about which we will come to know less and less the more the facts about him accumulate and interconnect, was certainly a part of his memory, along with a lot of sinewy life experience. Which is why he soon determined that he'd truly made an inauspicious start of his new life. In any case, this is the only way to explain the sudden change that finally allowed his neighbors to sleep more easily. For suddenly it appeared that he was really going to settle down here. One day, following the age-old customs of the local people, he began to rummage around outside his house. One fair day he went into town, quarreled with the toll collectors, haggled with the merchants, and ultimately drank himself witless. This was already an improvement. Now people could deal with him. He took on still other good habits. He spent time in church. He spoke about himself some. He worked some. Flirted some with the women. On a chilly, windy day he hoisted a child up onto his horse. He sang a foreign song to much laughter. He kicked a dog. Made a present of a cup. Fatted a pig and slaughtered it. Paced back and forth beside a roadside cross. Rang the bells. Gave up his wanderings through the swamps and fields. Moved some handsome furnishings into his house. Struck some deals with the town elders. Smote iron at the blacksmith's.

Except that the candle kept burning. And he kept gazing at the stars. And at times the dogs would still howl when his shadow roamed through the night.

In short, he made no promises, gave no real explanations, yet even so the whole business seemed to be quieting down. The people could tell that they would accept him, eventually. Oh, they would still grumble and whisper, but they would accept him even so. Slowly but surely they would reconcile themselves to his presence and perhaps he would even become one of them. But a bad start is still a bad start. People remember that.

He even bled a sick woman once and put an end to an epidemic of sickness. This is an important fact to bear in mind; otherwise it might be difficult to understand why people put up with and accepted him in this difficult time. Later, when events began to unwind in such unusual and startling ways, of course they whispered all kinds of things. That he had used his nimble tongue and fat purse to bribe Judge Joseph Albin and his colleagues. That even at the beginning the stranger was already in touch with some secret society. That there had to be some reason the authorities had left him alone for so long in these wicked days, in spite of all the signs. And remember that this was a time when it really wasn't possible simply to set out on a journey or move wherever you liked and settle down. People had far too sharp a memory of the physical and spiritual ills, inextricably bound together, that had been visited upon them year after year. Not a year had gone by without pesthouses being boarded shut, guards being put in place, and bodies being thrown into pits, for not a year had gone by without almighty God thundering his righteous anger down upon the sinful land. And he showed remarkable ingenuity in the process. One day he would send a horse trader, the next day a leatherworker, still another day a butcher, or some official or postman, even small animals and witches, to sow the seeds of plague among the people, despite all their security measures and all their precautions. If there was no other way, he would send a blue cloud by day or a poisonous wind by night. In short, fear was plentiful, and things were far from easy whenever the terrible sickness was preparing for its dance. And so it happened one sunny afternoon that the inhabitants of a cabin at the far end of town shrieked in terror as their mother lay dying. For the woman had a black boil in the pit of her underarm and sweat on her brow. She had collapsed in the yard all of a sudden, gasping and going pale. Some people ran into town for a priest, while others ran for a doctor, and still others locked themselves in their houses.

Who at that instant didn't think of the signs that people had been spying, not all that infrequently, in the heavens of late? Like the day when two subordinate suns had appeared in the sky? (The primary sun had been pale, as though ill.) Or of the night when they saw a blood-red moon gripping a fiery sword and a whip in its mouth? That night a woman had given birth to twins—one child black, the other white. And then there were the blood-red rainbows, and black dogs, and flaming church towers, and all the other signs and visions that passed through the land by word of mouth.

Perhaps Johan Ot was thinking of these things too. Perhaps he too had something trembling and throbbing around his heart when he was quarreling with the doctors from town and kept insisting that his was the correct diagnosis. The learned men wanted to isolate the woman and burn all of her belongings. But Johan Ot insisted that these weren't plague symptoms and that he had already seen this illness. Its one and only cause was an ailing organ overfull of blood, because too much stale, black blood had collected there. That blood had to be let out. They had to let it pour into the ground.

It's a known fact that in such circumstances blood must be let from a vein on the opposite side of the ailing organ, thus encouraging the stale blood to flow out. In rare cases it was acceptable to simply open a vein on the same side of the body on which the ailing organ was located. This method was less dependable. Altogether thirty veins had been identified from which blood could be let. The ailing organ itself could be laid open too, and then pungent herbs or medicinal peas could be placed in the wound.

The doctors knew all of this, all of these were familiar and trusted methods of healing. But the boil was black, and that was the whole problem. Still, they decided to let Ot try. Let him make the incision. Let him touch the boil. Let the newcomer perish, if he wanted.

Johan Ot did what he proposed. He made a nice, wide cut in the woman's flesh. True, she grew weaker and paler and she died a few days later, but she was the only one who died. There was no sickness. The signs in the heavens meant something else.

And so we could draw this tale of a stranger's sudden arrival in our midst to a close, because after this he gained our trust and lived his life the way people here had lived for ages. But we didn't accept him just so we could turn around and leave him in peace among the good and honest people of this land. He will drink his cup to the dregs, to the last drop. Because all of this—what he was doing, where he had come from—all of this still concealed some secret. Things are a long way from being as simple as they seem at first glance. Events yet to unfold will demonstrate this eloquently enough, although perhaps not quite so clearly to those who are strangers to the intricate ways of the spirit.

It started like this: a dissonant uproar came from the center of town, from the space where the bleak shanties huddled. Shouts, laughter, squabbling, all mixed together—that strange jumble of sounds when people assemble or are thrown together—unsettling. It was drizzling lightly and Johan Ot was all muddy when he came running up to the church. There was something for him to see there. Two hunched-over bodies, two naked human smudges, and gathered around them a taunting, guffawing, howling, bleating herd of other human beings. One of the two bodies was female, muddy, holding both hands over its crotch, which served as the crowd's principal object of ridicule. She squatted down and the screeching women just shrieked even louder. Let's see him mount her, they bleated, let's see him mount her like he's always trying to do. The man stared ahead, his arms limp, his head limp, his gaze limply fixed on the mud. With a pathetic little stump of a clapper between his legs in the cold and rain. Such were the wages of licentiousness. The righteous chastisement of the laws of God and man.

The woman looked up through the wet strands of her hair straight into Johan Ot's eyes. Her look ate into his pupils and its embers passed down into his entrails. He stood by and watched as the orgy of abuse by all the decent folk of the neighborhood went on and on. He heard a swallowing and wheezing next to him, followed by tortured, gulping, impeded speech, and he turned to see an old man whom the sight of this woman had completely undone. Lust had crushed him, as he grabbed onto his belly and chest. Ot felt that he ought to punch the old man in the face with all his might and then trample him, so that everyone would finally shut up and he too could at last be free of that warmth down in his guts.

But he didn't do a thing. He walked away. He never did anything. As always, something just drew him in and then pulverized him.

Some demon has a hand in this, that's all you can say, because on that day something like a demon must have got into him. He lay all night looking into the darkness. All the gloomy day, all the mud, all the herd, the rain, the two naked bodies, the stare through the wet strands of hair, those smoldering eyes, all the drink that he'd downed tonight, all that mess shifting and simmering and burning inside him. Toward morning the monsters began coming back, headless, tailless, shapeless, and bodiless they paraded around him, through him and out of him, so that he jumped up and banged his head on the wall. That helped, at least for a while. When he lay back down, the world began spinning its axis again and this lunatic room. He went outside to check on his guardian animal again, but outside, as the wind blew, nothing swayed over his doorway. The legless rat had vanished. Johan Ot froze and went pale with terror. His talisman against the prince of darkness was gone, long the guarantor of peace in his homestead. It was gone, and where else, but to the devil? He jumped to the ground and waded through the mud, grabbing and feeling each pebble, but in vain, Johan Ot, in vain, the little creature is gone. It escaped behind the house, uphill, into the forest, the wind swaying the crowns of the trees in its wake. He stumbled through the dark night until his muscles started to give out, until he felt a thin, slimy substance circulating through his body, until he'd expelled from his body all of the white-hot terror that nested in his chest and circulated through his veins to every extremity. He returned to his lonely dwelling limp, exhausted, despondent. He threw himself onto his bed, pressed his eyes shut with the fleshy part of his hands, and saw flames leaping everywhere. He took his hands away. On the hillside behind the house the underbrush was aflame. Bathed in its red glow, Johan Ot knew that some demon had a hand in this.

Nothing is concealed, everything is apparent—because there was someone else who knew about the demon too. He was standing outside the house, wearing a black cloak that reached down to the ground, his hair and face black, and holding a book. He smiled affably and looked at the bloodshot eyes and drawn features of the face before him, at the distorted and smudgy visage of Johan Ot, nighttime traveler. Something's not right with you, he said, something's badly amiss. Your mysterious wanderings at all hours, your face outside the church yesterday, the fire behind your house. These are signs. Trust me, you need to be aware of this. We don't care about your past life, we don't pry, but we're keeping watch now, here and now, so we do care about the why of everything. We're well informed, we're vigilant, and we know that these are dangerous signs. Every delusion, every anxiety haunting a person is a sign. It is up to you to submit to our aid and dispel the confusion inside you. With our collective power and the help of the Holy Spirit you can destroy that which is unclean. You run, he said, all the time you run. From whom? Tell me this, from whom? It doesn't matter that honest folk are weighing up the signs and the facts, that they say you fled from somewhere up north and then you fled from Carniola, that your family there weeps and laments your absence, that flesh of your flesh cries out for its father. What matters is that you always run and that the hill behind your house glows at night with fire. You are vulnerable. Let me warn you, there are dangerous nocturnal groups assembling in our land. The signs are that they'll come for you before long. I warn you, there is a spell on your house, and your books are suspicious. You are lost, the man said, caught in delusions and quarrels. This place is overrun with groups holding their bonfires at night. The red glow of those flames is everywhere. Let me make this as clear as possible: If there was ever a land where the prince of darkness ruled, furthering his designs through alchemists, sorcerers, and soothsayers, that land is ours.

Johan Ot tried to fix onto the black figure with his bloodshot eyes.

"Am I under suspicion?" he said. "A slight suspicion, a strong suspicion, an ironclad suspicion?"

"No," the smile answered. "Not at all. You're well informed. Those are indeed the different degrees of our system of law. It hasn't gone that far yet. But you've been warned."

More and more facts were reaching honest folk, more and more facts, although it wasn't clear where the facts were coming from and no one knew where they had been checked and confirmed. Ot had heard the emissary say that something wasn't right with him. Instead of living peacefully and enjoying the trust of the locals, he kept staying up at all hours and spending time with people of questionable intent. It was his own fault: he was digging a ditch for himself. Why did he need to go visiting Jewish homes or keep debating with doctors about the best medicines and incantations for various illnesses? What hellish curiosity drove him to barrage Judge Gregory Pregl with so many questions about the interrogations of secret brethren and the devil's other rebels? Why had he stayed up all night over wine trying to convince the learned and revered Doctor Ivan Gemmi that the mysterious inscription

S	A	T	A	N
A	D	A	M	A
T	A	B	A	T
A	M	A	D	A
N	A	T	A	S

was rife with meaning and a reliable defense against all kinds of disease? Why had he told Doctor Gemmi that populations about to fall prey to great misfortune and sadness are seized by unspeakable despair, and that the laws of God and man, the bonds of husband and wife, parent and child, brother and sister then cease to apply? That in the face of death by plague, man becomes a beast? That at some point on one of his journeys he had seen taverns full of people who, despite strict decrees by the authorities, drank with abandon, had relations with each other right and left, and generally carried on singing and shouting at all hours in their dens? That young and old had danced together like mad while bitter derision and frightful profanities were shouted out? That they had shamelessly, publicly engaged in the most revolting indecency? And why, after all, had Ot needed to ask the castle scribe whether Anabaptists really treated each other like brothers and sisters?

Soon persistent whispers streamed from house to house and such details began to draw a clearer picture of the taciturn newcomer as more and more was known about his life and deeds, his thoughts and dreams, his liaisons and enmities. He hadn't been in the area for long before all the trusted channels had produced a plethora of reliable facts.

What a criminal hole he must have grown up in! His mother a whore, his father a horse trader. He'd had the devil close by from the cradle onward, so to speak. He'd seen the inside of a jail quite young, in those lands to the north. He'd served various masters, beginning with adherents to the one true faith, followed by a series of heretics. He'd never been properly warmed by the light of the real truth. He'd gone on pilgrimages. What for? Certainly not in a true spirit of penitence. He had a wife and a child, but something had driven him out into the world. What precisely, no one knew yet. But they could guess. The hillside behind his house had been aflame and the fire went out by itself. A rat had disappeared, an animal without legs. His body had scars on it and carried a glowing fire inside. His eyes attested as much outside the church. His memory would get all tangled up and he would say one thing on one occasion, and something completely different the next. He didn't pay much attention to women, but he came running to the church when the punishment of fornicators was announced and carried out there. He often vanished inside a Jewish house in town. He would stay up with doctors and other learned people debating over their wine until late at night. About what, people would find out soon enough. The entire family of watchman Macel swore that one night a cloud of vermin of various disgusting shapes and sounds had hovered over his house.

And where did he go walking at night?

This question, the most critical question, in fact, will answer itself fairly soon. Altogether too many of these rumors had already entwined and entangled Johan Ot. So what if they were sometimes muddled, so what if the versions were illogical or contradicted each other, but they piled up nonetheless, people talked, and there was nothing good about that. Because it wasn't just anyone who was talking, but honest and upright people. And who was to be believed, if not them?

So now he had been warned. The man in black had made it quite clear. Now he would need to watch and wait. Something was going to happen. Something was going to draw him in.

In times like these it wasn't good if too many rumors, reports, and facts accumulated around a person. Sooner or later, somebody would sift and refine them, discarding the chaff and retaining the facts and the heretical fruit. But things just weren't that simple. There was no doubt that Johan Ot had been on the run. It was also certain that he had come to this place in search of peace. He wanted to be able to drink and eat and do what he pleased. But there was no peace, neither in this place, nor in him. Something was ablaze in his chest, something agitated the air around him. It's a known fact, of course, that the air contains not only the seeds of illness, but that evil spirits dispatch sinister thoughts on the zephyrs and whirlwinds the better to infect all the spaces that man inhabits, and that these insinuate themselves into people without their even noticing. All told, Ot had done a truly unfortunate job of choosing a refuge for his peaceful days. Perhaps he had thought that people had enough problems of their own—since they were continually beset by all the world's delusions as well as all the forces of good that did battle with them, the delusions—that they would scarcely even notice a newcomer. But it was just the other way around. He had too many bad habits and too many strange things happened to him and around him for them to be able to ignore him just like that.

For the land was truly being set to the torch. The smiling man with the black book was by no means mistaken on that point.

The prince of darkness really was looking to set up his bulwarks in the land, and righteous people had to fight him with all their means and might. This is why the illustrious and most upright of honest men, Justice Dr. Andrej Barth, had accused Margareta Klajdič and a certain old Julijana of consorting with the devil, causing illness, and submitting to Satan in all sorts of disgusting ways. Margareta was reluctant to confess, so the wise Dr. Barth had her stretched on the rack and her confession was not long in coming. Julijana died in jail. The good judge pardoned Margareta, and instead of burning her at the stake, as decent people expected and demanded, broken and battered as she was, he had her beheaded and only then burned. All of these facts must have been known to Johan Ot.

Six months later the renowned Justice Lampretič passed verdict in town on Urša Kolar. It was this trial that led to additional surprising discoveries that demonstrated just how widespread evil had become in this land. Urša Kolar denounced an amazing number of loathsome male and female monsters as molten tallow was poured on her feet and her face took on downright satanic features. It turned out that this brood was hiding everywhere, among Urša's friends and neighbors, among townspeople and merchants, among people whom no one would ever have accused of participating in any dangerous or heretical nighttime activities—though, of course, there was an especially large number of these conspirators among unusual people, people who were not very well known, or who had less settled routines. And the need to discover and destroy these wretches grew and grew. And miraculously, good fortune and humane treatment fell to Urša's lot too. She wasn't burned alive. She was garroted first, then burned.

Because of the wealth of reliable testimony it produced, the trial of Urša Kolar led to further investigations and trials. The labors of Lampretič and his cohort were not without issue. After painstaking investigations in the town and the surrounding countryside, they discovered a great number of men and women who, in league with the devil, had committed numerous criminal acts—thefts, murders of children, arson, the sowing of illness and storms, and so on. Some of these were drowned in the river that flows through the town, others were burned at the stake. The magistrates took pity on still others and merely had them bludgeoned to death. A few died during interrogation. Their corpses were then buried in remote, unconsecrated places.

Although this work had been successful beyond all measure, the evil had not yet been fully rooted out. Children would still disappear at night, and by day livestock were dying. There were fires, first here, then there. There were instances of honest, upright people being assaulted and beaten.

There was a great deal of evil.

Darkness and flames and blood everywhere, with people always concealing evil intentions.

And the worst of it was this: that groups were meeting which were proving difficult to detect.

One day Ot found he had restless legs, all day long his legs were restless—in the forest, in the fields, and at home. The heat pressed down so much on the shell of his cranium that the entire brain mass beneath it melted and sloshed, fogging his vision completely. None of the paths he struck out on suited him. He sensed barriers everywhere, everywhere he feared being intercepted by the dangerous delusion inside him, with no refuge in sight. His step was still elastic, but he could feel the tissues of his body giving out, the strength of his sinews dissipating, his heart beating louder and faster. He might not, might not, might not be able to take it.

He tried to run, but his legs gave out. He tried to sit, but that mysterious restlessness drove him out of his seat.

Nothing worked, absolutely nothing. He went inside and stretched out on his bed and listened to the beating and fluttering of his body.

Something touched his cheek, but it was so peaceful and quiet and delightfully gentle that he didn't flinch at all, he didn't leap to his feet or scream in terror at its moist touch.

He did none of these things. It was so quiet and moist and pleasant when it passed over his face, his forehead, his eyes, through his hair, touched and entered his chest, crept into his beating heart, into every restless fiber of his body, cooling his overheated blood, easing and quieting all of the voices so that he peacefully, effortlessly dropped off to sleep.

A deep sleep.

Johan Ot was within the grasp of sorcerous powers.

It was night when he woke up. The first thing he saw was the darkness, the window with dreamy stars glimmering in it, the black ceiling of his house, his peaceful, outstretched body, his limp arms alongside it on the bed. These things he saw first, and then he caught sight of those shining eyes locking peacefully onto his and then going farther and farther inside him. As soon as he saw those eyes he was completely in their power. They were so close to him that he felt a warm breath on his neck and his vanquished body happily hovered in space, minus its soul, minus its blood and aura, minus its heartbeat and pulse.

That moment lasted a very long time. Then she got up and in a flash of recollection he saw her humiliated body slumped outside the church surrounded by the multitude of respectable women, and he could hear the throaty rasping of the honest old man who was breathing audibly in the room just now, somewhere very close by.

All at once Ot was no longer surprised. She was here in this room full of ghosts and voices and suddenly he realized that this was the only possible world. She was here, and that made things so very simple.

That moment lasted a very long time. Then she got up and started walking back and forth, and he kept seeing her naked, humiliated, mud-spattered body, a beautiful body, as she walked back and forth faster and faster while the lights were being put out all around. This was the time of day when they locked the churches. She kept walking faster, but the room had her chained—she wanted out. Some of that restlessness he had felt during the day reentered him—the restlessness that had met its fulfillment in this moment, but now it was different, entirely different. She had come for him, she said, come with me tonight, and she drew strange symbols in the air, bending over him. You're ours, she said, we know that you're ours, come with me and you'll see where the real truth abides, the true face of the world and the spirit.

Outside the lights went out.

This was the hour of assembly.

He followed her out the door. It was a warm night outside. The wind drew through the darkness. Johan Ot could feel the symmetries of space shifting and he lost his balance as he felt his way after her. But she didn't even look back. With her eyes fixed firmly ahead, she was following a clear path toward her goal.

He saw some light up on the hillside and soon after that a silent group of people holding torches. He and the woman stepped into their midst and the faint, friendly murmur that followed was a fraternal welcoming. Lights approached from all sides, from out of the forest, over meadows and fields. Outside the village new ones were lit and merged into serpents rushing toward the same destination. Now Johan Ot was walking in line, blinded by the flame blazing before him, blinded by her body as it undulated with each lively step, and he listened to the panting and sighing of the wind in the crowns of the trees.

They reached a glade high up on a hillside. A man stood before him saying something. Johan Ot didn't hear a word of it, he just saw an oral cavity that kept opening right before his eyes and he sensed movement on all sides. This image: of a dark oral cavity right before his eyes, and all around the flickering of lights, and tiny figures in the distance that kept rushing closer and closer. The drumming of this shifting silence pressed down on his temples, causing him to reach his hands up to his head, to his hair and run his fingers through it.

Behind this cave of mouth, teeth, and tongue, behind this dark face talking and explaining things to him in every conceivable way, a huge fire was burning. New arrivals threw their torches into it and assumed positions on all sides of the visible glade, but most of all at its far end, on the edge of the forest clearing, where they merged with the shadows that flitted everywhere in sight.

Now the one who had been shouting at him, into his forehead, into his eyes, into his benumbed face, suddenly turned around and bent down to the ground. An invisible force pulled him lower and lower, causing his legs to shake and drawing him down with greater and greater force, until he collapsed, fell to his knees, and pressed his head to the earth. The whole multitude obeyed some command from the womb of the earth and even Johan Ot could feel himself being drawn down to the ground.

As he bowed, a razor-sharp thought flashed through his mind: is it here or deep in the ground? He set his head down as if on a block, and as he watched the flickering fire with wide-open eyes, he could hear.

There was movement and muffled drumming down below.

"I can hear it!" a woman with her hair let down shrieked at that instant and started dancing around the fire with abandon. From all sides the shadows replied, got up, and rushed toward her, toward the fire, and leaped into dance.

She lifted a burning heart high up in the sky and then set it beside the fire. At that moment the sound of bells came from a neighboring hilltop as the tongues of the fire reached up toward the crowns of the trees.

She leaped through the flames and landed, singed, on the other side. Now the dark shadows began wildly shooting through the blaze and then, embracing as couples, heading toward the edge of the forest.

He felt a damp hand on the back of his neck, then reaching down inside his shirt. When he turned around, he saw those shining eyes again, this time with the reflection of the flames in their pupils.

If he had known where he'd been that night, he wouldn't have slept the sleep of the dead like some bloodless corpse clear till midday. That afternoon he wandered around exhausted and confused and once again he didn't know which way to turn or what his mind was grinding down through all its crazy convolutions. He wanted some drink. Drink. But drinking alone at a moment like this, that would be even worse. He went to the tavern by the bridge. Some travelers had already gathered there—guards, scribes, and other employees of the local post and administration—the kind of people who've always visited taverns and will continue to do so for ages to come. When he entered, he felt a silence set in, and some necks craned at his arrival. He joined the guards at their table and soon discovered that his tales of derring-do, battles, and military campaigns weren't appreciated. Everyone moved to the far end of the table, leaving him alone.

He drilled into all the faces in the room with his eyes. Which of them had been there last night? The horse traders in the corner were gesturing with their strong arms and their wine-sodden heads. One of them spoke while the traveling merchant at the next table kept voicing agreement. Oral tradition, communication's state of the art. The new brotherhood was raising its head again. Horrible sacrilege. An underground organization with its headquarters in hell, with the devil himself. Its members were everywhere, hiding among the common folk, the townspeople, and the lords. There were bonfires up in the hills. This was just the beginning. They were assembling. Soon there would be assaults, murders, fires, revolt. The jails weren't full enough yet. Not enough of them had had their nails pulled out yet. They didn't talk, were as silent as the tomb. Satanic societies. Once people joined them, they were in them for life, with no going back. And, if that wasn't enough, black Madame Pest was wandering the land again. Roadblocks were up. And then there were the bonfires at night. Sorcerers. Very dangerous.

Ot's head began to spin from all the wine and information and the bizarre horror stories that these well-informed people were spreading from town to town. He wanted to pay and leave, when a familiar hand tapped him on the shoulder. He looked up and there, looming toward the ceiling in the dark, was the angular face of Doctor Ambrož, the master of medicine, connoisseur of logic and physics and fine wines. And now, Ambrož said, now you're going to need your amulet. What did you write on it? He gestured with his hand and winked an eye in the direction of the corner. Do you hear that nonsense, that gibberish that's flooding the world? And you're all alone. Not even the guard wants to sit with you.

Only Master Ambrož, that learned gentleman whom everyone needed, only he would sit with Johan Ot. To be quite frank, he said at the table, he had felt bad for him from the very beginning, since the day he'd first arrived. On account of those long nights over wine when he'd said and asked such strange things, and still more on account of those long nights when he'd gone wandering God knows where through the lonely forest.

Did he know, he asked, did Johan Ot know what a magic circle was? What casting a circle was? In these parts some people tended bonfires on Midsummer Night and visited roadside crosses at midnight. No, it had nothing to do with the brotherhood, good, ordinary Christians did these things, too. The ones who dared, who were brave, that is. The daring ones, the risk-takers would go there at midnight and summon the devil. They would draw a circle in the dirt with a birch rod and step into it. Once they were inside, the devil would come. He would bring money, anything a person wanted. But the thing had its own either/or. If you ran, if you got scared, if you didn't lash the devil with your rosary, if you didn't hold out inside your circle, you were lost. Your soul would be forfeit. So the moral was, you had to stay inside the circle or lose everything.

Master Ambrož had always listened to Ot's words, his tales from his wanderings, his experiences, and he would try to follow his thoughts. All those long nights over wine. Now, for the first time, he did all the talking. He said only this much and departed.

Johan Ot was left staring into his vinegary wine and thinking about this story and at last he understood. Now he knew where he had been the night before.

He had stepped into a magic circle.

The Karolina of Styria was serious business, which Ot would learn soon enough. So it should come as no surprise if the man in black with the books under his arm, the prayer books, catechisms, canons, and whatever else was stacked up there, if this time the man was no longer smiling. At all. He even refused the ham that Johan Ot ripped into with his healthy teeth. He looked at those white teeth, tearing and chewing the sinewy animal flesh, and the more he watched that steady, regular motion, the more unusual, if not downright suspicious, this whole business struck him. Who has teeth like that? Surely I don't. Strange, very strange.

Ot let him sit and wait. He said nothing. But the man was as cool and calculating as a serpent.

Then Johan Ot wiped the grease off his beard and looked and waited for the cold-blooded specter in the corner to speak.

In the meantime the somber, cold-blooded specter with the pale face drummed his fingers on his end of the table. Because the man knew well that the proverbial moment had come, and that now this business would get underway. So he kept his silence for a while longer, and only then did he speak, almost in a whisper.

There has been one warning, he said, and now here I am again. For the last time, in all likelihood. And not to chat, but on more serious business.

This time there would be no warnings, no admonishment. This time he would simply spell out the law for Ot. This time he would familiarize him with the fact that this land was governed by a law known as the Karolina of Styria.

And in article 109 of that law, we read (and he picked up a book and read):

Article 109.

If anyone causes injury or harm to another through sorcery, he shall be punished with death and that punishment shall be carried out by fire. If anyone resorts to sorcery without causing harm to another, he shall be punished as circumstance dictates, and the judges shall heed the counsels prescribed by the law.

The pages trembled slightly as the man held the book in hand, and so did Johan Ot.

What does this have to do with me, Johan Ot asked after a pause.

The other said nothing in reply. He just read his text.

Johan Ot knew full well that this was no joke anymore. The Karolina of Styria knew no loopholes, favoritism, or mercy. Its trajectory was sudden and straight. Judge Gregory Pregl had made him aware of this long ago during a night of hushed and persistent conversation. *In the beginning there is suspicion and that suspicion is recorded and noted. There is slight suspicion, there is strong suspicion, and there is ironclad suspicion.* This was not the time for him to reflect on the laws of this land, about its legal beelines, zigzags, and options. It didn't matter one whit anymore which of the suspicions now lay on Ot's scarred shoulders. Because for the Karolina, the signs alone were enough. It embarked upon each of its *stages* in quick succession: *preparation, presentation of proof, consultation and pronouncement of judgment,* and *execution of sentence.*

It was time that he pulled himself together, that he decided his own fate.

It was time that he waited for nightfall.

The brothers are with you, and so are the sisters, said the stranger who scratched on his window that evening on the side of the house facing the forest. Our group is united, no one will be left in the lurch. But I'm not being arrested for associating with members of some religious brotherhood, Johan Ot said, I'm being accused of some kind of sorcery. You're wrong, the stranger said, they're persecuting the new brotherhood, they're afraid of it, afraid of our old, deep, fundamental belief, our unyielding bond. Johan Ot didn't know that he was a member of some group, some brotherhood that was changing the world with fire and sword and faith in its own fanatical way. Whoever joins us for a night like that, the stranger said, is our brother. We'll rescue him, we'll always rescue him, even if we have to do it against his will. You were with us—our faith, the power of our faith will save you, our will, our unity, our community.

There were far too many words like that.

He had only gone there on account of that woman. Something had driven him there. All he'd heard was the drumming. He hadn't signed on for any program, hadn't signed any documents with the blood of his own heart.

Far too many words.

The man spoke too eagerly for Johan Ot to be able to believe that any sensible, effective association existed.

He left the chatterer and went inside.

No one, no outside help. He would clear his own path through the tangle of the universe.

His share of brains wasn't all that large, and it contained terrors, monsters, and hidden conspiracies. But at this moment his allotment was working well, the circulation through it was good, it thought ahead, and it thought fast. This was the moment when Johan Ot knew what to do with himself and where to go. His mind was working exclusively in his defense and for his benefit.

He was going to be accused, there was no doubt about that, and he might be arrested even tonight. Perhaps this was already the *preparatory stage*. He had been with a group of fire-jumpers. Now he was pledged to the new brotherhood. What did he know about them? Next to nothing. But he had been with them! They had leaped through fire and listened to the voice of the earth. They had gazed upon burning hearts. In the soft moss of a forested hillside he had sinned with a strumpet who had met with deserved punishment in front of the church. She had shaken the devil's own embers into his guts with her shining eyes. He would tell them this if they arrested him, if they reached the *stage of proof*. They had inducted him into their brotherhood, a dangerous, subversive cult. That's what he'd say if they arrested him, and a good deal more, too. He himself didn't know how he'd gotten mixed up with them, or how he'd gotten away, but these things didn't matter at all anymore. There were plenty of other dark portents and activities that he would no doubt turn out to be caught up in, if they arrested him. He was afraid of evil spirits, so he'd hung a legless rat over his door. But how that was going to be interpreted by the illustrious *iustitia*, headed by Lampretič, was a completely different matter. Sinister things were happening everywhere. Bonfires were blazing throughout the land and lone travelers were meeting their deaths in the most unusual ways. Livestock was dying. He was a stranger. The sentence would be pronounced. And carried out. The honorable Justice Lampretič was waiting for him with his men, who were paid on a set scale per number of needle-jabs, number of times the accused was set on the witches' stool, and every other method they could think up to hurt, burn, or break bones.

If they caught him.

By morning Johan Ot was already worlds away. He had given his horse free rein. The exhausted animal was contentedly pacing up a forested hillside, and he could feel its warm, pleasant, tired undulations, the gentle tensing of tendons and muscles, the twitching of its hide, and the smooth coursing of healthy blood underneath.

The morning, the trembling dewdrops on the leaves, everything was fresh, fresh. The mist shifting back and forth over the ground, the brush, the stream, not a path in sight—all true signs of the freedom that Johan Ot was riding into now, of the space that revealed itself to his eyes from all sides, with sheer openness everywhere. Behind him lay the night of that land, with all its evil deeds, its flames, its thefts, its witches, its beliefs, the evil spirits that its earth concealed in its womb, which went tramping about between the houses at all hours of the day and night, getting under people's skin and into their hearts, and taking possession of animals so that they dropped down pathetically onto their forelegs. All of this was behind him. All of the judges and doctors, the guards and peasants, the whole upstanding community, the man in black clothes and his damned, idiotic Karolina of Styria together with article 109, all the suspicions, all the stages, Lampretič and his men with their pay scale, the secret brotherhood with its beliefs and programs and bonfires and whips and leaps and sex. All of it, all of it behind him.

Before him was this morning with a dazzling white bell tower in the background, a blue sky into which the first rays of the sun were etching their golden colors, a morning with a night of flight and desperate riding behind it, this morning of beginning.

Flight—that was the only thing that could drive the anxious devil from your chest, the tendrils of magic spells from your blood, the fear out of your bones. Any minute he would begin anew, always afresh, always the next morning, always from scratch. Perhaps he would head for some new land, where warm, light-filled mornings like this one smiled, where the paths of righteousness are clear and good. Perhaps his path would lead him back to the mountainous northern land of his youth. Who knows?

Who knows the hour and day when, fresh of face, the night behind him and bright day before him, pure of heart and chaste of thought, he will enter his home.

This was the time of salvation, of firm resolve, glistening grass, and new paths.

By noon on the same day Johan Ot was walking back from that new world over the same forested hillside, except that now the sun stood high and all the pores of his exhausted body were wide open. Sweat streamed down his temples and face, and all he saw ahead of him was sun-blasted grass, no dew, no cool breeze, just glare and heat, and steaming lumps of dirt in the fields that shone in the background of this quite different scene.

So it was that Johan Ot was marched back with a court bailiff on each side and a worn-out nag behind him.

A swarm of fat, stinking, aggressive flies gathered over their heads, sticking to their sweaty faces, crawling under their shirts and under their skin, forcing their way into the fleshy folds and sucking Johan Ot's slime and his overheated, lethargic blood, only to continue their infernal, buzzing dance beneath his skin.

The swarming was unbearable. Ot longed to get into the forest, where it was cool and dark, but the threatening bucks on either side of him just laughed at his suggestions and pleas.

"You'll see how hot it can get, fellow," the first one said.

"All that drinking you did with our friends isn't going to help you one bit. You'll see how hot it gets," the other one said.

"When they slide the needle under your fingernails," the first one said.

"When they pour molten tallow on your feet," the second one said.

"When your bones burst and your jaw cracks," the first one said.

"When they give you another inch or two," the second one said.

"When, right at the end, they light the fire at your feet," the first one said. "That's the last time you'll be hot."

"When I beat and smash and bite somebody in their ugly face," Johan Ot said, and in the next instant both light and darkness collided with his eyes, as he heard a hollow explosion at the back of his skull, and then saw, way up above, in the glare, right next to the sun, a stocky face that was grinning and moving its mouth, as if saying something.

"What did he say?" he finally heard this oral cavity crackle from afar.

"That he's gonna stick it to that whore," he heard the other say. "I would, too, if I were him."

Did I say that, Johan Ot thought. While I was knocked out, from that rude and lawless knock on my head? Which is now the head of a lawless, criminal, worse than criminal beast? Was I just now talking about that damned, filthy broad?

The sun blazed past the swarthy face above him, which was just like the dark face that he'd seen against the background of the enormous bonfire. This sun dried out his mouth and made his cerebral cortex sticky and slippery. The flies beneath his skin went wild and pushed still deeper, into his brain tissue and eye sockets and through his arteries to his heart and the soft organs of his body.

Events had now taken on their own momentum and were transpiring so unexpectedly and yet so much according to the laws of nature that we simply don't have time for reflection or explanation. So we will keep our commentary for later and for now turn Johan Ot over to whatever future awaits him, despite his and our will. Save for the single observation that Johan Ot almost certainly would not have ended up in such unsavory company as this, whacking him over the head with a stick whenever it wanted and leaving him lying in the sun with flies swarming through his tender entrails—and just as certainly he would not now be on his way to see the honorable chief justice and interrogator, Justice Lampretič—if only he hadn't been betrayed by his own greedy nature, about which we've heard precious little till now.

The dewy morning through which he'd been riding toward his future had soon passed. Up went the sun and with it an emptiness and hunger in his stomach, because the refugee had taken very little food along. Coins and valuables, yes, and weapons too. But in the urgency of his flight and given the lack of ways he might have stowed it, very little food.

And so a void announced itself in his guts and got louder and louder, while against the morning backdrop a procession of white church towers passed by with little villages bunched at their feet. He stopped and stared at them for a long time. He still had some food left in his traveling bag, but how much longer would that last? And the horse? How far had he actually come? After a full night's ride, he must have gotten far. If he hadn't taken a wrong turn, that is; if he was still on the right path. So he stopped and stared and fretted. Then he wavered a bit. And then nature with its impertinent needs won out.

Close by on a gentle slope there was a house that surely must have contained something or other to sate his smacking lips, his mouth full of spittle, full of an eternal gluttonous lust for biting, chewing, and swallowing.

It was quiet and empty all around the house. The place smelled idyllically of human and animal shit. So there were people living here, so there was digesting going on: if they shit, they must also eat. At this Ot stopped thinking. He left his horse down below.

He walked uphill and into the house.

It turned out the house was empty. They're probably at work, gone early out to the fields. Normally he'd call out, he'd pay them something, but since no one was there, he would have to help himself. It was a nasty-looking place. Dim, stinking, dirty, all this obvious from the moment he walked through the door. The barest bit of light came in through tiny windows. When he entered he could see nothing. He walked around like a cat, feeling for objects in the dark. Then he straightened up and banged his head into the ceiling. He thought that something had moved in one corner. His eyes made out pots standing on some kind of built-in shelf. There's the food, such as it is, just as long as it's edible. He reached an arm out and his fingers took hold of some sort of dish. It slid out of his hand and crashed to the floor.

Now something definitely, very clearly moved in the corner.

He started and his eyeballs bulged from the strain of trying to see in the dark. Then he saw a heap of rags and some kind of figure on top of it, with two glowing lights up top, looking at him. Some kind of creature, something old and human was lying on the floor and flashing its eyes at him. He pulled the coin purse out of his belt and held it out in front of himself. I'll pay, he said, I'll pay, food—he pointed his fingers at his mouth—food, I pay. But whatever it was drew back on its rags out of fear, in mute terror it drew back and started to open its mouth. Ot moved toward it and shoved his purse out ahead and jingled it— I'll pay. Then the thing gave a throaty moan, followed immediately by such a blood-curdling scream that a shudder coursed through Ot's whole body, up his back and into his brain, and the screaming went on and got higher-pitched, making him panic—should I go to the door, run outside, or what? The shriek sliced through the air and suddenly, unthinkingly, he leaped over to the corner and slammed his hand down and struck something bony, and then he hit again until the screaming turned back into moaning.

That was better. Moaning is not screaming, at least, and it even sounded downright human, terrestrial, manageable.

Something very old and pathetic was shifting on the dirty mattress covered with rags. Shifting back and forth, it sighed and moaned, and at intervals hissed harsh, incomprehensible sentences at Ot. It could be a woman, a very old, very tired woman that they keep here to guard the house, as a guard dog, so to speak. His punch must have done some real damage. He could see that she was trying to scream again—after all, that must have been her job, they must have ordered her to do just that—and at that instant one last quick, lucid thought flashed through Ot's brain, that if he stayed in this house, things weren't going to go well for him. If it had come just a moment sooner, that thought—just a moment sooner—then everything, really everything might have turned out quite differently.

He turned on his heels and, hunched over, raced for the door. Outside he could hear voices, they're beating our Ma, somebody was shouting, somebody's beatin' 'er.

Too late.

The entrance was blocked by a thicket of bodies. You pig, we've got you now—the voices multiplied—smacking our Ma—and shouted over each other—get ready to meet your maker, you bastard, smacking and beating our mother, our poor, sick mother, and in her bed.

Too late.

He hadn't even managed to lift his weapon when the thicket tore into him.

They walloped him good. And once they felt they'd avenged their mother sufficiently and made him pay for her fear and pain—since they did all of this right before her eyes, while she hissed through her toothless mouth and moaned and even tried to take a swat or two at the thief herself, although this only caused her to fall back to the floor even more pathetically—once they felt they had done their duty, they even had him pay a fine for it all. They did this by relieving him of everything, absolutely everything he had on him. Then they locked him up in a pigpen, and that's where the bailiffs found him later.

They came around midday and laid a few more heavy, bloody lashes on him, but they didn't tie him up. That would have made it too much work to bring him back.

This is how Johan Ot found himself in such company in the noon-day heat, with flies getting under his ulcerous skin, as he trudged over the selfsame forested hillside whose fresh grass just that morning had been bathed in dew, where the first rays of the sun had streaked across the blue sky, where the morning should have been the morning of the beginning. He trudged over the forested hillside, down the path of his edifying story.

3.

The Declaration.

He sat hunched over, noiseless, motionless, in the black hole of the tower of justice, looking at the rats as they ran back and forth and watched him intently—the newcomer, the novice—with their tiny eyes. How long would he be here? When would he finally be lying here stretched out and barely breathing, unable to open an eyelid or move a limb, a nice, soft morsel for them? He sat there motionlessly, rooting endlessly through the strange muddle that had brought him here. Where was the stalwart fellow telling his tales of campaigns and battles, pounding his jug on the table, holding forth in learned company on all matters of mind and spirit, and speculating aloud on the healing arts, physics, and the beliefs of sects and societies? Where was the scarred and sunburned Johan Ot who carried his head high through village and town? This hunched-over shambles? Cowering and rooting about and thinking through this muddle, trying to identify the mistake that brought him here, digging and digging and waiting for questions without a clue as to how he would answer them? No, Johan Ot was not in an enviable position at all. Yes, he had a few things on his conscience that were causing fear, anxiety, and hope to gnaw and nip at his entrails. But otherwise, it's a good thing that he's here. Now, at least, we'll find out the who and the what and especially the why of Johan Ot. A thorough investigation has to produce a thorough answer, after all. We have plenty of tools at our disposal, and there is no shortage of basic facts.

Amazingly, Ot wasn't left to rot long amid the walls, the dampness, the cast iron, and the little black beasts. He was even fed. The investigation was to proceed apace. He was in their hands now and they wanted clear and quick answers to their questions. And they had quite a few of them to ask. They had the facts. When they first led him upstairs, he looked in vain among the interrogators and judges and other men for *his* lean face. No sign. Ot felt relieved. Because it became apparent from the very first questions that he was going to be able to answer them, and that fateful, decisive things were not yet at stake.

THE QUESTIONS

Had he been involved with a band of robbers in Carniola, prowled on lonely trails at night, attacked law-abiding people, and taken their money and other possessions?

Had he smashed a watchman's head into a rock on the bank of the Kokra River near Hoje, dragged him by the hair, and held him underwater?

Had he, disguised as a beggar, joined a procession of pilgrims at St. Lovrenc on pilgrimage day and tried to defile and violate a lady of the castle?

Had he stolen chalices from a church on an island in the middle of a lake?

Had he threatened upstanding people of the true faith by flashing the blade of a knife?

Had he beaten his wife, kept meat from her, dragged her by the hair while he was drunk, and taught her the false ways of a meatless life?

Had he taught his son to become a robber?

Had he stolen, and whence came the gold coins in his pockets and bags?

It wouldn't be necessary to stretch him on the rack, break his bones, beat him, hoist him on ropes, rip out his nails, or pour hot tallow on his feet. He was happy to talk. He talked on his own. He looked at the scribe who kept scribbling and scribbling, and on he talked. He knew that any instant things could turn serious, that any instant the trap could be sprung and that then his hide, his bones, his very life would be at stake. So he spoke well and wisely and precisely.

THE ANSWERS

I am Johannes Ott. I am from the Duchy of Neisse in Germany. I left my home because I wanted to live better, eat better, drink better, and sleep better. I wanted to earn my bread with hard and honest work. I have been an honest blacksmith, an honest wheelwright, and an honest cobbler. I have belonged to guilds and have worked in Bavaria, the Tyrol, Carinthia, and Carniola. I have served various masters and have learned to read. I have been in various wars against the heretics, but my hand did not shed human blood. In Carniola I learned the language spoken by the people here. I have never been involved with any band of robbers, as God is my witness, because I am an honest Christian. Quite the opposite, we would go hunting for bandits in the dark forests and at lonely crossroads. I have gone on pilgrimages, both to St. Lovrenc and elsewhere, this is true. But my wife and my family accompanied me. It is also true that I smashed a watchman's head against a rock on the bank of the Kokra, took him by the hair, and held him underwater, but only because he had stolen my sword and assaulted my wife. I did indeed go begging at St. Lovrenc once, but only because I had just arrived in this country and had nothing to live on. I did not steal any chalices, though I bought one at a fair in Loka. I have never committed any sacrilegious deed, not that time, not ever. I have never threatened anyone with the blade of a knife, or rather only in taverns and when I've witnessed fraud in the selling of indulgences. I've also drawn my knife when I've heard people preaching heresy. I did forbid my wife to eat meat, because she had vile meat-eating creatures in her belly that would sometimes come out in her stool. I beat her for the same reason—to drive those creatures out of her. I taught my son the true faith. I've earned any gold I've had with honest work. I have always greeted high-born ladies with respect and a bow from afar. I say all of this as the honest truth. I will gladly confess and repent anything of which I am guilty.

That part went well enough. He was glad to talk, and none of it was of any particular interest to them. True, during the questioning they scratched their chins, nudged, glanced, and winked at each other, studied and scrutinized him, turned up their noses, and leafed through sheets of paper. But they didn't lay a hand on him. They were merely trying to ascertain the true state of affairs, comparing the facts about him to his statements and really just beginning to prepare the actual investigation and presentation of proof. But we have managed to learn something about Johan Ot, even though his deposition did nothing to clarify the unusual sequence of events that led him so abruptly and so surely to the tower of justice, into the grip, the pincers of the legal process. Apparently we may assume that the peculiar fellow is not here to recount the convoluted paths of his past life. Though Johan Ot will speak on. Because next up are theology and metaphysics, those supremely serious questions about the ideas and beliefs of this era: fields expertly navigated by that famous master of the law, Justice Lampretič. This will be harder. Johan Ot belongs to Lampretič, and Lampretič will help him drive every unhealthy and impure thing out of his body. It will not be the first time that this worthy of the famous council of judges will ask such questions. It will not be the first time he solves a complex ideological riddle. Because the gaunt, bald, and pale little man who arrived the next day was the very man of whom history has recorded so many exceptional judicial feats. And that is why Johan Ot will speak on.

STILL MORE QUESTIONS

Had he often left home at night? When and how many times had he left home, and where had he been when he'd gone?

Was he also away from home on the night before the holiday of St. John the Baptist, the son of the priest Zachariah and his wife Elizabeth? Had Ot spent that night at a bonfire and in company that wished to use the holy day for their own wicked purposes?

Was he in the forest or out in the fields or somewhere else away from home that night?

Had he kept a legless rat hanging over the door of his house, and what did he think such an animal and such a sign meant?

Had he moved into an empty house and was there some spirit in that empty house, something in its air, had something crept in through the window?

In short, was that house bewitched and why had he moved into a bewitched house; why, of all houses, had he furnished a bewitched house for his sleeping and comfort?

Had he fled from Carniola or had he come here in good faith?

Had he also fled from the Duchy of Neisse, what and who, what kind of person and how many had caused him to flee from his homeland?

Had he given signals with his eyes to a strumpet being chastised in front of the church, had he subsequently led that licentious woman into his house?

Had he, for no known reason, struck an honest old man outside the church, and if he did not strike him, why had he wanted to?

Had he, for no known reason—for no reason known as yet—beaten an old woman in an empty house and shouted strange, unknown words that the honest mother of honest children could not understand, and which caused her to take fright when she saw his dark, angry face?

Had he drunk potions, what sort of potions had he drunk, and how had he prepared the potions?

Had he, to be specific, stood in a particular forest meadow on the night before the holiday of St. John the Baptist?

Had he held a burning heart aloft in his hand and reached toward the sky with it?

Had he listened to the language of the darkness and the earth?

Had he leaped through a fire?

In the forest meadow on that dark night, had he succumbed to filthy abomination and lust in the glow of that profane fire?

Had he on many previous occasions run deliriously across fields in broad daylight and in the dark of night, and what was burning in his chest and guts to drive him to run thus?

Had there been a glow and fire by his house?

Had there been above his house and above his roof a cloud of vermin of a welter of shapes and sounds?

Had he heard the swarming of a brood of flies buzzing beneath his skin?

Why had he fled from the Duchy of Neisse, that especially must be made clear, this was the key for Lampretič, why had he fled from the Duchy of Neisse, from the country in which so many things had happened?

Now his tongue got stuck. Now Johan Ot could get nothing to come out. He knew that they knew something. Witnesses had testified to something beyond the shadow of a doubt and under oath. Informants had whispered something in their ears. The ministries of information had gathered facts. This is why he refused to speak at first. This is why he gave ambiguous answers. They helped him along when Lampretič's man broke his nose just a little while they showed Ot their impressive, state-of-the-art equipment: the rack, the witches' stool, the tongs, molten tallow, pulleys hanging from the ceiling, and more.

They merely showed him the equipment, just took him on an informational tour of the tower of justice so he could see how perfectly it functioned.

He saw a live application of the thumbscrews.

This consisted of two small, sharp-edged boards connected by screws. A woman—from the looks of her it was almost impossible to doubt her sorcerous, demonic connections—a woman put both thumbs between the boards, which the executioner then screwed together, squeezing her thumbs with the regular motions of his steady hand. He squeezed and squashed both thumbs until blood came squirting from the nails and they became flat as a sheet of paper. She screamed and howled as the devil fled from her.

He saw a live application of the mancuerda.

Lampretič's man tied the same wench's hands behind her back so that the palms faced outward. Then he pulled on the rope so hard that it cut through to the bone and the wrist joints visibly lengthened.

This caused her to cry out, too.

He saw the witches' stool. This Styrian invention, known only in this country, was so perfect, so flawlessly and dependably and abruptly did it function, that it truly made a big impression on Johan Ot.

A bench about eight feet long stood in the middle of the room. On one end its legs were about four feet high, while on the other they were barely two feet high, causing the seat to slope. The seat also had multiple upturned edges which were sharpened from time to time. The individual was stripped naked, clothed in sackcloth, and set down on the bench's lower end, with his legs extending up toward the higher end. The legs were tied down so tight that the flesh bulged out from under the rope. Bound around the waist, the back and under both shoulders, the body hung from a hook in the ceiling. Thus the offending body hung in mid-air, unable to move. This wasn't painful to an individual with the devil inside him, or maybe it was—who can say. Johan Ot could tell it would definitely hurt him. He had no desire to try out Lampretič's apparatus.

And so he preferred to talk.

STILL MORE ANSWERS

I am Johannes Ott, originally from the Duchy of Neisse. I left my homeland because it had too many witches and the city authorities even had to build a special oven to burn them all. I have always been afraid of witches, so I fled to the lower countries, where I'd heard it was warmer and there were fewer liaisons with the devil than up north. Thenceforth I lived contentedly and went on pilgrimages and avoided all temptations. I left my home because my wife started eating more and more meat, which was being devoured by sorcerous spawn in her entrails. The other reason I came to Styria is because I'd heard that the sickness had left lots of abandoned, empty houses behind and that I'd be able to find a house here for nothing. I did not signal to that adulteress with my eyes and I did not beat the old man in front of the church, but ran away. I do not know if I was in the forest meadow, I slept poorly that night. I did not yield to lust with that woman. I had nothing in my body or my thoughts that caused me to run from country to country. It was underbrush that burned behind my house, I know of nothing else. I know of nothing else to say.

That may be so if you're a decent person, Lampretič said, if you speak kindly to people and treat them well. He said this and rushed out the door with his minions behind him. No, Lampretič was not happy with Johan Ot, far from it. The only truthful statement he'd made had been that there were a lot of witches in the Duchy of Neisse. But this they already knew—this was an old and widely-known fact. They wanted something quite different from him, they were looking for traces and tracks that would lead to a true motivation for Ot's actions. But because Lampretič was known for his persistent, yet humane investigations and means of uncovering fact, he held off giving the order to test Ot on one or another of the devices for finding the truth. Even though Johan Ot had already reached the proof-presenting stage as defined by the letter and spirit of the Karolina of Styria, even though Lampretič could have had him tried and tested there in good faith and in complete conformity with the law, the judge gave it one more try, out of the goodness of his heart. He summoned the witnesses.

Justice Gregory Pregl: I am deeply ashamed and repent the fact that on several occasions I spoke in private with Johan Ot, the accused, the facts of whose life are now being presented before this our court. I did this with the sole intention of enriching my professional expertise, because the accused knew a great deal about legal affairs in other countries. However, now, in the interest of legality, justice, and peace in our land, I must confess that Johan Ot took a persistent and unusually impassioned interest in the trials of the secret brethren that were recently conducted before our court. He was interested in the elements of their belief system as they confessed them in the course of the questioning that I myself conducted, for example why they resisted the established Church order, why they impose penitence on themselves, why they insist on behaving like brothers and sisters toward each other, and so on. He also declared that punishing sinners by setting them out naked in front of the church was a sad thing to do, and that it ran counter to the principles of true faith. Since we know that the brethren were proven beyond the shadow of a doubt to be Satan worshipers, Ot's fervent interest in them is undoubtedly proof of yet another of his murky associations. It is also apparent to me now that Johan Ot very possibly and, indeed, very probably is himself a member of one of these sects that we are so very persistently and fervently trying to uncover and prosecute.

Dr. Ivan Gemma: I discussed the healing arts with Johan Ot several times, particularly the sickness of the black death. Johan Ot lanced an old woman's boils and veins to allow the impure blood to pass. But the old woman died soon after, which was clear enough proof to me that he had put a spell on her instead of trying to heal her. At that time I was under the mistaken impression that Johan Ot had some medical experience, so I spoke with him several times after that. He spent most of this time telling me about the spiritual symptoms that occur among people in connection with said sickness both before and after it strikes. One night over wine he drew me the following sign:

S	A	T	A	N
A	D	A	M	A
T	A	B	A	T
A	M	A	D	A
N	A	T	A	S

I told him then that the best cure was dried and powdered toad with a pinch of sulfur or dried scorpion powder, carried in a small bag about the neck and over the heart. The accused then mocked me over this widely recognized and effective treatment and kept insisting about his inscriptions. He claimed that the sickness is the product of an impure spiritual state, which is true, but then he went on defending his secret inscriptions, which supposedly had profound spiritual connotations that could neutralize this state. Among others, he also wrote out the following inscription:

HAX—PAX—MAX—DEUS—ORDINAX

It was only my scientific curiosity and nothing else that drove me to discuss these sorcerous emblems and inscriptions. It amazes me that I did not realize at once how deluded the accused was and what powers must have taken possession of his mind and body. Surely this was all to do with some force dwelling within him—and we can only imagine who or what is responsible for putting it there.

Town Constable Anton Macel: Whenever I drank with Johan Ot, his eyes would be shining by morning like some animal's. I saw him roaming around aimlessly at all hours of the night. Once he asked me if I knew what caused miracles and what caused sickness. He said that God surely was not responsible for visiting both upon us. The best proof of his nature was the cloud of vermin that my wife saw over his house. It was right before sunset. Those vermin were swarming and shifting and thrashing, and it was so disgusting that she fled and told me about it at home. I propose that she describe what she saw herself.

So went the statements and testimonies. Dr. Ambrož, his neighbors, and numerous other respectable witnesses who were quite familiar with Ot's activities also had their say. There were so many statements that, altogether, it was more than enough to proceed to the next stage of the trial, the conferral and then the pronouncement of the verdict and sentence. But Lampretič wanted a great deal more. He wouldn't have lived up to his reputation if he hadn't taken things to their proper, logical, and reasonable conclusion. He wanted to establish a link to the trials and judgments taking place just then in the Duchy of Neisse, where Johan Ot had spent his youth. All evidence suggested that such a link existed. He just wanted a sincere admission of all Ot's misdeeds. He wanted to know what role the accused had in the secret brethren's movement. He wanted to hear where and how the movement communicated with the forces of darkness. He wanted to hear confirmation from Johan Ot that witches exist, because a causal connection required such confirmation. The *iustificatio*, which is to say the defense of the trial's legitimacy, had to be precise, logical, and exact—in other words, it had to be worthy of the prestige that Dr. Sc. Jur. Lampretič enjoyed among his peers and the ruling elite. And to ensure this he had to have a sincere confession and a legally unassailable statement from the accused.

He would get both.

Johan Ot was severely mistaken if he thought the plans he had cobbled together through all those nights with the rats in the tower of justice would allow him to outfox Lampretič and lead the judge by the nose, for even the patience of such a just and humane magistrate had its limits. The judiciary had had enough of Ot's feigned ignorance and evasions. They clapped the thumbscrews on him and twisted until his fingers were as flat as a sheet of paper.

Now they made progress.

A SINCERE CONFESSION

I am Johannes Ott from the Duchy of Neisse. From a land famed for the rampage of the devil's minions that went on there. The devil entered every house, he took possession of the people at all hours of the day and night, he caused sickness and fires, destroyed livestock and crops, his maidens flew around, met with him on forested hillsides, submitted to him, and kissed his stinking ass. He entered our house too, causing my mother to start behaving strangely. She would go from tavern to tavern and consort with drunks, while my father started to cheat in his horse deals. There was a great deal of evil everywhere, not just in our house. The city fathers had a special oven built that was used diligently to eliminate the she-devils. That first year they burned forty-two of them, and I learned later that they burned several hundred over the next few years. My mother was under suspicion and it was during the first stage of her trial that she died of the devil's own sickness upon her genitals. It had been passed to her by some drunk in whom Satan had sown his sick seed.

This kind of talk was to Lampretič's liking. On it flowed, and the accused was approaching the moment when he would have to deliver his confession. He was ripe for it. If the devil's seed had been in his mother, if the devil had rampaged in her womb, then Ot too must be infected. That would more than meet the requirements of sound judicial logic: the thing had precise origins and a clear continuity, and the more recent evidence, confessions, and testimony did a nice job of rounding things out. But then there was a momentary hitch. To his misfortune, Johan Ot started to bang his head against the wall and shout that his mother had given birth to him before the devil's seed was planted in her. The lucidity of this line of thinking took Lampretič by surprise. But now was no longer the time for such details, nor for philosophical debates. Now it was time to wrap up Ot's sincere confession as quickly as possible. Just a bit, for a very short time, he had the accused put on the witches' stool. And then things went on.

THE SINCERE CONFESSION GOES ON
I, Johannes Ott, born in the Duchy of Neisse, being of sound mind, sincerely admit and declare that some sort of devil was in me. It may have entered me from my mother's womb, or perhaps it migrated from there into my blood at some later date. I fled from Neisse and from everywhere else I have lived because the devil was constantly in me and went with me everywhere. May my attempts to flee from that evil be taken into account as extenuating circumstances. The devil soon lured me to Styria and showed me a house with a spell on it. I

remained determined to get rid of the spirit, so I hung a legless rat over the door, because I believed the animal would drive the devil away. But one day it took possession of me again through the smoldering eyes of a justly chastised adulteress outside a church. It also caused me to lift my hand against a poor, decent old man. That same evening it stole the animal from over my door and set a fire behind my house. It also stirred up a cloud of vermin of various strange shapes and sounds over my roof. All this time I have also aided the demon's earthly contacts by joining the brotherhood movement and actively participating in it. A proof of my wickedness are those mysterious inscriptions I wrote that I now affirm are nothing other than signs of the devil with sinister meanings. I did not respond to the warnings that were given to me about the Karolina of Styria. I kept up my activities and lured the honest people who have given testimony before this court to skepticism, and by doing this brought them closer to my prince of darkness. I struck an old woman. I held up a burning heart in my hands. I listened to the speech of the earth. I leaped through flames. I roamed aimlessly through fields in broad daylight and the dark of night. I felt the infernal, buzzing dance of a brood of flies beneath my skin. I shouted strange words. In short, I have been completely obsessed by the presence of the devil. I do not know if I have caused the recent sicknesses and misfortunes, but based on everything else that has happened to me, it is entirely possible to draw that conclusion. Let me also add that I beat my wife, led my son into the false faith, and went on pilgrimages with Satan inside of me. There can be no doubt that, along with all the other strange signs that have been appearing on earth and in the heavens, my actions have caused sickness and the death of livestock as a result. My participation in the assembly of fire-jumping brethren on the night before the feast of St. John the Baptist also has no other significance and no other possible explanation than that I was participating in a rite with the devil's own band. I would like to be able to say who the heretics were that were with me in that forest meadow, but I didn't know any of them.

At this point things came to a halt again, but this time Johan Ot couldn't continue because he truly didn't know the names. This happenstance, which would prove decisive for the subsequent course of events, can be ascribed to the haste with which Lampretič now wanted to bring this case to an end. Had he wished to take the trouble, he could have gotten the names out of Ot sure enough, but he had just concluded a number of terribly exhausting trials that had been initiated by Urša Kolar's endless denunciations. The court didn't want to invite that kind of drudgery again, which, though it produced good results, was costly and required a great deal of expert persuasion. Let the people relax for a while. The tale of Johan Ot would be edifying enough for the time being. And so both judge and accused, as well as all the other functionaries who had participated in the trial, were relieved when they heard the good fathers read forth solemnly and with witnesses present:

WE EXCOMMUNICATE AND CONDEMN
in the name of the Father and the Son and the Holy Spirit and on the basis of law all heretics from the protection of our Catholic church and we commend them to Satan. May they be cursed wherever they are—in towns or in villages, eating or drinking, asleep or awake, living or dead. May God send them hunger and plague and may they be loathed by all people. May Satan stand to their right hand, and on the Day of Judgment may they be condemned to eternal torment. May they be driven from their houses. May their enemies confiscate their property. May their wives and children rise up against them, and let no man help them in their need. May they be accursed with all of the curses of the Old and

New Testaments. May they meet with the curse of Sodom and Gomorrah and may they be consumed in their flames. May the earth swallow them up, just as it swallowed Dathan and Abiram for the sin of disobedience. May they be accursed as Lucifer and all the demons of hell, where they will remain with Judas and all the eternally tormented if they do not confess their sins and if they do not seek mercy and mend their ways.

The fathers with their pale, solemnly sage faces walked off, while other men dragged Johan Ot back down. There, in the dampness and with his beloved little animals, he had enough peace and time to consider the crimes he'd committed as a result of his innumerable transactions with the prince of darkness.

How did the suffering man conduct himself during all these events and disputations? As all people do who undergo the same process. He was broken slowly, but surely: surely he acknowledged all his errors and sinister associations and the evil circulating through his veins and racing through the tissue of his brain; surely he now understood many things he hadn't before.

Those instruments, these trials, those solemn speeches—all of them were simply balm for a sick spirit.

There he lay, the words of the excommunication echoing in his ears. Shredded to bits, individual frayed sentences crept through his skull and under his skin. He had said and confessed everything. It was obvious what was going to happen to him next. Only the formal declaration remained in order for Lampretič's process of justification to be complete. It was strange, as a matter of fact, that he had not yet been brought to make his declaration. After confessing all his secret associations and evil deeds! The end would come one way or another, with or without a declaration—that was just one more formality. And then?

But no, the man was not determined to die, not at all!

He wanted life, and the thought flashed through his head that the last sentences of the good fathers' solemn pronouncement might actually mean something.

This made him decide to do this one last thing.

Though it wasn't up to him to make the decision. When they brought him back up, it had already been decided. He just had to assent to it. He renounced everything. He assented to everything else. To his declaration:

DECLARATION

I swear that I believe that all heretics and sorcerers suffer eternal hellfire and therefore I renounce heresy—more accurately, disbelief, which falsely and sinfully claims that there are no sorcerers or witches and that they cannot do harm, for disbelief—as I now confess—explicitly contradicts the findings of our mother the Holy Church, of all doctors of the Catholic faith, and of the imperial laws that prescribe death at the stake for such transgressors.

Now one more dangerous thought flashed through his brain—that he had believed this all along, his whole life long, but that he was confessing it to his own detriment—but in this he simply saw one last attempt by the forces of darkness inside him. So he lowered his eyes and did so swear.

He had nothing further to add.

The case of Johan Ot had come to an end.

4.

The mysterious disappearance of Johan Ot. Should the people meekly wait? A heretical sect makes some decisions and takes some steps at its headquarters. The delusions of public opinion.

For Justice Lampretič and like-minded individuals in the courts and in the halls of power, this case was closed. For the judicial and theological experts it was closed. It was closed for Lampretič's zealous colleagues, for the investigators, the scribes, the provocateurs, the denouncers, the spies, the guards, the jailers, and their bloody assistants. At least this is what they thought. Actually, the fellow hadn't given any of them much trouble at all, and yet the case of Johan Ot was instructive, supremely instructive. Now the people would know for whom they had to be on the watch, from whom they had to protect their property, their wives and children, their fields, livestock, and crops, their souls when it came down to it: from foreigners, above all from foreigners. And also from locals who behaved like foreigners, who roamed around in the dead of night, who had rodents nailed to their doors, who drank and kept their lights on until late, who sought contact with members of the new brotherhood, who spoke of the hidden, deeper meanings in strange inscriptions. The devil had a hand in everything—he was hiding in you, in your neighbor, your friend, your wife, an animal, the air, in rivers and streams—everywhere. Now righteous folk wanted to see that beast, who had undoubtedly caused a lot more evil than could be proven, be punished in human form. Now they wanted to see Johan Ot in a fire that would sizzle his depraved body and soul, whose leaping flames would hail yet another victory by upstanding, wise Justice Lampretič. And so the fate of this man with his murky connections and covenants both here and in the beyond continued to interest the peaceable, disciplined, and hard-working people of the area, and this is why, as far as they were concerned, his case was not yet closed.

The people knew altogether too much about the affair of Johan Ot. His not-so-numerous evil doings, proclaimed far and wide by the court's dutiful heralds all throughout the prolonged presentation of proof, had been talked about altogether too much. This is why the people were unable to simply shut up and change the subject when they realized that this agent of the devil wasn't being delivered to them either on a pyre, or drawn and quartered, or drowned, or in any case finished off. The problem assumed quite serious proportions when, at the city gate, a group of townsmen and peasants started stoning two city fathers and a magistrate's scribe passing through on official business. Burn Satan's lackey at the stake, the outraged mob shouted, refusing to be placated. By evening they moved their raucous assembly indoors, to the taverns, until eventually the local watchmen had to disperse them with the help of the castle steward and his assistants.

Why the devil's footman was still alive, why the judiciary had not yet carried out the sentence it had pronounced, why it hadn't already prepared a pyre or a drowning or a drawing and quartering was a question that only came to bother the overheated heads of these respectable subjects and freemen more and more. Even a few high-placed functionaries weren't clear about the thing, since punishments of that sort were entirely natural and ordinary in these kinds of cases. But the latter chose to remain silent, assuming that something must have come up—a stay of some sort, perhaps. All the same, they were getting worried, because after all, it was dangerous to toy with the people when they got into these moods. Were they supposed to wait around meekly until some new plague or blight or some other pestilence or tribulation was visited upon them? Just because some bigshot was reluctant to drive the soul right out of this spawn of hell? Lights started burning well into the early morning hours in a number of houses, and voices, cursing, upset, could be heard through the windows.

Which is why Lampretič was badly mistaken if he thought that the case of Johan Ot was closed when he pronounced the verdict and signed and sealed the writ of judgment. His men, who would continue to have to deal with Johan Ot, were no less mistaken. Though they would now have to deal with him in a different way—they would have to deal with his name, his specter, stirring citizens up to the point where actual disturbances and eruptions of dissatisfaction began to be seen.

No, it's not going to be easy to untangle what was going on with the strange fellow from the Duchy of Neisse—if that, indeed, is where he was from—Johan Ot—if that, indeed, was his name—and why people weren't seeing and hearing his skin sizzle and his soul wail as it fled into the lap of its dark master. Was it possible that the redoubtable Justice Lampretič and his colleagues had made a mistake? Why had Lampretič suddenly taken off for the seat of the duchy instead of taking his usual seat on the square and waiting contentedly for the pyre to signal the true, solemn end of his case?

No, a mistake was out of the question. Because for Lampretič and his people the case really was closed. Even though it apparently wasn't for anyone else.

The documents from the trial prove as much: the infallibility of Lampretič's *iustitia*, its precision and procedural punctiliousness. There is no judicial error in these documents. The only thing missing is the report on the execution of sentence. Everything else is there, from start to finish, with all the *i*s dotted and the court's seal affixed. The sheets documenting the investigation, the presentation of proof, the consultation and pronouncement of verdict all end in an unmistakable, robust flourish that could only come from Lampretič's hand. A footnote indicates that the convicted man, who by his own confession had had dealings with the forces of darkness, was removed to the town of H. in the hill country of Styria, where even now the guilt of a large band of women who had met with the devil on Mt. P. was being determined with the help of the usual juridical tests and tools. There the convicted man would assist by giving testimony at the trial.

But in the records of the town of H. there isn't a trace of a report of any Johannes Ott from the Duchy of Neisse participating in the hearings and trials that took place at that time.

So what happened to our fellow?

Somebody was thinking about him. Somebody was pondering him night and day and bringing people together to consult and advise. Help comes when you least expect it, and indeed, in his dank abode with the rats in the tower of justice next to the river gurgling its tales and dreams past him at night, amid his thoughts of the cosmic misunderstanding he had stumbled into, Johan Ot could scarcely hope for things to take a different turn. But they already had. In the town of R., a command center was already plotting the next moves of its rescue party. For them the case of Johan Ot was far from finished or forgotten. Hadn't this man listened to the speech of the dark forces of the earth in the company of accursed, excommunicated heretics on the night before the feast of St. John the Baptist? Hadn't he leaped over bonfires with them? Hadn't he joined in their secret covenant at the hour of assembly, the hour of burning hearts and impassioned love-making on the hillside next to the forest clearing, awash in the glow of the warm and purifying fire? Johan Ot always had his doubts—a fact that had momentous consequences for him. But that one night, when a stranger came with a promise to rescue him, he doubted too much. Well, actually, it's not so much that he doubted. He didn't be-lieve a single word of it. His unknown visitor promised to help him. Surely he knew his business, given the fortitude and conviction with which he had given his word. But Johan Ot wasn't the sort of person to enter into covenants or join secret societies. Just dealing with his own problems was too much for him. There was no question he had been among the new brotherhood. But why should that cause them to conspire and plot his rescue from fire, water, and noose? He had been with them that night and it didn't matter one bit whether he was informed about their subversive programs, whether he knew about their muddled heretical concepts or not. He didn't have time to get into that sort of thing. What was certain was that he had struck an old woman and ended up safely in the custody of Lampretič's colleagues. What was certain was that he had lost a fair amount of blood, sat on the witches' stool, and made all kinds of confessions and statements, right and left.

But these were frighteningly adept and dangerous people. You never knew where their allies and confederates were, or where, with all of their power and influence, the branches of the brother-hood reached.

They believed too fervently, therefore they must have been in league with the powers of darkness and were undoubtedly the worst possible heretics. They leaped through bonfires, set fire to hearts, and talked about the unity of souls. They listened to the earth. They walked down deserted paths at night, carrying torches. Miracles happened around their bonfires. They brazenly, fearlessly made love around the fires or, as was correctly noted in one document at the time, they "do shamelesslye engage in fornication." A judge once asked them, "Is it true that you recognize no differences amongst yourselves? That you share all with each other? That you treat each other as brothers and sisters?" But they made no answer. They preferred to die. At one time they'd had their own church in R. They had taken refuge at the edge of this beautiful land. They knew how to keep silent and they kept close together, for they knew that the Karolina was near and could scoop any one of them up at any moment.

But it didn't even occur to Johan Ot, as he now lay in his dim hole with rats for companions and thought about all the devils in his blood, that he was a member of such a splendidly organized society, whose eloquent and decisive leader Jakob Derzaj had once clearly said, "Soon new, unheard-of things will take place." A man capable of enacting a program like that wouldn't find it too hard to spirit his brother out of Lampretič's and the Karolina's deadly embrace.

For Johan Ot was their brother, after all. He had been with them, he had been with their sister. He knew what the earth said. He had learned the language of shadow and flame. He was a brave, silent, and stalwart man. He had acted decisively in front of the church. They knew all of this and were waiting for him to cave in in the face of the thumbscrews and pulley. Even the most stalwart cave in if they're not grounded firmly enough in the faith and the covenant.

Johan Ot said nothing. He betrayed no one.

It no longer mattered at this point that their brother, kissed and squeezed as he was in the hot and cold embrace of the Karolina of Styria, was incapable of giving anything away because he simply didn't know anything. He had followed the woman that night, he had watched that inscrutable face with the bonfire in the background, he had turned away some raving stranger the night before he fled—and just what could he have told them about any of this?

Nights passed and days passed, but nobody came to bang on their door, shouting they were under arrest. So he hadn't betrayed them.

He endured all the torments. He had pledged his bodily pain and his blood in covenant to them.

And so the conspiratorial mechanism got underway.

It will never be entirely clear how far its feelers and organizational threads extended. Had the incorruptible Justice Josef Albin decided that the convicted man was to be transported to the town of H., where a large group of witches was being tried? Or had somebody else made that decision? Had the hints and whispers been traded higher up? Had perhaps some member of the society who occupied a high position in the judicial or administrative hierarchy been responsible for this whispering and hinting? Why had Lampretič so abruptly left for G., even though he had completed his court documentation so thoroughly—absolutely to the letter—that there would never be any doubt of his unwavering commitment to the law?

We will never get any answer to these and other questions. All we know is that the brethren leader Jakob Derzaj stated much later that his conspiratorial command center at R. made plans to rescue Johan Ot. And so we shall meet Johan Ot again on his path through the convolutions of history and metaphysics, but this time calmer and braver than before. He lives to fight another day.

That morning, as they transported him, pale and ugly to H—for his nose had clearly been broken, and not just one time—to take part in further presentations of proof, there were more than a few warm and friendly—and above all, grateful—faces in the crowd. He didn't see them, of course, because a throng of respectable folk who were simply unable and, more to the point, unwilling to tame their rage and hatred was crowding around the cart. And why not? Why shouldn't they spit and flail at this man who had, after all, been proven guilty? Silently and with downcast eyes he endured the people's righteous anger. He was guilty of everything they had proven, and probably quite a bit more. Directly or indirectly, he had inflicted some evil on each of these good, hard-working people. He had caused the death of this one's livestock and that one's child. Another was sick because of him, and yet another was tormented by vile monsters in his sleep. He had afflicted this one's eye, and that one's bowels. Look at this old man, shaking and limping and spitting through what few rotten teeth he has left as he rushes toward the cart with the monster on it. Wasn't he the one whose sexual powers Ot had blighted, causing him to sob into his pillow night after night? And look at that deformed girl sticking her head through the gap at one corner and snarling as she tries to bite him. Isn't she the one whose hands he crippled, hadn't he confused and twisted the thoughts in her head? And look at the fat fruit vendor, panting as she pushes her way through the crowd, red in the face, with spittle and foam on her mouth and a cane in her hand. Who was it defiled her daughter in the dark of night? Him.

He had done these and other horrible things. He had caused people to wake up at night feeling a great weight on their chest and sweat on their foreheads and palms. He had clambered over their roofs, slammed their shutters in the dead of night, tiptoed around their beds, afflicted their bowels, rotted their teeth, taken away their appetites, caused them to rave with fever, and implanted boil-like formations in their bodies.

Him and others like him.

In view of all this, whatever Lampretič and his men had done to Ot was hardly enough. They'd broken his nose, but why were his arms and legs still in one piece? Why did he still have eyes to see and ears to hear? Why was that black tongue that he used to pronounce curses still lolling around in his mouth? Why did he still have the fingernails he used to scratch at their front doors? Why did he still have his skin stretched taut about his body, with the swarming nests of vermin beneath it?

What great, good fortune that all of this would soon be frying and baking, twisting, sizzling and crackling. Thank goodness this nest of hell-spawn would soon collapse into dust, and Satan, howling like thunder, would have to abandon the stranger's body.

But why, oh why were they taking so long with the fire? Where were they taking him under armed guard? Why didn't they just finish him off right there and then and tear him to shreds?

No, amid this eruption of righteous popular anger Johan Ot was unable to see the surreptitious glances that would have given him hope and turned his thoughts away from the seed-buds he could feel in his blood and the flies buzzing beneath his skin. The best he could hope for was that they wouldn't tear him to tatters and gnaw him to bits right there on the cobblestones of the town's main street. But the town authorities wouldn't allow such a disgrace. If there had been a direct order to transport him to a different trial in H., then that was where he had to go. Let him meet his death there.

But the glances went with him. From village to village, from one assembly of righteous popular rage to the next, they kept passing along their secret message. For he couldn't be under the devil's command, and he hadn't committed all those horrible deeds. He was theirs and he had proven he could keep silent and endure.

The conspiracy was doing its job.

The final document says that Ot was sent to H., and after that all trace of him in our land and the neighboring ones vanishes. Likewise all trace of Johannes Ott of the Duchy of Neisse, but that, of course, doesn't necessarily mean anything. Certainly nothing conclusive about our man's life, or his mysterious fate. Yes, that final court document says that Ot was sent to H. But in all the court archives of H. there is no mention of his actual involvement in the trials there.

So what happened en route?

The procession, bearing such a renowned traveler as it did, moved very slowly. Not just because of the two old equestrines that drew the cart and the entire devil's parade with it—not just because of that. It was primarily because of all the respectable people in every town, every village, and at every bend in the road who had to spit at Ot, hit him, and even bite him if they could. Johan Ot and all his wicked deeds, as well as countless other evils caused by others connected to or like him— these were not the only hardships that the people had to suffer and endure. There was sickness, there were bloody wars, there were ferocious janissaries—their own sons—there was every imaginable iniquity, so it's easy to understand that they hated the enemy within—who is in fact the most dangerous enemy, the enemy that is here and in the air and in the blood and can get under anyone's skin at any time—that they hated this enemy most bitterly and profoundly of all.

But the sea of grief that was their lives also had certain demographical consequences—namely, that many of them died, many more migrated away, and as a result there were numerous houses and sometimes whole settlements standing empty.

It was in one such settlement that the procession stopped to rest. At the only house that showed any signs of life.

Later the guards tried to defend their rest stop using all kinds of excuses, but this did nothing to spare them a variety of punishments and floggings. They said it was impossible to sustain such a relentless pace, when in every village the wrath of the people faced down the guards' efforts to keep the malefactor alive for the trials to come and the stake. They said they simply had to rest.

This much was understandable, but it was harder for them to explain the fatal error—or at least the negligence—that followed. At first they tried to cover it up, but then it came out when one of them let down his guard. Some good-willed but ominous-looking strangers had approached the house. The fact that they looked ominous and that something clearly wasn't right with this band of people were things that became clear only later. It wasn't apparent when the guards first saw them. They were happy to have them around, their women and their drink. They even threw the monster on the cart some bread and gave him a drop.

That was all they could say.

Toward night some sort of witchcraft must have taken place, because the prisoner Johan Ot vanished with the party of unknowns.

When they realized what had happened, the guards staggered drunk around the village, searching for him everywhere, but the earth had swallowed up those figures of the night.

Once again, some devil must have had a hand in this. And that was probably true, because the villain, bound and beaten as he was, would not have had the strength to run.

The guards hurried on to H. that same night, to avoid having a disappointed populace spitting and biting at each stop along the way. These were dedicated men who, despite this incident, were conscientious about their work and had even pitched in to beat their prisoner whenever they got bored.

The authorities in H. were incensed, and so was Lampretič, when he got the news in the capital.

The people wanted a burning.

But Johan Ot was gone. Vanished. It was a terrible scandal, because didn't letting the devil's servant slip out of your hands mean that you were in league with him too? An investigation was begun. Who had sent the condemned man to H.? Had that move been absolutely necessary? But here the investigation stopped. The move *had* been necessary, because establishing the causal connection between the witchery and Satanic cults in the Duchy of Neisse and the evil here would have produced significant and useful results.

The authorities tried to hush up the scandal. In order to assuage the fury of the multitudes, they managed quickly to get all the necessary confessions out of the witches of H. Admittedly, to accomplish this they used the Spanish boot, which was forbidden, not just the prescribed methods of a humane judicial process: the rack, thumbscrews, the pulley, and the witches' stool. But because of the urgent need, those in charge turned a blind eye. Then they quickly set the accused out to roast atop various hilltops around the countryside, in order to achieve the maximum propaganda effect.

They narrowed the focus of the investigation in order to simplify the process: the ashes of the witches who'd been burned could hardly point out all the other houses where their fellow witches and warlocks lived. Fortunately, reports from the field assessing the mood of the people yielded—after detailed analysis—quite an encouraging picture. Among other things, reports came in that the rumor had begun that Johan Ot had indeed left this world on one of those pyres, howling.

So things couldn't have worked out better.

For a while there continued to be differing opinions on the entire affair: some radicals, particularly the more conscientious officials, were audacious enough to say, late at night, over wine or in bed next to their wives, how suspicious the whole thing seemed to them. Others nursed their doubts for a while and tried to pump whatever sources of information were handy. But gradually a view came to predominate that originated in a healthy, grassroots concept of justice: namely, that Ot's sort of evil would eventually have to meet its punishment somewhere, and if not at this stake, then at some other one, and if not by fire, then underwater, or at the blade of an ax.

5.

A plaintive autumn wind. The 12,672 demons of Elisa Pleinacher. The old brotherhood eats at the roots. So many passionate words, so many original concepts. A unified spiritual community. Where is this dangerous mission whirling him off to?

But the fellow still had his head firmly attached to his neck. Here it is, he would say whenever memory took him back, here are the tendons, the muscles, the bones that hold it up. It was solidly fused to his body and now no one could take it off. His skin was whole, too, perhaps a bit scarred, but whole and stretched nice and taut over his usually powerful body, over that weakened but still generous jumble of guts that shifted gently back and forth as he sat in his hovel, shoving heaps of meat and bread down into them and pouring down jugs of wine.

All present and accounted for, all body parts hale and hardy. That's important, he would say and guffaw, sending jets of wine streaming out through his teeth and onto the table.

The Karolina's cold hand still had a grip on his heart. He could feel that hand in his chest and he could feel its rigid embrace. He had been finished. Fire, the pincers, the hangman, the judge, and the pious, righteous people—all had been pointing the way for him to the other world—and not upward, toward the glittering stars, but down, into the earth whose voice he had listened to, toward eternal fire and brimstone, torments, pain, howls reaching into every bone and fiber.

How many days had they passed now in this dimly lit place on some forested hillside? How long had it taken to get here? Where had they brought him? What would be the price of his rescue? What he had done to earn it? What would be next?

He hadn't stepped out of the house, just like he'd been ordered, but the questions kept boring away at him. His body recovered and began to fidget again. Restless to move onward, away from here. But where?

He listened to the baleful autumn wind bending the tops of the trees and announcing the coming cold. The days grew darker and the sky pressed down to the ground. Its vault stretched right over the forest and closed off the space of the flatland opposite. They would have to come from there, through that door of a landscape. He waited in his cozy hiding place and brooded, appreciating life and his intact hide less and less. They couldn't have rescued him just to leave him to rot in this shack.

There wasn't another living creature. Only the wind with its song and the shifting trees, only the long empty nights when the spirits and their shapes would awaken in his dreams. He started to run out of food and had to manage what was left of his supplies wisely. Time became excruciatingly slow. One day Ot was standing at the window when he heard branches crackle in the forest above the house. The sound of human footsteps drew closer until it seemed as though it was about to walk right into the house. Then Ot caught sight of a human figure moving slowly and carefully uphill between the trees. A shabbily dressed peasant loaded down with firewood was looking toward the nominally abandoned house. At first Ot was so overjoyed that he nearly ran outdoors to invite the man in for a bite of food, for a visit, to exchange human words. But he froze at the door. Hadn't they told him: there was a risk of denunciation. Hadn't they told him: wait, we'll come when the time is right, we'll come back for certain. He listened to himself panting, listened to the wild beating of his heart urging him outside, and he listened to the memory that nailed his feet to the floor. The screaming old woman, the toothless hag in the corner whose loathsome shrieks had driven him into the paws of Lampretič's men. The peasant would get scared, run, report. Then Ot would be finished, then nothing could save him. He stayed where he was.

The other kept looking downhill for a long time, as though deciding whether to go in, then turned around and vanished into the trees. What would have happened if he had come back? Would Ot have killed him? Buried him behind the house? Burdened himself with human blood, a crime?

He flung himself on the bed and listened as his restlessness pounded on the walls and against the vault of the trapped sky. He couldn't take it any longer. It was time for him to leave.

That evening they came. He watched them through the twilight as they rolled their way across the flatland in the wind, ever so slowly creeping toward the house. One man on horseback with two men on foot behind him. For an endlessly long moment they vanished in the ravine below the house, then suddenly they were on the ridge and at the door.

That night a light burned in the lone house at the edge of the forest as the four men bowed their heads in learned discussion. That night the true face of the world was revealed to Johan Ot. The things he had only sensed until now, that had entered his consciousness in brief bursts of knowledge or experience, these things now took solid shape and were filled out. As he mounted his horse at morning's first light and shook hands with the men, he knew that this was a derelict land, paying a bloody tribute night after night.

Fire and blood and chaos were the order of the day. The cruel, bloodthirsty Turk was still skewering innocent Christian children on his pike before their parents' eyes. He had been beaten back a hundred times, but still he wouldn't relent. Rebellious peasants were being condemned to death and the galleys. The nobles were undermining the Emperor's and the Church's authority with their plots and feuds. The Church was perpetrating the worst sacrileges. Barely had it managed to subdue Luther's false prophets than it was once again overtaken by greed, sin, and viciousness. The theologians were haughty, the monks were worldly, and all of them were as rapacious as wolves. Hanging courts were convicting innocent people of crimes and transgressions. Daughters were denouncing their mothers as witches. A council of judges would get drunk on wine while watching torturers go about their business. Nuns swept up in mass sexual hysteria would have the demons driven out of them with all available means. Bishops who had been educated by Jesuits would have professors, law students, parish priests, canons, vicars, seminary students, and the most beautiful girls imprisoned and burned at the stake in large numbers. The granddaughter of Elisa Pleinacher had 12,672 demons driven out of her. A ten-year-old girl had given birth to two children of the devil's and even confessed as much. Six women had killed a child, disinterred it, and boiled the body down into devil's fat. In four years' time Dr. Ivan Tillerich had condemned thirty witches to the stake. Peter Schatz and the aforementioned Doctors Barth and Lampretič were no better. Was everyone who had been convicted as a sorcerer really a sorcerer? Had witchcraft really been proven in the case of all these witches? Hadn't many heretics, particularly members of the brotherhood, died on this pretext? Didn't the system point its finger at them as Satan worshippers? Wasn't anyone who expressed doubts about this mass insanity likewise charged as a heretic and Satan worshipper? Witchcraft existed, there could be no doubt, but was witchcraft the only pretext that this or that nobleman or Church official or local judge could come up with? Did the new brethren have to be the object of their thirst for blood? And how about the devil: whose side was he actually on? In whom, in what people and institutions was he lurking? Things had gone so far that after a Turkish incursion the people of Styria had been forced to swear allegiance to the sultan. Things had gone so far that Christians had slaughtered each other for thirty years over a false dilemma, while in fact neither side was any better than the other. Lutheran or Papist, both were terrified of any legitimate religious fervor, of any excessive passion for the truth. Both asserted that a Christian had to endure violence and wrongdoing from his masters. They were afraid of the new churches. They were afraid of the old community and fraternity of the people. They were engaged in a battle to the death and, at least in our parts, the Papist had slain the Lutheran. Now it was the turn of others. Thousands of people were to be purged and made martyrs, and were their lives supposed to be the devil's handiwork?

But the old brotherhood was still alive. It was corroding this world of darkness at its roots. It's true it had been involved in the uprisings. It's true it had been a part of conspiracies. For aren't all means permitted when one is destroying a world built on chaos and error? But the organization's real strength lay elsewhere—in the mind, in faith, in equality, in a profound and boundless devotion to the shared cause. Today's world was a world of terror, governed by a grander conspiracy still. The new brotherhood would put an end to that.

After long days of isolation Johan Ot had taken in so many passionate words, so many explanations, so many impassioned looks and handshakes in one night that now, as he rode into the new morning, his head really was spinning a bit. But he had been present, overwhelmingly convinced and decisively committed to new concepts that until now he had only intuited, but which now abruptly and inexorably entered his consciousness as self-evident, as the one sure and uncontestable truth. He traveled the land as a herald of the one true covenant. Fires would burn on lone hillsides, people would haul stones on their backs, and new churches would rise up on holy sites where miracles had happened; throngs of pilgrims would honor the true saints, and the organization would be linked and united as never before. An agitated people would then find the true path to salvation and authentic Christian community. The oppressors would cease oppressing, farmhands and maidens would quit their work, children would leave their parents, and fathers would abandon their families. No one would rule over anyone any longer. No one would preach about the Pope's God. All would be as brothers and sisters, without Masses or sermons or false saints. It would be a united spiritual fellowship. A community. The power of spirit and faith, the committed work of one man for the other, endlessly interlinked. This was the way. This was the goal.

So many passionate words, in fact, so much fervor, so much decisiveness all at once on behalf of this new cause, that it becomes downright difficult to believe that our man's sincere. He had warmed to the ideas of the brethren, their concepts and programs, to their gnawing at roots, to the disintegration of the body and soul of the existing order, to their underground and conspiratorial activities, in fact. And he warmed to it suddenly, in the course of a single night, even committing to an active role. True, they had saved him from death. True, he had had plenty of time to think about *iustitia* and the spiritual constitution of these people and this land. All this is true, but it is also true that not everything was quite right with the fellow, after all.

His actions and his accounts attest to that. He had followed far too many and varied temporal and spiritual paths until now to be able to reverse course so suddenly and resolutely. Perhaps he simply enjoyed his new assignment, this traveling business from town to town, from village to village, this apparent business designed to conceal his true mission, which was to connect adherents, transport messages, and collect information. One way or the other, he had made his own decision. Let him face the consequences. As long as he doesn't change his mind. As long as he doesn't get driven and whirled off somewhere else yet again.

6.

A broad, light-filled space. The quiet slaughter of a large animal. Heavy night breathing in a dark, conspiratorial hole.

The plain that he had earlier looked onto from the cabin was not nearly as expansive as it had seemed when the vault of the sky was pressing down on it and closing it off from the inside. In the brilliance of sunrise its furthest extent was clearly visible, where it began to lead sharply uphill. The good, doughty animal they had so carefully selected for him was used to having a rider on its back. The horse's footing was sure, and it avoided the trail's sharp, frozen edges. Johan Ot looked at the sunrise and felt the warm, breathing, living mass beneath him as it throbbed together with him in a single desire— to travel, to conquer distance. He watched the sunrise and saw that morning was starting again, as it always did, over and over, blazing a new trail, always starting from the beginning, regardless of what end of the path you were on, whether here at the start or at your destination, regardless of whatever trap might be yawning out there, no matter how dangerous. As though nature too had decided to set out anew, along with Ot. The somber vault of the sky that had previously been pushing down to the ground and touching the crowns of the trees was now open, with the sun glowing bright and round and red over the chilly landscape. Ot contemplated the glow of the red light as it began to refract and scatter over the hilltops.

As he approached the foot of the hill, the sun vanished, drenched in cold shadow. He spurred the horse more quickly over the narrow path past the barren trees, their cold branches jutting like daggers. When had the howling wind driven the last yellow leaves off of them? During the long days when he was perched in his hideout, waiting for the moment when his pursuers would finally lose his scent and with it any will to find him? Or before then? He could feel this countryside just as he could breathe in the bright light of the sky, which was now blue and clear. Every moment he glanced up, and with every breath some of that clear sky settled in him. This is how newborns breathe and feel.

It turned out that the path led through a kind of depression. On the far side another hill rose, looking downright black in the morning light with the ribs of its stripped tree trunks, which it displayed insistently. It took Ot so long to ride through this hole that he sighed with relief when he saw a broad, illuminated space at the far end. There the sky reached down with its blueness, revealing a whole world. Now this was going to be nice, and safer too. Now there would be villages and isolated farmsteads—human dwellings, in short—of the type that on a similar morning some time ago had abruptly turned him back, against his will, to where he had come from.

There was still no wind, no clouds either, but the birds had already come to life in the fields. Black, cawing, and poignant in this gloomy, autumnal countryside, in this sublime fall morning awakening for Johan Ot. He passed through the fields slowly, over pastures with brownish frozen grass, until he finally entered a sparse, grayish wood.

Perhaps it smelled like snow, even though it was a clear day with the sun rolling across the sky's vault up above. That's precisely when snow comes—such cold, clear days stand in wait for it. Somewhere far off on the horizon, dark, dense masses were forming to shut off the vault of the sky once again and narrow the horizons.

This barren countryside, this exhausting ride over desolate trails—was this the freedom he had so longed for? Even though there were horizons and picturesque scenes wherever the eye roamed, even though clumps of houses stood etched in the distance at pathside, their smoke rising straight up to the sky, suddenly Johan Ot was once again ill-tempered and sullen.

All too soon had he forgotten the damp tower of justice, where on every side only the brick of the walls met the eye. In a single day he had forgotten the endless days of waiting in the cabin behind him, where his only human contact had been a startled peasant peering toward the house and then vanishing.

He longed for people, carefree discussions, taverns, lots of live, warm bodies in a small space.

Toward evening he caught sight of the settlement where he was heading. A black cluster of houses stood pressed under the ridge of a hill, as if hiding from the wind and storms that blew over it. Tired and in a foul mood, he kept his eyes fixed on those simple shacks with their tiny windows, which for the longest time remained unchangingly distant, with unchangingly small windows, unchangingly high up the hill. His horse moved only with difficulty, listlessly beneath him.

When he got up there, it was already dark. Here and there faint lights shone out of the black openings, with an occasional shadow darting past. At last, these were real, close-up traces of life.

He heard voices coming from a tall, spacious shed that stood next to one of the houses, rising several meters up over it. He climbed off his horse slowly and walked toward the sound with a tired, staggering tread. A door opened, sending a shaft of dancing light out onto the courtyard as a short shadow darted out through the opening and slammed the door shut behind it. Someone let out a high squeal and the light showing through the cracks went out. He stood in front of the door and listened to the sudden silence in perplexity. Not a thing was moving inside.

Now he was entirely on his guard. He pulled a long dagger out of his belt and squeezed it tight. He couldn't turn back. Not riding that tired nag and at night, laden with leather and silver. There were traps everywhere. And what about here? What was going on with this sudden silence on the other side of the door? Had he taken a wrong turn? Come to the wrong address? His nerves stretched taut, he stood at the door and thought. He would try to sweet-talk his way through this one, provided this was the wrong address. Otherwise he would put the fear of God into these damned frightened peasants huddling behind the door. That's what he would do.

He stepped up to the door and banged his fist on it twice. The sound of it echoed through the room inside, but there was no answer. Not a single voice. Nothing. And yet they were standing right at the door. He gently pushed it open and the rotten wood gave a heart-rending squeal. The bright night moved inside until moonlight illuminated a strange scene. A huge, spread-eagled, bloody mass of meat hung from under the ceiling down to the floor. Some sort of animal head was bobbing beneath a throat slit to a palm's breadth, out of which blood was still seeping and dropping into a bucket on the floor. The skin had been sliced down the middle and forcibly pulled apart, leaving the blood-soaked, fleshy innards exposed in the harsh moonlight. Six or seven men with glinting eyes stood all around, ready to pounce. As though they had been caught in some dishonest deed, ready to defend themselves. The one who stood closest to the animal, the legs of which were tied and hidden somewhere up by the ceiling, was holding a long, bloody knife.

They stood like this for an infinitely long moment. Ot in the doorway, the moonlight to his back, his face dark and a long dagger in hand, the men startled and illuminated, ready for whatever grim action was necessary. The young boy who had stood lookout moments before and had informed them all about the new arrival was now standing just a pace away from the door.

Even though the mutual inspection and recognition had taken just an instant, the men had had more than enough time to reassure themselves. The stranger was alone.

Johan Ot could feel the tension subside, which was not at all to his advantage.

"Good evening," he said, and instantly realized how stupid that had been, how badly he had just ruined things, how he had demolished the barrier that had stood between him and the men gathered around this clandestinely slaughtered animal. What's all this then, that's what he should have said, what are you up to, something like that, but under no circumstances should he have said "good evening." Because there had been no "and good evening to you too, sir" sent his way in return, no answer, not so much as a word—they just relaxed a bit and gradually, placidly started moving toward him, toward the door. The one with the knife looked like he was ready to cut another throat, even a Christian one, and Johan Ot's dagger suddenly seemed like a ridiculous, pathetic weapon faced by these threatening looks that had already witnessed such herculean slaughter.

"Stop!" he shouted, and nobody stopped. Stop, he shouted, taking a step back. "I'm here for Urban," and he knew that he couldn't turn and run, because then it would be too late, because then they would chase him and tear him apart, for certain. "I'm looking for Urban, Urban Posek." One of them raised a hand and stopped them.

"I don't care about your butchering," Johan Ot said. "What do I care about your illegal nighttime butchering. I'm not a spy." Which was as good as saying, "I'm a spy and I've been watching you, and Urban Posek is just my excuse. I've caught you and now you're mine."

Someone toward the back grabbed the one with the knife and tried to stop him, but the latter shook loose. There will be time for that, the one toward the back hissed. There will be time, do you hear, and he called out over his shoulder to Johan Ot, who was staring confused at the melee that was building, "Speak up, now! What?"

Then, amid the general confusion, Johan Ot had a flash of insight. In a clear, but faltering voice he began to intone the words, "For thus saith the Lord of those who keep my Sabbaths, and choose the things that please me . . ." And in the next instant a response came from inside:

". . . and take hold of my covenant."

The butcher's hands relented in disappointment.

Somebody sighed in relief and someone else said, clearly and forcefully, "He's one of us."

Johan Ot slid his dagger back into his belt and went in. The looks on the men's faces were more hospitable now as they sized up the newcomer. Only now did Ot smell the sweetly intoxicating scent of blood and steaming flesh that filled the whole shed. Someone struck a flint and light filled the killing room. The warm, intoxicating stench reached into Ot's guts while his eyes avoided the white, slashed gullet that jutted out tubelike, white and gristly. He began to feel sick.

"I'm tired," he said. "Thirsty."

A young fellow picked up a bowl spattered with blood and ran somewhere outside with it. He came back with water and offered it to the traveler. When Johan Ot took it in his hands, he could feel something smooth, dry and slippery on its bottom. There were red drops on top of it, too, on the rim of the bowl where he would have to set it to his mouth. They were all watching him and now there was simply no way for him to say I'm not thirsty anymore. He closed his eyes and sent several gulping swallowfuls down his throat.

"We came pretty close to having more sausage," the butcher said, and all the others guffawed.

"Take him to see Urban," said the man who had responded to the password, and Johan Ot followed the young fellow.

Several houses along, the boy knocked on a door and hurriedly babbled a few words when it opened. The rotund figure in the door-way made a welcoming gesture and Johan Ot stepped into a smoke-filled room that was lit from one side by some glowing embers in the hearth and from the other by an oil lamp that was about to go out.

"What messages do you bring?" the rotund man asked grimly, even before Johan Ot had a chance to get a good look at the room. He didn't feel the least bit comfortable around this peculiar fellow. Covenant or not, outside on his horse there was silver and goat leather, and he had gold coins stashed in his belt, and who could say if the people in this village didn't take the notion of Christian community, sharing all wealth equally, just a little too seriously.

"The new brotherhood is rising up," Ot said by rote. "The sea that concealed the holy tomb has begun drumming underground. The bonfires will flare and the paths of the martyrs will come to life. It's the time of assembly once again."

The man paced nervously about the room. He's got something up his sleeve, Johan Ot thought. I'd better keep my dagger under my pillow. They're not getting me again. I don't care if they're the head, legs, and arms of the brotherhood.

"Was there nothing else," the peasant asked. "Nothing specific?"

"Yes," Johan Ot said. "Jakob Demšar wants Urban Posek to know that construction of the church and altar of St. Fabian on Gorca Hill is about to begin."

"Is that all?" Urban Posek asked.

"That's it," Johan Ot said.

The door opened and a tiny female creature dashed in. It looked at the stranger, went to the hearth, and warmed its hands there for a moment, and then withdrew to the bed in one corner.

Show him the barn, Urban said and the maid abruptly jumped back to her feet. She nodded toward him and Johan Ot followed behind. Without a word she led him out back and showed him a place for his horse in a sort of outbuilding that was chained shut for some reason and covered over with boards and stones.

They'll get along fine together, Johan Ot tried to joke at the expense of the cow and horse, two pathetic creatures that would have to spend the night in that cold place through which the wind was blowing strong.

The maid giggled something in response and ran out the door. Ot took his pack off his horse and dragged it back into the house. The maid served him some variety of warm stew, while Urban Posek, the man he'd heard was an important link in the chain of the movement, was already tossing and turning in his bed. Johan Ot had expected a hailstorm of questions and an exhausting debriefing, but to all appearances Posek wasn't interested at all. Was he just inured to these visits by messengers? Or was he really hatching plans behind that beetle brow of his?

"Your daughter?" Johan Ot asked, pointing to the maid who was grating something over a black pot beside the hearth.

The other made no reply. Here, he nodded toward the place where the stranger was supposed to spread out his bedding, and then he turned to face the wall. At this point Johan Ot would just as soon have packed everything back up and left. He would just as soon have slept in the stable next to his animal, if it wasn't so cold out. Who knew if his horse would even still be there by morning? If it wouldn't be hanging by its legs in that shed with its throat slit? Ot plumped up his straw bedding and pulled his blanket over himself. What squalor: this bed, this stinking room, this village, these sinister people, he muttered to himself unintelligibly; this is where we send Johan Ot as our messenger and herald?—to these hicks, into this poverty? These are the people who are going to set the world on its head? Who are going to set up new altars and build a richly spiritual society? These beaten, benighted people?

Let's have some quiet, it's time to sleep, his neighbor barked into the wall, and Johan Ot swallowed hard. He had set both of his packages in front of him on the bedding and now curled himself around them, and he hid his dagger beneath where his head would lie. At the hearth the girl poured out some liquid that went splashing into an earthen container. Some loud voices went past the house. And then everything was silent. Ot didn't even give a thought to where the maid had gone, listening only to the grave-like silence, the infinite black peace that had reigned in those lands every night since time immemorial. His ears rang, and in his mind's eye he saw an enormous forest with its fat-trunked trees stripped bare, a horse and rider slogging and stumbling through it.

Then came a sort of hissing and hushing sound, through which he could hear barking in the distance. A fox, Ot thought and opened his eyes. A ray of moonlight shone through the window, yet despite this the room was completely dark. Where am I sleeping? he wondered, half-asleep, where am I, and at that instant something hissed into his ear again and he could feel a live body moving next to him. He flinched, grabbed his dagger, and propped himself up on his elbows. Under the blanket was a wagging thing slithering toward the wall like some enormous insect. Ot jerked the cover aside and saw the outline of a tiny body. He reached his hand out and felt some long, strawlike hair, then felt a finger placed on his mouth: Shhh, hissed the shape. The maid, thought Ot, that pale, shadowy creature that was standing at the hearth before, what the devil is she doing here? It's a trick, he thought, they're up to something, he thought and said, half-audibly, "What is this?" At the other wall the lumbering body of the rotund peasant responded by shifting in its sleep; Urban Posek even began working his jaws vigorously, as if trying to reply. He grumbled and his teeth clamped together and started to grind like some creaky door. The woman reached up toward Ot's ear until he could feel her warm breath, and she whispered so quietly that he could barely make out, "Quiet, he's dangerous. But he sleeps like the dead."

So that's how it is. Johan Ot felt greatly relieved, although he couldn't entirely rid himself of the insistent thought that there was something behind all the maid's recent fidgeting under the covers. Had she wanted to rob him? What did it matter? Here she was now, daughter or wife, maiden or whore, filthy or louse-ridden; sidling up to him with some clever plot under those patches of clumpy hair that covered her face, or perhaps with nothing more sinister at work than her feminine instincts and needs. Ot stretched out on his back and put his dagger back under the straw. He reached out and drew the maid's head close to his ear so he could hear her warm, rapid breathing. She wrapped herself around him and stroked his face. She stank a little of long unwashed sweat, and her hands were rough, but in such surroundings it all seemed right. She was warm and her hands squirmed like some little, skittering animal's. She stroked Ot's chest and reached down toward his trousers. He grabbed her by the wrist. The rough-hewn door of Urban's teeth had started to creak again. It was too distracting. What if he wakes up, Ot whispered. He won't, the maid breathed into his ear. She already knows, she has experience, she knows that the heavyset fellow never wakes up in these circumstances. Her fingers were already wiggling their way back down, toward Ot's genitals. Now they reached far down, to his knees, and then reached back up along his thighs. He could feel something coming to life and moving down there, and he could feel her grabbing greedily, hungrily at his hard stalk, grasping it as she breathed loudly into his ear, as if the winds were heaving against the walls of a wooden house. He turned around to face her and felt the slightly shrunken, slightly limp breasts of a young woman, while she held onto him through the cloth of his trousers and squeezed so that it hurt when he next tried to move. She had some odd swelling down below, and when she let go of him and suddenly pulled her clothes up to her chin, he could feel a nicely rounded, taut belly beneath his hand. She's with child, though not far along, only a few months, said Ot's hand as it was already reaching into her lush growth with its remarkably long hairs. It was too late now for doubt or second thoughts, too late for the fear of God. Now Ot's hand felt something wet and soft that expanded and warmly drew it in until it wanted the whole hand and wouldn't be satisfied with anything less. Then, suddenly, she pressed her legs together and got up. She undid Ot's belt with both hands and loosened his trousers. She knelt down beside him on her hands and knees. Her hair hung down in hanks. He crawled behind her and with much loud gasping whooshed into her. It was a short, gnarled, spasmodic, twisted dying away. She moaned so loudly that Urban really ought to have woken up and scrambled to his feet.

But all he did was go on grinding his teeth, sounding like an old, creaky door.

"Do you people always do it like that?" Ot asked the woman later, as they neatened up his bedding and picked off the hay that had made its way into every pore of their bodies and stitch of their clothes during their vigorous activity.

"Like what?" she asked, not comprehending.

"You know, from behind," he said. "Like dogs."

"Can't you see I'm pregnant, you fool?" she said. "Do you want to crush my child?"

"Do our messengers come here often?" Ot asked.

"I'll say," she answered.

"And do you crawl into bed with all of them?" he asked.

She gave no answer. Then she pulled her clothes back down to her heels and got up.

"Oh, you," she said. "Do you know what you are? A thick-skulled little merchant." And then her shadow skittered into the far corner and disappeared among some rags.

Urban started grinding again and said something out loud through his teeth.

7.

A night in the highlands. The new brotherhood rears its head. Ot is drawn elsewhere. Adam. A record of the eye-gougings, murders, and other crimes of Ana Jelenko, the witch. Interminable battle songs.

The next morning Johan Ot rode off. His horse was hale and hardy and both it and its rider were happy that it wasn't hanging by its legs in the shed. The weather was still clear and chilly, and frost crunched under the horse's hoofs. As the path began to lead downhill, Ot dismounted and carefully led his horse by the reins. Now the animal was valuable to him beyond all reckoning. He couldn't afford to have it slip and injure one of its legs. At the bottom of the hill the forest gave way to a meadow and when Ot looked back, he saw that same compressed cluster of houses on the ridge beyond the forest, smoke curling merrily out of their chimneys. Outside one of the houses a female figure in a long dress was watching him ride off.

He rode north for about half a day and when he came to a river he turned his horse toward the west. He was scheduled to deliver his next message somewhere on the border between Styria and Carinthia. Probably in precisely the same kind of hamlet again. Though

Johan Ot hoped that this next stop wouldn't have any startled night-time butchers or pregnant women visiting messengers' beds in the teeth-grinding presence of their sectarian leader.

This damn country is just crawling with people, he told himself as he looked down a hillside at a road upon which a group of armed men was traveling with some slow-moving, heavy-laden horses swaying in step between them. Merchants. With an armed guard. And here I'm riding alone like an idiot. In one of these villages someone's going to separate me from my silver and leather, if not do worse. Quick, he thought, I've got to join that group of armed merchants as soon as I can.

He set his horse to trotting straight uphill. It was the right direction. The red glow of the afternoon sun glinted through the tops of the pine trees. No fields, no crows. Probably not even any animals, including wolves. The path wound steadily uphill toward a ridge. He stopped to rest several times. Somewhere he was going to have to find a human habitation. Not much more time passed before he caught sight through the trees of a cabin with wooden boards for a roof. It stood in a deserted glade, fairly high up the mountainside. From the forested slope that surrounded it on all sides Ot carefully inspected the terrain. There were no signs of life. It was probably a shepherd's cabin for summer pasturage. The perfect spot to bed down for the night.

The shack was indeed empty, yet amazingly well designed and sufficiently well built that it provided enough warmth. But what would Ot do with his horse? The door that he painstakingly pried open with his dagger was certainly too low to let the horse in as well. And if he left it outside? Wolves? Other beasts? The devil's own emissaries? Werewolves? And why not werewolves? He took another careful look around at the interior of the shack. In fact, the roof was high enough to accommodate both man and horse. Shepherds in summertime obviously didn't need a ceiling. There was just the roof up at the top. At first Ot tried to coax the horse into hunching down, in order to get it through the door, then he tugged at the reins, but it was useless. He looked for some tool he could use to knock the cross timber out from over the doorway. He found nothing. Whoever had stayed here had taken everything with them. All they'd left behind was some dirty crockery and rotten hay. Ot found a big, heavy rock outside that he heaved at the doorframe with all his might, so that the wood groaned and the impact echoed off the mountain and then vanished into the trees. He heaved it once more, and now the whole assemblage was a shambles. Just as long as the damned shack doesn't collapse on top of me. He led the horse back up to the doorway, then he managed to pry some planks and timbers out of it. Still not enough. He would have to remove the cross beam. He tied a heavy rope around it and attached that to the saddle. Then he swung at the horse's hindquarters with all his might, causing the animal to leap forward and the doorway to crack.

Now there was enough space, but this solution had led to additional problems. Would he now have to sleep with the door open? Ot collected all the broken wood and took it inside, where he set it on the floor at the doorway. This'll make a racket if somebody tries to get in, he told himself.

It was a long night with little sleep. The wolves soon started howling outside, and they were in excellent form. What sort of place have I come to in these damned highlands? he wondered. Why am I still steering clear of people—who said it was necessary? He went on listening to the hungry howling that announced the arrival of winter. In this day and age, he said to himself, in this modern age, with the countryside as settled as this and with a well-organized system of roads, to think that there are still packs of wild, howling beasts at large in an age like ours! And soon, whether because he was afraid of spending the night alone up in the highlands, or just on account of the howling outside, Johan Ot once again took to thinking of all the evil spirits that probably haunted such places—themselves in the form of wild beasts. Should he pray? Would the ardent faith of his new coreligionists, more powerful and more ardent than any other faith of modern times, save him from this anguish? Or should he seize onto some amulet, some inscription, some symbol—about any of which he could have held forth at length not so long ago? Profound, unyielding doubt lodged in him that night.

When he woke up in the morning, he was greeted by the dark curtain of the sky and a pasture lightly covered with snow, and snowflakes here and there still tumbling down from the sky. The start of the new day was none too encouraging. Snow in the highlands and steep paths downhill. How would he manage with the horse? He lit a small fire in the middle of the shack and warmed up some wine on it. He gulped it down hot, and everything around him now appeared less hostile and unreliable. But Ot's worries were justified. Right over the ridge the path started down the hillside in switchbacks, and very steep ones. The animal took fright and resisted, so that Ot had to pull it by the reins and shout orders at it. Somewhere halfway down, when it was no longer snowing and the smoke of the next village showed in a momentary burst of light that shone out of a rift in the sky, the path started to rise again gently just before it plunged twelve feet straight down to a narrow ledge. Johan Ot wiped the beads of sweat off his forehead. There was no going forward. To his left the hillside swept steeply downward between stones and scant trees, while to his right the slope was so overgrown with brush that there was no getting through it. There was quite simply no way out. The path led in only one direction—back, which at his present rate of speed meant another night spent on top of the hill, because the descent waiting for him on the other side was no less demanding. Should he leave the animal to the wolves or just put a bullet in its head and continue on foot? Nature was playing a cruel game with Johan Ot.

He decided to leave the horse in the shepherd's hut and come back for it some day soon with one of the villagers to show him the way. And this he proceeded to do. He didn't reach the hilltop until just before nightfall, because the horse refused to move quickly over the frozen and slippery earth. But at this point it would have been risky to try going back even by foot. Ot resolved to spend one more night at the shack. There really was no other choice.

He dumped out some oats for the horse and poured some dirty water into a pail and flung himself down on some straw. He pulled up his blanket and, exhausted, fell asleep in an instant. In the middle of the night he was awakened by a shuffling and clatter as the horse anxiously kicked and prodded at the pile of wood. Ot sat up and listened, all ears. Something squealed outside, and then, just on the other side of the thin wooden wall, Ot could hear this something feeling its way along the exterior of the shack. Something was breathing deeply and forcefully. Ot hit the wall with a stick and the howling on the other side retreated toward the woods.

After that there was no more sleep for weary eyes. Have I got something haunting me again, Johan Ot wondered, some devil sending his werewolves after me? Has some damned Fate gone and decided that I have to spend yet another night on this snowbound hilltop?

He was still awake, though numb and terrified, when morning came. He had no desire to warm up his wine and just drank it down cold. Bottoms up. Now he was strong and steadfast again. What wolves, what hilltop, what snow? He would see the valley floor this very day. As if heaven were taking pity on his foolhardy undertaking, which in these circumstances could easily leave him at the bottom of some precipice, where foxes would trot off into the woods with his bones, the sky suddenly cleared. The sun shone through bright, warm, and cheerful, and there was no doubt that the trails would be softening up soon.

He set out around midafternoon, and roughly a hundred yards before the treacherous ledge his clever animal sought out a safer path of its own accord, veering off through the brush on the upslope from the path.

In the morning Ot reached the village, incredulous yet with eyes that shone with the hungry look of a pack of wolves.

He paid the mistrustful innkeeper in advance, completely confounding the man, who would never have expected this lone, armed traveler to pay for room and board for his horse and himself in advance. And copiously.

Ot woke up around midday. His fingers trembling, he untied both his bags, but nothing was missing from either one. Even his horse was shuffling contentedly in the barn, well fed. It's a miracle, he said to himself, another miracle. I haven't been robbed and I'm still alive. But I can't depend on this kind of miracle anymore.

A while later it dawned on him. That band of merchants had also spent the night at the inn, accompanied by its armed guard. The guards had kept watch all through the night. This was the explanation. For experience had taught Johan Ot that a lone traveler bearing silver and a small mountain of tanned goat leather, staying overnight at a remote village's desolate inn, could not count on seeing another bright, healthy morning under ordinary circumstances.

He lost no time in engaging the merchants in conversation. They were traveling to Tyrol. They would sell wine, grain, oil, linen, and other goods in the lands to the north. They would come back with fabrics, canvas, wool, leather, and metal goods—stuff that really sells. The profits were extraordinary, as long as you could handle all the problems and obstacles that the authorities, willful townspeople, bands of robbers, bad weather, and disease dealt you along the way.

So could Johan Ot travel some of the way with them? Why not, if he didn't mind being part of their armed guard.

They would be setting out in the morning. What they needed now was a good rest. Their plan was to cover a large distance without any stops.

That afternoon Johan Ot took a walk through the village. He looked at the nicely built, modest, well-kept houses. If not for the mud that the autumn sun had melted after the previous night's freeze, and which the locals had done a thorough job of kneading and churning up, the village wouldn't have created quite the ramshackle impression that he'd got coming down the hillside. But there was something else that drew Ot's attention. As soon as he left the inn at the edge of the village, he saw a woman running somewhere toward its center, her skirt flapping between her legs. She looked bewildered. A few paces on and he heard footsteps coming from behind. An old man wheezed past taking deep breaths and not even looking his way, with a child, possibly a grandson, who knows, running in his wake. Something was happening there. The herd had already stampeded, with all the healthy ones in the first waves and now the feeble and the procrastinators hurrying to keep up. Don't tell me I'm about to see another naked woman in the mud, Johan Ot thought and paused for a moment. Don't tell me there's some new humiliation in store.

He could hear loud voices coming from just beyond the next house. When he rounded the corner he almost ran into a large group of people crowded tightly together, every one of them a proper hayseed with a solemn expression on his face. All of them were staring ahead to where a stern-featured man was standing, waving his arms ardently, which alone would have conveyed his fervor even if he'd kept his mouth shut. But no, he was preaching something to the assembled townspeople at the top of his voice:

That their procession had been broken up. That the town guards had forcibly intervened in the affairs of faithful Christians who were in the midst of a pilgrimage, undertaken honestly and in good faith. That the bishop had issued a terrible proclamation, stating that no processions had been sanctioned for this day, least of all one prescribing the use of whips by its pilgrims for purging their sins and emulating the martyrdom of their Lord.

Behind Ot's head, against the black background of the mountainside, a colorful banner with some sort of holy image on it waved in the wind. The people listened in silence. No exclamations, no signs of displeasure, nothing. They just listened, and their silence amid such fiery words was all the more eloquent.

That despite all decrees, the man went on, those heretical Lutheran apostates were still being allowed to christen themselves with ordinary water, take communion under two signs, and lead shameless lives. That shameful pacts and treaties were being struck with the heretical Turk, even as he continued to rampage through our lands. That the Lutheran lie of a pure gospel was being tolerated. And yet, while all of this went on, the most zealously faithful believers were being persecuted, interrogated, and tortured, and their processions were being dispersed. That it was time to put an end to all of this, and that surely the Duke and Emperor knew nothing of these goings-on, the speaker concluded to a subdued murmur of assent.

He's one of us, Johan Ot thought. No question about it, the procession was one of ours. Then it was true what they said: the new brotherhood hadn't died out. It was still holding on in remote settlements and villages like this. And it had the audacity to raise its head up and be seen. Ot thought of going up to the speaker and telling him that they weren't alone and that the organization was at work elsewhere, too. He knew he ought to do it, but he also knew that this particular group had gone too far. This group was out of control.

Things were going to get nasty in this village by tomorrow. Maybe even sooner, depending entirely on how long it would take the spy in the audience to reach his destination, how long it would take there to write up the warrants, and then how long it would take the guards to get here in this bad weather. Still, there was no question: they would be here by tomorrow.

Ot spun around and headed quickly toward the inn. He went upstairs and flung himself on the bed. Our people? he thought. Our people? The doubt that had first got under his skin up on the mountain now grabbed him once more and bored into him. Were these monstrous, fanatical questions of life and death really his as well as theirs?

Yes, some skeptical devil had taken hold of Johan Ot once again. Once again something started to knead and worry at something in his brain. How many times had he already paid for this unbearable weakness? How many times would he have to pay yet?

It gnawed and bored into him, until he started pulling his beard out as he nervously paced back and forth in his room. Then a sudden stop, and a shudder: was this really the time for questions like these? Was this the moment for second thoughts? He had to decide, to take action. He didn't dare set out at once: guards might intercept him, or he could get mistaken for a spy and killed. These coarse peasants wouldn't think twice about shoving a knife into the back of a member of the brotherhood before bothering to ask questions. Ot would stay with the merchants, stay at the inn till morning—that, after all, was the surest way of getting out of this crazy village, into which who knows what demon hellcat had lured him on this dangerous, this chaotic day, of all the days he might have chosen. He would stay, and that would be how he would get out of there with his hide intact.

That's what it's all about, he thought, isn't that what it's all about, Johan Ot? That and not a thing else in the world.

He had a flash of insight that day, and later he found it hard to shake off the thought that if this country really was such a mess, if it really was the miserable hellhole it seemed, then the brotherhood shared responsibility for that fact, with or without its good intentions.

That evening over drinks the conversation took a turn that Johan Ot would just as soon have avoided. The merchants had been drinking all afternoon and by now their tongues were quite loose. They had no interest in shop talk now and were talking more and more about past and current events. One of them, with the unusual name of Ivan Adam, gave vent to his thoughts most volubly, and apparently without any fear of consequences. He had drunk so much wine that it dripped down his beard and onto his clothes, and he pounded his mug on the table to underscore his words. Another man, who was apparently the group's leader, was caustic and gloomy. He observed the goings-on around him with his cat eyes and spoke solemnly to try to bring Adam and the other loud drinkers to their senses. But Krobath—that was his name—didn't meet with much success. The company was predisposed to be anything but constructive.

"Who thinks," Adam banged his mug against the table, "who thinks that this snot-nosed little emperor with his pack of bought and paid-for bureaucrats, obstinate nobles, greedy clerics, and then all his good will and frailty, who thinks he'll ever be able to bring order to this accursed, anarchic country? Anyone with half an idea in his head can give it to him up his powdered ass. Here and abroad. The French, the Turks, the Hungarians, the Venetians, the Lutherans, the Papists, the merchants, the nobles—anyone can do with him whatever he wants."

Shivers went down Johan Ot's spine. He hadn't heard verbal abuse like this in a long time. But it was just drunken babble. The ones earlier today, at the assembly—they were more serious and more dangerous.

"And those buffoons," Adam shouted, "this afternoon. Did any of you hear that insane, incoherent speech they gave? Now there's a crowd that will hack and hew each other to death, flagellating themselves like madmen, leaping through flames, and all sorts of other idiocies."

"They're capable of a lot worse than that," Krobath added coolly and clearly. "Not far from here there's this strange custom, a pilgrimage they call Vierbergen. Every other Friday after Easter they run up to the top of four mountains. They run like mad through horrible terrain, over rocks, through barrens, through nettles, with gashes on their feet and legs, their bodies lashed by switches. They run to the top of each mountain and they scoot around its church on their knees and then they run on to the next. I saw them, once. They were so lean, bloody, exhausted, and battered that it made a person want to vomit."

"Are you talking about the new brotherhood?" Johan Ot asked quietly, in order to conceal the shivers that had just coursed through his body again.

"New or old," Adam shouted. "Nobody has figured out how to stomp on their fingers. Least of all that shitty little Leopold. The man just can't give up his hobbyhorse. It's a fucking shame, the kind of emperor we're stuck with."

"That's right," a short, bald man with a squeaky voice said. "That's right. If people can speak about him like this, out loud, then he must not be worth very much." The little fellow was happy with his clever remark. Then he bowed his head back down and disappeared in his mug.

"No," Krobath said. "There really isn't any way to teach those lunatics a lesson. The rack is probably too comfy for them. By god, near Cologne the inquisitors burned some bishop at the stake for having had his way with some nun. And they did it with his highness's permission.

Who's to say that some conspiratorial devil didn't have his claws sunk into that business?"

"Drop it," Adam said, calm now, so he could steer the conversation back toward his powdered sovereign. "That was a long time ago, under a different emperor."

"Whichever one it was," Johan Ot said cautiously, "he knew what he was doing. You can be sure that bishop had some demon in him. They're everywhere."

Startled, the group fell silent and all turned to look at Ot.

"Sure," Adam said, "I suppose there's no harm if the big shots roast each other now and then."

"They're no use to us, anyway," Krobath added. "These theological and political feuds of theirs only hurt business."

"Let them roast each other, let them slaughter each other," Adam started getting worked up again. "For thirty years they slaughtered each other like cattle over one image or two, over some 'pure gospel.' God help them. Now the French have got them scared out of their pants. Tomorrow it will be the Spaniards, and the day after that it will be that bunch there." Adam pointed his finger at the wall and beyond it.

"And uppity peasants," Krobath said.

"Who keep bashing each other's bloody heads in for nothing," the little fellow interjected.

"Well, all right," Adam said, "so they strung up some nuns and ladies of the court. At least that much was worthwhile."

"But not for business," Krobath said.

"You goddamned pragmatist," Adam shouted, again legitimately incensed. "You don't care a bit about those pampered idiots so long as you can buy them off."

"I care about business," Krobath said.

"I care about Leopold's powdered ass," Adam said.

"Let's drink," Johan Ot said, and pitchers of red wine were handed down the length of the table again.

He wasn't anxious anymore. These men know what they're doing. Everyone needs their money. Everyone kisses up to them. They keep everyone else aloft. They travel. They stay informed. The flow of information is in their hands. They are the conscience of their time. Everything else is just secondary or tertiary or less. Everyone else is trapped in their various conspiracies. But these men are with all and against all. For themselves. For their pockets. For wine.

"To Dorotea," the little fellow suddenly exclaimed. "I drink to Dorotea, to her health. May she and her white tits be waiting for me."

"Me too," Adam said and winked. "To her health, and may she not be getting diddled right now by some night watchman."

Johan Ot was relieved. The dangerous conversation was over. There would be no further mention of the insane, heretical brotherhood. Nor the emperor's ass. Now it was time to drink. Now it was time for their heads to clunk down on the table, warm inebriation coursing through their veins.

Only Adam and Johan Ot held strong. They ate, swallowed, belched, spat, shouted, threw coins around, and slapped the innkeeper's wife on her backside. Something inside Johan Ot opened up, some volcano erupted down in his guts. Something broke, causing him to plant his dagger in the wooden tabletop and spew out such curses, such oaths, such vulgarity that the innkeeper's hair stood on end.

As the first light of day appeared outside, the two of them were left alone muttering among the pitcher shards, among the gristly pieces of meat flung and smeared around the table, among their early-morning delusions.

"You're good," Adam chuckled into his beard. "You spoke well. I like how you just spat things out. Listen," he said. "What I'm telling you now is dead serious. I've had it up to here with this lunacy. These burnings everywhere you go. Do you understand?" he asked. "Do you understand?"

Johan Ot was silent. This person really did have some sort of demon inside him. He just wouldn't give up.

"I'll show you," Adam said, getting up. "Wait here, I'll show you."

He pushed off from the table and stumbled creakily up the stairs. At the top he slipped and crashed down onto the wooden floor, and it took a long time for him to get back up.

In the meantime, Ot was succumbing. He looked through foggy eyes at the table with its puddles and the shaft of light falling on it. His stomach was upset. He felt nauseated. He put his head down on his arms and fell asleep.

Adam poked him in the ribs with his dagger. Ot raised his head and saw Adam's face grinning down at him, framed by the ceiling.

"Are you still conscious?" Adam asked. "Listen."

He unfolded a sheet of paper and sat down next to Johan Ot.

"Listen," he said. "I'm going to read you something." He pushed the paper toward the middle of the table, where the beam of light was now shining. He began reading slowly and with emphasis. Every trace of drunkenness was gone from his voice.

"Ana Jelenko testifies that in Gorjansko Marija Drajnar plucked out the eyes of the Christ on the cross and consequently went blind. Ana Jelenko further testifies that Marija Drajnar prepared a special dish made from some strange plants. They couldn't have been medicinal plants, because they stank terribly. When Jelenko tried the dish, her face became ugly and distorted, as though someone else had crept under her skin. Ana Jelenko also witnessed Marija Drajnar preparing a dish made of lizards, vipers, slugs, and toads. When Jelenko tried *that* dish, her skin started to peel. Together the two women were responsible for the livestock in St. Ana succumbing to pestilence. Once they took eight stones, breathed onto them, and thus caused a hailstorm. But Ana Jelenko and Marija Drajnar aren't just guilty of the damage that they've caused and they aren't just guilty of being in contact with the forces of evil. While under investigation, during the stage of proof, Ana Jelenko testified that other witches—whose names she has not yet produced—had killed a peasant named Jakob. As of now, Ana Jelenko has not yet testified as to the method used for the aforementioned murder. Apparently the witches had set out vipers and toads to dry on top of a beehive built by this Jakob. There is probably some connection between the drying of lizards on the beehive built by Jakob and the murder that occurred shortly after- ward, though this remains obscure for now. And then: the witches Lužnik, Rosenkranz, and Marjeta bathed in a tub. The three evildoers were ordered to empty the water from the tub down the side of a hill, shortly after which a severe hailstorm ensued. The aforementioned witches, whom Ana Jelenko named under intense interrogation, will be included in this investigation immediately. Ana Jelenko testified that she had been in communication with an evil spirit that went by the name of 'Blackie.'

"All of the witches, according to Ana Jelenko's testimony, had bells and a ram's horn. It is obvious what they used these implements for— summoning their demons. The peasant woman Neža, who was in- terrogated during these proceedings, admitted that she drank wine with a certain Marjeta (determine whether this is the same Marjeta as the defendant Marjeta Luegendorfer) and then went with her to a crossroads where Marjeta (Luegendorfer?) called out, "Chick, chick, chick!" which brought forth a devil who gave her money. Regarding the interrogation of Ana Jelenko, townswoman Krautner must also be summoned and charged in the poisoning of four individuals who died last September. It is quite conceivable that this Krautner and her associates baked a cake into which they mixed poisonous substances and thus ended four respectable Christian lives. And further, in connection with Ana Jelenko's testimony, the witch Lužnik, who is already under investigation, must be asked whether she and the wife of the mayor of Resnik told fortunes with a band of Gypsies on All Saints Eve. And did she go that same night to a crossroads near Resnik and grind up human bones? Her testimony will tell us why there was such a hailstorm the night before All Saints Day. And on the night of Three Kings' Day, Ana Jelenko and an individual whose name she does not know blew bits of human bones to the four winds while holding up a crucifix. Ana Jelenko further testifies that she learned from a certain Marjeta (Luegendorfer?) how to induce mothers to kill their children. The spirits of various dead witches, named Pfefferl, Kuhschwein, Prokvas, and Magerl, are black as cats, according to Ana Jelenko, and kept in corked bottles."

Adam drew these last two words out emphatically and then fell silent. Eventually he added:

"And here's a brief note written in a different hand:

"Determine what kind of bath was prepared out of wine, water, milk, and salt in Gačnik. Perhaps used for provoking a storm? Determine who exactly seduced the peasant woman Neža and who taught her the incantation she used to dry up the milk of cows at pasture. Determine in greater detail how they were able to make themselves blind by plucking out Christ's eyes. Was the plucking out itself sufficient? Was some incantation used? Was some demon directly involved? Determine—since no mention is made in the testimony—which mothers killed their children under Ana Jelenko's influence. A.C., special commissioner."

The two men noticed that the morning sunlight had now expanded to reach every side of the room and was illuminating several drunken men from the armed convoy. Until now they had been utterly still, sleeping in their corners without so much as a murmur, as though the steady sound of Adam's voice reading had charmed them. Now one or another of them moaned in his sleep. And now the unrelenting sound of interminable soldiers' songs was coming from the stable. The same song with its endlessly repeating melody drifted in through the windows, around the room, and all through the village, reaching into the restless, skittish sleep of the villagers, refusing to stop. The pensioned soldiers had drunk straight through till morning, until broad daylight. All through the night and into the morning shadows had gone to the windows and nervously looked out at the road. The morning sunlight woke them all to a new day. It expanded every-where, illuminated everything.

"Did you hear what I read to you?" Adam asked.

"I heard," Ot said.

"And?"

"Nothing."

"Nothing? What do you mean, nothing?"

Johan Ot stared absently at the swelling sunlight.

"It's nothing new, Adam," he said. "There are so many of those sto-ries. So many witches and nooses. So many judges. So many hang-men. They're at each other's throats constantly."

"So, my dear saint, or whatever you are, since you know how to swear so elegantly," Adam said. "Do you know how old this docu-ment actually is? And do you know that they're burning witches to this day over nonsense like this?"

"Yes," Johan Ot said, attentive now and sober. "Yes, diabolic nonsense."

"Damn it, are you just another one of these damned fools? Tell me, can an evil spirit be stored in a corked bottle? Tell me what mother kills her own children! What 'chick, chick, chick' brings you money! Tell me!"

He looked Ot straight in the eye and his gaze reached deep inside, to where doubt and belief struggled inside. Johan Ot did not reply.

"I'm not saying there's no witchcraft," Adam said. "Listen, I'm not trying to say that there are no evil spirits or that the devil doesn't have a hand in all kinds of evil plots. But a spirit stored in a bottle, plucking the eyes out of a wooden statue of Jesus, devouring your own children—these things have nothing to do with witchcraft. These things are either just the products of incoherent raving, or filthy opportunism. Do you understand?"

"I understand," Johan Ot replied wearily. "But what I don't understand is why you keep yapping about these things. Sure, sometimes they overdid it. But what's one witch more or less when there are so many of them to deal with? Did you know that in the Duchy of Neisse they started out burning just forty-two of them at the stake? But when they saw how productive it was to fry up the little she-devils, they incinerated more than a thousand of them in ovens over the next few years—in ovens, mind you, not at the stake."

"You cretin. You perfect medical specimen of a cretin," said Adam, making Johan Ot smile. "'One witch more or less'? Are you really such a cretin or did they ram so much fear up your ass that you don't dare even squeak? 'One witch more or less.'"

The innkeeper and his wife were fumbling around on the upper floor, and the hollow thumping of it echoed down the stairs.

"It cost me a fortune, not to mention a lot of trouble, to get hold of this document. It means a great deal to me," Adam added.

Johan Ot tried to stand. Was he really going to get up from the table and leave this senseless, empty conversation and head right back out, sleepless, on his long journey? Was he really not going to get a minute's sleep? All he could think of was bed.

"It means a lot to me," Adam repeated.

Johan Ot tried to stand. Bed. Oblivion.

"Doesn't my name seem strange to you? A bit unlikely, perhaps?" Adam now insisted with clenched teeth.

"On the contrary," Ot said. "Not at all."

"But it *is* unlikely. In fact, it's completely made up." Adam took hold of Ot's arm with an iron grip. "It isn't my parents' name. Their name was the same as my grandmother's. My grandmother's name was Ana Jelenko. She and the Luegendorf woman taught mothers to murder their own children. They probably killed their own, too. That is, my parents. Get it? In cahoots with Kuhschwein. She produced storms. They say my grandmother roared and howled at the stake so horribly that not only Kuhschwein but at least a dozen other evil spirits must have still been with her at the time. Or maybe it was a hundred?"

Vertigo of a sort began to churn through the room and embers started burning Johan Ot's eyes. He could see the walls shifting and spinning around the distended face right in front of him, this face with its clenched teeth and bags under its eyes. All of this shifted and spun and churned inside Ot's skull, collided with the ceiling and walls and collapsed on itself. A nasty, spittly curse croaked to his lips.

The drunks in the stable kept singing their interminable battle songs.

8.

A clot and purgatives. A coincidence and investigation. A dark, empty oral cavity with no tongue inside. The struggle with nature. Adam's dangerous thoughts and hatreds.

Their departure was delayed. Not just because of the nasty hangovers they were collectively treating with some sort of broth, a hot concoction with pieces of fatty meat floating around inside it. And not just because the little bald fellow—the one who the night before had stared into his mug at the image of his Dorotea with her great, white breasts—not just because he hadn't returned from the stable after retreating there saying that something was lying heavy in his stomach. At Krobath's recommendation the bald fellow had taken a purgative, but probably too large a dose. As he reported later—actually quite some time later, that afternoon—he had endured such never-ending, watery shits that you could have sipped the stuff with a spoon. Until finally he discharged a clot almost as big as a pear. But, as we've said, neither of these facts was the actual reason for the delay. Because the thing that Johan Ot had anticipated did in fact happen.

Soldiers came galloping in on horseback that morning and disarmed the whole woozy company, corralling them into the ground floor of the inn. Upon his arrival in the village, the district justice was assured that this time his investigations would produce outstanding results. How curious that a group of merchants were overstaying their welcome at just the time a rally erupted protesting against the dispersal of a procession of flagellants. What links existed between these two facts? Clearly the enemy within was allied with forces from outside the country. And here is where they decided to meet. A village known for its outbreaks of heresy. Wherever you find flagellants who don't even bother to hide their convictions, but gather in public to protest official orders and decrees, there you won't just find heresy, but out-and-out rebellion. It was hard to believe that the convoy and demonstration could both have arrived at the same time simply by coincidence. There was almost no way this could be happenstance.

At first, the merchants and their humiliated convoy, eyes cast down to the ground—how could we let them disarm us like this!—weren't able to grasp what was happening. Was it contraband these soldiers were after? Were they going to bleed the merchants for tribute? Certainly they weren't going to be arrested for strolling over the mountain, braving the wolves and snow? But there was someone among them who knew what was at stake and what the authorities wanted. There was someone among them who kept his fear in his chest and was still working to think up just the right excuse. And that someone was Johan Ot, his head heavy and filled to the brim with the ugly thoughts and memories that Adam—he of the clenched teeth and the vague jumble of skeptical ideas—had conjured for Ot in the dim glare of daybreak.

As their predicament became clear, some of the convoy members were seized with panic. The little bald fellow had to run out for additional shitting, while two others began importuning the well-fed district justice, pleading with him and trying to persuade him how implausible it was that upstanding merchants working for His

Majesty might have anything to do with any demonic conspiracy. Adam threw a jug on the floor and spat out some curse that miraculously did not contain the exalted name of Leopold, let alone anything about his powdered ass. Still, they seized him and one of the soldiers whacked him on the back with the flat edge of his sword so hard that it went clunk and Adam moaned from the pain.

Only Krobath kept a cool head. With his face a picture of composure, he negotiated with the justice to have his hotheaded soldiers let go of Adam, and then Krobath went about calming his hysterical colleagues. With great dignity he invited the judge upstairs to his room to discuss things. He was volunteering himself for questioning. The red-faced justice took a drink from a jug, looked first at his soldiers and then at the stunned assembly, then nodded to his scribe, and the three of them went upstairs. Not much time went by at all before the scribe came back downstairs. His face an insouciant mask, as though nothing at all out of the ordinary had happened, he sat down among his own people and ordered wine.

It took a good long while for the two upstairs to come to an agreement—or rather, for the district justice to question the merchant Krobath about possible connections between his group and the heretical, rebellious peasants. In the meantime, the atmosphere in the inn became downright pleasant. No one, after all, had forbidden His Majesty's soldiers or the merchants and the members of their convoy to drink. So the former fortified their spirits and built up their courage for the new exploits awaiting them in the village—and especially those exploits having to do with the female part of the heretical population—while the latter tried to allay all the unpleasant feelings caused either by the long night they'd just spent, which should have been given over to restorative sleep, or, in the case of the armed escort, by the fear and humiliation inflicted on them by these greenhorns. The soldiers of the convoy were for the most part old, experienced hands who had fought on all the battlefields of Europe, under every possible commander, and in every possible uniform. Now all they were good for was frightening highwaymen—who were hardly known for their courage anyway. But they would be needed again, and soon. The French were already scheming, the Hungarians rebelling, the Turk once again sending his troops out on forays. And you never knew from one day to the next which way the otherwise formidable and courageous Croats were going to turn. No, there would never be a shortage of wars. So, really, both sets of fighting men, young and old, had more in common with each other than they did with either the merchants or officials. Really, there was no reason for these fellows to be threatening their own comrades with swords and blunderbusses. Far better that they drink together, rouse old memories, and get ready for new wars.

When the judge at last came flying out of the room upstairs, he beheld a scene that did no honor to an oath-bound ducal army. Swords and blunderbusses lay strewn over the tables and benches, wherever their owners had dropped them when they decided to exchange an iron handle for the round, pleasant contours of a wine jug. His boys were unbuttoned and talkative and their eyes shone. All down the line they had made friends with their bedraggled elders, with much mutual back slapping. Only the merchants sat silently at their own table off to the side, mentally counting their gold pieces, their goods, their holdings, which could soon very easily become someone else's property. Meanwhile, the innkeeper was about to lose his mind. His wife was almost in tatters, and no one, absolutely no one intended to pay for all this wine.

"What's going on here?" the justice roared from the top of the steps. "Where is the captain of the guard?"

Such a silence now ensued that the coughing of a single boy—which had stuck in his throat at the sound of the judge's shriek from above—could be heard echoing off the walls.

A fellow with a potbelly hanging out over his belt untangled himself from the innkeeper's wife's skirts and tried to approach the judge at attention. The official stared daggers at him.

"Fall in!" the captain shrieked, to make up for the bad impression, and everyone in the place obeyed the order—even the men from the convoy, who withdrew to their employers' end of the room. Now the two sides were facing each other again. One with weapons in hand, albeit standing on slightly wobbly legs, and the other up against the wall, jostling each other and chortling. Between them, on the battlefield, were half-empty pitchers and the innkeeper's wife, maneuvering her dress abashedly to cover her ample bosom.

Government authority had been reasserted and the judge was content. He walked down the stairs and rushed out the door, the iron decorations on his chest and around his waist bouncing and jingling.

The soldiers, now at ease, shrugged their shoulders as if to say "what do you expect, work is work," but the captain wasn't going to allow another slip. He marched into the center of the room, turned to face his men, and sized them up with a harsh, turkeylike glare. Silence took hold, once and for all.

Johan Ot bent down to a low-placed window and looked out. There were soldiers in the street, outside each house. The judge was running through the village giving orders. With much shouting, which was audible even here, people were being rousted out of their homes. The soldiers shoved the men with the butts of their guns and dragged the women by their hair. Someone hauled an old man out by his leg and pushed him into the mud. They were forcing them in the direction of yesterday's rally.

Krobath was nowhere to be seen. Adam got up and headed toward the steps, but he was immediately intercepted and put back in his place.

They could hear wild shouts of abuse outside. A woman's screams were so piercing and her voice so strong that Johan Ot thought in spite of himself of a slaughtered pig that just had its throat cut and is running around squirting blood everywhere.

Would there be blood? Would blood flow?

Would there be fire?

Then everything went just as quiet outside as in.

It must have been well after noon when Johan Ot saw through the window that people were slowly, quietly returning to their houses. Some soldiers were walking between them. Showing no inclination to rape, plunder, or start fires. Though clearly they had not been discouraged from so doing. Surely the village deserved some sort of collective punishment, a blow that each individual citizen would feel on his own skin, the better to dislodge the evil spirit that was squatting within each of those flagellant sectarians. Yes, something had happened back there, some measure had been taken, and now they were all coming home, as though from some solemn commemoration.

The people eventually dispersed. Not a soul could be seen, except for a bunch of soldiers clustered around the front door of the inn to keep warm and await the order to depart. It was obvious there was nothing left for them to do here.

A short time later the judge came waddling back up the road, his medals and insignia swaying. He came indoors and, brow furrowed, bounded up the steps. A moment later he came back down with Krobath. All the judge was able to say was "It's over," or something like that.

At a sign from the judge the turkeylike captain lifted the siege in the room. All at once everything collapsed. Everyone was in a hurry to get somewhere. The company of merchants pulled its bags together and loaded them on their wagons, the soldiers shouldered or sheathed their weapons, fastened the straps that held them, and saddled their horses, all of this taking place without a single word being said. The little bald merchant came in from somewhere, buttoning his trousers, as if to apologize, as if to say he'd really had the worst runs of his life. Damned purgative.

Soon the column was setting out. Johan Ot and Adam each upended one more pitcher of wine. It dribbled down their collars.

"You'll see," Johan Ot said, "it'll freeze and leave you some nice armor on your chest."

"A day like this has to be washed down with wine," Adam said. "This isn't the first time I've been in that sort of quarantine."

They tossed the innkeeper a bunch of coins, and he bowed to them all the way out the door, which made Johan Ot uncomfortable. They mounted the horses made ready for them and raced after the caravan. The road was hard now and almost frozen. The village looked abandoned and dreary. Not so much as a shadow moved behind any of the windows. From far off the riders caught sight of their party in the open space in the middle of the village—the same place where the rally had taken place the previous day. The convoy was completely motionless. The men were looking at something.

When Ot and Adam got closer, they saw what it was. The first was bound to a freshly hewn stake. His hands had been bound right up at the top, so that he hung more than stood beside it. He was trying to get to his feet, but collapsed each time. His whole back had been lashed open. The skin was bloody and broken, with plenty of white dermis showing through. Another stood in exactly the spot where the speaker had thundered yesterday. Instead of a nose, which they must have sliced off expertly, with a great deal of precision, he had a bloody mass, with two tiny black holes gaping at the viewers from inside the partly dried tissue. This one looked at them crazily yet hopefully, opening his mouth and grunting. His eyes gave him away. It was indeed the speaker. He would never again spread his dangerous ideas.

He would never again speak ill of the authorities, their decisions, or their actions. There was no tongue inside, just a dark, empty oral cavity which would never again produce anything but the "aaaaah" with which even now he was trying to preach or protest something.

"He won't be wiping his nose anymore," Adam said, but nobody laughed. Johan Ot felt as though he ought to have a good retch now, once and for all, to vomit out and expel all of the hellish insanity that simply refused to stop welling up around him.

The party moved past the figure silently, leaving him gurgling and groaning behind them.

Toward evening the air gradually began to warm as the black vault of the sky again pressed down on the earth with all its weight. The countryside was enclosed by mountains on every side, but the road that led through the barren lowlands was a good one. Its rises and descents were gentle, so that the horses—the only truly well-rested animals in the party—made easy progress. By contrast, the air was dense and heavy, like freshly kneaded dough. It swelled and expanded in the lungs and blood, causing people and horses alike to pant for more. It wasn't a strain to breathe it—but it passed through the body like some dense substance, concentrated and coarse. This black accumulation that pressed down uniformly onto the ground, as if a single mass, was a sure sign that something would happen. Soon a wind came up, and a mournful whistling that spanned all notes of the scale blew through the stumps of the trees and the crowns of the pines in the distance. The convoy decided to keep moving forward, regardless. They needed to be past Šentvid by morning. There would be no stop—they would eat and take care of their other necessities along the way. Krobath made this decision in the interests of all the allied merchants. They had wasted too much time in that sad little village they had chosen for their rest. This assessment was a wise one. After the effort it would take to get through these highlands—by no means inconsiderable, even though the merchants had chosen the most easily negotiable road—a more leisurely rest stop in the next village, at the base of the mountains, would provide the perfect starting point for their big push. No one could have anticipated that things would turn out quite differently.

After a while the wind abated and a semi-silence ensued, though the rushing air remained clearly audible as it withdrew over the mountain to the far side and began to plow through the valley. At this point the road began to rise slightly toward a passage between two great mountains. At the top, where the way led down again, the convoy encountered its first snowflakes. A soft breeze that the first wave of air had left behind drove the flakes lightly and finely into the men's faces, so that they stuck to their eyebrows, clung to their skin, and left wet traces.

"A man might crack without wine," Adam said and pulled the cork out of a flask. He took a swallow and handed it Johan, who returned it wordlessly when he felt the familiar swarming sensation suffuse his stomach walls, easing the tension of its cells.

The imperturbable men endured the fluttering snowflakes wordlessly all through the dark night that enfolded them. Now they could hardly see two paces ahead. The advance guard, into whose ranks the entire body of soldiers rotated regularly, would indicate with prolonged shouts at precise intervals which direction the road led and what the conditions were like up ahead. The convoy made slow progress. Then it began to snow even harder, and the flakes grew unpleasantly wet, finding their way down the men's necks and under their overcoats. The little bald fellow, Baltazar Kazelj Locatelli, whose guts had evidently begun cramping up again, lay among sacks on the wagon. Despite the comfortable and privileged status his illness brought him, he couldn't contain himself—at first he was just muttering to himself, then he began to complain out loud.

"Aren't we the clever ones," he called out into the darkness where Krobath was likely to be riding his horse. "Didn't we pick just the right day to rest and the right day to hit the road."

Adam growled something to the effect that he was going to give Locatelli a nice, warm punch in his wet face.

"Shut up," someone barked at the same time, and then for a good long while they could hear nothing but the singsong calls of the advance guard and drawling commands to the horses.

The skeins of snow were so densely woven now that the riders couldn't even see the crackling, smoldering flames of their torches. They were hacking their way through an out-and-out blizzard, struggling with the forces of nature.

Morning was still far off.

One of the merchants suddenly dropped out of his saddle. Two nights in a row without sleep, the first spent with wine and the innkeeper's curvaceous wife, the second in a battle with snow—even for a man who had endured a great deal in his life, this was too much. And with few exceptions, the merchants were hardly a cosseted class. Each of them had had to fight his way to his wealth, each was familiar with late-night ambushes, had led columns of stout pack horses into the Karst's winter wind. Each one knew of inns with bodies buried out back so deep that even the foxes couldn't dig them out. Each one knew how to handle a sword and fill a harquebus with gunpowder. Each knew how to chew dried bread and kindle a flame in a windstorm. Even though the days when you had to travel through wilderness for days on end were long past—for the land was thick with populated towns now and crisscrossed with reliable and vigorous lines of communication—you still met with frequent human and natural hazards. But this one had nonetheless reached the end of his tether and passed out. They set him among the bags next to the little bald fellow, who went from complaining to wailing and lamenting.

"We're not getting out of here alive," he sobbed. "What fool decided we were going to cover this much distance at one go? At night?"

And he began to rattle off a series of mournful prayers.

"If it weren't for Dorotea," Adam said to Johan Ot, "I'd really let him have it."

Johan Ot had a quick flash of the little female in the hay whose name he never even learned. However much he may have longed on this unbearable night to submerge in thought back to that shack with its smoke-saturated stench, he nevertheless drove this intruding scene away. It was too much connected with the image of Urban Posek, and with Jakob Demšar and the building of the Church of St. Fabian in Gorca. And with all the people he had yet to settle with, and who were responsible for his being here, whether he liked it or not.

The little man's monotonous prayer was infectious. A few of the others joined in, and their babble, mixed with the orders and oaths of the others, filled the deep night.

This felicitous harmony of prayers and curses in the midst of a blizzard was one of the most beautiful things that Johan Ot had ever heard.

The snow stubbornly refused to abate, so they stopped and briefly made camp under some firs with dense branches. They started two fires and warmed some wine on them. One thing was clear—only by sticking together would they make it through to morning. Adam lifted a mug and drank to Johan Ot.

"Admit it, you've never drunk in as pleasant a setting as this before," he said.

"I have," Ot answered. "Two nights ago, in the highlands."

"There's something I've been meaning to tell you," Adam said. "While we were busy drinking last night, they were waiting in their huts. They stayed up all night waiting for yesterday morning to come."

"I knew there would be a search," Johan Ot said.

"How's that?"

"I just did."

"You're an odd fellow," Adam said.

"Yes," Johan Ot said and went to tighten his horse's saddle, which had become loose after so much intense riding.

"I get the feeling you must have gone through a lot," Adam said with a note of curiosity in his voice a while later, when their horses were swaying their way through the snow again.

"If it all ended this minute, it would be too much," Johan Ot said. "But it won't," he added a moment later.

And it didn't. When morning came, the roofs of a town that had gotten quite close, without warning, showed through the curtain of snow.

Although they were dead tired and had, with great effort and the help of some house servants, dragged their cargo into a special room, and although the soldiers from the convoy had begun unfastening their broad belts even before their employers had finished this procedure, Krobath and the little fellow carefully inspected the goods. The sheep's cheese for Bavaria had all gone bad, water had got into the scorpion oil, and even the linen and linsey-woolsey were soaked. Only the wine and ironware were still usable. The losses were significant, especially considering the scorpion oil, which had been a major investment, bought from Carniolan peasants at a premium. But there was nothing they could do about it.

Johan Ot couldn't have cared less about his silver and goat leather. He tossed both bags in a corner and stretched out on his bed.

When he woke up toward evening, he tried to put his boots on, but they were soaked through. He tore off a piece of dry fabric from the bed cover and used it to wrap his feet. Shod like a beggar and dressed in his crumpled clothes, to which only his leather belt lent a shade of dignity, he went out into the dining room. Adam was already sitting there with a pitcher in hand, while Krobath was sipping some soup. They laughed when they saw him. Ot sat down. The innkeeper looked at him mistrustfully before bringing some hot soup and a jug of wine.

The men were in good spirits, even though their nighttime passage hadn't come cheap. Krobath turned to Adam and said, "Looks to me like you've read it to him, too."

Adam shrugged. "Sure, seeing as how he swears so nice."

"What do you mean?" Krobath asked.

"Come on, Johan," Adam coaxed their new companion. "Do it again. It was so nice to hear."

Johan Ot sipped his soup.

"I have to buy boots somewhere," he said.

"All right, I'll tell you. But it's a shame, because I don't do it nearly as good. He said he didn't give a shit for Papists, Lutherans, members of brotherhoods, witches, or doctors, but that he especially didn't give a shit for those masters of theology who go around whoring and drinking for nights on end and then start religious wars. He said they should pump an enema up some Lampretič's ass, so that he shits and shits till he drowns in his excrement. He said that the very existence of the court of inquisition is itself proof of godlessness and Satanism, and that he wasn't sure which one was stupider, the church or the state. I'll tell you, he said it beautifully. I can't remember it all. It's a shame he didn't say anything about Leopold. Johan, don't you want to say something about Leopold's majestic ass?"

"I was drunk," Johan Ot said. "I don't know what I said."

"Oh, you know," Adam laughed. "You know perfectly well." He got up and went to his room.

The other two were left alone. Krobath's eyes bored into Johan's face.

"He's obsessed with it," Krobath said. "Don't you see, he's obsessed with it. He reads that court document to anyone who strikes him as even a little bit independent-minded. It can't end well."

"No, it can't," Johan Ot said.

"And now it's not enough for him to make fun of the witch trials. Now he's become one of those people who promote sedition against Leopold in both the written and spoken word. Which is not quite as dangerous as the other thing, but there's no way any of it can end well if Adam keeps letting himself get drawn into this sort of business. And that's too bad, because he's a good businessman."

Adam came back. He was holding something behind his back.

"Speaking ill of me again, huh?" he asked Ot and continued in the same breath, "This, you see, is worth more than all our squabbles." He tossed a pair of firm, well-polished boots on the table.

"Take them," he said.

This sudden outburst of friendship didn't please Johan Ot one bit. But he really did need the boots.

9.

Has Johan Ot forsaken his covenant? Has he vanished into this colorful, merry merchant's life? Is it time for doubts to gnaw and eyes to roll? A person can't hide like this. A man can't escape his fate.

Winter wasn't easy for the band of merchants. The paths were just short of impassable and they had to change horses often. Each time a few guldiners would disappear in the process. Not that business flourished at this time of year in any case. Linen and steel from the iron works were the most saleable items. Krobath had a well-developed network of sellers and buyers, but they still couldn't point to any particular profit. On top of everything else, robbers multiplied like rats in this lean time and would try to strike at them whenever they came upon the next lonely place on the road. For this reason Krobath managed after long negotiations to attract three additional copper merchants to the convoy. He also tried to link up with a shoemakers' and leather goods guild to distribute all their products, but the potential collaborators walked away from the deal, deciding to establish their own network for sales. Whether or not highwaymen would ever risk attacking such a well-defended column, the imposing sight of the large convoy made any robber think twice—though perhaps the risk wasn't so great as might be assumed. Size notwithstanding, the party still traveled with the utmost caution. The authorities had already begun recruiting again for this or that new war, and the old soldiers were disappearing one by one. They were enticed by the prospect of another lazy winter of hanging out in the towns where the units were stationed, drinking, fighting with the townspeople, and whoring.

But life on the convoy didn't bore Johan Ot in the slightest. With the help of Krobath's sage advice he soon became a proper businessman himself. He managed to move his silver and goat leather. He acquired two more horses and in Salzburg bought some fine porcelain as well as knives and daggers. He sold these items in Carniola and Styria, bought up some white linen and leather, and when he went back north his assets increased quite respectably.

Now we see him in a Jew's countinghouse, his cold, calculating gaze drilling into the miserly, stammering man's forehead, trying to read his thoughts. You have to be firm with him, Krobath had said, they're an exceptionally capable people—greedy, but capable. Disgusting, Adam had added, with the Emperor's consent every last one of them was driven out of my hometown on the Drava, because they'd become such skinflints that no one could stand them anymore. The story goes that peasants dug one of them out of his grave and threw him over the fence for the wild animals to enjoy. The message was clear to Johan Ot: BE FIRM. The little man minced here and there through the dark room, while Ot sat calmly, speaking in a clear, brusque tone. Bargaining. Then Ot got up and went to the door, the little figure mincing after him. Money, he wanted the money, and his hands, which had become rather puffy and oily, stuffed it contentedly into his pockets and saddlebags.

Now we see him, Ot, in a tavern. Fat and wine glisten on his shaggy beard after he's wolfed down big slices of meat and sent wine in after to help them settle. He calls out orders with his mouth full. He hums some indecent songs. He spits, curses, throws money around, and slaps a fat whore on her rump. He and Adam have drilled more than their share of them. Krobath shakes his head. This is no good, it's no good at all. That kind of life is for soldiers. But the flow of capital doesn't dry up. In spite of the winter and the taverns and the wine and the women.

Now we see Ot trading horses, sampling salt in a coastal town, cutting a deal with a peasant at a village fair, pulling leather out of a bag and testing it in his powerful hands, holding fabric up to the light, closing a deal in a tavern.

That winter he was frequently seen all over the highlands and coastal region—in taverns, on desolate roads, in snowdrifts and on sunny days. He was involved everywhere, he was a partner everywhere, and everywhere he managed to finagle some advantage and profit. He never questioned what the purpose was of all this transporting, buying, selling, trading, and tricking. It was good. It made his pockets jingle.

One evening he said to Adam, "I think I have it better now than I've ever had it in my life."

You wouldn't have recognized Johan Ot, the gazer at stars, in this man—not easily. A beard had covered his face, he kept his hair oiled and brushed flat, and his nice little belly was cinched up in a wide leather belt. Where had he learned to rub his hands and roll his eyes like this, and to rattle his sentences off at such a clip? He would haggle with the municipal judge and let him slap his back. It was downright embarrassing to watch the words spit out of his mouth and his hands fidget about his body as though searching for something. To see him wipe his forehead and dart his eyes this way and that.

But winter was soon over and the merchant convoy stepped into the first mud of springtime on the mountain paths. For Johan Ot, bad times had always come with the arrival of spring. They came bit by bit, yes, but once they had assembled, they were there in force.

One night he yanked at his own beard and hair and banged his head against the wall. He cursed so much that Adam turned pale. These were no longer the brilliant curses of the day of their first acquaintance—this came from deep inside, from a bad conscience and bad memories, from terror and wine.

The time came when Ot couldn't sleep and his gaze would wander over some landscape inside him. His eyes would dart around erratically and invisible forces took control of his body. Spasms jerked him around in bed and he grimaced in pain and bit into his lip. His teeth dug in deep, and then there was blood on his probing fingers. He stared at his fingers close up.

Around Easter the processions of flagellants awakened: a banner with a holy icon reaching to the sky over bent figures lashing and lashing each another in their quest for grace and purification.

Armed detachments sent by the authorities dispersed them. For these lashings concealed deep and dangerous spiritual impulses. And ideas. The authorities knew this. And Johan Ot knew it, too.

The sleepless nights became more and more frequent. Yes, Johan Ot knew that they hadn't forgotten about him. One of these days some stranger with his face covered would confront him.

True, the beggar's cart in which he'd been paraded from village to village like a vicious, wounded animal was far behind him now. Forgetfulness had done its work there. But what about the promises he had made in the cabin at the forest's edge? And his assignment? The devil's bait had seduced him into disappearing and forsaking his secret covenant forever. The devil? Yes, we don't mention the prince of darkness's name for nothing. Because one thing is clear. Whoever the devil takes control of, once his seeds have been planted in that person's blood, can never shake him loose. Either the devil has to be driven out by fire, or the victim will go on committing evil deeds in the world. What else is he good for, except harming righteous and pious people and stealing their health, their property, and their sleep at night?

No, Ot needed to keep on the move. This latest lapse had first overtaken him up in the hills. The next time his conscience had failed him was in the village with the rally and those reprisals.

That time he did the right thing. Why should he have delivered himself and all those good people into the clutches of the law?

But now?

Why had he failed to do the right thing this time?

No, a man can't hide like this. A man can't escape his fate. Justice, in one form or the other, was waiting for him once again.

10.

A blaze in the midst of the sky, the breaking of light, a twitching at the core of the body. The grim day-to-day life of merchants. Adam's curses, provocations, and continuing descent into some sort of dangerous rebellion. The man is bound to go too far.

The blaze was exactly in the middle of the sky. The fireball of the sun had become so inflamed on that day that its edges were melting. Far beyond the center of the blaze, its unbearable yellow light turned the blue sky into a harsh, dazzling-white surface. All during that unbearable day people cast their eyes to the ground, to the stumbling of their horses' hooves, where each step sent up a cloud of dust, as though they were traveling in light fog. The road was seemingly without end, as the column of merchants staggered and straggled forward. The linen on bent backs was at once soaked and dried to the point of stiffness. The sweat streamed from their underarms, but there were patches behind that dried in the heat, leaving bunched-up traces of salt. The soldiers, beltless and stripped to the waist, wandered helter-skelter between the carts of the caravan, cursing and then hocking big gobs of spit that were thick with the dust that shone and hovered in the air in thousands of barely perceptible particles. Even the grass no longer seemed to be breathing out its green freshness—instead, specks of dust and heat rasped through its veins.

This was the time of traveling and deal-making. There was scarcely a path that needed avoiding. Everywhere firm, reliable ground met their feet. Krobath's group had now shrunk significantly in size. After long consideration the merchants had split up, since this way the costs of maintaining their convoy—the drovers, wagon drivers, and armed guard—were also reduced. Adam and Ot, who had squandered the better part of their holdings in taverns, couldn't afford to separate themselves from Krobath's wise leadership. Clearly, it would have led to the ruin of them both. Sooner or later they would have squandered what was left in yet another tavern, if—that is—they weren't robbed while out drunk first, and their bodies even thrown, perhaps, into some deep well already containing the bodies of the countless foolish merchants who had come before them. Krobath was right to warn them that they'd been letting things go lately. Johan Ot's nights became longer and more difficult, with less and less sleep and more and more anxious and aimless staring this way and that. One day he made a decision. He selected two dependable soldiers and gave them horses loaded with silver and goat leather. They came back within a few days, having performed their task well. They had taken back the goods with a message from Johan Ot: Returning your loan. Deliver these goods to Jakob Demšar. Johan Ot felt relieved once it was done. But he was sorely mistaken if he thought he could fulfill his covenant so easily. The message the two soldiers brought back from Urban Posek was succinct: That's not all you owe.

He took to pacing about nervously again. He had attained absolutely no closure in this business. He had evaded nothing at all.

Adam's drinking bouts began to surpass all limits of reason. There was hardly a morning now that he woke up in bed. Wherever he went, he would start one of his provocative tirades that he rarely managed to finish. Not all of the people were against their young, handsome, and beneficent emperor, as Adam claimed in his delusion. Nor were all taverngoers so firmly convinced that it was impossible to get evil spirits into a bottle, which was one of the most frequent questions in the surveys that he undertook, the better to study nighttime public opinion. Everywhere, it seemed, there were decent, pious people who were supportive of both the secular and ecclesiastical authorities. As a result, there were more than a few nights when pitchers and chairs went flying through the room, or an angry sword cleft a table in two. How many times now had Krobath, who was sick of Adam's behavior, had to use his influence, his guldiners, and who knows what else with the municipal judge to rescue his companion from the latest mess? Business and politics do not go together, certainly not in the way that Adam conceived of them, and this fact began to show in his holdings. Of the nine pack horses he had originally owned, he now had just two, and it took him enormous effort to maintain even them with the help of Jewish loans, which were no longer so abhorrent to him.

The only one of the company who made any real economic progress was the little bald fellow, Baltasar Kazelj Locatelli. His holdings had grown and multiplied, turning him into quite a wealthy and respectable man. Perhaps even his Dorotea, who still has quite an exalted and important mission to perform in this story, would have fallen in love with and come to respect him, if not for his all too frequent digestive problems. Yet again he took too large a dose of purgative when Adam and his incendiary babble managed to get their Landsknechts and Swiss Guards into a brutal fight with the local watchmen. The townspeople were outraged and besieged the tavern all day, with the convoy's soldiers and, by chance, Krobath's group of merchants trapped inside. Of course Baltasar Kazelj Locatelli's digestive tract suffered for a long time after that, and he even had to seek refuge at home in Dorotea's care for a good month thereafter. By coincidence, Adam, who at the moment was in no hurry to get anywhere, spent part of that time as a guest in Baltasar's house.

So here was the convoy on this hot day, on this trail exuding dust that crept into every pore of their bodies. The horses farted loudly from the strain, and there were no stops, no water, no shade, no rest. Whenever Krobath decided they needed to cover a certain distance, they covered it. They always, or almost always, did right to listen to him. Whoever's not up to the journey, whoever can't take the strain is not meant for business, Krobath would say, and had better just stay home and sit with his wife.

The blaze was precisely in the middle of the sky.

This was the moment when time stops, when that ball over your head simply refuses to budge, when there's simply no movement to it up there in the sky. Johan Ot stared through the milky fluid splashed across the countryside. The vivid figure of the horseman in front of him swayed before his eyes. He could feel his skin folding and tautening scale-like under the pressure of the heat and he thought how one day all this travel would come to an end. Time stands still, he said to himself, and suddenly you're stretched out across a trail, and then maybe it goes on without you. Then on some other trail it stands still for someone else.

It's standing still for me, he now said almost out loud. It does on all of these trails, which are actually just a single one. And just a single damned ball in the sky, which blazes till the end of your life. In a refraction of the motionless light he saw a beggar's cart with a tall cage on it, hauling the miscreant who had inflicted so much evil on the populace. And he felt a strange twitching at the core of his body.

Wait, he said, didn't I already come to a stop on a hot day just like this one? Wasn't the same blazing ball in the sky, with shadowless trees in every direction? Wasn't there some vermin fidgeting under my skin then, just like right now? Yes, didn't I have some verminous brood squirming under my skin? But back then the blaze of light was followed by darkness. Back then something went pop at the back of my skull.

High up above, next to the sun in all the glare, he saw an oily face grinning and vaguely moving its lips, as if speaking.

He heard shouts up ahead. Someone had stopped the column and issued an order. Then he heard the tread of horse hooves, and somebody was trying to pull his hands from his head. But his hands kept their iron grip, to keep everything from flying and gushing apart when the blow came.

"Why have you stopped?" somebody asked. "Why have you dismounted?"

In the infinite, hot landscape he had stopped and was squeezing his cranium between his hands.

Then all of it abated, and he felt he could loosen his grip: everything had congealed and would hold together now.

"It's all right," he said and took a swallow of the warm, foul wine that Adam offered him.

"Heatstroke," Krobath said calmly a while later. "Too much sun and too much of your damned gluttony," he said to Adam.

But it wasn't heatstroke.

It was a memory and some germ in Johan Ot's body and mind that absolutely refused to leave him.

They rode up a shallow rise and from its top, on the plain far ahead of them, they saw miniature black figures moving around and bending down slowly. When the convoy drew close, they realized that these people were being made to do something to the road.

"These are even worse peons than us," Adam said. "These are real peons."

But Krobath was overjoyed.

"They're fixing the road. I can't believe it."

Krobath and the other merchants were by no means unaware of the fact that the roads of the outskirts of the empire were in a deplorable state. It was often impossible for a team of horses to make it over even the most negligible hill. At that time things were much better in the German lands and, as a result, German and Dutch merchants were getting much richer much faster. After all, on a wagon you could transport far more goods than on some old nag, which at most could carry three hundred pounds and would probably collapse under that in bad weather. Nor were they unaware that the local noblemen committed a scant 326 guldiners per year to road repairs, enough to patch up some insignificant bridge at best. So the sly old merchant's joy at his visions of stacks of newly minted coins in his pockets was not without foundation.

Indeed, these people were digging and hauling stones off of carts on this unbearable summer day. Though the master of the road works, thumping his stick on his back and expelling fine streams of spittle through his teeth, was not the least bit talkative about his project. How far along would the repairs go? By how much would they widen the road? Why were they doing this useful work at all? Who had commissioned it? Krobath showered him with questions, but the man just kept spitting.

"Somebody," he said in answer to this last question, and kicked the poor devil next to him, who then straightened his hunched-over back.

They met several more such groups, but got no more sensible answers from any of them.

At a building works and tollbooth, everything was revealed.

Later that year His Imperial Highness would be making a visit to these lands, once the road was wide enough to accommodate his coach.

Adam broke into a cold sweat. Him and his powdered ass, he said. Now we've got him.

11.

About the judge with a real devil inside him. About a ridiculous scuffle and hurt feelings in the Locatelli household. About innocent scenes with ugly consequences. About people with vinegar running in their veins.

Johan Ot's gurgling brain may have been cooking the thought that this moment of his journey was eternal, but in fact it passed. The blazing white molten ball rolled on toward the mountains and acquired sharp edges. Its color changed too, leaving a nice, firm ball glowing red over the hilltops. Thus illuminated, they drew westward to the ducal city by evening. The closer they got, the larger the busy human anthill became, tirelessly digging in the earth and hauling stones around. It looked as though the workers were going to keep grinding away well into the night, provided the moon lit their workplace. The road had to be ready for the holiday. Only a few months still separated these loyal subjects from the great moment.

The city was in an upbeat, holiday mood, as if already filled with anticipation for the great day when His Ducal and Imperial Grace would shine on their comings and goings. Lights were shining in windows and boisterous voices could be heard from the taverns, causing our group's throats to itch in joyous expectation. Traffic was heavy, with numerous carriages, craftsmen with their wares, peasants returning from selling or buying, merchants beckoning the passersby into their stores, soldiers on foot or on horseback, as well as numerous distinguished townspeople, guildsmen, officials, apothecaries, solicitors, scribes, and more, all of this crowd shifting and jostling back and forth, as though it were a torrential, eddying river. Johan Ot listened to the gurgling speech wafting toward him from all directions. The emperor could be proud of the capital of his duchy, a truly European city. His elfin, bald, but most especially respectable business associate, the one who had trouble with his intestines and purgatives, but also had a stunning house and a stunning Dorotea to compensate, Baltasar Kazelj Locatelli told Johan later that this place had Carniolans, Styrians, Carinthians, Croats, Italians, Tyroleans, Bavarians, Saxons, Franks, Swabians, Silesians, Moravians, Czechs, and even Danes, Pomeranians, Dutchmen, and Frenchmen living in it. Locatelli wanted to make it perfectly clear that he hadn't stumbled into making this city his home by accident—no, he had deliberately chosen it as the place where, as soon as he'd amassed enough guldiners, Dorotea and he would spend magnificent days boating, drinking, and listening to Italian singers. Of course he didn't hear Adam's comment on all of this: "That is, if she doesn't take off with the first Italian vagabond with a little more staying power than poor, pathetic Baltasar Kazelj Locatelli."

But the little fellow really did belong to the upper crust of town society. It wasn't for nothing that he'd spent arduous days and nights on desolate trails, fought his way up and over mountains, slept and eaten in filthy inns, and slowly but surely increased his stack of coins. His house truly was blessed with affluence, which he wanted to display in all its glory to the colleagues with whom—as he was later to say—he had faced all sorts of mortal dangers. Adam suspected that the little fellow would have preferred to stuff his coins in a safe and live more modestly, if not for Dorotea, who had surely insisted on a place that measured up to her beauty.

He had arranged for an exquisite dinner. In addition to the four merchants—their drivers and armed guard were already happily chasing skirts and imbibing in a number of the city's dives, much to the envy of Johan and Adam—the guests included some sort of master craftsman and his wife, the owner of a nearby inn and his wife (whom they called father and mother, in keeping with local custom), and who else but a municipal justice with his wife and daughter. When the latter appeared in his dazzling attire, something yanked at Johan Ot's guts. It took his appetite away to look at this ruddy-faced carouser with his sneaky, darting eyes, hopeless jokes, and low forehead, concealing a peasant brain all wound up in a scroll of writs and decrees and orders. His wife and daughter were spitting images of each other, all buttoned up to the neck and as dull as the law itself.

"Thank God," Adam said to him later, "that he has two women like that, picking away at him day and night."

The feeding was endless—buckwheat groats, soup, corn pudding, boar, roast pork, cheese, and southern fruits.

Johan Ot watched the townspeople gulping and gulping and knocking back wine as their famous bourgeois restraint steadily vanished. One thought kept drilling at Ot, and with every bite that the justice smacked between his lips, with every swig that he audibly gulped down, each time he hiccuped or belched, the thought drilled deeper—how can I make this lout suffer, somehow?

Because the fellow was singing his own praises. He was much too busy, there were far too many evil deeds being done in this corner of our beloved land for him to take any time off. First one fellow refuses to pay his taxes, then another beats up an innkeeper (mother and father audibly gasped), then there's a theft, then there's a murder

(Baltasar Kazelj Locatelli belched angrily, as though his stomach and guts were in tip-top condition), then some blackguard rapes a virgin (Dorotea cast her eyes up in despair), then heretics defile a holy icon (the justice's women crossed themselves), then those same heretics stone the justice's deputy who was sent to investigate the matter (the justice angrily banged his fist on the table)—his work is just unbelievably demanding and hard and consuming. And watch out, we're going to have problems with witches again soon. There aren't any in the city, but they're multiplying in the surrounding villages like vermin, like locusts (with looks of horror, all the assembled washed down this bad news with wine, while Adam, his hand trembling, knocked over his wine goblet and walked over to the window). Confounded scoundrels and murderers and criminals, the justice concluded his speech.

And as though suspecting that his words had not left a deep enough impression on the company, he added:

"Do you think it's easy to decide to have a thief's hand chopped off, to condemn a robber to rot in jail, to commit a rebellious peasant to row in a galley for life, to have a sinner's back thrashed with a stick till the skin splits and the flesh protrudes, even—and I've had a case like this—to order a criminal sewn up in a bag and thrown into a river?"

With this he hit his mark. Now the faces looking at him were respectful to the point of terror. He probably would have babbled and boasted on until morning, if not for Adam, who ruined it all for him.

"How very responsible," he suddenly called out, loud and clear from the window. "And dangerous."

A silence ensued as meaningful glances intersected: What's his problem? Why is he shouting at our nice, pleasant dinner? Dorotea tried to rein him in with the scolding glance of the all-powerful hostess, but it was too late. Adam was off and running.

"I know of a case," he said. "I suspect you're familiar with it too, judge. In Lower Styria there was a judge who sent countless witches to the stake. Actually, to be precise, he had some of them drowned, which, as I've heard, is also your own favorite method of execution. This man racked up one decoration after the other. All the signs were that he was on the verge of a brilliant career. In the district capital his zeal was well known and it was an open secret that he was going to be promoted soon. Nobody doubted that he would be made district justice—one of the most prominent men in the land, if you will, and in these difficult times practically its administrator."

The judge felt flattered to hear such recognition of a colleague and he nodded vigorously and raised his goblet. Before he had a chance to drink, though, something got stuck in his throat.

"But do you know what happened?" Adam continued. "The revered judge himself had a nasty demon inside him. He had the devil in him, you see. The man went a bit too far in his zeal, just a single step, you might say. He discovered evil spirits in the bishop's nephew. He tried to wring them out of him—you know, the rack and all the rest of it. To make things even worse, he used the Spanish boot, which is forbidden. But the bishop's nephew was not a sorcerer and he didn't even have a single demon inside him. When the judge found out that he had the bishop's nephew on his hands and not some spawn of the devil—because then the investigation would have had to proceed to the bishop himself—he put a stop to the trial right in the middle of the presentation of proof. And then an investigation was launched against *him*. It soon turned out that the justice did indeed have a devil inside him. Just one, but a confoundedly industrious one. They would have roasted him up for sure, if one of his former colleagues hadn't opened the jail door for him. Now he's a fugitive. Has anyone seen him? He's easy to recognize. It's his eyes. They're hot and bright from the spirit he's carrying inside him."

For a few moments there was painful silence in the room. Baltasar Kazelj Locatelli looked to Dorotea in despair, mother and father looked baffled that everyone was suddenly so quiet and wondered what was going on, and master and mistress craftsman awkwardly heaped meat on their plates to avoid doing nothing.

Dorotea tried to break the tension that was on the verge of bursting in all the silence. She cast a furtive but furious glance at Adam, who was standing right beside the judge's chair, with one hand on its back and the other on the table as he looked straight into the deathlike face from which every drop of blood had drained, the same blood that, just moments before, had provided those same cheeks with a robust and ruddy complexion. Johan Ot could feel Krobath's concerned and attentive gaze resting on him, as if asking "what now?"

Dorotea found her bearings. She stood up, raised her glass, and said, "To our industrious and righteous judge!"

But these words produced the opposite of the intended effect.

The judge's pale face flushed bright red. He stood up and pushed his chair back.

"Industrious? Do you mean to imply that I have some industrious demon lurking inside me?"

Then he turned to face Adam, even as his two women tried to pull him back down into his chair, and he solemnly declaimed:

"My dear sour wine merchant—or whatever it is you sell. The case you've cited does nothing to incriminate my rank or our judicial system in general, if that's what you meant to imply. We are people too, and subject to the devil's wiles, if we don't know how to fend them off. And let me warn you as well that you have just accused me of abetting a fugitive."

The judge's wife tried to minimize the scandal.

"No," she said. "That's not what he meant."

"Oh, that's what he meant all right," the judge raised his voice. "He stood right next to me, his breath blowing right in my face and stinking—you'll forgive me—stinking of sour wine, and he could only have meant me when he so pointedly asked, 'Has anyone seen him?' That's . . . that's . . ." the judge searched for the right word.

"Slander!" he finished and sat down in satisfaction. Thus, to all appearances, he had rescued his honor, the more so since Adam had wandered off and was silently pouring himself some more wine. Thanks to the concerted efforts of all present, and after a few more explanations and another glass of wine all around, the whole affair might have turned out well, if it weren't for something else occurring that nobody could have predicted. Baltasar Kazelj Locatelli, who out of sheer joy at hosting such a splendid dinner in his own house had drunk a substantial quantity of wine that evening, leaped to his feet, all red in the face. A few pieces of porcelain crashed to the floor behind him.

"I beg your pardon, judge," he exclaimed in a trembling voice. "But our wine is not sour. I cannot permit that to be said in my house."

The judge tried to clarify his insult.

"I wasn't saying that your wine is sour," he said. "His is."

"But we, we . . ." the little fellow began, on the verge of tears. "We all sell the same wine."

It was no longer possible to avoid a full-fledged scene.

"Then that means we sell sour wine, too," mother tavern keeper squawked. "We've been buying it from Kazelj for the past ten years."

And now the judge's wife could no longer restrain herself.

"It's not just bad," she hissed across the table. "It's diluted with water!"

All of them leaped to their feet as all hell broke loose. Father tavern keeper grabbed his wife by the waist from behind and held her back so that she wouldn't jump down the judge's wife's throat. The judge realized what a terrible disgrace it was for his wife to be bickering like a produce vendor with mother tavern keeper—with people, in other words, who ought to have been enormously proud of having spent an evening with him at table. Baltasar Kazelj Locatelli went hopping from Krobath to the judge and back, entreating both of them, his hands fidgeting. Master and mistress craftsman tried to continue eating, but with all his jumping around the little fellow managed to knock their plates onto the floor. They both got up, offended. Dorotea howled in falsetto, cradling her head in her lap and shaking, while her careful hairdo came undone and her multi-hued make-up smeared on her face, so that when she cast her eyes back up to the ceiling—toward heaven, in other words—to redouble her lament, she looked for all the world like a rainbow. Adam guffawed and ran into the kitchen to fetch the servants. These crowded around the doorway and giggled until Baltasar noticed them and ran over for a second to send them packing before heading back onto the field of battle. To add to the chaos, an Italian singer of glabrous visage and slicked-back hair, cradling a mandolin in his arms, appeared in their midst at that very instant—most likely by order of Locatelli: the evening's crowning glory. After standing in the door for a while and gazing dumbstruck at the fracas, his southern blood came to a boil and he walked straight into the epicenter of the battle. With a silken kerchief in hand, he bent down to brush the makeup off Dorotea's face and white bosom. At this point, Baltasar Kazelj Locatelli, who was beginning to realize what a colossal scandal was taking place in his house, one that would be the object of gossip for the next decade or at least until the emperor arrived, well, when he saw the damned Italian bending over his virtuous wife, he lost it completely. He dashed over and shoved the singer in his protruding ass, so that he went flying full force into Dorotea's breasts and practically tipped her over with her chair. Then Locatelli's stableman came running in and applied several kicks to help the poet decide to depart. As if the sudden blow to her breasts—used as they were to nothing but gentle caresses—had jolted her awake, Dorotea now leaped to her feet like a lioness.

"You miserable pygmy!" she roared. "Don't you lay a hand on me!" She lunged at Baltasar Kazelj Locatelli, who immediately quieted down and turned submissive, and shrieked a shower of spittle in his face. Adam tried to separate them, but then she just as suddenly released the little man from her grip.

"And you," she hissed at Adam. "You're damn wrong if you think you're going to get anything out of me tonight. Go look for it in the street. Or make a date with your fist." And then she broke out in uncontrollable sobbing again.

Hostilities gradually ceased. The combatants, out of breath, disheveled, unfastened, doused in wine, sat opposite one another staring daggers at their opponents. Mother tavern keeper was still banging her goblet on the table and the judge's wife was sobbing and pushing her husband to get her out of this nightmare as soon as possible. Father tavern keeper stared wordlessly into space, grinding his teeth. Baltasar Kazelj Locatelli, Adam, and the Italian singer, who had two black eyes from being worked over by the stableman and greasy hanks of brilliantined hair flopping down over his face—all three of them were leaning as one toward Dorotea, who was still emitting heartrending howls as she lay on a settee by the window.

Then the gentle voice of the mistress craftsman interrupted the hostess's sighs and moans.

"Where has your Matilda got to, Mrs. Judge?"

All of them looked around. Matilda was nowhere to be seen. She had vanished.

"Poor thing," the judge's wife said in a changed, most of all worried voice. "Poor thing, she probably ran home to escape this shameless spectacle. She's very sensitive, you know."

Even so, her words didn't sound too convincing, because Johan Ot was also nowhere to be seen.

The next morning Adam discovered Johan Ot in a tavern near the city gate. He was resting his head in his hands and staring vacantly into the mug before him as he sat in the midst of the convoy's soldiers, who were happily banging their mugs on the tables and belting out military marches. Drained, Adam sat back on the bench and took a drink of wine.

"I've been hard at it again," Adam said.

"With Dorotea?" Johan Ot asked.

"Behind her, beneath her, and with her a little bit too," Adam said. "She's not easy. Gets all excited, especially when she's been upset."

They were quiet for a while as they looked into their mugs and at the excited faces around them that just kept singing and singing.

"How about you?" Adam finally asked.

Johan Ot abruptly shook with joyless laughter.

"I don't know if I've ever done it with so much pure hatred," he said. "All evening I was trying to think up some way to hurt that lout of a judge. And then it came of its own accord. Thanks for inciting the fight—it was great."

Ot was speaking as freely now as if some numbness had passed.

"I suggested that I should escort her home from that horrible scuffle. She accepted immediately and we hadn't yet started down the steps when she lifted her skirt."

"So, you showed that gawky Matilda a good time. I couldn't have done it. She's already got a judge's face, like some fettered statute."

"It wasn't easy for me, either. But still, I did good. There'll be no sleep for the judge's family for a while. She was still a virgin, so the battle will rage on at their house. But, listen. When I put it in, you know, it squeaked. These people have got vinegar running in their veins."

12.

Is that his head throbbing after a bad night? The time leading up to great events. Filthy and happy. He smells of semen and sex and has that look in his eyes.

There was a hollow bang bang echoing in his head and reverberating through the room like thunder. These brutal blows banged through his capillaries toward his eyes, which were now filled from top to bottom with sharp, prickly light coming from somewhere up high. What sort of light is this, Johan Ot wondered. What's this stabbing my eyes, beating my head? For a long time he looked out the window, which admitted a real glare that originated far away and above, up in the sky. It's afternoon already, Johan said, and that's my head throbbing after a bad night. But it wasn't his head throbbing, because at that same instant the bang bang thundered again from its hollow depths, so that Johan Ot was forced to admit that he had no idea what was thumping. In the sullen wakefulness that follows a long night and too much wine he glanced around in search of the source of the sound. Adam lay on the other bed with his mouth wide open. Again came bang bang through the static gloom and this time

Johan Ot jumped. It's not in my head, he said. Somebody's banging on the door.

He got up, picked a jug of wine up off the floor and poured roughly a swallow's worth of it into Adam's gaping maw, which caused the latter to stop breathing. The wine got stuck somewhere and he spewed a showery stream of red up toward the ceiling. But then Adam was on his feet, running around the room, waving his arms and looking confused.

"Sorry," Johan Ot said. "I didn't mean to scare you. It's just that the judge's guards are banging on our door."

Adam came to his senses immediately. He pulled on his trousers, grabbed his sword, and ran to the window.

"We're too high up," Johan whispered. "Hide behind the door, instead."

Adam pressed close to the wall, holding the jug in both hands, so that he could smash it over their visitor's head, or whichever part of him he could reach.

The door drummed again and Johan Ot threw the latch. He yanked the door open and a stream of light poured from their room into the hallway. Standing in the doorway, his hand raised and ready to knock on the wood again, was Baltasar Kazelj Locatelli. His eyes were sunken and his bald head freshly scrubbed and pomaded.

His whole body was shaking. He came in and sat down on one of the beds. He didn't even turn around to look at Adam, who was still standing against the wall, holding the jug aloft.

"I nearly gave you a real whack on your bald head," Adam said.

"If only you had," Baltasar Kazelj Locatelli lamented. "If only you had, once and for all. What a mess! What a scandal!"

"Oh, come on, it can't be that bad," Johan Ot said.

"Oh, it's much worse than bad," Baltasar Kazelj Locatelli whimpered. "The whole town is talking about the fight in my house—my house. They're saying that mother tavern keeper told the judge's wife that her husband is utterly corrupt and crooked and nothing more than a lackey and I don't know what else. I'm supposed to have assaulted that lickspittle Italian singer out of jealousy. And then the judge and father tavern keep are said to have been tussling under the table, biting and pulling each other's hair out. They say the windowpanes at the judge's house were rattling all night, because their Matilda behaved like a slut in our house till morning. And on and on it goes—there's no end to it. Oh, dear God," the little fellow moaned, "what have I done to you that you punish me like this? Dorotea refuses to look at me. She says everything is my fault. I suppose it is. Downstairs, before I came up here, I heard that the judge's days are numbered. He shouldn't have got mixed up in this. His reputation is finished. They're going to fire him."

The little fellow was truly pitiful. His entire world had collapsed. So many years spent slowly building things up, so much effort accumulating his estate, respectability, and prestige in this town—and now a single evening had destroyed it all.

"Maybe something can still be salvaged," Adam said compassionately.

"No," he sobbed. "Nothing can be done. It's all over. Finished."

Johan Ot was thinking. Baltasar Kazelj Locatelli was indeed in dire straits and the judge's career was no better off, but the magistrate still had enough power and connections to get his revenge and make life very difficult for them all.

"The two of us had better just get out of town," he said.

"Wait," the little fellow said, jumping to his feet. "Don't you move. Don't you move one inch. We're going to get your things out of this miserable tavern and move you into our place."

"What?" asked Johan Ot. "I don't understand. We were part of the mess at your house. And I can imagine the judge would especially like to have Adam's head on a platter."

"Not one inch," Baltasar Kazelj Locatelli repeated emphatically. "Dorotea insists. It will only make things worse if you stay in this miserable inn or scamper off like dogs with your tails between your legs. Then it will be the drunken houseguests I pick up on my travels that get blamed for everything. And finally it will be just me—me— because I make friends with people like that and even invite them for dinner with the judge himself—I'll be the one who carries the stain for the rest of his life. We have to do just the opposite, is what Dorotea says. We have to put you up in our house—Krobath, too, of course— and lavish comfort and attention on you as though you were the most distinguished guests. And then things will be different."

"Very strange, indeed," Ot said. "But maybe he's right. We can't leave him in the lurch now."

"Dorotea, either," Adam sighed.

Reluctantly they began packing their things.

"Stop!" Baltasar Kazelj Locatelli exclaimed again. "You're not going anywhere like this," he practically ordered. "Not all scruffy and stubbly like this. First baths. Shaves. The very best clothes."

And so Johan Ot suddenly found himself living in one of the foremost houses in town—a very tall house with a studded front door and carved shutters and numerous rooms inside. After all the barns and stinking brotherhood huts and miserable taverns and even worse places he had lived in—with small, black animals scampering underfoot—he had earned this. He wasn't happy about accepting the offer, because he didn't want to be part of Dorotea's exhibition of make-believe, with fictitious wealthy (and correspondingly well-mannered) merchants in the featured roles. In fact, with the exception of Baltasar Kazelj Locatelli, they were a rather pathetic band of merchants. Perhaps Krobath still had some assets under wraps, but Adam and

Ot had long since given up the thought of owning anything like so splendid a house, managed by the charming Dorotea. But now Ot had accepted this role and would have to play it to the end, whatever that was to be. He knew it couldn't end well. It never had before.

But Dorotea couldn't have cared less about his doubts and fears. She threw herself into the work of transforming the two traders and itinerant dust-eaters into respectable and even commanding figures. Adam was no problem—he took to it like a fish to water. But Johan Ot was an ordeal. Everything bothered him, all of the silks and mantles, all the fine fabrics and scents they poured onto his neck; all of the oils they worked into his scalp to get rid of the smell of road, barn, and tavern, and to cover over the smell of the cheap grease he'd been using for his hair; all of this cinching up of clothes around his waist, and the tailor's hand reaching up to his crotch to make sure his newly tailored trousers hung just right—all this activity bothered him immensely, and he had a hard time hiding his unease. Who can turn a wolf—and a hunted wolf, at that—into a poodle? he thought. Only his belly lent him a modicum of distinction. Everything else—the features of his face, his gait, his movements, everything—only underscored what an alien creature was concealed by all this glitter.

He would be spending his nights with the dreary Krobath, according to Dorotea's plan, because Adam, thanks to who knew what exceptional service to the house, had been given his own room. It turned out that Dorotea had made an astute move when she invited her husband's business partners under their roof. Now no one could claim that it was just some transient lowlifes who had provoked the scandal. The lights were lit in the Locatelli house every night, and numerous distinguished guests came to visit—court magistrates and healers, master craftsmen, merchants of course, and others who simply couldn't refuse an invitation from Dorotea Kazelj Locatelli. Her little husband looked askance at all this profitless frittering away of

158

money, but that was as far as his displeasure went. It was clear that Dorotea was aiming high. She was going to advance the prestige of the firm and house of Locatelli a long way.

The little fellow also felt he should somehow compensate for at least part of the financial loss the company was now sure to incur. Not just the merchants, but their whole convoy was sitting idle in the city and living it up, rather than pushing down some dusty road. And the soldiers had become greedy. One of them had already made a few scratches in some charlatan's chest with his knife and there was reason to fear further incident—not that such a little scandal was at all significant in comparison with the one that took place that unhappy night in Locatelli's house. Still, for all of these reasons, but especially thanks to Dorotea, who had nothing against her husband heading out on a new business trip—on the contrary, she thought it would be good if he went on the road again, just without Adam, who had to stay in town and defend himself if there was a suit with the judge—for all of these reasons, one morning Baltasar Kazelj Locatelli set out with the entire caravan. Even Krobath was unable to resist the temptation. They loaded up on tin dishes that they would convert into money in the towns along the coast, and also large bolts of linsey-woolsey that would find their way to Senigallia near Ancona. Dorotea persuaded her beloved husband to reimburse Adam and Johan Ot for the use of their pack horses and equipment. They were reluctant to accept the money, since, after all, they were living in their house for free, but Dorotea said "no debts make good friends." Baltasar made a sour face and counted out their guldiners.

If poor Locatelli had known what was to become of his money while he was off making deals in far-off locales, sleeping alone in wretched inns, he most likely would not have allowed himself to be talked into taking that trip so readily. He might even have done something entirely unforeseen, something like what he did that one evening when he was filled with the courage of a lion. Indeed, Dorotea had most likely taken just such a possibility into account, which is why she behaved most prudently and wisely while her husband was away. There were always other guests present in the house who would be able to tell what a respectful distance the two guests of honor kept. Even the cook and the servants could confirm at any hour of the day that everything was on the up and up with their mistress. Upon his return, Baltasar most certainly got favorable reports about his Dorotea's moral integrity. Only the Italian poet was allowed to shower attention on her, but this, after all, was only in tribute to her beauty. But as the last guests left at night, so too did the door close in the singer's face, leaving him to sigh and moan under Dorotea's windows.

Johan Ot found the continual feasting and drinking quite to his liking. He sat up until late at night with the learned men who frequently visited, discussing the topics that had once been so dear to him—the healing arts, physics, and trade—but he kept clear of theology, metaphysics, and current affairs. He did not write down, draw, or interpret any symbols, markings, or words with deeper spiritual meanings.

Adam, on the other hand, began attending their hostess's soirees less and less. With each day that passed, he paced around that much more gloomily. Something was eating at him and drawing him away. His cheeks caved in and he developed dark circles under his eyes. At first Johan thought he looked so drained because of the arduous nights he was spending with Dorotea, but soon Ot realized that something else was to blame. In mid-July one of the emperor's ministers came to town. Quietly and without fanfare. He held long discussions at city hall, the content of which would be discussed every evening at Dorotea's salon. The minister was preparing for the arrival of Emperor Leopold, who was to be welcomed, as everywhere else along his route, by all the states general. The minister was checking on the preparations and arranging the details of the reception. He was, in short, a kind of chief of imperial protocol. By asking exceptionally cautious questions, Adam tried to find out the date of the emperor's arrival, but in fact no one knew anything definite. Even Dorotea was unable to help him. Immediately after this event Adam vanished for several days without a word of explanation. When he came back, he was even more withdrawn and preoccupied than before.

Johan Ot tried several times to drag out of Adam what was going on, but with no success. All he knew was that Adam was swimming in dangerous currents, beset by rapids and rocks. Ot didn't want to press the issue, because at the time he had enough on his hands dealing with Matilda. The girl had basically begun to stalk him. In church and on the street she would give him signs whenever she could, and eventually she started sending him messages. Despite the exceptional vigilance of her parents, who had already recovered from their social blunder, thanks to the pending imperial visit, which put everything else in its shadow, she had managed to lift her skirts for Johan Ot again. It happened one night when he got a message saying that she would be waiting for him on a side street in the wee hours. Ot was tired of all the feasting and palavering, which had grown exhaustingly monotonous, and in his drunken haze he decided to punish the judge once more, even though he really didn't even hate him anymore. The judge was, after all, merely a useful tool in these difficult times, when everyone had some lapse to account for.

It happened on a sort of trash heap, among some slippery food remains, with cats yowling around them, a fast and slippery experience that left Ot panting. But Matilda was happy. Filthy and happy.

Whoever smells of semen and sex, whoever has that look in his eyes, is already beyond hope. He gets tangled up in a woman's skirts and breasts and thighs and sweaty hands, her impassioned sighs and gasps, and the nights fly past. This is how, in the days before the great historic events that were fast approaching, Johan Ot forgot himself and his caution, which had long been leading him safely past the hazards that in fateful times like these lie in wait for a person at every step. Because one morning, when he was coming back from seeing Matilda, there was a white figure standing on the steps leading up to his room. It was holding a candle and its hair was let down. In short, a familiar scene. Dorotea did not step out of his way. She didn't even move. Thus they stood looking each other in the eye, and something nasty and scurrilous, something raw, something common, some perverse-smelling thing must have emanated from this man, who wasn't even all that handsome or young, certainly not enough to tempt a respectable woman who already had two lovers in addition to Baltasar Kazelj Locatelli, to shamelessly stand in his way like this. Then, without a word or a sound, without a smile or a nod, she followed Ot up, and in the early morning light he watched her milky white, smooth, rounded, captivating body bend over him, approaching him from above, then retreating, those great breasts now let loose and moving over his skin, her fingers that skittered and caressed and reached every sensitive part of his body, that bit of her face he could see way up above framed by her loosened hair, those teeth biting into her fleshy upper lip—he watched her prepare and arrange and adjust the motionless and aroused male body beneath her, so that at last her strange, intoxicating mass could mount him and lie upon him, so it could move and squeeze and milk and finally burst, explode, subside, and collapse all over him, enveloping him in its fleshy omnipresence.

13.

The longest night. Thighsthighsthighs in sight, sound, and touch: the simulacrum of death in a woman's softness. The great rehearsals. Pamphlets. Arrests. Abrasure. Two organisms. A dangerous intention casting about in his breast. The emperor twitches in his sleep. The accused not sure if he'll live to see morning.

And it truly collapsed all over him, it truly enveloped him. Gone from his grim view were the lone fires, the deserted landscapes, the highlands in the first snow of winter, his lonesome homestead, the walls of the tower of justice, soldiers' faces in taverns—flushed, drunken faces, the jeers of the enraged mob, the filthy rooms of dilapidated mountain cabins, the smoke, the sun, the snow, the vast hindquarters of horses in their steady, undulous rhythm, the entire swarming anthill that till now had coursed through his brain each night as he went to sleep—all of this was now strained out, drained, gone. The bitter memories had melted into the brilliance of this naked female body, the flit and flutter of delicate fabrics, the movement of white limbs, the nocturnal sighs and gasps that knew no end, a merging of sounds and sensations, the taut excitability and contact, approach, movement, and joining of bodies, their suction and sweaty slipperiness, the opening and penetration of the blossom, a single, uninterrupted budding of the organism, that savagery and destruction and dying in a woman's softness. Thighsthighsthighs in sight and sound and touch. Everywhere in his thoughts and awareness nothing but naked, white, moving female thighs.

He had truly gone astray, truly got himself wedged between Dorotea's and Matilda's thighs, the dark deltas above them, the endless migrations from one to the other and then back again, this monstrous delirium of desire devouring the solitary traveler to the last. Gone were any thoughts of his secret covenant, gone was the tumult of past and future events. No pricks of memory or commitment jabbed at him in the early morning hours, jolting his body and mind awake and causing his eyes to wander over the ceiling, lost. Incessant debauchery and dissipation so thoroughly squeezed and wrung out Ot's mind and memory that he no longer knew where his own space, his beginning and end were. For although the world of thighs and their allures may be delusional, it is harmonious and self-contained.

This is why he was not in the least bit interested in the discussion one evening in the house of Baltasar Kazelj Locatelli concerning the approach of the great day, when His Highness's presence would illuminate the local human squalor and ignorance; nor in what was being said about the dangerous rabble-rousers who were polluting local souls with their outrageous outbursts, both written and spoken, and compromising the integrity of His Majesty's itinerary; nor in what was said about the dangerous political and heretical dregs of their society that would have to be destroyed, dispersed, locked up, hanged, or expelled before His Majesty arrived, definitely before he arrived. Even the fact that Ot was able to flounce about the beds in the judge's house unhindered, lured there night after night by his daughter, no longer seemed all that meaningful to him, though it could have. For

Matilda had told him more than once that a great hunt for all kinds of demonspawn had begun yet again. The judge was on the road day after day. Tired, weary, and shaken by all the innumerable crimes that he had to punish, he would return home gurgling and coughing and wander around displaying his woeful, work-burdened face. Here Ot was ensconced between thighs that coexisted quite peacefully and took turns contentedly swallowing him up. This is where he'd wedged himself in, and from this perspective he couldn't see the powerful, sudden changes, the historic changes that were happening all around.

The town filled up with newcomers. Some of them, well appointed and distinguished, found lodgings in the houses of the townspeople and fraternized with the locals. Others, with narrow faces and well-trained eyes and ears, crept into every pore of the town's daytime and nighttime existence. You could see them everywhere—in all the taverns and shops, at market and in the courts, at meetings of guilds and soldiers' drinking bouts—everywhere they were present, they took part. They listened, inquired, investigated, consulted, observed, and took notes.

The town was all lit up. Day after day there were festive Masses and ceremonies at town hall. At night the firing of cannon was often heard. The great rehearsal for the great day was well underway. Now it was clear: Leopold was coming and could be expected any day. An obedient people awaited its ruler. By ancient custom they would swear their allegiance and loyalty to him anew. The people had not been afforded such happiness in ages and it would be a long time before these magnificent scenes would be repeated.

Johan Ot looked at all this bustle and pomp, all this scurrying and swarming of the human anthill, he listened to the talk of dangerous, rabble-rousing conspiracies that burgeoned at Dorotea's table, he looked bemusedly at Matilda as she told him about her father's hard work chasing down heretics, but as far as Ot was concerned, all of this was happening in some other world. He was someplace where no spy or judge could find him—wedged between thighs, in their safe harbor night after night. God bless women's thighs, the lone fugitive's last safe refuge.

One night, as he drank wine in bed with Dorotea at his back, breathing deeply in her sleep, there came a light scratching at the door. Something was moving on the other side, like someone nervously, impatiently shifting around. When Ot got up, the cup was trembling slightly in his hand. It was as if a choke-pear had been dropped into his throat, and his knees gave way slightly as he put his ear to the wooden door. Outside he heard movement and scratching and whispering: "Open up." It was Adam. Then Adam was standing in the doorway, gaunt but grinning, with dark circles under his eyes and the shadow of some hazardous plan on his face.

With awkward, useless hands that didn't quite know what to do with themselves, Johan Ot invited him in.

Adam took a look at the naked female body on the bed and grinned again. He sat down at the table and poured wine for himself. There was movement in the bed and then Dorotea, her eyes wide, hair tousled, and plenteous breasts exposed, was gaping in amazement at this unbidden midnight ghost. A sob of some sort convulsed her while, at a loss, Johan Ot pulled on his trousers.

For a while there was silence in the room, with only Dorotea's sobbing to punctuate it—a startled silence mixed with her moans and tears. Adam just smiled. He looked at Johan Ot, caught red-handed, pacing awkwardly around the room as he buttoned up his trousers, and he listened to Dorotea's contrite sobbing and he smiled and said, "It's all right, it's all right."

"It's all right," Adam said. "Don't be embarrassed, there's no sacrilege in a little bit of friendly back and forth. And anyway," he added after a pause, "somebody has to help the poor girl while Baltasar is out gathering guldiners and taking his purgatives."

Dorotea continued to sob, but Adam had already moved on, as though nothing at all was wrong, as though they were sitting around the dinner table or the like—he changed the subject without hesitation. Now it all glowed and spewed out of him.

His Powdered Assness was arriving. They were in a state of siege. There were disturbances in the empire that nobody could tame or control. There were armies on the way. There were informers, guards, and spies. There was a group that was planning to do something. Bloody justice was reaching its hand into every village. There was panic spreading before His Majesty's arrival. There were the authorities still hoping to reassert order. There were the interests and objectives of the French king and the Venetian Republic, and of course there were the sultan's intrigues. There were liaisons being made everywhere. There was a network. There was a well-woven network that reached high and low, that involved the states general, the church, and the common people. There were conspirators and terrorists and secret societies.

"Societies?" Johan Ot asked. "What kind of societies?"

He had been away from the thighs for barely a moment and something in him was already coming around. Some recollection, some tiny needles jabbing and glowing inside him as he listened to Adam's impassioned words. Hadn't he heard something like this somewhere before? It had been formulated differently, but the essence, wasn't this in essence the same thing? The echo of distant words moved in Ot and suddenly, against his will, in this night, which was dwindling away in the narrow streets outside the windows, in this room with Dorotea putting up her hair as she poured herself another glass of wine, in this disheveled den of sin, where Adam was sowing his wild ideas, Ot began to speak all at once, and he could hear his voice saying:

For thus saith the Lord of those who keep my Sabbaths, and choose the things that please me . . .

He stopped short, amazed at the words he had suddenly spoken, and he could feel Adam's sharp eyes piercing him and rummaging around inside. But Ot just stared back at him darkly.

"What," Johan Ot said. "What? Don't you know how it goes on?"

"How what goes on?" Adam said, as though he'd understood nothing, and in fact he hadn't.

"The call to arms," Johan Ot said.

"There is no goddamned call to arms," Adam protested.

". . . *and take hold of my covenant,*" Johan Ot finished, devastated, because now it was clear that Adam had nothing to do with that business. "The new brotherhood," he whispered a moment later.

"The new brotherhood?" Adam roared. "What crazy, stupid, goddamned new brotherhood? It's craziness," he said, "craziness. The brethren are fools, fanatics, groundless malcontents, illiterate peasants, rogues, rascals, scoundrels, a bunch of crazy Alpine goiter cases—that's the new brotherhood for you. Stay away from those masochists, lashing their own bodies, running over fields of sharp stones. All their talk about equality and brotherhood—it's pointless, destructive, meaningless."

Adam spoke loudly, violently, furiously, with spittle flying from his mouth.

"Some insane contagion has burrowed into the Catholic and Protestant lands," he thundered. "Insanity in every possible shape, heresy in every possible disguise, chicanery and stupidity of every sort. And at the head of this mess stands a man with a brain as slow as a cow's. Don't you see?" Adam stood up and raised his arm high with his index finger extended. "Don't you see that we have to put that sniveling runt down in order to end the madness and finally have peace? We don't need some addle-brained, swindling brotherhood, and we don't need belligerent peasants—no, what's needed is a conspiracy with a clear goal, a single conspiracy with a clear goal."

Johan Ot went as pale as a sheet. Dorotea leaped at Adam and put her hand over his mouth.

"Have you gone out of your mind?" she whispered. "What sort of madness is this? To shout like that at a time like this."

"That's right," Johan Ot said. "He must be out of his mind."

Adam pulled away from Dorotea's embrace and calmly walked over to the window.

"Do you see?" his voice was calmer now as he pointed outside. "There's nobody, this house is safe."

"You're crazy," Dorotea said in a scolding voice. "You'll come to a bad end."

"That's what Krobath says too," Johan Ot said. "And Adam, there's something I have to tell you at last. You take your conspiracy and your secret society entirely too seriously. These days everyone is in some conspiracy or other. The modern world is a world of chaos and terror. Everyone has some role to play in that. So you don't have to go around and make such a point of setting your head on the executioner's block."

Dorotea nodded emphatically and pressed her hand to Adam's hot forehead.

"Oh, you poor, dear, babbling little fool," she said as she tried to catch hold of his arm, which was fending her away. "At each of our evening gatherings there's talk of provocations and conspiracies and dangers, of fanatics and malcontents—every single night," she said. "And not one thing has changed as a result of all these societies and discontents, has it, Johan?" she said as she pointed Ot toward the door, because Adam really did need to be helped, he really was in need of medical attention, and what could be more salutary for so impassioned a conspiratorial soul as thighs? Johan Ot understood this all too well himself, and so he obligingly, quietly went out the door, and once he had closed it, he could already hear the bed start to creak. O, thighs, best of all medicines for all the reckless conspirators of this world.

Morning light. Ot took a walk through the morning light. The sun was already coloring the roofs of the houses, and he could sense how hot things would get up above and how much cooler it was down here. Up there the flame of bright day was already flaring, but down here the dark passageways of the streets were only now receiving their first, grayish light. Ot filled his chest with the chill morning air and a fresh burst of energy coursed through his body. His senses awakened. He listened curiously to the sound of hammering. Mallets and axes. A group of workers was busily knocking together some sort of makeshift construction. A master builder was running between them, giving orders. Such diligent activity at such an early morning hour. Both here and back in the house, in bed. They would be panting and snarling. Adam would be disgorging all his conspiratorial fury between Dorotea's thighs or onto her belly, and thus would be sure to save his head, which was otherwise already bobbing on quite a slender stalk. Ot stopped outside the church. The door was open, with a black, chilly void gaping inside. Go in? Think things over? But he continued on his way and headed down toward the river. He watched the lazy, almost motionless shifting of its thick waters, its viscous crawl, and now even his brain awoke. There was a thumping in his head like the sounds of those hammers and axes before, and it mixed with the rapid gasping of the two lovers in bed. No, this wasn't jealousy or anything like that. It was a strange uneasiness that gnawed at and hollowed out the inward parts of Ot's body, of his tired and drained body—an organism drained and dissolved by wine and an infinitude of thighs. What about all this chaos, something in his head click-clacked. What about this muddle from start to finish, from Lampretič to the brethren and wolves and desolate trails and mountain villages? What about all these events, this pointless, perpetual shunting around the countryside, what about these judges and soldiers and nobles and vicars and bishops and Leopold and all these women? What did Johan Ot want, where did he come from and where was he going and what, in fact, was he doing in the middle of this moment that seemed forever to turn back on itself? Surrounded by dangers and pleasures that, to tell the truth, had absolutely nothing to do with him? What brilliant notion did Adam have inside him that his eyes burned bright and his mind spun and spun, and all he craved was action? And Ot's covenant—hadn't he once been a member of a group that also wanted to create and order things in this world? He had? A horrid shudder went up his spine. He had? And a sharp realization shot through him, one that had already pushed him out into the world so many times before: get going. Bad things are brewing here. Blades are being sharpened here, and ropes are being braided for necks. Get going. Away from this place. Here he would only rot in some tower of justice again, some joker would put on the thumbscrews and he'd be paraded through the streets on a cart like some exotic beast. That morning by the river he felt the whole of the chaos of the universe within him, and it shifted and jostled and collided inside him, sharpening into a single, clear thought: get going.

But Johan Ot didn't listen to the voice of his intuition. And he would regret it.

As he walked back from the river, he chuckled to himself like some eccentric, carefree idiot. Now they've probably come, he said and entered the first tavern from which he heard raucous laughter. Old soldiers—Croats—were tying a last one on. They're here because of Him, Ot thought. Adam is here because of Him, too. And his confederates. So are the nobles. And the judges. And the clergy. The guards, the military, the merchants and musicians, the singers, drinkers, smugglers, thieves, robbers, muggers, peasants and intellectuals, the Italians and the Saxons. All of them elbowing each other aside, all of them busy, all with a plan, each with his share. Because of Him. Even the judge on his bloody rounds through the countryside.

The dress rehearsal was drawing to an end.

The great moment was approaching.

Toward noon Ot staggered uncertainly up the steps of the Locatelli residence. That morning's supply of wine had flushed his cheeks nicely and a contented smile stretched across the shaggy thicket of his face. Dorotea was furious. She dragged him into her room. Where had he gone? What was all this drinking in broad daylight about? There was the reputation of the house of Baltasar Kazelj Locatelli to think of. And there was his own reputation too, after all. Everybody was on the watch now. Everyone was keeping an eye on everyone else. Nothing escaped notice. This was a fine situation she'd gotten herself into. First a fool determined to set his head on the block, who was going to get the rest of them in serious trouble, and now a drunkard who kept showing up night after night beneath the window of the judge's spindly daughter. Who had no idea what was going on around him. Who sat gaping and scratching his belly in her respectable salon. One fool and one drunken womanizer, that's what she was harboring under her roof.

Dorotea was furious indeed. And not without reason. Johan Ot had only just realized the prodigious scope of her social ambitions. This woman knew what she wanted and how to get it. The two of them could easily screw up all her plans. And at last it occurred to Ot that, so long as the two of them were around, their hostess was on the verge of destruction. Not just social, but complete and utter—even physical—destruction. One of these days, when Johan Ot and Adam would be discovered to have . . . and consequently their entire social set would be discovered to have . . . then no amount of reputation, no social connections and no influence would have any effect. The judiciary has its laws and its ways of enforcing them.

"And what about Adam," Dorotea said, he'd been waiting for Ot all afternoon. Adam hadn't come to his senses at all, he hadn't calmed down one bit. He wanted to speak to Ot. He was proposing some sort of collaboration. That damned fool, Dorotea nearly burst into tears, he left some papers here. She pulled a sheaf of papers out from under the bed and threw them on the table. Something behind that forehead of Johan Ot's sharpened at once and gained focus. He picked up a sheet and read it. The big, distinct letters swarmed before his eyes. Once he managed to arrange them inside his cranium, he leaped back to his feet and glanced fearfully around.

"These are pamphlets!" he shouted. "The fool, these are pamphlets."

"He says we should hand them out or stuff them under the front doors of houses," Dorotea said.

"The fool, these are pamphlets agitating against Leopold!" Johan Ot exclaimed. "This will get us hanged. Into the fire, throw these papers in the fire right now!"

Dorotea grabbed the stack of papers and ran out the door.

Johan Ot held his head in both hands, feeling as though something inside it was being squeezed and split apart. It was going to explode. Something ugly is about to happen again, he knew.

Sleep, he decided, I've got to sleep.

But Johan Ot was mistaken if he thought that sleep was going to drive away the thoughts and incidents that had begun to tear him away from the safe and comforting shelter of thighs. He had idled and vegetated and cavorted in their embrace for long enough. Now the wheels had begun to turn and this very day something would happen that would buzz through his entrails and portend a very different sort of life and a very different sort of future.

It was dark when he awoke, and now his head truly was splitting— in two, in three pieces. He held it under water for a long time to try to coax the pieces into coming together again. Then he began to rearrange his crumpled clothing—in vain, because Dorotea's servant arrived with a message: Dorotea did not wish to see him at supper that evening. His presence in tonight's company would be, quite simply, superfluous. Is that so? That's it for one set of thighs, so how about the other?

He went to Matilda's, because tonight, on the evening before the great event, the judge was unlikely to be home. There was no question that he would be out conducting the last of his hearings, because the district had to be completely cleaned up by morning. And he would spill every last drop of blood—not his own, of course—to make sure that was so.

So Ot was out for another walk through the bustling city, waiting for the streets to empty a little. But it wasn't easy to get to Matilda's that evening. Countless men from out of town were milling about on every street corner and it was only with great difficulty that he managed to scale the usual walls and press through the usual courtyards to get to the girl's window. He knocked for a long time. Then, at last, the outlines of a skinny and slightly stooped figure appeared in the moonlight. Tonight? it snapped. Not tonight. Johan Ot stood paralyzed for a moment. Why was all the feminine femoral softness in the world conspiring against him tonight? He turned around to go, but as he did so the righteous man's daughter changed her mind. Come on, she hissed.

"But make it fast," she said when he got upstairs. "I have work to do."

Johan Ot was stunned. Since when did a judge's daughter have work to do? What kind of work? He'd put in a lot of time in this house, and he'd never noticed a trace of any work being done, either physical or intellectual. In any case, the judge's business and his daughter's business had never interested him particularly. Well, maybe the first time it had seemed a little strange to be rummaging around the local Lampretič's underwear, his wife's perfumes, and their daughter's skirts. But with time Ot learned to turn a blind eye. He knew the judge's business and had no interest in his papers—Ot had already been on the receiving end of that sort of justice. And as for his daughter, it was more her external and internal physicality that interested him. But not her work, and certainly not her mind.

But now this younger bastion of righteousness really was working at something. She had some papers spread out on the table by the light of a candle.

"I know how to write, you know," she said proudly. "So I'm helping Father today."

Johan Ot couldn't wait to get into bed, and yet some unfortunate curiosity was tweaking his temples. What work? What writing?

"The accounts," Matilda said. "Business expenses, travel expenses, scribe's expenses, expenses for the . . . the ones who hurt people . . . He's done a lot of traveling and a lot of work the past few days." She sighed deeply:

"He hasn't been able to take any time off."

Johan Ot grabbed the first sheet of paper lying on the table.

	_fl._	_cr._
For cutting off all body hair (abrasure)	1	
For examining a sign of the devil	1	
For chopping off a head or a hand		15
For nailing a chopped-off hand or head to a gibbet		15
For garroting		15
For applying red-hot tongs (per pinch)		30
For cutting off a nose or an ear		30
For burning a subject alive	5	
For burning a subject alive if the victim is difficult, i.e., if he has to be taken by force to the stake	10	30
For burying ashes	1	
For the trial banquet		48

"That's an expense account," she said. "Ah, you wouldn't believe how many of these expense accounts there are. Each one is different and each one has to be written up separately."

Ot looked at the glow of the candlelight and the shadows dancing on the girl's face. He saw that carefree, distracted administrative look in her watery eyes and felt not only the paper shaking in his hands, but a shudder traveling all through his body, to the point where the old throbbing and pressure returned to his head and eyes. He had never before noticed how hopelessly that dilapidated clump of slicked and oiled and pinned-up hair perched on top of Matilda's head, how repellent her jutting cheekbones were, how twisted her nose was, and how thin and compressed and lost her lips were in the middle of her face. In the middle of the pale, bluish, withered face on her skinny neck, above her high lace collar, above that black dress, underneath which hid her bony limbs and hunched back and concave belly and stench, which he could smell now, which wafted into his face when she lay down on the bed and lifted her skirts. He looked into that face, into those watery eyes with their fatuous look directed from nowhere outward at nothing, unlit by a single thought or experience. His hands shook and something throbbed in his eyes while in his chest a thick and concentrated pool of vomit was collecting that he would soon have to spew straight into the colorless smear of her eyes.

The slush reached right up into his throat as he looked down at that exposed body, at those legs spread out on the bed like a couple of motionless white snakes, with clothing bunched above them, held up and together by two hands. Those skinny calves and knock-knees, that dark delta up above, that headless beast living its independent life and waiting for who knows what, probably for some red appendage to shove into its sheath and stubble, for some mechanical operation, for some repetitive act, no different from any other act in a bureaucracy. This bodiless beast with two limbs and a dark delta on top—and above that a heap of clothing, patches and lace and between them a narrow, emaciated, pinched, and pale face with watery eyes fixed on the ceiling—these two separate organisms lying apart on the bed, each one waiting for the blood in the other to quicken . . . while Ot stands there still holding a piece of paper that flutters as though rustled by a breeze, stands there with a catalog of every executioner's bloodiest deed in his hands, with his sudden disillusionment in his hands, with all his fear and memories and sudden recognition in his hands.

A dangerous spark was stirring inside him, and a strange criminal intent was moving in his chest and skull. The throbbing in his eyes intensified, until the two beasts on the bed grew anxious. It swarmed, some limbs connected, its hands tended to something, and then both organisms reunited in a single form. Over its emaciated cheekbones the watery eyes looked at Ot from close up, and below them the thin line of its lips opened up to whisper: What's wrong with you?

Yes, some Satan, frightened and aroused, was running wild through Johan Ot's body. Some devil drove images of lopped-off noses and burnings at the stake in front of his eyes—of an official burying god-less ashes in unhallowed ground behind a wall, and then of a trial banquet. Some devil was driving monsters and tentacles into his thoughts and his blood, throbbing in his temples.

The moment of the crime, the classical setting of the horrible crime perpetrated in the judge's house presented itself at that moment, in that space, in Johan Ot's bloody eyes, as his trembling hands dropped the document and reached toward her, toward her neck, toward that gristly snake that needed to pop in the clutch of his unyielding fingers.

The thin lips opened and revealed a row of black teeth, the dark cavity of the mouth and finally the throat squeezed and squeezed as it tried to scream something out.

Something inside Ot grew quiet and peaceful and cool in view of this strangulation, in view of this low moan unable to convert itself into a scream, in view of those watery eyes that only now acquired some color and expression. Something had been slaked—at least the worst of this powerful lust to do evil, at least the worst of the demon's wild provocations from within. At least to the extent that his arms relaxed and he turned around and ran outside. At least to the extent that he could hear behind him and inside him her breaking voice saying over and over: My how you frightened me where are you going, my how you frightened me where are you going, frightened me going, frightenedmegoing.

It was night outside and a ray of warm moonlight shone on the sooty roofs of the houses. Outside there was peace. The dark creature inside Ot had stopped its thrashing and somersaults. All that was left of its fury was a little anxiety and some tension in his chest. He leaned his back against the wall of a house and looked at the blue cast of the moonlight. From the far side of town, from the vicinity of the city gate near the bridge, came a sort of confused chatter. A multitude of voices and shouts merged in a solid roar that sounded in the night like the river thundering beneath the bridges. Ot set out after the voices and after he'd turned the first corner saw flames and good-sized crowds of townspeople, visitors, soldiers, teams of oxen, horses, the shifting and swarming of the night's human and animal multitudes. There were lively discussions and shouts stretching from there as far as the walls and beyond. The great gate stood wide open, allowing this living river to pour through it with its roar, which sounded so strange in this peaceful town in the middle of the night. Nobody stopped Ot when he passed through to the other side and into the fields, where there were innumerable bonfires with shadows passing between them, where there were tents and horses being led by the reins—where, in short, the bustle of an entire military encampment shone in his eyes.

Old soldiers, officers in armor, long pikes, guns, swords glinting in the glow of the bonfires, straw strewn all over the ground, the rattle of metal objects—all of these elements, all of these tasks, this bustle, this army, all this commotion in the city and its environs—all of it was living in anticipation of the coming day.

This is the night on which Johan Ot, anxiety in his chest, wanders among the flicker of images, people, and things. This is the moonlit night, so long awaited, that would be longer than all previous nights, because this is a night of anticipation.

This is the night when the emperor sleeps peacefully somewhere close by or far away, or gets drunk with his retinue and courtesans, thinking with disgust of all the endless protocols and ceremonies, all the lickspittle bowing and servile looks concealing an infinitude of conniving and personal interests, all the shoving and endless empty word-mongering he will have to endure tomorrow.

This is the night when Adam and his cohort sit somewhere in silence, practically choking on their fear of the coming day. When they sit in a roadside tavern, stare into their mugs filled to the brim with wine, and swear allegiance to each other one more time. This is the night when their people in town go stuffing pamphlets under front doors.

This is the night when knives get sharpened for the emperor's neck.

This peaceful, moonlit night when the emperor turns over in his sleep with a sudden terrible premonition; this night when spies lurk in every tavern and street trying to note down every word that's spoken and every suspicious person; this night when a now calm Matilda scribbles in the light of a candle, copying expense accounts for hangmen, judges, assessors, scribes, prosecutors, and advocates; this night when her father, drained and exhausted, with dark bags under his eyes, interrogates a suspect in the tower of justice; this night when the lights go out in the house of Baltasar Kazelj Locatelli and the Italian poet creeps panting into Dorotea's bed; this night when the little fellow sleeps a fitful sleep with his coins in the barn of some inn in the Karst; this night when all the soldiers inspect and oil and polish their muskets, when they buff their new leather straps and carefully fold their parade dress uniforms; this night when no one sleeps well, when the suspect's fearful eyes wander all over the ceiling and he has no idea if he'll live to see morning.

This is a night without sleep that will finally have to pass.

14.

A gently undulating and throbbing human sea. A harmonious crawler
with a thousand legs that sways and beckons and babbles and gasps in
unison. The emperor and the whore and the real live little dead man.

Down below moved a crawler with a thousand legs, flicking its countless limbs and thrumming with a multitude of voices. A crowd, an
enormous crowd gathered in the streets and squares, clumps of bodies at windows, on balconies and roofs, a crowd unanimous in its taut
yet fluid waves, in its high-spirited, uniform anticipation. What unknown, bizarre link had assembled so many individuals into a single
caterpillar with a thousand legs, so that it pulsed with a single mind
and a single breath? What thought had so totally submerged each
one of these men and women into a single hot and sweaty crowd, all
beatific from the glory of this historic moment? The entire organism
quivering, thrumming, waiting for Him, the One, the Absolute. The
dazzling, intoxicating historical fervor melting each one of them in a
unified, gently undulating, gently throbbing human sea. Townspeople
and nobles and soldiers and peasants and vagabonds and beggars—all
of them, all in it, all in one, all with red and sleepless eyes after a night

of milling around lost through the billow and surge. An uncertain night, the last night, full of unease and uncertainty, had passed. Each one had done his part, each one had come up with his scheme, and now the long-awaited day was here, now it would all come to pass.

Even Johan Ot with his troubled soul had awaited this most illustrious day of the decade, perhaps of the entire century, this day in late summer, this September afternoon that the chroniclers would describe for years to come in the choicest, most dazzling words—yes, even Ot had waited excitedly. Now he was leaning out a window of Locatelli's house and watching the ebb and flow of the human bodies, of that creature with a thousand legs which swayed and beckoned and babbled and gasped in a bizarrely harmonious way. He too was gripped with excitement, even though he had spent these great, historic moments of anticipation in so ignominious a way, between women's thighs, all the way until this last night, when in a flash he finally realized that there really was something important taking place here, something he had never experienced before and never would again.

He too was drawn into the crawler with a thousand legs. Some unknown force bound him to this organism too, each of whose units was fraught with the tension that for so many nights had trembled and buzzed in the air, in the streets, in the fields, on the river embankment, and in the houses. The pamphlets stuffed under the front doors of houses, the nighttime arrests, the denunciations, interrogations, and eavesdropping, the numerous strangers walking the streets, the military that over the past few days had assembled just outside the city walls, the crowds of noblemen who had taken rooms in townspeople's homes—all of these striking and crass and horrible developments did nothing at all to debase the festivities to the prosaic level of some earthly, comprehensible event. On the contrary, all of it smelled of some strange historical uncertainty, everyone living under the spell of a great historical moment, seized by a slight mass hysteria in which they had lost their footing and the universe had parted, and was now eluding all sober, reasoning minds.

Their ruler, that supernatural being who was present every moment of their existences, hadn't walked among them in person for centuries, and probably wouldn't again for centuries more. Who could grasp the glory of this moment? Wasn't it worth it for a single moment like this to throw ten times, no, a hundred times more people in jail than they usually did, and wasn't it worth the greatest possible splendor, the greatest excitement, the most profound fervor, and the most thundering VIVAT?

This is His arrival: glory, splendor, bells, cannon, Te Deum, and earthly wonder.

At four that afternoon the cannon atop the castle walls thundered. For a moment a motionless silence ensued, and then the millipede started to wriggle again in excitement. Down below things started to gurgle and whirl, causing Johan Ot's head to spin. The cannon had been the signal. He was coming. And indeed, a while later, bright-colored, fluttering banners began to appear over the heads of the crowd in the lower part of the street. A surge of shouts came from there, while here the millipede was still gasping in the extremes of its excitement. Johan Ot flew down the steps and shoved his way into the crowd. The drumming drew closer and the flushed faces all around him were staring into blank space, at the empty place where something incredible was about to appear any second, something that human eyes had never yet seen. A detachment of Croats rode at the head of the procession, all of them with long lances and tiger skins over their shoulders. They were followed by a large, nicely arrayed group of other horsemen. Then came a huge multitude of local noblemen, whose horses kept bumping up against the millipede's body and pressing it up against the walls, for after them, after them He rode in on horseback. Leopoldus Dei Gratia Romanorum Imperator Semper

Augustus Germaniae Hungariae Bohemiae etc. Rex Archidux Austriae Dux Burgundiae etc. by Himself. Alone in a broad empty space encircled by grandees, alone in his armor and with lace around his neck and a huge wig on his head. With his hooked nose and bulging eyes, with the light bristle on his upper lip, with his boyish face and his insouciantly pouting thick lower lip.

He appeared for just a moment and then He was gone—the millipede concealed the emperor from Johan Ot's eyes and then engulfed him, leaving nothing but gasping and shoving, and it was all Ot could do to grab onto the Locatellis' door handle and squeeze into the dark, cool entryway.

He stood there for a while, checking the limbs that the millipede had tried to crush in its grip.

And that's it? he asked later when he'd caught his breath. That's all there is? he asked as he passed through the dining room, where a meal was being prepared for some fourth-class bureaucrat from the emperor's retinue who was billeted in the Locatelli house. Ot went to his room and took off his boots and thought of Dorotea's thighs, which after all were the most beautiful thighs in the world, and he fell asleep.

This is how Johan Ot spent that historic day. He slept, exhausted by the great moment, heedlessly wasting the chance to be part of the ongoing festivities as they roared outside late into the night. The millipede had almost entirely dispersed and was now indulging in its happiness, which embraced and engulfed the city and its environs, reaching into every corner of even the most obscure side street and secluded tavern. And there were strange dreams in which Adam's face unexpectedly appeared, talking about abrasure and nailing chopped-off hands onto gibbets—that wine-flushed face was in the street beneath Ot's window, part of the millipede, opening its mouth in the terrible din, and Ot could make out every one of its audacious and blasphemous words distinctly—and these strange dreams jolted

Ot awake, clammy and frightened, at an hour that should have been nighttime, even though there was light still fluttering at the window. Ot went to the window and saw the city below radiant, illuminated by countless lights as the now woozy and decimated millipede continued to move through the streets. Ot looked for Dorotea and her white thighs, thinking to win her back with a kind word, but the house was empty. In the dining room he found the remains of some hastily consumed food. He poured himself wine and went back to bed. He listened to the drumming of the magnificent pageant, looked out the windows that were all radiant in His glory, and he thought of Adam, who had somehow found his way into his peaceful dreams.

Somewhere Adam's beguiling face was being sizzled and stabbed and disfigured. Somewhere someone had gotten him into their clutches along with all his conspiratorial cohorts and plans. What sort of subversive ideas, what sort of seditious plans were blundering through these people's heads, what sort of senseless resistance to the Imperator, graced with his laurel wreath, the EmperorKingDukeandPrince? Where did they get the idea that his brain was as slow as a cow's? Why did they make fun of his powdered ass? History would forget these naysayers and malcontents, these bedbugs and voles on the body and field of the empire. What will be written is that conspiracies were forged and that malcontents distributed pamphlets against His exalted person—that's all that will be left, whilst the men themselves will leave their bones sitting in the jails and towers of justice. What will be written about Him, however, will be something else entirely—the kind and wise emperor, who, though he did little for his obedient people, ruled his millipede wisely and well, especially with the help of his most useful and favored educational tools—the block and the ax. He would drive his millipede into one war after the other, and it would swarm after him obediently, shedding blood wherever he wanted.

This is how Johan Ot drifted back to sleep, his red eyelids etched with the image of that afternoon's noble horseman, who had changed the life of this place so completely—with that enormous wig on his head, its curls cascading down over his neck, with his hooked nose, his slightly bulging eyes with the whites showing around the irises, and the light bristle on his upper lip—that boyish face with its thick, fleshy lower lip. And so Ot slept, and this is how the image of His Majesty would have remained in his eyes, this would have been his memory of that historic day with all its drumming and the ever so slightly tense undulations of the sea of people, the crawler . . .

Yes, that's where things would have remained if only they hadn't taken an abrupt and surprisingly different turn. If not for the fourth-class bureaucrat from the emperor's retinue who had been billeted in the house of Baltasar Kazelj Locatelli. If not for Dorotea, who knew from the very outset that she had a supremely exalted and important mission to carry out in this story. And so Leopoldus Dei Gratia Romanorum Semper Augustus Germaniae etc. did not pass from Johan Ot's life in this form, most glorious, on horseback, surrounded by his delirious millipede, but in a quite different, quite strange, quite human, and quite intimate form instead.

The next morning, when Johan Ot awoke from his restorative sleep, which had succeeded in banishing the last dark, skeptical demon from his thoughts, it turned out that the great merchant's house was still entirely empty. Out in the courtyard a servant was cleaning the stable, but he didn't know where everyone was. The house was empty and the remains of the previous night's gluttonizing still sat on the table, stinking.

Ot's footsteps echoed hollowly up and down the stairs. He walked perplexed through empty rooms, sat down on Dorotea's rumpled bedsheets, and thought hard. What had happened? Had Baltasar Kazelj Locatelli come back and taken Dorotea and the others back on the road with him? Had Adam and now all the other lodgers been arrested and put in thumbscrews? If so, why hadn't they taken him too? Ot's panicked mind couldn't get to the bottom of this mystery, which gaped at him emptily from every corner like the aftermath of some plague.

He headed into town, which was now resting exhausted and getting ready to launch into further festivities on account of the emperor's presence. Ot looked for his acquaintances from Dorotea's salon, but he found no one, because the caterpillar had thoroughly shuffled its limbs the night before—the chaos was total. This person had spent the night at that person's house, while the next person wasn't home but had some strangers staying there. In short, Ot's search was futile.

He went back to the empty house and waited. He had no alternative.

Toward evening the city came back to life. The streets filled and the glow of the lamps lit the bed where Johan Ot was lying, alone again after such a long time, and in such unusual circumstances to boot. He couldn't stand it anymore. He went out to a tavern where he joined some peasants who had come to celebrate the great event, and he drank until morning.

Two eyes were staring at him sharply when he woke up. There was a hot light in the background, but close up were those two greenish eyes that peered at him without moving. At last Ot himself moved, and the two eyes bounded away, howling. A dog had been sniffing at Johan Ot as he lay in a ditch by the road.

He didn't go back. He didn't seek out his warm bed and refuge. He was afraid of the empty house with its lone servant, the groom from the stable, gesticulating and cleaning, he was afraid of receiving some new pitiless and unexpected piece of bad news. So he kept drinking. And there were infinite opportunities for that. Because on the third day there came a report that passed quickly by word of mouth. His Imperial Highness had decided to extend his stay in the city. The millipede was exhausted, but days like these only come once in a hundred years, so it kept wriggling and carousing away. On the fourth day the imperial chancellery for information announced that the Imperator and Rex had gone hunting. On the fifth day he was out boating. On the sixth day he rested. And only on the seventh day did word come that the king was departing. He disappeared practically without ceremony. The millipede was simultaneously agitated and honored. What was going on, that their lord had so extended his stay in their provincial capital? What an honor for the local population! And why did he then leave so suddenly, without any ceremony, almost in private? He had bidden farewell to only the most prominent local nobles.

Rumors abounded and began colliding with each other. Urgent affairs of state had kept him here. A conspiracy of the nobles had kept him here. An assassin who climbed through his window with a knife between his teeth had kept him here. Illness had kept him here. There was no end to the rumors.

The chroniclers and historians say nothing about the unexpectedly prolonged sojourn of the Rex Archidux Austriae etc. in this provincial capital. There's no explanation.

He left quietly. Of course, the millipede was already so exhausted that it couldn't have given him anything resembling a glorious send-off. The peasants went back to their homesteads after a few days, the merchants began counting their profits, the innkeepers cleaned up their broken dishes and chairs, the judges began to release detainees and suspects . . . the holiday couldn't go on forever, after all. Only the soldiers, who now no longer had any real work to do because there were no more parades to march in—only they were still living it up in the early morning hours, the last ones to leave the stage of history. All the other limbs of the exhausted millipede dragged themselves off to their duties and rest.

Including Johan Ot, partied out, tired, worn down, uncertain, and curious. Including Ot as he dragged himself down a pitch-black street, bumping into baskets, getting his feet caught in some fabric on the ground, slipping on vomit, and generally making his way through all the squalor that the swarming caterpillar had digested and left behind following the interminable celebration that would go down in history. A skein of the morning sky twisted and turned between the dark roofs above him. But he had questions throbbing inside him. And he will get answers. He will get explanations for which the historians and chroniclers would be grateful, but alas, he'll take these with him, on to new adventures and landscapes, onto the seas, and then into the eternal darkness of history. But before all that, he will find out and remember.

For now, upon his return, the Locatelli house was occupied. Dorotea was back, the servants were back, and apparently even the master of the house, Baltasar Kazelj Locatelli, had slipped into one of the rooms that night, falling asleep in an instant, exhausted from his long and difficult journey.

And this is how the moment finally arrived when Johan Ot found out what mysterious things had been going on, the moment when everything would be given an explanation and the truth would shine forth in all its objective, radiant, and wholly proper light.

Incredible things had happened.

In the days that followed Dorotea began to tell about them.

Dorotea liked to talk. This had been her great moment, the high point of her life's story. She couldn't keep such secrets to herself, even though she had been ordered and threatened a hundred times to keep quiet, or else . . . But saying something like that to a woman of Dorotea's ilk was like pouring oil on a fire. The parts of the story fit together and they added up. So thoroughly did the story mesh with events that Johan Ot had to believe it. And so, that famous image of

Leopold Dei Gratia Romanorum Imperator Germaniae etc. riding on a white horse and being embraced lovingly and faithfully by the millipede marched away. Forever.

On that special day, about which the history books say that such glorious scenes never again took place in the duchy's capital city, the Imperator, Rex, and Archidux attended Mass in the cathedral and listened to the bishop's fine baritone as he sang his Te Deum more beautifully than at any of the rehearsals. Once he had performed this formality, His Majesty was conducted to his quarters in the bishop's residence in the very strict and very boring company of his uncle and two exceptionally dreary ministers. In an instant the remaining multitude of his fun-loving courtiers dispersed among the city's various houses, where they had been assigned quarters and where some truly enjoyable diversions were waiting. One of the emperor's bureaucrats, Count Rossini-Schlossenberg, found himself assigned to the home of Baltasar Kazelj Locatelli—Dorotea's house. This unambitious fellow, who ranked quite low in the court hierarchy, was entirely satisfied with his accommodations, and of course particularly with Dorotea, who was more beautiful that evening than ever before. After supper they quickly agreed on a visit to the house of one of the municipal councilors, where a large group of the emperor's courtiers had assembled. Apparently Dorotea had given the servants permission to take that special evening off and join in the general merrymaking. So it was no surprise that Johan Ot, upon waking that evening, found the house empty. At the home of the municipal councilor Dorotea drew the attention of all the guests. So it happened that next morning she was sitting in the garden with Count Christoph Starnburger, who was to all appearances quite a bit more important than Rossini-Schlossenberg. Christoph Starnburger invited Dorotea to his house, where she rested and was introduced that same day to Count Johannes Massheim, who was practically the right-hand man of Minister Count Lorcia. Minister Count Lorcia was delighted by Dorotea's appearance, and especially by the abundance, grace, and intelligence of the upper part of her torso, up to the neck. And this circumstance was decisive for the subsequent course of events. Minister Count Lorcia was staying with the emperor in the bishop's palace, from which the clergy had decamped for the occasion. The next afternoon, Minster Count Lorcia introduced the anointed Imperator and Archidux of these lands to his discovery. He mentioned it only in passing, during a conversation about the greediness of the local nobility, the roads, and the intrigues of the Venetians. The anointed one was, after all, a young man still, and he didn't have water flowing in his veins, which fact was attested to by his slightly bulging eyes with their shifty gaze and his distinctly sensuous, fleshy lower lip, which in old age would turn into a downright ponderous lump of flesh hanging from his jaw. But despite his youth, he was a cautious ruler, so he took his time sizing up the dreary minister, who must have had something up his sleeve to make such an offer. Surely the man must have intended to win some benefit for himself out of the deal, if nothing else. But bargain or no, life in the bishop's palace was wearing frightfully thin. Discussions with His Majesty's ministers, interrupted by ceremonies at the city hall, a discussion with the local estates general, and other affairs of state, but otherwise sheer dreariness in this boring Alpine country where the day and night before the people had gone completely crazy over his arrival. He'd had to plug his ears so as not to hear the prolonged wailing that passed for singing in this part of the world, and that sounded continually from the taverns near and far. And so the side of His Majesty's nature that his appearance so eloquently betrayed won out over caution. He inquired in more detail and he was instantly in the palm of Count Lorcia's hand—and in his ministerial snares. The count went on at such impossible length about Dorotea that His Majesty simply had to put an end to his babble. It was decided. After all, the emperor needed to get to know his people—even the ones here, such as they were, up close and intimately, so to speak.

From that moment Dorotea Kazelj Locatelli became an affaire d'état and state secret number one. The office of protocol and the security apparatus were set flawlessly in motion. No information: the public was to be kept out. This business was too precarious. A commoner in the anointed one's bed, and on top of that a commoner about whom they'd had no time to collect any facts, and didn't dare do so at this stage, assuming they didn't want to endanger their ongoing conspiracy investigation in some way. The personnel from the secret service who were given this unforeseen assignment grumbled a bit—such a dangerous matter, so suddenly, on such short notice—but the plan was in place and the order was given. They had to carry it out. For the emperor wanted to do some research on the positions of his subjects in these parts, and he wanted to do it tonight.

Dorotea didn't even suspect that such an exalted mission was awaiting her, or that so many people were already carrying out official duties on her account. She bore her enormous mountain of hair and feathers uncertainly in the company of the brushed and scented Johannes Massheim. She felt special, but infinitely insecure on those slick floors, in that brilliant candlelight, among those silken shins—amid all the silk, the jewelry, and the tightened bodices; and she kept thinking that in spite of her well made-up face, in spite of her flounced skirt and her bounteous breasts—which truth be told were the only really dignified thing about her—that despite all of this she couldn't conceal the stench of the road and the slimy patter that all those traveling merchants had brought into her house. She sensed that in the company of these distinguished cavaliers who had invited her to their private party, where other townspeople, especially women, were present, and despite the fact that the differences between the various social classes involved were being downplayed in this company on account of the mutual goal awaiting them at the end of the evening, she still had thick beads of sweat on her forehead. She would have preferred to leave all those powdered wigs tied with ribbons, all those bows and nods and the smooth talk that seemed incapable of saying anything directly, or even somewhat clearly, about going to bed with one another—she would have preferred to leave all of it behind and go be with her Baltasar, or rather Adam, or rather Johan Ot, or at least her Italian singer.

Which is why she brightened up when she was suddenly, quite discretely, unobtrusively, and politely led to an empty room. Her acquaintance of that afternoon, Minister Count Lorcia, was waiting for her there, and he informed her confidingly, but also quite officially, that from this moment on she was now state property in service to a higher mission and that she simply did not have a say in the matter. That she had been, so to speak, commandeered. No, she hadn't expected anything like this even in her dreams. She dropped down into a chair. One ordeal was over now, but what was to come?

The servants, ostensibly at her order, had been dismissed. A courier was on the way to meet Baltasar Kazelj Locatelli with the message that she had been given an important government assignment. Her guest, the merchant Johan Ot, about whom they were collecting information, was being kept under watch. And her? She would presently undergo a brief preparatory procedure, and after that it would be off to work, because there was little time. The next evening the ceremonies were scheduled to end with the solemn pledge.

She had no time to think things over and no time to faint. She followed her entourage, who explained how she should act and what she should do, but with such a refined vocabulary that she couldn't make much sense out of it. She would handle things her way. If *that* was what it was about, then she had some experience to work with, after all. Some skills. It's not about anything other than *that*, she thought. When is it about anything else? And her confidence grew.

When they finally led her onto the stage, she determined immediately that the main piece of furniture here was a bed—a big, luxurious bed— but just a bed nonetheless. A familiar battlefield. Here nothing bad could happen to her. Here she could feel safer and less awkward than on those slick floors among those fragrant, brushed, and pomaded cavaliers.

She poured herself some of the wine that was waiting on a table for the covert lovers, and the trembling in her hands subsided. She sat down on a chair and arranged herself in as dignified a pose as possible. Once she found the most comfortable position, she froze in it. But her emperor and master by the grace of God was nowhere to be seen. So she poured herself some more wine and froze in place again. She was beginning to hurt all over from this uncomfortable position when the door finally opened. He came in. That is, Him, wearing some lace clothing and in tightly fitting trousers. But the heavens didn't part and angels didn't sing. Leopoldus Dei Gratia Romanorum Imperator Semper Augustus Germaniae Hungariae Bohemiae etc. Rex Archidux Austriae Dux Burgundiae etc. was mildly drunk, and as soon as he walked in he began to unfasten his pants. Dorotea looked at those bloodshot, bulging eyes and the trousers her lord was now holding in his hands, and at that instant she forgot to fall to her knees as she'd been instructed. She just sat there, staring at the Rex Archidux Austriae etc. in bewilderment as he stood in the middle of the room with trousers in hand, his tiny pupils gawking at her from within their huge, bloodshot eyeballs.

Dux Burgundiae etc. was standing and waiting for Dorotea to move, but she didn't move a muscle. She sat on her chair like a baroque statue, and His Highness suddenly flushed red. He refastened his trousers. He paced about the room. He poured himself wine. Then drank it. He was silent. He pondered. What should he do? Should he call his minister to come explain to this woman that she was supposed to undress, that she was here for *that* and nothing else?

"So," he finally said. "What have we here?"

Dorotea said nothing in response. Something strange was building inside her and she no longer recognized herself. Some terrible obstinacy had taken control of her, some horribly dangerous obstinate notion was pecking at her brain.

"So," the Imperator Augustus Hungariae said again. "Are you getting undressed or not?"

Yes, some devil was acting up inside Dorotea, because she just kept staring stubbornly ahead and neither said nor did a single thing. Something was building inside her, some sort of whatdoyoucallit, who knows, but she would be damned if she'd be the one to get undressed first, ofallthings!

"What are you staring at?" the Imperator Bohemiae suddenly roared, so suddenly in fact that a gulp of wine caught in his throat and he started to cough uncontrollably.

When he regained his breath, he dashed to the door and threw it open with a bang.

"Count Lorcia," he bellowed in imperial fury. "Throw this damned whore out. And think of the consequences," he added more calmly when he saw his minister's frightened face.

Dorotea could see the walls and floor shaking from the ruler's terrible rage, she could sense the cosmos collapsing in this room.

Horrified at her own blasphemous resistance, she stood up and leaned against the edge of the table. Count Lorcia stood in the doorway, piercing her with his gaze, first giving her an imploring look, then shifting his focus to the emperor's back, whereupon terror appeared in his eyes. He approached Dorotea and seized her angrily by the elbow. He pushed her toward the door, but at that instant a new gear must have turned in the anointed's head.

"Stop," he shouted. "What are you doing with that woman?"

The famous fleshy lower lip shook with righteous anger.

"Where are you shoving that woman?" the emperor stammered in agitation. "Why are you shoving her? Who told you to shove that woman?"

It was unlikely that this outburst by the ruler had been precipitated by some faux pas on the minister's part. In all likelihood, the thought had simply occurred to the emperor—he always had to think quickly—that he was going to have to spend this night drinking alone after all, or at best with only this dangerously capable and dangerously cunning man for company, this man who did nothing all night and day but hatch new political machinations.

It was also unlikely that Dorotea interpreted the emperor's sudden favor as stemming from anything other than the anointed's own weakness. Because now, instead of her, it was the minister who went flying out of the room, and this fact could only instill confidence in her. Ultimately, it was a kind of affirmation of her behavior up to now. Yes, she had always known how to handle men.

Or that's what she thought.

And that's how she stayed.

But, even now, things didn't proceed as smoothly or as simply as they should have. Dorotea had now undressed, albeit not completely, just enough to cause the Imperator's lower lip to start trembling again. But the moment she approached the bed and pulled the covers off of it, she screamed in fright. In the bed lay a tiny creature, a real live little dead man with a beard and hair between its legs. The Archidux, who was once again holding his trousers in his hand, tried to calm Dorotea. He's not alive, he said. He's been embalmed, he's from India, you see. He's my guardian and mascot, he's always with me, stammered the emperor as he tried with one hand to stroke and sooth the sobbing Dorotea, his other hand continuing to hold the royal trousers.

No, this was beyond Dorotea's ken. It was too much even for her. To lie in bed with this bizarre, shaggy dwarf, with this real live little dead man shrunken down by some chemical or other to miniature size, with those eyes bulging vacantly out.

"No," Dorotea said. "May Your Majesty forgive me, but with this, this corpse around I cannot, how should I put it, engage in intercourse."

The Archidux Austriae etc. began buttoning up his trousers again.

"Listen," he said, his voice trembling with the effort of remaining calm. "Listen, I can't be lenient with you endlessly. Who are you that you don't want to lie with me?" And his words sounded convincing and powerful indeed, reinforced by the din of the pageantry and merry-making that were tearing the millipede apart outside. Singing and shouting came in the window, the crash of jugs breaking and the echo of distant gunshots.

"I do," Dorotea said. "I do want to lie with your grace, but I refuse . . . I refuse to lie with that strange monster."

"It must be with both," the Imperator shouted in a terrifying rage. "With both!"

But Dorotea's feminine pride awakened in her again.

She refused. She would not sleep with both of them. She wouldn't permit it.

The ruler and emperor by the grace of God now completely lost control. In his mind's eye he reviewed the opulence of that bounteous baroque bosom that he had seen with his actual eyes just moments before, but which was now covered once more and disobedient and rebellious. With both hands he seized Dorotea by the shoulders and tried to push her down on the bed. But the girl was used to far more powerful arms and aggressors, and she shoved her own hand in the emperor's face and pushed him away. The Imperator Dei Gratia Romanorum Imperator etc. then charged at her like a bull, burrowing his head and hands into her clothing such that she could not shake him off. They pulled each other through the room this way, they panted and sobbed and kicked and bit as they rolled over the floor in a furious ball. It was a bitter and determined battle. The emperor nearly burst into tears. You'll let me, he sobbed in exhaustion, trying to pull a mountain of clothing off of Dorotea and over his own head. You'll let me. I won't, Dorotea hissed back at him, I won't, as she yanked his hands off her with remarkable force.

There was a cautious knock at the door. Someone had heard the clatter of broken pitchers caused by the otherwise quiet if bitter scuffle on the floor. It could have been an assassination attempt. Anything was possible.

The emperor and his quarry flew apart and adjusted their clothing while catching their breath.

"May I be of assistance in any way?" Count Lorcia asked discreetly from outside.

"No," the Imperator called out, simply because his panting prevented him from saying anything more articulate or at greater length. Never yet had the Archidux Austriae etc. experienced such a defeat. Outside his loyal people continued to raise their voices, at this very instant his soldiers were defeating the Turk somewhere in Bosnia, at this moment his enemies were sighing in jail and facing the uncertainty of seeing another morning, at this moment he was one of Europe's greatest rulers. But here he was, sitting on the floor, his trembling hand shoving his shirt back into his trousers and then wiping the sweat off his brow. And over there was this miserable wife of a merchant, procured for the emperor by Count Lorcia—God help him—to humiliate and torment and possibly kill him. To his horror, the Imperator acknowledged the situation he was in. It was a terrible comedown, all told, and this was its lowest point.

Dorotea slept in the bishop's palace that night. Count Lorcia showed her to her room and turned a key in the lock behind her. Goosebumps of fear and despair went down his back. He, after all, was responsible for this mess. He would bear the displeasure of the emperor, who was even now destroying the furniture in his room and pacing back and forth in a helpless rage. Yet when Count Lorcia contemplated this business thoroughly, he realized that his position had not worsened—on the contrary, all indications were that soon it would even improve. For the art of diplomacy would now come in very handy. The furious Imperator was calming down now and thinking of ways to lessen the likely consequences of this debacle, but once he was calm again, what would come next? Next he would want to have Dorotea, and he *would* have her, and the count would be the one to make it happen. The emperor would never leave this city with such a defeat on his soul.

And that is what happened. Soon Count Lorcia had to launch his diplomatic initiative. Long, exhausting negotiations got underway. He went from the emperor to Dorotea and back. He tried to persuade her. The negotiations were not easy. Dorotea was gripped by a terrible obstinacy. She simply would not relent. It's either the dwarf or me, she said. One of us has to get out of that bed. But the emperor could hardly retreat. With both, he said. It must be with both. Of course it was easier to say this than accomplish it. The minister sweated. He used all his nimbleness and all possible promises to try to persuade Dorotea. He begged her. He threatened her. He cajoled her.

Toward morning his nerves began to fray. He approached the emperor who was sitting at his table. His head slumped on his chest, wine trickling down his chin, he was staring blankly ahead without any hope of victory.

"Perhaps, after all," the count began hesitantly, "perhaps you might consent to command Somebody to come here."

Dux Burgundiae etc. raised his head. He looked at his servant half dizzily, half absently.

"I think," the minister went on, "that if we could just apply a little pressure . . . a little force," he said. "Not too much, just enough to soften her a bit."

The emperor shook his head.

"No," he said. "That would be meaningless. She must let me willingly," he said. "She must climb into this bed on her own initiative."

He heard his own words echoing somewhere far off in the room. He saw a new historic day of his rule shining in through the window. And he thought what a humane ruler he truly was, and, contented with his decision, he sank into a deep, drunken sleep.

The next part of this story is truly dramatic. Events were developing in a way that should never have been permitted. The clockwork of history had been knocked off its track.

First there was the confusion at that morning's reception for the local nobility. A number of extremely serious matters of government had to be dealt with at this session with the local grandees. Some quite considerable quarrels over property had to be settled, involving vast expanses of land and hundreds of souls. Certain privileges had to be revoked and still others bestowed. A dispute over unpaid wages provoked by the commanders of some border-guard units had to be settled. All this and still other business had to be dealt with.

But the ruler was absent. Even though his ministers had already prepared the documents, his authoritative presence among these willful, stubborn, and greedy landowners was essential. But the ruler was absent, because there was no power on earth that could get him out of bed. When he finally did wake up, he had such a hangover that he truly wasn't fit to decree anything wise and just.

Despite grumbling by the grandees, the reception was postponed till that afternoon, causing that day's entire edifice of protocol to sway. After issuing a report that the emperor was feeling ill after all the strains of his trip, his organizational staff set to work at full force. The solemn pledge that was supposed to cap the visit was postponed to the next morning, together with the ceremonial departure.

At the same time, Counter Minister Lorcia and his closest advisors began their diplomatic battle in the most crucial theater. The Dorotea knot had to be untied or nothing else was going to move ahead. The count ordered that facts be gathered immediately, in hopes that he might be able to make clever use of some piece of information from Dorotea's rich biography to soften her obstinacy. Beyond that, he tried buttering her up with expensive gifts. Both efforts were fruitless. When the facts were presented to him, the count was horrified. If the emperor found out what sort of person his minister had gotten him involved with, compromising his prestige for years to come, the count's career would be over. So he hushed it all up. The gifts were equally pointless. Are you trying to bribe me? Dorotea said. You won't get anywhere. When the dwarf goes, then we can talk.

In the meantime they had managed to bring the emperor around, so he could be present at that important meeting, hear the news, and issue several decrees. On the agenda for that evening was a boat ride with music. Before he left, the emperor gave Count Lorcia an ultimatum: Tonight without fail. Of her own free will, he emphasized.

This time fortune was generous to the minister. Although he managed to accomplish nothing with Dorotea—she started to cry and insist that they let her go home—the Emperor by the grace of God came back so drunk that he slept straight through the night.

But first thing next morning, his head aching again, the ruler summoned his minister. Is it taken care of?

Alas, the minister was unable to answer that question in the affirmative. Luckily, the emperor had too strong a hangover to throw his man out immediately, or break the first thing he could lay hands on.

The solemn pledge was once again postponed. The head of the ministry of information arrived and asked in a humble, yet slightly peevish voice, "What should we tell the public? The people are a bit upset."

"What do I care," the Rex Austriae etc. growled. "Tell them I've gone hunting."

"But," the head of the ministry of information persisted, "if you'll permit me this observation, if Your Majesty isn't out hunting, this will be known."

He went flying out the door. But His Majesty had to go hunting. There was no other option. His court shook their heads. Hunting in mid-morning, just like that? They were stuck in the middle of this town, among all the flush-faced townspeople, among hicks from the countryside bellowing out their endless songs. And there was still no sign of their leaving.

Count Minister Lorcia was in a fix. He incessantly conferred and debated with his staff how they might get Dorotea under the emperor, onto him, or regardless of position into his bed with the shaggy dwarf still present. The secret service delivered some unpleasant information to him. The nobles and municipal councilors were grumbling.

The costs of the emperor's visit were mounting to horrific sums, while the solemn pledge kept getting postponed from one day to the next. The imperial retinue was whispering that the emperor had come down with a serious illness, or perhaps had gone slightly mad. All affairs of state came to a standstill. The coastal regions awaited some news of the imperial arrival. Receptions had been scheduled everywhere. The secret emissaries of the Venetian Republic who were supposed to meet with the emperor in a small town along the way reported that they could no longer wait. The crowds were still making merry, but their merriness was going flat. The millipede was staggering under mass outbreaks of drunkenness. The most incredible rumors were spreading from one tavern to the next, including a report that an assassin had injured the emperor and that the conspirators had been caught.

Count Minister Lorcia decided to take swift action. To spread word that urgent matters of state had detained the emperor. A fierce dispute with the sultan. That would work well. The people hated the Turk. Further, to keep the conspiracy around Dorotea secret by whatever means necessary, albeit with some exceptions. To summon under oath some of the city's most respected municipal councilors and consult with them. There was no alternative. The count had run out of ideas. Perhaps they would know how to change Dorotea's mind. The meeting was tumultuous, but a resolution was indeed reached. To send swift couriers after Baltasar Kazelj Locatelli. He could persuade her.

But the count couldn't stand around with his arms crossed, waiting for the little fellow to arrive. He approached Dorotea again. Either she was acting a role or she had actually gone slightly mad in her terrible, mixed-up obstinacy. She was making noises now about some supposedly untouchable feminine honor or other. She threatened a scandal.

The count thought he might turn her over to some of his men, without the emperor's knowing. How she'd make a run then for that bed and that damned dwarf that His Majesty had insisted and insisted upon, just like her with her feminine honor. Things will not end well for this whore, he vowed. She'll pay. Just as soon as this lunacy is over.

The fifth day of the state of siege arrived. Baltasar Kazelj Locatelli was nowhere to be seen, yet even so the negotiations suddenly started to move ahead.

The dwarf would not be in the bed, but would be sitting in a chair by the window. With its face turned away from the bed, Dorotea insisted. The Imperator would not be drunk and would not walk around holding his trousers, Dorotea added as a new condition. Agreed, Minister Lorcia reported back, even though he wouldn't have dared face his sovereign with such a demand, even if he were dead drunk. There would be no untoward consequences for anyone as a result of the unfortunate events of the past few days, Dorotea demanded of the intermediary. Nothing would happen to her, or Baltasar, or anyone else. The prestige of their house would not suffer, and damages would be paid. Once again, Count Lorcia drew on his diplomatic guile. He gave his personal word. While grinding his teeth.

Dorotea took some more time to think things over. She couldn't give in so quickly. She would leave this battle holding her head high. But the minister was pulling his hair out. The discombobulation was complete and it seemed even more confusion was threatening to wash over them. No doubt this obsession of the emperor's, or his original, hasty, ill-considered decision, or else just this senseless wench, one way or the other, would eventually lead to some uprising or a local war breaking out.

Not until evening of the fifth day was the white flag unfurled over Dorotea's fortress. As naturally as she had resisted, she now agreed to collaborate. She was calmly fixing her hair when the minister, woebegone and sleepless, bleary-eyed and exhausted, came to get her.

Even Leopoldus Dei Gratia Romanorum Imperator Semper Augustus Germaniae Bohemiae etc. was in a bad way. He was sitting in a chair, staring into space with a defeated look. How many nights, how many months had passed since he first saw that baroque bosom, that beguiling smile, that first graceful disrobing, that resistance that revealed a real woman with a woman's dignity and pride, how many nights since Dorotea had granted him a look or a potion or anything? He sat there in his chair and waited for a knock on the door. All afternoon he waited. Then she came. He was drunk and his trousers were unbuttoned.

Then they lay down as simply as old lovers.

In the morning Dorotea held the dwarf in her lap. She laughed and said it wasn't scary at all. In fact, he was a cute little guy.

On the sixth day the emperor attended the solemn pledge at the courthouse. Everyone sighed in relief. An exquisite meal followed. The Archidux Austriae etc. left it abruptly. He had to rest before his journey, he said. But he didn't rest. Dorotea was waiting for him and had kept herself occupied by changing the dwarf's clothes.

On the sixth day the emperor left, quietly and without ceremony. Affairs of state started up again. The clockwork of history was back on track. The provocateurs who had spread false rumors about the emperor's delay in the city were arrested. A few conspirators of an earlier vintage were pardoned. The Venetian delegates hadn't left after all. Neither a rebellion nor a war broke out. And Count Minister Lorcia slept for twenty-four hours.

15.

Who's that standing beneath the window? Who is that spitting seeds? Panic in the depths of night. Flight. Poisonous thorn apple. More flight. Something's throbbing in his innards and the whole countryside all the way to the horizon replies with a mighty din reaching from heaven to earth.

A few days after these events Adam reappeared. He was tattered and beaten, but alive and in one piece. Johan Ot was delighted at the sight of this pale ghost. They hadn't used the vice on him. To all appearances, though, his group hadn't accomplished anything worthwhile or significant either. So many worries, Johan Ot said, and so much fear on account of some feckless debaters. Distributing pamphlets and chattering late into the night. But no action. Adam was in a foul mood. He snapped at everyone around him and he refused to respond to any of his friend's acid comments. Only when he found out about Dorotea's extraordinary story did he lose control. How could you, he shouted, how could you let our woman lie with his Powdered Assness? He even attacked Baltasar, seizing him by the collar and breathing his vinous conspiratorial breath upon him: You jumped-up little con-man, he gasped, aren't you ashamed to have your wife slutting around so shamelessly? Baltasar Kazel Locatelli shook loose of Adam's grip and rearranged his clothes. I am proud, he announced ceremoniously, to have had such an extra-fast courier sent to summon me.

And so life in the distinguished household of Baltasar Kazelj Locatelli resumed the same course as before, like all things in the country and empire. All that was needed was for merchant Krobath to reappear and they would be ready to hit the white, dusty roads on business again. Johan Ot was yearning to travel again. But he needn't have been in such a hurry. He will have to set out again all too soon, and against his will.

He was sorely mistaken if he thought his indirect encounter with the great ruler wasn't going to have any consequences, or likewise that his behavior on the strange night when he saw Matilda's ledgers and tried to strangle her, but then left—that *that* would go unpunished. But he was most mistaken of all if he thought that the days of his involvement with the heretical fraternity that he'd so knavishly abandoned for the sake of women's thighs were past. Now and then, late at night or in the early morning hours, the thought of his pledge still came to him—a thought that nipped and snapped at his innards until the kind embrace of white sheets and women's bodies flooded and extinguished it.

Someone with Johan Ot's past and connections couldn't sink so easily into bourgeois comfort and insouciance. Someone like that will have to continue his hopeless battle to the last breath. To the dark pit of the grave.

The net surrounding Baltasar Kazelj Locatelli's household and company had begun to be woven a long time before. The good, honest, and respectable man simply couldn't have known what a viper he was nursing at his breast. The judge and several municipal councilors had long since wanted to learn more about both of the gentlemen who were sitting idly in the merchant's house, prowling around town at night and disturbing the peace. The events before and during His Majesty's arrival had thwarted this interest to some extent, yet it was precisely then that things began to unravel for the strangers, and the noose began to pull tight. Trouble came from several directions. The bureaucratic apparatus that fought against any kind of illegal, subversive, or heretical activity, although a plodding organization that gathered its information slowly and sometimes drew hazy conclusions, nevertheless functioned dependably in all its plodding certainty. The Dorotea affair had put the household into their sights, and provided the basis for an investigation.

It came when Ot least expected it.

One night a trembling hand on his face woke him out of a peaceful sleep. The hand felt its way over his temples and hair and crawled over his eyes as if it wanted to do something warm and pleasant, as though it were trying to wake him gently. He felt the fingers worm their way over his eyelids and in a sudden instinctive act of self-defense he grabbed the hand by the wrist. He could hear an excited whisper in the midnight silence. The gleaming face above him was wheezing excitedly. Through the darkness he could make out Adam's face all crumpled together with worry. Ot woke up instantly. Adam pulled him over to the window. He pointed anxiously at the corner of the neighboring house. There some shadow or other, clearly bored, was shifting its weight from one foot to the other. It would walk back and forth quite calmly, stand still, wait, reach into its pocket for some seeds, spit and sketch on the ground with its foot. Been there for two nights now, Adam whispered. We're being watched. Something moved in Ot's solar plexus and a piercing chill went down his spine. Fear. That was fear coursing through his body and mind. Adam and Ot sat on the bed like two tired, worried lovers and said nothing.

They sat silently in the dead of night, each with his hopes and each with worry drilling, sobbing, raving through his insides.

Ot had suspected for a long time. For a long time dangerous, distrustful thoughts had been hacking and gouging out their pathways and warnings. Now the object of his fear had arrived. He couldn't think clearly. Why? Who was behind it? Who were they after? Who were they hunting? Who did they want to get in their grip? And again the memory of his recent encounter with that dead and trembling piece of paper in his hands, his encounter with that soulless price list came to mind. More than any recent experience, that damned piece of paper made his stomach churn and encouraged his unease, driving the tedious thump of Ot's heart in the night. It was proof that just on the other side of the street—yes, that close—where that figure was drawing something on the ground with its foot and spitting out seeds, reason and understanding that respond to another person's reason and understanding cease to exist, and all there is is a cold, patient, swollen apparatus mindlessly, senselessly pursuing its task. And carrying it out. The task is all—an administrative process already underway, leading inevitably to one Lampretič or another.

Needles of fear jabbed Ot continuously. All day and sleeplessly into the next night.

Panic ruled the house then. They all stood at the windows looking out at the shadow that kept shifting around and had no intention of leaving. Adam cursed. Treachery. Some damned spy had reported the pamphlets, and maybe a lot more. Locatelli sobbed, wondering what on earth was happening, what on earth did we do, honestupstandingloyaltoemperorandcrown as we are. Dorotea said something about Minister Lorcia, that lying pig. Johan Ot said nothing.

His bad conscience was gnawing at him.

Why and for whom was that shadow standing on the corner?

For Adam? Probably for Adam. All his bluster and swagger in taverns was bound to lead to no good. His nighttime forays. His pamphlets. And his whole seditious gang wanting to carry out who knew what atrocities while people slept. And then there were his connections, which reached who knows how far and who knows how high.

For Dorotea? Probably for Dorotea. She had gone too far during her tragicomic tale, with her feminine self-importance, her arrogance. Why didn't she submit, why didn't she let him? Why had they needed to set affairs of state on their head on her account and send for her husband so urgently? Some devil must have possessed her to cause her to bicker and negotiate with that slimy, no-good count.

For Johan Ot? Most likely for Johan Ot. Someone had produced some information. Someone had sifted through his entire life. Someone had tracked down and found out everything. What tied and held him to this house, to these women at this time, at this uneasy time when everyone was being watched and everyone was being researched by secret councils? They knew about everyone. This one has human contacts, and that one has supernatural ones. This fellow is going to commit one crime, and that fellow is going to commit the other.

It was another long, sleepless night.

The shadow on the corner kept drawing on the ground with its foot. With the tip of its boot. What kind of emblem was it drawing? A gallows?

And then hysteria. Baltasar's moaning and sobbing got louder. As the rest of them went on standing by the windows in silence, his sobbing rose and beat against the walls of the room, frayed everyone's nerves, and then beat against the walls some more. It grew louder and louder, turning into groans and yells and shouts until Adam shut him up with an angry snarl. Baltasar went quiet and in the renewed silence stared at Adam with eyes wide. You, he shouted, you're at fault for everything. Out of my house. Outoutout he shouted and stammered and tore at Adam's clothes. Adam shoved him in the chest and Baltasar rolled on the floor and howled, not in anger or in pain, but in despair, pure despair. Then all at once he went quiet, as though sobering up. He calmed down and stepped into the center of the room.

"Whoever is guilty," he said, "should go outside and turn himself in."

All the others were silent.

"You should go outside and turn yourself in," he continued ominously. "Otherwise I'll go turn you in myself."

He walked right up to Adam and looked him in the eye.

"I know what you said," he whispered. "I was always there when you'd complain and call disaster down on us. Krobath is my witness. And that man is my witness too," he said, pointing at Johan Ot.

There was a dangerous tension in the room. Panic was baring its teeth. Something heavy and evil was moving through the house.

"Criminal," Baltasar whispered. "You're a criminal. You're a wanted man."

Adam glanced around uncertainly. Dorotea was leaning her elbows on the table and had her head buried in her hands. Johan Ot was looking out the window. The figure outside was shifting nervously and looking up.

"You hell spawn," Baltasar hissed, taking a step back and pointing his index finger at Adam. "You've got devils in you. You're not just a malcontent. You want to destroy us. That's why you're here."

A chill and a wave of vertigo passed through Johan Ot. He could see that something heavy and clumsy was moving inside Adam now. Something was gnawing at the man's guts, and some new poison was burning through his veins. Ot could see that Dorotea had moved and was lifting her cold eyes to the two men as they stood opposite each other, surveying the tension flowing out of the empty space between them. Ot saw her put her hands to the sides of her head and yelp quietly.

"I'll turn you in," Baltasar trembled. "It's my duty."

She walked calmly across the room and stepped behind her husband's back. Ot saw her trembling lips and hands as they all opened wide at the level of Baltasar's head. Then they dropped down and were motionless for a moment. Then they leaped back up, up toward Baltasar's sparse hair at the top of his head. They latched on tightly, and the little fellow's face twitched and his eyes darted strangely left and right as his taut skin drew his eyelids up and together. Dorotea gave a crazed shriek and began yanking on her husband's hair, causing his head to bob and sway all over. What are you doing? Baltasar shouted, what are you doing? At that moment Adam too leaped into action. He jumped forward and hit the little fellow in the gut. Shut up, he gasped, shut your mouth, shut it. She won't, we won't, do, anything, to you, you hear, nothing, just, shut up, be quiet. Baltsar howled and with catlike agility leaped up into Adam's arms and bit him, murder, they're trying to murder me.

Johan Ot noticed the shadow on the corner growing agitated. The figure kept looking up and then suddenly turned around and vanished. Ot ran now toward the knot of tussling housemates and tried to untie it. He held back Adam's hand as it tried to reach for his dagger to cut, stop, end Baltasar's horrible shrieking and biting which thundered through the room and was squeezing his brain into a crazed muddle. Ot kept reaching deliriously for the one hand that kept eluding him while Adam's other arm continued squeezing somewhere around Baltasar's neck and he kept pushing Dorotea away feverishly as she repeatedly got up and reached for Baltasar's hair and scalp, frightful sobs shaking her distracted face all the while.

Ot heard a commotion in the stairway outside. He jumped and let go of Adam's hand as something calm and somber passed through his forehead and he suddenly found himself standing outside of the frenzied circle, outside of that horrific bundle of blows and moans and shouts. Suddenly he was simply observing this crime in embryo, which had been set off by the tension that all the panic and fear and other insidious germs in the souls of these deranged people had managed to beget out of nothing.

Yes, he jumped and listened to the clatter of the servants in the stairway and to the razor-sharp words that were now passing through him: no more, never again with the rats in the tower, never again crushed fingers, no trials ever again. He turned almost against his will and took off. In the doorway he ran into a giant footman whom he knocked to the floor. He could feel the other's hands trying to grab him from behind. In two leaps he was in his room. He grabbed his weapon, flung the wardrobe doors open, and shoved his coin purse under his shirt. He ran back out into the hallway and came to a stop in the sudden silence that had flooded every corner of this deranged house.

There was a hollow banging on the front door. The sound coursed through the hallways and streamed through Ot's eyes as they felt their way through the darkness. He ran downstairs and in his peripheral vision saw a figure opening the door from inside. Then the glow of flames flashing. The back door, then, the courtyard, the stable. Ot's head hit the doorframe. He groaned. He ran to the wall opposite and tried to pry off a board. It refused to give way. Noise, shouts, clattering inside the house. At his back a voice gasped heatedly. It's me, it said. Adam. Break it down, he said. They'd had the same thought. Run. Both of them took hold and it started to give out a hollow squeak. A familiar voice at their backs. To the stable, it shouted, get to the stable. They both squeezed through the opening. The voice kept giving orders and shouting relentlessly. Krobath, Adam snorted, that pig, that squealer. He snorted this and then his shadow flitted into the garden, past the trees. Krobath, Johan Ot repeated as he helplessly watched Adam suddenly, wildly, hopelessly disappear into the darkness and out of his life.

On instinct. His entire body was operating on instinct. Get away. Run. Faster. Things lashing at his face. He felt warm blood. Trickling. He could feel it in the corner of his mouth. Blood. Run. He raced downhill. Through gardens. Toward a gap in the wall. A gate. A familiar gate, a way through. Farther down is the river. He ran to the river. Stopped, out of breath. Shouts coming from behind him. Endless shouts. Krobath giving orders, calling out. Krobath's face before his eyes, the dogged face of that calm, reasonable man before his eyes. At the burbling river Ot dashed upstream. He followed its dawdling current, slow as an ox.

He found himself wedged into some bushes. Swampy ground beneath his feet. His heart was hammering, roaring inside his ribcage. It wanted out. The hammers were falling furiously in there. And in his head too. Such dizziness and confusion in his head. Such an abrupt turnaround. From a peaceful, a comfortable, spoiled, lazy, pampered life to desperate flight. Into a swamp. Into these reeds that go on forever. His legs were moving on instinct. Forward, forward. His hands parted the reeds that kept lashing at his face. Only keep going. Get out of there. Hide.

His mind couldn't keep up.

Something inside him was spinning and crumbling and stopping. Getting in the way. Everything was getting in the way and going crazy in this sudden chaos.

Bluish moonlight settled on Ot's eyelids, mixing images, voices, and words. It burrowed in past his eyes. Here was Krobath in front of him. Suddenly here was his face in front of him, big, reasonable, pure, stretching from horizon to horizon, from those mountains awash in this bluish light all the way here to his eyes—Krobath's face, enormous, bright, and translucent. Adam, he said, he's taken a wrong turn. All his ridicule, he said, not good, not good. Did he read it to you? he asked. Did he? A winter night. Krobath's loud, harsh orders.

Krobath in cahoots with the district judge. Matilda. Standing in front of him. Abrasure, she says, for nailing hands to the gibbet, if force is required to take the condemned to the stake, she said. The moonlight crushed him. Down this hill, downhill. Per pinch, Matilda calls to him, waving a piece of paper, per pinch. The trial banquet, burying the ashes. A smoldering killing ground on the hilltop. Whoever inflicts injury or harm by witchcraft. That dark fellow holding the breviary under his arm. The prince of darkness rules in this land. Chaos and fire everywhere. Get away. Through the gorge, the gorge is the only way out. Then to the highlands. The highlands in winter. Wolves are breathing, breathing audibly on the other side of the wall. Next to him. Right next to him. Questions. And still more questions. Answers. And still more answers. We excommunicate and condemn. A peddler from the market reaches her fleshy hand inside, through the laths. Dorotea in candlelight, wearing her white blouse. Suddenly she turns around and grabs Ot by the hair. Absent eyes. Adam has a knife in his hand. We've got to shove it in, he says, we've got to give that snot-nosed little powdered ass a good going over.

Get away.

The body's instinctive motions. Its flexibility. The movement of air. Shadows of trees. A field. Coming in waves, thundering. The sea. A millipede, a murmuring millipede all around.

Get away.

She is standing before him. Her slack, girlish breasts. Her belly, taut. An enormous skinned animal hanging behind her. Urban Posek sends his greetings, she says. My Sabbaths, who faithfully take hold of my covenant. Are you taking hold of my covenant, she asks. You pathetic little merchant, are you taking hold of my covenant?

Get away.

He's a bird. He flies like a bird. Far below he sees a rooftop. A small, dark square. He descends, onto the peak of the roof. He stays there.

They've assembled down below. He calls something out to them and laughs. Come on up. And makes obscene gestures. Spits at them, shames them, abuses them. That whole crowd with their enormous faces staring upward, turned upward like vast flat surfaces with elongated noses and weirdly distended eyes. All of them are assembled. One next to the other. They climb up, they lean a ladder up. They lay siege. I'll fly away, he says, I'll fly away. At that instant he slips. He tries to hold onto the peak of the roof. The straw is smooth, slick. He slips. He's drawn down. Farther and farther. I have to take off, he says, take off over those faces, over the roofs, over the tower of justice, over the killing ground, over the smoldering fires. But his arms don't obey. His body collapses into itself. Not one part of it obeys him. There are no juices left inside. He collapses, down, to the earth, cool, into the grass, into the grass.

Something cool and damp stuck to his eyelids. A shiver coursed down his back and the wet linen stuck to his skin. When he opened his eyes, there was fog all around him. It clung to the ground and rose up the banks of this dark ravine. He lifted his head and saw that he was lying in the grass in a kind of gorge that rose up steeply on both sides. Below him he could hear the murmuring of a brook. The landscape was saturated with moisture as the faint glow of early morning came through the trees into its darkness. He propped himself up on his elbows and then lifted himself up laboriously till he was sitting. There was a pain in his back that he'd got from lying so still and that now, as he hunched over, jabbed at him sharply. His legs hurt, and he felt a burning and stinging on his hands and face. He was shivering from the morning chill. He looked around and noticed a dagger not far off in the grass. He felt under his shirt. His coin purse was gone. What dreams, he said, what a horrible escape, and now I'm here. Now he's done for. With nothing. Alone. In the wild. The dampness was unpleasant. He got up and everywhere he looked there was moisture glistening on the leaves. It wasn't dripping. So it hadn't rained. The morning dew in a steep, narrow gorge. He inspected his clothing. It was soaked. His trousers were whole, but his shirt was in tatters. Cuts on his skin, even here. He'd had a good lashing. He headed down to the brook and washed the mud off his boots. On the other side of the gorge he climbed up past sparse trees on the hillside to where the light shone, up at the top. He grabbed tightly onto bushes as he climbed. Despite that, he lost his footing several times. It was slick, muddy earth. This is where he'd nose-dived the night before. This is where he'd slid down from the ridge.

Once he'd climbed to the top, a green, undulating, and unfamiliar landscape opened up before him. How long had he run? How far could he get in one night of incessant running? The sky glowed red against the background of this green expanse, sparsely dotted with trees, with the brown line of a plowed field to the left and a copse of bent, twisting trees to the right. Somewhere over there the sun would go up. He climbed and sat down for a rest. He was lost in the tall grass. Not even the slightest breeze rustled them in the early morning silence. The twittering of some birds awakening in the treetops only underscored the limitless peace. He listened intently—no roosters crowed, no dogs barked. Fear and flight had driven him into this soggy desolation, the instinctive functioning of his body had found him this hiding place. Only that field at the edge of the countryside betrayed a human presence.

He got up and waded through the grass. Its tall blades clung wet and chilly to his legs. Green gnats, awakened, flew up from under his footsteps. There wasn't the tiniest dry space. Dampness was everywhere, dampness that soaked into Ot's clothing and skin. In a little while the sun would cast light on this landscape and dry it as far as the eye could see. Only the hollow, alongside which he was walking toward the copse on the right—only it would remain dark and damp. This hiding place should have a stream flowing through it and snails clinging to its roots. He would come back here.

He didn't dare step out onto the level ground that separated the hollow with the stream from the copse with its bent, twisting trees. He stood under the crown of a tree for a long time, looking around. There wasn't a living soul anywhere. Then he ran out like a meek, frightened animal. He only caught his breath on the far side. Now he could hear a rooster in the distance. Out of the glowing part of the sky came a barely audible cry that smelled of people, a house, dryness.

He sat down on a thick branch that was slightly blackened in the morning dampness and he waited for that old glowing ball to launch into the blue sky's circuit. Some sort of plant with a squashlike head and orange blossoms was growing in the ferns and moss. He didn't know its name. He broke off one of its yellowish green pods, which consisted of soft flesh surrounding a yellow heart. In his fingers it turned into an oozing, stinking slime. The heart appeared to be edible. He bit into it, but some bitter, white milk trickled through his mouth. He spat it out. He would look to people for food, not the forest. It wasn't safe here. Even in nature the dark forces of the earth set their traps. Poisonous thorn apple. How many witches had eaten things so they could live and dream and rave through their witch's adventures. Something was swarming on the leaf that was still in his hand. He shook the tiny, greenish little dots into his hand. The leaf lice perched on his skin and moved slightly. So much swarming, so much dampness, so many slimy and flickering substances in this morning. In this forest, in this grass, in this vegetation and in this hollow, where he would hide for a day. To wait for the hunt that was undoubtedly still going on to die down. Among the gnats and the lice that God had conceived for the earth, who knew what for, for whose benefit and to whose detriment. Or perhaps somebody other than God was responsible for them. Wasn't everything on the earth and of the earth in fact the creation of somebody else? Poisonous thorn apple. This oozing, stinking slime. These green, swarming little creatures. Gnats. Snails. Salamanders. Snakes. Toads. In the dampness, dripping from the trees, in everything wet and slimy. Between water and air. What is this revolting transformation that's overcome me, he wondered. What sort of thoughts are these, this morning? Fear of renewal? Of the night that's behind me? Of a repetition of the events that brought me here, among these flowing and shifting or fixed but living substances?

What had happened, in fact? He looked back through the twisting branches at the red ball that had finally risen in the sky. He thought, collected, and organized his memory under its glare—drying things out, clearing things up, glowing. Who was the hunter, who the quarry? Had the hunters really been after him this time, too? Or had his skittish body, so used to weathering every woe and misfortunate, simply scampered away on its own, for no good reason, running amok through the courtyard and gardens, and eventually into this gorge and forest?

No, Johan Ot would never understand the chaos that had brought him here, that had driven him into this new flight, this wild, animalistic flight from unknown pursuers. Krobath—what was Krobath doing among the hunters and trackers? That solemn man who had rescued Adam from unpleasant situations so many times before. It must have been to his benefit in some way. He had connections. He must have done it to maintain his good connections. Krobath knew all about Adam's subversive plans, his revolutionary activities; but then why had he protected him so often in the past? He had always been with Adam, always watching, his eye ever vigilant. Krobath would watch and take mental notes about how things were developing. And this time it had gone too far. So Krobath had exposed him. He'd shown his true face. The face of a goddamned informer.

Or else. There was another possible interpretation. The authorities had been collecting information about Dorotea and her friends. They had picked up Ot's scent and gone wild. Wanting nothing more than to arrest him and shove him back in front of that monstrously grim, cold-blooded tribunal. And then there was the covenant of the brotherhood. Couldn't it have its fingers and claws in this somewhere? Ot had withdrawn, he'd quietly withdrawn and forgotten about his rescuers, his promises, his oaths, his mission. Were they applying pressure to him? Everything was hazy. Indecipherable. Complex. The ways of the authorities and the courts were complex, the influence of secret societies was complex, all earthly works and then most particularly the spiritual ones were complex, indeed impenetrable. Where did all these events and ways and threads meet? Where was the focal point? Where was the place and when the moment that one might find truth and clarity?

The less Ot understood, the more the space inside his skull fretted and stewed. Had a crime been committed, in fact? In their deranged panic had Dorotea and Adam battered, had they needlessly, pointlessly pounded that poor little fellow to death? What fear, what insane fear had driven them into that wild, horrible, relentless tangle? Had the guards been waiting outside? For what, for whom were they waiting, who was it they planned to arrest? Had the shouting and smashing and all the commotion in Locatelli's house encouraged them to come sooner?

What had happened, what had happened? What dark forces had set events on this pointless, insane course again, causing everything to get less and less clear? Why was it necessary to keep running and running through this unhappy country, through this insane and bloody country? To the point where only a single certainty remained: he was a beast, a beast on the run, incessantly on the run since he'd first been aware of himself—on the run.

No, Johan Ot would never understand the chaos that drove him through the world. He wouldn't understand that he carried an evil seed within himself. Within and upon. Why otherwise would he show up again and again in places where there was darkness and confusion?

If, at one point, things had been clear, if it had been possible to explain them with the help of facts, events, and phenomena and put them in a precise and proper perspective, now the chaos of the universe had seized this unlucky soul once and for all, dragging him into the center of its vortex.

Had Ot any hope of understanding who he was, what he wanted, and where he was going?

He stared at that ember in the sky and listened to the unsteady beating of his heart. It hammered. It pounded and pounded. It thundered. In his entrails too it thundered and the whole countryside as far as the horizon responded with a mighty clamor reaching from earth to heaven.

16.

The cold, the unbearable blows of the rain. The people pursue an escaped beast, an outlaw. The toothless red mouth of the shaggy face on the right hand.

When he woke up, the sun stood high in the sky. It burned through a narrow belt of blue with unusual force. Dark clouds pressed in from both sides, while in the distance, at the edge of the countryside, the sky was black from an accumulation of dense watery and airborne substances. With his dagger Ot cut off a bunch of branches and dragged them across the empty expanse into the hollow. He crawled into the space under a rocky overhang and spread the dry branches, ferns, and shrubs out on the floor of his dank skunk hole.

A hollow drumming sound rolled from beyond the edge of the horizon all across the plain. Then it began pounding and raging in the distance in earnest. The tops of the sparsely planted trees were all sent into a prolonged fluttering. Then everything went quiet, even the birds and the buzz of the insects. The drumming was coming closer, and now Johan Ot knew that there was nowhere, including here, in this desolate place, that he wouldn't be forced to fight to survive.

He crawled into the shelter and silence of his grave. He waited. Then whatever it was struck close by. Far above he could hear the patter of the first drops, as for a short time they tickled the leaves and reached down with their chill air, until the dam burst, and water gurgled through the darkness into sinkholes and channels. Ot watched the muddy, viscous stuff that foamed off the overhang and went spraying and pouring precipitously down, inches away.

It poured and poured and with all his senses Ot yearned now for the miraculous beauty of a quiet, dry peasant homestead. Far off and unattainable. He tried to go to sleep, but the chill set his whole body shivering. The torrent had extinguished the last of the daylight and only high above toward the top of the hill could he make out the outlines of trees. Soon even they sank into the darkness and he stared into emptiness with eyes wide. Moisture had melted his surroundings entirely, and it struck him that outside, at arm's length, the distinction between water and air had been temporarily abolished, and that it would no longer be possible to breathe in that chilly, thick mixture, that the only place where there was still air left was here, in his dank, stuffy skunk hole. The downpour, this cosmic deluge refused to stop. Now he could feel something cool penetrating beneath the branches and there was a gurgling behind his back as well. He put his hand to the wall and everywhere on its smooth surface he felt a wet, creeping coldness. The water had percolated down through the earth and was collecting in a pool under the branches. It was going to flood him. He couldn't hold out here. Rigid from the cold and from lying still for so long, he slid rather than crawled out of his lair. He climbed up toward the edge of the gorge, but now it was more difficult. The rain was coming down in rivers and kept undermining his step. When he finally did manage to drag himself up to the top, he was thoroughly soaked and chilled.

Dampness. Cold. The unbearable blows of the rain.

He headed out over the plain toward the place where he had seen the brown earth that morning.

He dragged himself over the soaking landscape in a kind of lethargic half-sleep, without any goal or plan.

Should he beg, should he pray, should he call out for mercy?

To whom? The forces of earth or heaven? Who had the upper hand on a horrible night like this—diabolical powers or sacred?

Hang on, he said, you just need to hang on a little longer. Someone will rescue you. They have to.

Overcome with hunger, exhaustion, dampness, and cold, he collapsed. But his dull and unrelenting will to survive persisted, and he kept crawling forward.

Suddenly he realized that his fingers were feeling something vertical and hard. It was a fence. The work of human hands. He stood up and climbed over its wood. Farther on there was a low wooden building, and persistent movement inside—the stamping of many feet. Ot staggered toward it and felt along its wall. He stopped at the door and banged on it feebly. No echo came from inside, no word was spoken. Just the stamping, louder now. He leaned into the door and pushed forward. Then his elbow collided with a bolt and his whole body lurched through the hole that gaped before him. He felt something soft and warm and living. Sheep, somebody had taken pity on their small livestock and driven them from their pen into this shelter. An entire little herd was jostling and shifting position in these close quarters.

Ot stared into the second morning of his unreasoning flight. The sheep had made a welcoming space around him. They were crowding around and looking at this thing that was moving on the floor. It was warm and light inside. There was a pail full of curdled milk standing on a wooden shelf. Ot swallowed the entire, enormous volume of the bucket's contents in rapid gulps. He filled his rounded belly—which had grown used to entirely different and far more plentiful food in recent weeks—all the way to the top.

Outside it was a well-scrubbed, sunny morning. Beyond the carpets of yellow fields that stretched up over a small hill in the vicinity, he could see dark, thatched roofs. Very close by a lark darted up at a sharp angle into the sky.

Here was the fluttering of this happy bird, after all. Following the night of floods and cataclysms, there was life, after all. No one had been drowned, no one asphyxiated in the deluge of that dense, endlessly flowing substance. But how close had his white, exhausted body come to being drowned in that badger den, or whatever that flooded hole under the overhang was? One day they would have found the disintegrating corpse, or what was left of the disintegrating corpse, for most of it would have been carried off by animals. Yes, one day somebody would have shrieked in horror. A stranger, they would have said, a victim of murder, witchcraft, the plague.

Even in death Ot would have struck fear into the bones of honest, devout people.

He went inside to have a closer look around the shed, but hardly had he crossed the threshold than he heard voices outside. He reckoned they must be somewhere to the right, where a narrow path wound through the high grass. But he miscalculated. When he stepped out through the doorway again, the voices had already come around the corner of the building and were in front of him. Two youngish fellows, shepherds by the look of them, one of them barefoot, the other wearing some kind of wooden footwear, both of them in oversized, fluttering linen shirts. Startled, they stopped, and even Ot couldn't think of any quick or smart way to react to this sudden encounter. So they stood and looked at each other, until Johan Ot said, the storm . . .

took shelter . . . in your, and he pointed a finger back at the shed. If there had been just one of them, he might have been able to convince him. Perhaps they could have had a nice chat. But here with their two heads together, round and slow as these may have been, like oxen's, they summoned up some courage. He's a tramp, the one in the shoes said, he's been stealing.

Johan Ot tried to explain he hadn't been stealing: the storm . . . took shelter, and he pointed at the sky and inside the shed, but it was pointless, they understood him too well.

"Thief," the one in the shoes said. "Robber, vagabond." The barefoot one nodded swiftly and decisively. They stepped back from Ot as he approached them, gesticulating broadly and using many words to try to persuade them, to explain. The one in shoes tripped but then picked up a stick and got up off the ground. The barefoot one ran to the fence and tried to pull out a board so he could bang Johan Ot over the head with it.

There was no way out. Ot drew the long dagger out of his belt and shifted it from hand to hand, so that it glinted brightly in the sun.

"A killer," the one wearing shoes said and dropped his stick.

"He'll kill us," the barefoot one said and let go of the piece of board that he had jerked out of the fence.

With a skillful flourish that he had observed among soldiers, Johan Ot waved the knife through the air, shouted and leaped forward in a threatening, crouching stance.

The barefoot one was first to run for it, while the other tripped and stumbled in his heavy shoes, until he bent down, picked them up and ran after his partner.

Johan Ot looked ahead, frightened and defeated. He remained alone on the field of battle, but soon they would come running back with swords and pitchforks and, God help him, they would hunt him like a boar through the underbrush.

He ran indoors, pushed the pail with the milk aside, and felt several loaves of cheese lying toward the back of the shelf. He grabbed one of them and shoved it under his belt. The sheep bleated and scattered to all sides and then came trundling through the door out into the open after him.

He ran through the stubble of the field and thought of his boots, which the sharp points down below were slashing and destroying mercilessly. He listened to his heavy breathing and waited for the moment when the commotion would start up around the cottage. He was already quite close to a sparse wood when he glanced back and caught sight of them. They were compressed into a tight bunch outside the cottage. One of them called out and the group opened up. They stretched out in a broad arc and started running toward the woods, calling out loudly to each other as they ran.

Ot finally remembered the gorge. The plain, he had to make it over the plain in short order. They wouldn't be able to see him from this side. The woods are in the way. If I can manage that, he said to himself, I'm saved.

He drove himself through the grass at full tilt. The shouting was getting closer. Now they're near the woods. Now they're in it. They've spread out, looking for him. He reached the edge and hurled his whole body over it so that he slid smoothly down to the creek. He came to a stop. Where was his emergency lair with the rock overhang? Ahead or behind him? Without thinking he started to follow the creek downstream and a few paces later caught sight of the rock. He crawled under it and onto the wet branches. He breathed deeply. His hand was still squeezed around the dagger hilt.

Before much time had passed he could hear voices up above. Fragmented, abrupt, harsh, snapping. The peasants were in a killing mood, all right. Ot held his breath, even though he was certain that nobody could find him in his den. When you looked at it from the outside, it was completely dark inside. Surely my eyes don't shine, he thought.

The commotion and bloodthirsty shouts gradually shifted uphill and then vanished.

He waited a while longer, then he dragged himself out. Only now did he get a good look at himself. He was dirty and in tatters, and through the shreds of his clothing he could see dried blood on his body. He was a tramp, a real tramp. No wonder they had come after him. Fear had caused them to close ranks. He recalled his band of merchants and the scares they would get traveling desolate trails. Lots of fugitive criminals from the lands around Venice, all sorts of bandits were constantly harassing the local populace. The land was full of dangerous foreigners, morality was disintegrating, and even the judges were afraid. Thefts and all sorts of violence were so common that decent people were no longer safe even in their own homes.

That was it. Fear had united them against him. Now he was a real tramp. He had to get clothes and a horse. Then things would be different. Then people wouldn't chase after him giving out those frightened, bloodthirsty cries. It wouldn't be easy.

He climbed back up and had a good look around. The band of men had dispersed. He couldn't see the shepherd's hut from this side. He descended alongside the trees that grew along the edge of the gorge.

He must have walked for a long time, because the sun was already reaching toward evening. The creek emerged from its gorge and as it entered the flatland expanded into a placid current several paces wide. Willows grew on both sides of it. At the foot of some hills at the far end of the stream there appeared to be a good-sized settlement. First fields, then a small bridge, then houses. It was close enough that he could hear dogs barking and a child crying.

He would wait here till evening. He found a place to sit among some bushes, which put the flatland and any unbidden visitor who might be inclined to sound an alarm directly in front of him. He pulled the loaf of cheese out of his shirt. He chewed and chewed until he got sick of it.

He listened to the echoes of the sounds of evening that came to him with the gusts of a gentle breeze. People were coming home from their fields, fussing around their houses, calling their dogs and children, getting ready for supper. The life of a peasant settlement, always and everywhere the same. They've worked so hard they can barely stand on their feet. Their eyes heavy, they throw the bolts on the doors of their stables and houses. Now they're going to stuff themselves with food. Then they'll have brief conversations in those dim houses of theirs, with beams running the length of the ceiling. Monstrous images will nest in the black woodwork under the roof, as the wind drives at weird creatures above it. Inside it will be warm and safe. Then, sweaty and exhausted, in a house swarming with young, old and little creatures, they will mate. Laundry will be dried on lines next to the stove, and in the far corner a crucifix will respire with them. Everything will breathe in this safe space, filled with humidity and sanctified peace.

Why don't I live like that, Ot asked aloud, making himself flinch at the sudden sound of a human voice in the willow-laced darkness. Why don't I live like that, why do I have to flee and then wander about with this fear and confusion in my chest? What power, what unknown force drives me from one escape to the next?

He tried to think back in time to the motives and reasons. Far back to a homestead and peace of his own, but everything in that remote past was so uncertain and dark, so vague and strange that he couldn't be sure it was true. Maybe they're just dreams, he thought. And maybe I'm just dreaming this dark cluster of houses and the dogs barking and this stream murmuring peacefully in its motionless current and this urge I feel to go and break into that house jutting out on the river bank, just waiting for me.

He walked carefully alongside the stream as far as the bridge. There he stopped and listened. No voices. He could proceed. Slowly he climbed up the bank and looked at the dark windows behind which people were breathing and snoring in their leaden sleep. He shoved some trap door or other and was suddenly on the other side of the fence. At that instant something started howling and snarling. A dark shadow bounded toward him, and at the last second, in an agile, cat-like maneuver, he jumped out and pulled the gate shut behind him. On the other side the enraged animal howled and jumped at the fence. Its call was picked up outside the other houses. The whole canine village mustered its courage by barking wildly and howling. Damned mutt, Ot thought, could wake the dead with that kind of racket. Ot crouched alongside the fence and waited. If they set the dogs loose, he thought, I'm done for. He heard the door of a house farther up the hillside opening. Someone came outside, walked around, and then called out loudly to his dog. It quieted down. And the animal on the other side of the fence calmed down too. But the dog remained alert. It could sense Ot's motionless presence. It was padding around and sniffing. It's afraid. It's afraid, too.

Ot remained motionless for an infinitely long time. Then he moved slightly and waited for the dog to go wild. Nothing happened. It stayed quiet. He moved alongside the fence and reached the corner of the house. This was where the fence met up with the dark timbers of the building. Ot reached up on tiptoe and listened by the window. Breathing. People are sleeping in there. Around to the other side. There was a thicket of bushes behind the house, with an opening for him to pass through. The house was built into the hillside, which rose up steeply behind it. He reached his hand into a window and felt around. Empty. It couldn't be far to the floor. He tried to shove his head and shoulders inside, but he couldn't make it through.

He sat down on the ground and thought desperately. A shirt, just give me one shirt, good people. And some food.

He rose up again in a rage. He rushed at the window and wedged his head inside it. Now all he needed was to get his shoulders through and he was as good as in. But he wasn't. He managed to get his shoulders through, but then got stuck at the hips. He panted and cursed and pushed. There was no way. Someone must have heard him, because there was motion inside and some words spoken in the room ahead of him. Then he distinctly heard a voice ask, "Who's there?" Ot pushed backward with his whole body. He had to moan, because the wood cut sharply into his skin. Somebody's in here, the voice called out and the house came to life. Ot felt the presence of that male individual who had entered the room and was feeling his way through the dark. Then he felt his head being grabbed by the hair.

"I've got him," the man roared with all his might. "He can't get away."

In the desperation that followed, Johan Ot shoved somebody in the belly and then in the crotch, so that the hold on his head was released. Go around, the voice bellowed. Go around the house. The front door slammed. Voices. Squeals. The barking of dogs. And Ot never understood how or when he ended up back on the hillside. He had been scuffling through bodies and shouts in the dark, dozens of tentacles latching on and snatching back and forth in that darkness. Ot's fists pounded away all around him and he growled like some wild beast, because that's just what he was now, a beast.

Up on the hillside, with the rocks and sharp thorns, he caught his breath as tears of anger and tears of despair welled up in his eyes. There's no place, no place to go. He would have to wander from house to house forever, and everywhere he would be chased and beaten.

There was no salvation in sight.

No way out anywhere.

He could just flee. Flee from no one and flee from everyone. Flight in its most savage and senseless form. Flight pure and simple. From that chaos in Locatelli's house to this insane flight from these hicks, wild with fear, amid cold and dampness, onto these cliffs where every frightened beast of creation has retreated. And before? What was there before? Had there ever been any kind of steady, peaceful homestead anywhere?

He couldn't think of any. But his mind was uncooperative. Stuck and spinning uselessly in a desperate desire for deliverance, deliverance. Down below him was an enraged and frightened crowd. Here there were rocks and thorns. He was out of hope and out of determination when the thought came to him: I'll get out of this yet.

He wandered among those rocks all night. Faint, scratched up, and tattered to shreds, he finally lay down and stretched out in the grass.

In his sleep he could hear distant bells, gunshots, and shouting. Indeed, a large bell had started ringing very close by. It rang steadily and persistently. Here, too, there were human voices with their terrible shouting, and it made him want to get up and run, run back through those thorns, but his body wouldn't obey. When he opened his eyes, he saw between the trees in the morning light high above a pale, utterly pale and motionless face. It was looking straight at him with its expressionless eyes. A bloody face, red rivulets of blood on its cheeks. They streamed down its forehead and eyes. But this stream was motionless. A crown, there was a crown up on top, a real crown of thorns. The Savior was looking at Ot in his death agony. Nothing was happening, all of this was perfectly still as the bells went on ringing, and yet Ot felt a human presence. Something was moving—yes, there was motion down by his feet. He propped himself up on his elbows and at that instant a shadow scuttled into the undergrowth beneath the cross. Beneath the crucifix. What am I doing here underneath the bloody, crucified Savior? Bells are ringing, and there's a mob after me with swords and pitchforks and flails.

He tried to get up, but groaned in pain and exhaustion and dropped back down into the grass. There was movement in the undergrowth again. His eyes shifted from the Savior's face, traveling all the way down the wide, planklike wooden cross, until they encountered a peculiar human shape at the bottom. In tatters. Carrying skins and beggars' sacks. Slightly hunchbacked. Male, shaggy, bearded. Nervous, frightened, dancing gestures. Insane eyes darting in their sockets, so different from the peaceful, vacant eyes up above.

It stepped forward and timidly approached. Now, high above, next to the Savior's bloody, pale face, Johan Ot saw an overgrown mass with curious eyes first looking down at him, then left and right. Ot looked at those two faces in the morning sunlight. Then the shaggy face spoke, while the pale one remained silent with its rivulets of blood and tight yet drooping lips.

"Forgive me, brother," said the red, toothless oral cavity of the shaggy face on the right. "I thought you were kaput for sure."

With an awkward gesture that also contained a certain regret, he pulled a well-preserved, cuffed leather boot from under one arm.

"Mine," Johan Ot gasped. "My boot."

"Yes," the shaggy face said. "Yes, yes, you can have it back. I don't take them off living bodies. Never, ever."

Johan Ot tried to smile at him thankfully.

"Damn, you're a mess," the shaggy face said and leaned over him. He lifted Ot's head up and poured some water into his mouth, babbling the whole time.

"They made a mess of you, you're worse off than I am, what can you do, what can you do, that's how things are for us. But boots like these, how did you ever manage, where did you steal them, it's really a shame you woke up, because I thought you were a goner for sure. At least you came to the right place to die," he said. "Right here under our Lord."

"The bells," Johan Ot gasped and nodded his head toward the hill where the ringing came from. "What for?"

"Oh, that?" the babbler said. "Every night," he said. "They're hunting witches. They go walking over the fields draped in a sheet and steal the blessing from the fields. *Ar-zhek, ar-zhek* those witches scream, a person could go mad with fear, and then they vanish and reappear at some crossroads with a cross beside it, like here. That's why you're safe here, you'll always be safe here. Nobody dares come here. They just assemble up by the church and ring the bells and shoot if they have something to shoot with, or else they just scream for hours on end without stopping."

"Dangerous," Johan Ot whispered.

"Dangerous?" the babbler rattled on. "Of course they're dangerous, but only around their own houses or near a church. No place else. Everywhere else there's tremendous fear. At crossroads, beneath a cross, whoever comes here late at night or in the early morning hours can lose his mind. They know that, every child knows that, that's why there's nobody here, that's why you can rest here without any worries. And thanks be to God," the shaggy fellow crossed himself and cast his eyes up toward the crucifix, "that you still have your boots on your feet. Mercifully, He woke you up just in time. I thought you'd already passed on, that the witches—and there are plenty of them around here, as you can hear, right?—that the witches, down below I mean, were already dragging your body around and lashing it."

The man picked up the boot and tried to put it back on the foot off of which he had pulled it. With great effort Johan Ot sat up and helped.

"I'd give them to you," Johan Ot said, "but without boots . . ."

"I understand," the shaggy one interrupted him. "I understand, without boots there's just no getting by in our profession, is there?

You're grateful to me, aren't you? I'm the first person in a long time who hasn't sicked dogs on you, aren't I?" His toothless mouth chortled. "I know it, I know it well."

Johan Ot gnawed on the dry bread that his rescuer gave him and he watched the bright and solemn morning light that was rising in the east as he listened to the shaggy fellow chortle in the silence that had suddenly fallen, for the hunters had ceased their hunting for one night. Ot watched and listened and marveled at how quickly and miraculously his strength could return.

"Where are we?" Ot asked all of a sudden, as though he were already back on his feet, as though he felt drawn back out onto the road, onward, toward some destination.

"Close," the other said enigmatically. "Close to St. Anthony, my patron. A nice little village," he whispered confidentially. "Lots of pilgrims, lots of good, heedless people. My Anthony helps, he preaches to the fish, and he'll help us."

Johan Ot got to his feet. Once he had taken a look at himself, he realized he was in no way better off than his shaggy, cheerful companion, that he was no less of a vagabond. He had to laugh.

"Is there water anywhere?" he asked. "I need to wash."

He leaned on the hunched figure, and the two of them slowly wobbled off down the forest path. In a scratchy voice his companion began to sing merrily:

Saint Anthony of Padua
Give us aught to forage on.

17.

Time disintegrates. Intentions evaporate. The wheels of fire. Days of old returning. A sorry backwater. How do you feel in the desert, Anthony?

This funny-pathetic life, the cheerful and melancholy and strange life of a vagabond, a tramp, a beggar. Spent between kicks, chunks of meat set out for dogs, a loaf of bread in your shirt, some stolen cake in your beggar's bag. Dodging the snarls and growls of guards of the hearth, spending nights in the hay and the barn, on errands in the monastery orchard. Amid banquets and hunger. In squalor, in the cold and the wind. On moonlit nights. In the silence of an empty church. Philosophizing with your vagabond and brigand friends. Fleeing the shadow of the hangman and judge. In the security of your saintly clothes. On ways of the cross, on pilgrimages, white, radiant, and high. In arduous processions.

At a carefree village celebration.
The yodel of the pipes in their regular rhythm. Male and female figures moving rhythmically under a village linden tree. A holiday.

Festively dressed. The men in broad-brimmed hats, beneath which the sweat pours and pours onto their faces flushed with exertion. Wearing their wide trousers made of dark homespun cloth, all of them hot and serious as they go anxiously through their motions. The women with pleated linen on their heads, wearing broad skirts that move and flutter with the gentle undulation of their bodies, with shining eyes and seductive gestures.

Swords. Swords held in knobby peasant hands. Iron and dogwood walking sticks.

The yodel of the pipes. The rhythm. It transports them and drops them and spins them into their days of old.

A circle that loses its regular spin, loses its rules. Hands hitting wood, to the rhythm. Faster. Across and together. This strange peasant dance. Wine from a pitcher, down a beard, down a chest. In shirts, now they're in shirts and together, bunched together in the crowd. They hold onto each other's shoulders and hands, let go and scatter like a startled flock, then back together, a safe bundle of limbs, grips, and breaths, sweaty faces, shifting bodies, deeper bending, leaps, to the beat, to the yodel of the pipes.

They sat behind a house, inconspicuous, unneeded, pointless rejects of creation. Anton was stuffing tiny pieces of bread into his toothless mouth and then grinding and grinding those bits in his jaws. Johan Ot was staring ahead. Evening was coming and the frenzied dance out in the square was calming down. He heard the giggling of girls and the swaggering blather of drunken men. The two of them had nowhere to go. They had come from nowhere. They feared no one. Time had disintegrated, intentions evaporated. A cool breeze bent the grass.

"Did you ever have a home?" Anton asked.

"Somewhere I did," Johan Ot said. He saw a field of stubble. Harvested grain. A hill darkening as daytime withdrew. Was that here or there? Was it sometime in the past or now?

"Do you miss it?" Anton said. "Does it torment you and make you anxious? Begone! Begone! I always think: How would you feel in the desert, Anton?"

At a carefree village celebration.

In an abandoned house one day at noon.

Two soldiers stopped. Infantrymen from who knows what division. The first with a sword and a long pike. The second with a sword at his waist, a musket over his shoulder, and some kind of stick, both to lean on, and to load the musket, attached to his belt. Wearing broad, floppy trousers down to the knee. The trouser legs are bunched up and flounced, until they get squeezed together with broad red ribbons far down below. With a hat and an ostentatious feather tucked into the hatband. Dusty, tired, with weary faces and vacant eyes. At a neighboring house they ask for water. The two beggars mutely perch at a window and watch the village as it empties. Their lookout has reported back. Soldiers are coming.

The hopelessly monotonous, hurdy-gurdy refrain that the soldiers are singing draws closer. A fine voice, clear and sonorous, accompanied by a second deeper voice that gives it support and a base for its heights, with a third scrambling around on its little footsteps— together they sing the same short refrain over and over, hurdy and gurdy. The barking of dogs interferes, punctuating the refrain of their lament.

Then they came into view. The three singers out in front on horses. Beside them a musician who had his bag and pipes hanging over his horse's hindquarters, where they bounced carelessly like the udders of an empty, infertile cow. Even so, they sang. Staring far out ahead, they wailed their shapeless, rhythmless song, as boring as the road itself. Officers rode behind them, with straps and gold bands hang-

ing down from their faded uniforms. They chatted and spat indiffer-
ently. Neither they nor their horses paid any attention to the frenzied nipping, growling, barking, and howling of the peasants' dogs
as these huddled around them. How many villages had they ridden
through, with how many dogs growling and howling around them?
In the rear, the enlisted men were hobbling through the dust. In no
particular formation, they stared wearily at the ground or looked
around at the facades of the houses with bored and listless eyes. They
appeared to be exhausted and sick of everything. They're homeless
too, Johan Ot thought. They're on the road and they're fleeing too.
Pursuers or pursued, it makes no difference. There is no heroism,
no sign of their great battles, cannon fire and blood, there's none of
that in their eyes. Just boredom. What coastal region are they from?
Where are they being driven? To Bosnia or Hungary or Bavaria?
It doesn't matter. Wherever they go there are villages on the road,
dogs barking, then a short battle, and then fall in and march, and so
on endlessly. They've become indifferent and deadened same as us.
Their mountain homes, the church bell ringing to Sunday Mass, the
Christmas walnuts and warm holiday bread on the table—they've
lost their last memories of these things, too. All they have left is the
road and the hurdy-gurdy up front with its long, feeble refrain. With
an exhausted musician piping in now and then. Orders. Rest. Sleep.
March. Overandoverandover. A millipede moving from battle to
battle, from village to village, accompanied by the terrified looks of
peasants: please God just let them not stop here. A millipede on its
endless journey in service to a great ruler.

Ot noticed that the village remained silent. Only a few children
went running toward the soldiers, and even they were brought back
to the safety of apron strings by their mothers' worried she-beast
shouts. Only the dogs kept running behind the soldiers for a while.
All that was left was the cloud of dust raised by their running about.

Nothing else. And that faint, long hurdy-gurdy sound disappearing in the distance and proving that they'd gone, that they weren't here, and that they don't even exist.

"Howling and cranking their hurdy-gurdy," Anton said, chortling through his red gums. "Howling in despair."

"They'll end up bloody and broken in some field," Johan Ot said.

"We're better off," Anton chortled.

"Nobody's better off," Johan Ot said. "In this sorry backwater? Everywhere the same sorry, bloody backwater."

In abandoned house one day at noon.

After work, in the monastery orchard, song flooding from the church.

He leafed through some of the papers that a Capuchin monk had left on a bench. Anton was philosophizing and talking to himself and making strange gestures in the air. A powerful chorus that reached to the sky was coming from the church. Ot's eyes slid over the dark teeming letters. Then they stopped and his pupils fastened onto a particular passage. He shuddered. He read. And then again. Aloud:

"The aspiration and drive to build churches on desolate sites in the mountains and forests originates with vagabonds, organ-grinders, and other wastrels who live lives of idleness and debauchery, who own nothing and seek personal gain through dishonest means. Criminals, dreamers, tricksters, idlers, and the demon-possessed, fit for nothing but the galley, choose suitable sites in forests or valleys, clear them of their undergrowth, and entice honest people to go there, saying that these are the sites of miracles."

"Is that what it says?" Anton asked.

"Yes, it is," Johan Ot said.

"Miracles are nothing to scoff at," Anton said. "There was a staff once that turned into a serpent."

"Dreamers, the demon-possessed, and tricksters," Johan Ot said, as he pictured a house at the edge of a forest, men with their heads bowed in heated discussion—Urban Posek, he thought. Somewhere Urban Posek and Jakob Demšar are walking through the world and somewhere in the world they've got a razor for my neck.

After work, in the monastery orchard, song flooding from the church.

On the road, hoarfrost and ice underfoot.

A call came from the right, followed by powerful shouting. Ot's feet automatically sought someplace to hide, but there was nowhere: a village green with sparse shrubs all around. Figures of human beings followed the voices. They rose up out of a hollow like ghosts and in this dreamlike sprint of theirs approached the road. A large group of men and women. The men were waving their bare swords in the air and hacking branches off the trees. They cried out, while the women shrieked. A bride accompanied by married women on one side and a groom with his best men on the other headed home through fields, the village green, and unfamiliar places.

"They're chasing off evil spirits," he said. "That way the marriage will be a good one and there'll be happiness in the new house."

"What for?" Johan Ot said. "What for? But tell me, why does everyone run in this damned country? Why does everyone flee?"

On the road, hoarfrost and ice underfoot.

In a dark stable, the warmth of animal bodies.

They crawled indoors, away from the harsh, chilly wind that blew outside. It was warm and it stank of manure, of fat, of powerful animal bodies. Bodies that ate and gaped in the darkness and noisily disposed of their waste, all of that shit dropping to their feet with a noisy smack. In the middle of the night the stable door squeaked. Two shadows slipped inside. Blowing warm air on their hands, whispering. Then things grew louder and more agitated. The animals grew agitated. Something white, bright, and feminine shone in the dark. It stretched upward and a warm shadow covered it in its powerful embrace—holding the fragile female body in its arms and pressing it to the wall. It leaned against the wall and delicate legs like tendrils locked around its back. They moaned and groaned and grasped each other. The animals were shifting anxiously around when the woman briefly, indistinctly swallowed her muffled aahhh and then drew it out with her uneven breathing into weird, prolonged calls, interrupted, cut short, as though her breath were being taken away. The man was panting regularly and gradually losing control, squeezing the legs wrapped around his hips and pressing toward the wall with all his might. His gasps became more frequent and then turned into a prolonged cry, after which his arms relaxed and the white tendrils eventually slid gently down. They released and unlocked one another and collapsed into a defenseless dark heap on the floor. The shadow with the broad back, with its deep sigh of relief, still covering the other. Wordlessly. Everything was wordless. Even afterward, when the two shadows stirred and went out the door, allowing a sharp jolt of winter chill to blow in.

The beggars were lying half-asleep in the stinking hay. They didn't close their eyes all night.

When the first pale sunlight hit their beggars' bedding, Anton sat up and then leaned over those empty and strangely hollow eyes of Johan Ot, which were staring peacefully at the ceiling. As though they were the bulging eyes of an actual corpse.

"That's how they make love," he said. "That's how these people make love."

"That's how they mate," Johan Ot said.

"You're bad off," Anton said, exhaling a voiceless chortle through his toothless mouth. "Your guts are on fire. You're bad off. You didn't pass this test very well."

In a dark stable, the warmth of animal bodies.

A mournful procession.

Bare-heeled monks walked in the lead, with a huge, black cross wavering above their heads. They were followed by a dense, undulating crowd of bodies that jostled each other. In their movements, in their motion, in their incessant strain. With torches and candles in the glow of evening as the night devoured it. Shouts and whippings. On their knees, on all fours. Prayers like a moan and prayers like a curse. Some of them beat their heads on the ground, beat their chests with their fists, behaving as if they were demon-possessed or feebleminded. This night the two wanderers came to a stop on a forested hillside. They watched the wheels of fire that the pilgrims launched into the valley in the black of night.

"It's come back," Anton said. "Under the wings of the Capuchins, in a new sort of way. Different, but it's back."

That night an illness came over Johan Ot.

"Frightened people," Anton said. "Morbidly irritable, confused about faith, new prophets, apparitions, miracles."

That night an illness came over Johan Ot.

"False prophets have arisen," Anton said. "The end of the world is nigh."

Ot was shaking with some sort of fever and cold beads of sweat emerged on his forehead. He watched the wheels of fire and the people gathering around the church at the top of the hill. Their bodies shaking and writhing, as if they were in the grip of falling sickness. They rolled on the ground, some on their bellies, others on their backs. They lashed themselves with whips and writhed in bizarre ways. Those criminals, dreamers, tricksters, demon-possessed, he said, this insanity from one end of the land to the other. One minute it dies off and the next it's come back to life. One minute it's wheels of fire and the next it's a new beginning. Fire. The earth drumming. Days of old returning.

That night Anton had unusually clear, deep eyes. He observed the fever and illness that had inhabited Johan Ot.

That night Anton spoke to the sick man in a calm voice.

"You're bad off," he said. "You've seen everything but you've understood nothing. Everyone is getting slaughtered and flattened in these times of ours. Other people know why. You haven't passed any of your tests very well."

A mournful procession.

After that night there were no peaceful moments left for Johan Ot. Fear sat on his shoulders. The two vagabonds dragged themselves from one village to the next, endlessly, until Anton could no longer keep up.

And this is how they will part ways. Things kept going farther and farther downhill for Johan Ot and he couldn't conceive that the bottom was still a long way off. That the beggar's staff was not the last station, that the end of his fall was still farther down. The labyrinth had swallowed him whole and irrevocably into its earthly inferno, driving him relentlessly down the path of his dark fate. What drew and shook him that night? To what destination? Why does he veer off, why does he insist on fleeing to the rim, only to have the gears draw him back to the center again and again? He wants to be master of his own fate. Why doesn't he join in, why doesn't he make up his mind and follow God or the Devil and their associates on this earth? Why does he forsake his brethren in covenant, abandon his friends, why does he roam the world in his accursed isolation, fleeing or loitering? Why does he bear within himself all the delusions and spiritual ills of his time? Why does he not resist, why doesn't he vanquish them, why doesn't he participate anywhere, passionately and with conviction? He ought to accept his new vagabond beggar's life. He ought to beg and steal, sleep in barns and granaries and forests, and share these people's joys and sorrows. He should try to understand their happiness and suffering. He should make peace with this vagabond life of his.

That he couldn't stand Anton anymore is what he shrieked one day at a forest crossroads, that he simply could not bear to see, hear, or feel Anton's constant presence. His damned toothless oral cavity philosophizing and chewing and muttering and gumming, his screechy voice, his hump, his skinny thief and beggar's hands that were destined to be chopped off on some block someday, leaving him with stumps for begging in front of a church. The revulsion and those garbled thoughts and sayings of a goddamned crazy vagrant and thief and Judas. Ot would become like that soon himself, he would go crazy too if he let things go on as they were.

Startled, Anton watched this rage and shouting and pulling of hair. Then he cast his eyes to the ground. He was silent, silent for a long time. Then he raised those unusually clear eyes, his suddenly unusually intelligent eyes and spoke in such a pure voice that a cold shudder ran down Johan Ot's back.

"I understand," Anton said finally. "I understand perfectly. But tell me one thing before we part. You have some secret idea you're carrying. Some idea is driving you through the world. Tell me what it is."

Johan Ot was struck dumb for a moment. It was as though the pale, cold face of that bloody sufferer on the crossroads had spoken.

"What sort of idea?" he demanded angrily. "I don't have any damned, stupid idea. Jakob Demšar and Urban Posek, now *they* have an idea. Lampretič has one. Adam is gadding about with one in his beggar's rags somewhere, like the two of us here, hatching and plotting something. But me—no. I just see one thing—this sorry country and this terrible mess. This mental illness that's crossing through the land and drenching it through and through—the land, the air, the people. I said that once somewhere. They tried to butcher and obliterate me once for that. So I'll say it again: *spiritual anguish is being forged into human substance. That's why all of this has to collapse, disintegrate, and rot.* Along with me."

"You've said it," Anton's pale face with its amazed and gentle eyes said. "You've spoken your *Mene mene tekel upharsin.* The invisible hand has written on that white wall you see."

Anton's face had become shaggy and greasy again. His voice had grown all gummy and that bright inanity Johan Ot first saw in the morning twilight had settled in his face again.

"Vulture," Ot said. "You were going to take the boots off a dead person."

"You don't understand a thing," Anton chortled with that red oral cavity. "Not a thing."

He turned slowly around and hobbled off down the forested hillside. Johan Ot watched his hunched figure bob and sway, becoming smaller and smaller. He waved a hand in disgust and turned resolutely around. Let's hit the road, down along the trade roads to the sea, I'll start from scratch and do everything differently this time.

Although he thought he must have gone a long way, Ot could still hear distinctly the monotonous, long refrain:

Saint Anthony of Padua
Give us aught to forage on.

18.

The secret society of Magic Jack.

That night as he stood on the hilltop looking down, the last bit of clear sky drained into the vast expanse. Somewhere out there, way at the edge, sea and sky met. That peaceful and infinitely quiet surface seemed dangerous. Dangerous, but enticing. For down there, where the surface ate into land, was the shore and a city, a place where roads crossed. This was the site of everyone's hopes and beginnings, going back ages. Yesterday, today, and tomorrow. One or the other trick, a quick head, and industrious hands would always allow you to board, shove off, travel. To start over again, eternally. The worst was behind him. Dirty bunks, desolate paths, dangerous crossings, forests, journeys, wind, and dust. Now Ot wanted noise, people, crowds, chatter, shouting: warm, peaceful human figures. First the forest at his feet started to darken, then the cool shadow reached out into that peaceful surface and up into the sky. He saw a bit of light down below and was drawn to it. Bright, decisive of step, he headed down toward it, farther and farther down in the direction of his fate.

But there was no noise anywhere. Just silence in this familiar meeting place of sea and dry land, no voices or shouts, no footsteps, nothing.

There was the city gate, its maw, gaping wide open.

His heart beat a bit more quickly and his eyes widened a bit in surprise. There had been no news about this in the interior, or even in the County of Gorizia, or among the freighters in the Karst. No real reports that something was happening down here.

But something was happening down here. Without any doubt, something was wrong.

He stood for a while and stared into the black hole of the gate, and then he dashed inside, into the darkness. His muddy boots squished beneath the vault of the gate and then in the narrow street between the tall houses. In a small public square a few lights were burning—torches stuck into holders outside some doors. So there was life after all. So there were people after all. But it was quiet. Only the crackle of the flames and the gentle breeze that bent them.

Silence devoured him. He stopped, put his hands to his ears, and heard the ring of noiselessness in them.

It was so quiet that it gnawed at the house walls.

He walked down a narrow street that had some small bridges with windows stretched over it, then came to a stop in a larger empty space. The same sight. Three or four torches casting shadows that flitted and flickered and danced in the gusts of the wind, forming crazy, horrendously shaped monsters on the facades of the houses. He approached a wooden handcart leaned up against a wall and threw it to the ground. The clatter shook its way across the walls to the other side of the square, came back as an echo, and then fled into the darkness, into the dark streets, where it was swallowed. A moment later there was some sound over his head. He looked up and saw a bearded face that instantly drew back inside.

"Hey," Ot called out. "Hey, you up there in your hole."

He was overcome with an unusual, overly daring playfulness. As he'd approached, as he'd come down toward the coast, he had wondered where he was going to beg for bread, work, a place to sleep, in his humblest voice. Now he had suddenly forgotten his vagabond appearance, here in this skittish empty town with people huddling and hiding behind its windows, oppressed by some fear, perhaps of the plague. In this town he had suddenly sensed his former powers inside him.

Whether it's sickness, he said, whether it's fear, or whether it's hard times, so much the better, so much the easier. Even if there's a quarantine. Their ranks will have been decimated and they'll need new men.

There was no answer. He walked on, creeping through those pitch-black streets and pushing on the door handles. One of them would open somewhere. There would be a vacancy somewhere. He tripped over a heap of garbage. Some cats squealed and bristled behind him.

He was tired and exhausted, his throat caked with the dust of his journey, and he was confused by the unusual quiet of the town. Some crazy excess of daring driving him from one door to the next. He had to find somebody.

Then it struck him that he had run out of ways to go, that the narrow streets were intersecting strangely, merging with each other, that all the passageways were identical and all the façades the same one over and over. He walked faster, throwing himself at doors and looking up at that same window, framed with garlands of statues, saints, and naked cherubs on every house, a dance of these peaceful, tiny bodies around every window. He walked faster, despite the fact that his feet already hurt terribly. Suddenly he was running, somewhere there had to be a damned exit or entrance, he banged his head into a low overhang, causing blood to trickle down his forehead, and then he didn't know which way to turn. In the darkness he sat down on a smooth stone bench alongside the wall of a house. Where have I come to? he wondered. Where am I groping and crawling? He looked out ahead. He squeezed his fists and mumbled something to himself.

He got up and just past the next house the street broadened. He looked around in amazement. In some inexplicable way he had got back to where he had started. On the big square, outside the house where the bearded face had slid back into the darkness.

The wind began blowing more strongly and almost put the torches out. On the far side of the houses he could hear the rhythm of the first waves. The words of the big, dangerous sea.

He had come to challenge that monstrous liquid surface stretching all the way to the edge of the sky. Now it was gently moving, slapping against the shore on the far side of the houses. Now it was answering him in its muted voice.

He stood in the middle of the square in the dance of shadows and the wind that crawled through the black holes of the streets. Alone.

He had no choice. He banged on the doors.

Silence.

No answer.

He dropped his arms and looked around helplessly. On the far side of the houses the sea was pounding and he felt a kind of fear and a kind of fury, anger rising in his chest.

He caused a terrible racket by dragging the overturned handcart and slamming it into a door.

Eyes were glaring at him.

From everywhere, eyes, innumerable eyes were palpating his body and watching his wild behavior in silence.

The thing in his chest grew, expanding into his throat, and again he grabbed the handcart and pulled it back and shoved it on its wheels into a door like a battering ram. There was a horrible bang, the silence was cleft in two as though a huge slab of granite had split, the façades of the houses shook and bent down over his head.

That helped.

He took deep breaths as he leaned on the broken door. He felt a slight movement under his hand. The door had opened slightly. He pressed his face against the opening to smell the breath and hear the voice of the human being on the other side. But the voice came from deep within.

"What are you trying to do, you fool?" it said, so quiet and so human. But then Ot heard quick footsteps behind him. He turned around and saw three male figures with obscure weapons in hand running across the square and pushing through the dancing shadows. He hesitated in the doorway, for some reason, wondering if he should say something, if he should try to explain to the men who were approaching so quickly. For some reason he stood there, and in the next moment they were there and on top of him.

That's how it happened. All of it, that simple and quick.

The worst things always happened this quickly and senselessly. And he was back in jail.

The First Day.

A tramp among tramps. Tattered and shaggy among the tattered and shaggy. Among the louse-ridden and mangy, bandits, thieves, and scoundrels, among the blistered and filthy. One of them had no nose, another no ears, and a third had a deep scar that stretched across his face. They welcomed him with a contented murmur. As one of their own. It was a long, stone passageway with a thick iron cage to the right. Bodies jostling in this hole. The voices of their guards came from the passageway and in the morning some light came through from God knows where. Because there were no windows: no blue sky behind them nor stars in the sky.

On the first day a guard brought some food and water. Excellent food, in fact—some slimy mixture of intestines and corn. It was cold and stale, but Ot leaped on this food like a wolf. He devoured it, paying heed to nothing else.

The guard stood beside him and watched with unusual interest. He ignored the others. He stared at Ot swallowing and at the apple bobbing up and down his skinny neck.

Then he bent down over him and hissed into his face, "You pig, you filthy pig."

The Second Day.

The rogues chatted. Slowly, leisurely, and with great focus, as though time were at a standstill. About the judicial system in the Venetian Republic. About sentences. About the prisons. One of them told a story about a fish that they used to rip the flesh off the bodies of convicts. Everyone stared and waited for the newcomer to start talking. But the newcomer remained silent. He understood nothing of what was going on. Toward evening a scar-faced giant approached and shoved Ot in the ribs.

So, he said, what are you here for? Robberytheftmurderrape? Ot shook his head. Assault? No, the bowed head shook. Fraud? Nothing, he shouted, I haven't done anything, I don't know what I'm here for, I'm not guilty. Hey, the colossus said, there are no snitches here. You can talk. Ot shrieked and shoved the scarface in the chest with all his might. I don't care, he howled. I don't care about any snitches. I don't know why they've shoved me into this hole. The giant began to move threateningly, but then thought better of it. He started to shake with laughter. You're not guilty, he said and then the whole band of brigands burst out into guffaws so violent they were snorting with laughter and bursting with laughter between those dank walls.

That evening the guard came and led Ot away. He shoved him through a tiny, dark opening. Alone. That day there was no food and no water. He banged on the door. The guard looked in through the grating and said, "So, you want to eat? You want to eat, you poisonous pig?"

The Third Day.

On the third day the guard dragged and kicked Ot around the narrow space. The guard shouted so that spit sprayed out of his mouth. "You poisonous pig, you were going to infect and kill every living thing. Now we've got you, you Salzburgian dog."

Now the space under the hot periphery of Ot's skull really began to boil and cook.

The Fourth Day.

On the fourth day Ot had another serving of corn and cold tripe gruel. He listened as the crazed guard shouted. Now it was clear: this guard was the crazy one, not him. Certainly not him. Ot didn't say such demented things.

But the jailer—he was crazy.

The Fifth Day.

They came first thing in the morning. Three of them. They led him down a long corridor with harsh daylight shining in through some window. The glare went straight to Ot's pupils. Then his eyes and his whole head burned, and his temples and scalp itched peculiarly. Even later, after they had put him back into the larger room. When he rubbed his eyes, he saw the gigantic scar-faced vagabond, who was laughing merrily at him. The prisoners were sitting on the floor here and waiting for something or somebody. The men chattered in all the languages of Babel, but the gurgling of Italian dominated. Ot could understand the scarface. Don't worry, the brute said. Everyone here is guilty. Toward noon the guards came back. Keys jangled menacingly down the corridor. Someone dragged the blade of his sword along the wall, causing a sharp metallic rasp and a clang at each seam.

The one with sword in hand opened the door.

He looked Ot straight in the eye as he called out:

"Hans Debelak!"

Ot looked around and waited for someone to reply, but the other just kept staring at him. Then louder:

"Hans Debelak, I said!"

No one responded. Maybe the giant was the one who ought to step forward. Why the hell didn't he speak up? And why did the crazy jailer keep looking at Ot?

The jailer put his sword in his neighbor's hands and approached Ot. He grabbed him by the shoulders and first forced him to the floor, then with all his might he shoved him out into the corridor. Damned poisoner, he said, you pretending to be simple, or what?

"This is a mistake," Ot shouted. "It's a mistake!" He struggled and kicked as they dragged him down the corridor. At the end of it there was a narrow stairway that led up to an iron door. That's where they stopped.

"Now just watch," the crazy jailer said and buckled his sword back on. He put on a stiff, official expression, a mask that stretched across his entire face and must have been fastened tight somewhere in back.

When they entered, an enormous multitude of figures blazed at Ot in strange poses, colors, images—the terrifying chaos of nature. It was a painting that stretched from one wall to the other, before which they stopped. The jailer walked on with his mask on his face and gently knocked on a door. He went in and the sound of a conversation followed. Questions and answers. Meanwhile, Ot and the other guards stood before the gigantic image and its teeming multitude. Countless human bodies in the chaos of nature. A furious sea and sky and, in the distance, the wreck of a ship. Above it a red flag with a cross that twisted and turned, fluttering down into the depths. In the foreground a multitude of bodies. Hands lifted in prayer or a curse, to beg or to threaten. Fingers spread out in life's last hope, fists balled in a final effort. The staring eyes of a face right up in front that was looking at Ot. There was terror in those eyes and they were filled to the brim with otherworldliness. The red of a brilliant lightning bolt splashed across the face. A female body, white and bared, and the faint and submissive face above that body. Tousled hair, a downcast look, to her feet. Black layers of the thick sea washed over these bodies and drove upward, toward the sky, casting spray. Tattered clothing carried off by the wind into the pandemonium of sea and sky. Lost bodies, all of these huddled, tense figures right before their destruction. Muscular men, their mouths gaping, here teeth clenching a fist. He's bitten into himself, into his body. These monsters and colors and chaos and the flag with the cross fluttering into the abyss.

This was the end of all paths. This was where water and land and sky met. This painting over the wall. This chaos. This entrance to hell.

Past the painting to the door, which has opened, and into the room, which has high windows rounded at the top. The light falling through them, the calm figure in it. At a table a man with lace around his neck. With lace and questions.

It was a brief dialog.

The questioner's eyes sized up the figure before him.

"You look like quite the vagabond," he said, and his lips stretched toward the fellow looking out the window. "This could be the one."

"Tell me," he said after a moment. "Tell me, have you ever been in Salzburg?"

"Yes," Ot replied. "Traveling on business."

"Traveling on business," the other repeated, smiling. "Oh, were you now."

"But now you're a beggar," said the bearded know-it-all. "You were robbed on some desolate trail, and now you're looking for your people and looking for work, isn't that right?"

"Exactly," Ot confirmed when he suddenly realized that it didn't matter what answers he gave, because everything here had already been determined by the logic and mechanism of some hidden system.

"What about underground networks, what about secret societies," the man in lace asked. "Have you heard of them?"

"Well, sort of," Ot hesitated. "I mean, everywhe . . . everyone has heard that the whole world is full of them."

"Ever heard this name," the other said, getting up. "Magic Jack? Does that mean anything to you?"

"No," the tramp responded decisively.

"Oh, really now?" the other drummed his fingers on the table, leaning a hip on it. "Come on. Mag-ic Jack."

Ot was silent.

"Magic Jack," the other almost sang in his monotone voice. "Magic-MagicJack."

Ot said nothing.

"Listen, Debelak," the belaced investigator said. "You know perfectly well what Magic Jack means."

"I don't," Ot said in a voice that rose slightly in pitch, but was tired and apathetic. "My name is not Debelak and I don't know what Magic Jack refers to."

"Come on," the man smiled, moving to the other side of the table. "Why don't you tell us what you are, then. And who you are."

"Johan Ot," he said, though it didn't sound very persuasive. "Johan Ot from the Duchy of Neisse."

"And you haven't heard of the name Magic Jack?"

"No, I haven't."

"And you have been in Salzburg."

"Yes, I have."

The figure at the window shifted and with a nervous motion turned to face the room.

"That's enough," came from the window, as a white, smooth hand laden with rings waved impatiently through the cone of light.

Enough.

As they led Ot back and he glanced up at the painting, he heard music. Somewhere in this building, on one of its upper floors, someone was busily working a stringed instrument, a viola, producing clear, beautiful sounds that even coming from a distance poured across the picture.

At the bottom of the stairs the jailer took off his mask and relaxed his face.

"Still lying, pig?" he said. "I'll teach you to keep lying."

The whole time, all the way down the corridor, he shoved Ot in the back, hissing indistinct accusations at him.

In the holding area Ot saw the scar-faced giant again.

"Did you see how scared they are?" he whispered. "That's a state of siege out there. This is the only building that still has life in it. The city is empty. It's a state of siege. They're scared stiff, so they take it out on us."

Ot didn't have the impression that any of those people were scared. They had seemed perfectly calm and collected to him. Almost bored. As though they'd been sitting here for ages asking questions—and would for ages to come—as though they knew everything, understood everything. They weren't afraid. But he was, to the bone, and he understood nothing.

The Sixth Day.

On the sixth day he said, "Dear God, what sort of vile trick are you playing on me?"

Nothing is so well hidden that it isn't still in plain sight, because
on the seventh day Ot heard the keys jangling first thing in the
morning. Now they're going to take me out of this damp iron pen,
take me upstairs to people who deal with paintings and music, he
thought. But they didn't. On the seventh day they led him through
the empty town. He looked at the dark streets, the bridges with saints
and cherubs across them, the hollow windows. A wind was pulling
through all the openings of the empty town. There was no life, indeed. There was some sort of state of siege here, indeed. Ot paused for
a moment beneath the window of the house where once a man's head
had ducked inside. When had that been? In what dreams? He saw the
demolished door. Someone had hurled a wooden handcart at it.

They brought him before the judges. Behind their heads that great,
blue surface of the sea moved slowly and dangerously.

Now the belaced men performed their work quickly.

They knew everything about him.

Magic Jack.

His name was Hans Debelak. He was originally from Carniola.
He had roamed through the world in disguise. One moment he was
a beggar, the next he was a merchant. He was and still remained a
member of a secret, murderous society of brigands that was undermining the foundations of a healthy world, that was trying to destroy
whatever was healthy, just, and sacred in the world. It was gnawing away at the foundations of the German, Austrian, and Venetian
lands. Debelak was a terrorist, a poisoner and an alchemist. Since
the recent wars the Society of Magic Jack had gained much ground.
An underground organization. One of many roaming the countryside and killing. Underground. Terror. Using all means available to
eliminate spiritual and temporal leaders. Now it had begun poisoning

wells and wine and food. Somebody was supporting them. Somebody was paying and inciting them. The society had been hunted to the verge of extinction, but its members still wandered the world in a last terroristic, poisonous effort. People were barricading themselves in their houses. Strict safety precautions had been introduced. No one was going outside. There was a state of siege.

Ot denied and stubbornly resisted this obvious truth. Listlessly, but persistently he objected: That's not true. I am Johan Ot, there's been a mistake in your investigation, in your system. I was in Salzburg and in the Carniolan lands, but I've never had any contact with any secret society of robbers.

Magic Jack.

But it was pointless. Ot's lackluster answers had no effect. Hans Debelak, the Carniolan beggar, the well-known member of the well-known Debelak family, who had given himself over heart and soul to the secret society of Magic Jack, was also well known for his evil deeds, here and elsewhere. At St. Lorenz and at Huje, where he had committed numerous punishable acts—assaulting an executioner, attempted rape, theft of holy objects from a church, heresy; an endless number of evil acts. And now the secret society of Magic Jack had sent him here to sow confusion, idiocy, and death in the towns of the Venetian Republic.

Some sort of lunacy jabbed at Ot's eyes, some sort of madness came over the face of this shaggy vagabond. He opened his mouth and tried to speak, but all that came out was a strange babble, the indecipherable speech of a deaf-mute. It was as though all he had was the stump of a tongue, as though his ability to think and make connections was as broken as the look on his face.

Magic Jack.

The modern world kept well informed. Information circulated dependably and speedily. The appropriate agencies cooperated with each other. Ot shouldn't think, he shouldn't even begin to think of trying to deceive them with his lies and his babble. United they would stomp on the fingers of terror and all underground organizations.

They had found out, in time, that in the Salzburg trials the illegal association of vagabonds, tramps, beggars, miners, and who knows what other suspicious types—they had found out in time that the society of Magic Jack had not been completely eradicated. The danger lived on in Carniola in the Debelak clan of beggars and vagrants. The whole swarm of them were moving toward the coast like plague rats. Like vermin bearing the germs of confusion and madness, like locusts, like decay itself. They carried out their destruction using alchemy and magic potions. Hans Debelak was here, and his accomplices had already fallen into their nets, or would do so soon.

They had him now.

They would question him.

Their indictment was brief.

First. That he was an active member of the secret society of Magic Jack.

Second. That he had acted as a member of said society, disguised as a beggar and a merchant.

Third. That he had come to their town with the poisonous intent of sowing confusion, fear, and madness among the people.

Fourth. That all facts and circumstances pointed to his earlier evil deeds, which were also punishable by the laws of all lands.

In view of the state of siege now in force, let the verdict be pronounced after a quick trial, honoring the principles of justice that apply in such cases.

There was no shortage of proof.

He didn't object.

The sentence: the galleys.

For the rest of his natural life.

Phrases that were impossible to pronounce, all the words and all the thoughts that it was no longer possible to form and deliver through rational speech, ravings without order or sense coursed through Ot's brain tissue and welled out through the room, over its walls and through them. About the limits of reason, that this went beyond the limits of reason, that what they wanted with him made no sense anymore, that the unspoken words wrapped around him and were crawling back inside him, that one minute he was a fire jumper, the next minute a minion of Satan, one minute a merchant and the next a conspirator in a heretical brotherhood, one minute a member of the secret society of Magic Jack and the next a village fool and walking dead man. This is a dream, his words hit the stones below and bounced back distorted, this must be a dream.

But the real stuff of dreams was only now beginning. He will dream out his dreamlike life to the end, because now the man is about to board a galley. The galleys, the judge had said. The galley.

19.

It's calm and glints gently, and its surface moves treacherously in large chunks. Carnivorous animals below, one eating the other. The galley slave between his sea and his sky.

On one side is the coast with its tall cliffs, bare of vegetation, without trees and without settlements. On the other side water and sky join together. Out there, somewhere beyond that line, the Western Sea begins.

But even the sea here, which is the forerunner of the Western Sea, warning of its dangers and terrors, is extremely forbidding to people. Just the look of it: it is calm and glints gently, and its surface moves treacherously in large chunks, as though someone below had his heels dug into the sea floor and, with a titanic effort, were lifting up huge layers on his back. Those aren't waves. There are no waves here, because there's no wind. Only this quiet, glinting, treacherous motion. You could barely get across it rowing and sailing for four months. Not even a wisp of air moves the boat forward, the wind of this lazy sea is that indolent. There is much sea algae on the surface. The water is heavy and sea monsters continually circle back and forth—all these wild beasts swimming between the slow, lazy boats.

Such is the entrance to the Western Sea.

But the Western Sea itself is so great and terrifying that a bird can't cross it in a whole year. If boats were to cross it, they would advance into ever greater darkness and impenetrable fog, and finally they would come upon a horrible, chaotic jumble of water and sky, where whirlpools and yawning depths draw the traveler into a dark world from which there is no return.

It is endless and terrifying and it wraps the whole world in its fog, its darkness, its gaping maw.

At one time it was also called the Sea of Darkness.

The owner, a red-cheeked, well-fed Venetian, paced nervously back and forth for days in the narrow space of the gallery affixed to the stern of the boat, continually looking out toward the line between water and sky. The *comito*, the galley's first officer, drove the rowers on and beat them. The captain spat and swore. He sensed and sniffed— smelled the wind and the air, sensed them being drawn day after day toward the line. It wasn't visible, because the coast shrank only gradually, but day by day the crags got shorter, so slowly that even a trained eye could barely perceive it. That's why he spat and swore and drove the crew and the slaves. The crew would huddle together. Who the hell had got them stuck in this calm? They worked, sweated, and waited for the ship to come out of it. The merchants conferred with each other and talked smut. The soldiers yawned and pointed out the sea monsters that circled the boat, showing their hungry maws. The carpenters and pitchmen joined up in shared tasks. They shouted wildly to each other first here, then there, for help or tools. They had much to do, because a gently shifting sea is more dangerous, surprisingly, than rough water. Planks would break in every imaginable spot as the sea clutched the boat in its wide but convulsive embrace. The ship crackled and groaned constantly. Day and night the axes sang and the mallet blows echoed, while at night a fire was kept burning in the middle of the deck, with a kettle of pitch burbling like some witch's brew.

Only the galley slaves were not involved in the life of the ship. They were simply a part of it, its driving force, mindlessly, automatically fighting the inertia of water and air. They worked according to a rule of thirds: rowing on benches in three shifts. One third of the men rowed while the others rested. The handles of their oars were fastened to the benches and jutted in the air like lopped off branches. So it would go for twenty hours at a stretch with no rest. At that point all their driving force was exhausted and used up. The ship would come to a stop in the motionless sea, which clutched at it once more and caused it to crackle. Then the ship began to move again. Without rhythm or spirit, the men drew on those heavy logs that would get stuck down below in the algae. Even the *comito*'s whistle had long since gone silent. Each of them fought with his piece of wood bitterly, paroxysmally, against the slimy, sticky substance below. Silently. Until the next shift. They went and threw themselves on their bunks and slept.

Despite overwhelming physical exhaustion, our galley slave had not given up on his stargazing. At night he would look up and say something, a few incomprehensible phrases, horrifying any chance onlooker who witnessed his deranged face churning words out through its mouth. By day he would ask aloud and with sudden clarity of thought in his voice: What's down there?

None of this had happened by accident. Well he knew that this nasty, slimy, sticky sea was here on his account. That it moved slowly and treacherously because of him. Ever since he first glimpsed its dangerous motion and its gnawing erosion of the shore, saw it from the hilltop above the city. From the first day on. All because of him. But now, now the water was performing especially and most assuredly because of him. Why else would the ship have suddenly gone off course several days before, why would the wind have so suddenly filled its sails, why else would the waves have come that drove them here to these doldrums? The old sailors put it clearly enough: the movement of the sea was caused by a spirit hidden in the depths. A vague thought kept stinging and jolting the galley slave: was this spirit the same monster that had chased him around the world, that had kindled the flames above his house, sent the cloud of vermin over his roof, dispatched him to a forest clearing toward a secret pact among burning hearts, sent crazy Anton and the crazy jailer, prodded him down to the sea and into the empty town with dead silence in its walls, where there was life in only one building out of which a path led in just one direction, to this boat and its scabrous and criminal crew? If it was the same spirit down there in the deep, it would give a sign. Which is why the slave asked: what's down there? And the guards heard his questions. One day when they didn't know what to do with themselves, when they had oiled and buffed the cannon for the hundredth time, when they didn't know what to do with their hands anymore, with their footsteps, with their heads and mouths and thoughts, one of them said: Maybe the fool senses something. Let's have a look at what's down below. They tied as much rope together as they had and fastened a large piece of lead to it, then they made their bets. Some said the sea was shallow and the bottom near the surface, covered with algae and other growth. Others thought that the sea was deep, with a layer of algae only floating on the top and containing it, with the spirit of the depths down below, treacherously, gently moving the water so that ships groaned in its tight embrace. Who else could be moving it? They dropped their sinker. It went deeper and deeper. The boat grew so silent, not even the oars could be heard anymore. Everything came to a stop. The carpenters and pitchmen joined them, followed by the captain, the *comiti*, and the merchants. The ship perched silently in the strange terror of anticipation. Only the timbers continued to creak. The rope went deeper and deeper into the dark depths and no one dared look anyone else in the eye, because they knew they would see them filled to the brim with fear. The rope ran out and the lead still hadn't reached the bottom. The captain remained calm. Now that's an odd sea, he said. Now no one could guess what might be down there. The galley slave was silent and looked straight ahead. Oh, there were terrible, carnivorous animals down below, one devouring the other. That much was known.

But what else? What else?

Then things took a different turn. The galley slave looked in amazement at the shrieking people around him. They were howling and laughing and crying. Suddenly everything had reversed itself. The motionless peace of this outcrop of the Western Sea had shifted at last. They drank wine, all of them, from the highest to the lowest, from the convicts to the volunteers. Is it possible, the galley slave wondered, is it possible that we didn't get pulled into the Western Sea? That would have been the end of us, once and for all, down to the bottom in infinite peace with the animals and whatever else. For once fortune had smiled, just for once. Down the face that had looked so many horrors and abominations in the eye, down the face that had had known a thousand secrets, over the mouth that had spoken secret formulas, down this dark, sunburned face warm tears of happiness flowed.

For once there'd been good fortune.

They were moving, and in three days' time they caught sight of the Spanish coast.

The encounter with the Western Sea, or Sea of Darkness, wasn't the most difficult thing the galley slave experienced on the ship. Then everyone was afraid, fear lurked in everyone's eyes—the captain's, the *comiti*'s, the merchants' and quartermasters', the sailors' and the galley slaves'. They were together and united, the bottomless depths binding them all into a terrified ball. It was a terrible and shared terror, whereas before they had been hell for each other. Where was the day when they had been dragged onto the ship, shackled like animals being carted to the fair? On board their comrades, and the salaried sailors, and the volunteers awaited them. These last would be paid, free of chains, almost proper crew members. But our galley slave counted as one of the *schiavi* and *forzati*, the prisoners and convicts, the last, dirty, most worthless work force. With chains at their ankles. Five of them to an oar. Day after day. Drill. Every day they sailed out, they drilled the fine art of their new profession. Rowing and touching the bench, when the ship sails out of the harbor or enters it, a kind of parade step, in fact, with rhythmical, serpentine flourishes of the oars through the air. The rake stroke, a more demanding parade maneuver, where the oars are in constant contact with the water, churning a foam around the boat. Rowing alternate benches, for long hauls, at half strength. Rowing all benches, which was their usual, day-to-day driving effort. Even after they had adapted, the work went on endlessly. Now they had to harden their muscles. Every day, even when the rest of the crew had shore leave, every day they had to set out to sea. Their bodies could not be allowed to slacken, their limbs had to turn stonelike in their incessant functioning. The slave swabbed and cleaned the ship, carried water and food, and washed his comrades' clothing. This was a simple process. He would tie their canvas rags onto a long rope and drop it into the sea. The clothes, wet and stiff with salt, would then be dried as they wore them. And he prepared food: bread dipped in wine.

The galley slave got to know the work and routine and his new life. The *comito* with his whistle and the *aguzzino*—the galley sergeant with his whip. The merchants and the captain. He recognized his terrible, new beginning, and that's when it was worst. Not at the edge of the Western Sea, when his frazzled brain shaped a thought that got planted like a spear point and dug in: hold out. I'll get out of this. Hold out.

The galley slave rowed for what seemed like ages. His eyes, full of the plant life of home, never grew accustomed to the endless, flat glare. Over and over again green hillsides, blue lakes, gray mountains, and deep, cold snows outside a church on Sunday would appear in the glitter.

He saw the springtime sea. The wind howled and crackled in both sails and drove the galley across it. There was no rowing, no bloody palms. He looked at the sea and the multitude of fish it contained. They rushed toward the shore. Every spring. They rushed home, into the mouths of rivers, onward, uphill, into the mountains, where shepherds gathered their sheep on green hilltops, their calls echoing in that finite, manageable space. That's where the fish journeyed. Up the Danube, the Sava, up countless green streams.

He saw a small island. Birds gathered on it. They could fly away whenever they felt like it, wherever they wished.

He saw a summer night. Its sharp, mysterious glow illuminated the sea. Its points shifted and the galley slave's little share of brains focused, squinted, and moved back and forth through his skull, trying to decipher the mystery of light. But there was no understanding it. Everything here had its own mysterious laws. The most elemental of all. Everything here was still at its beginning.

In autumn the waves burned. On the tips of the agitated sea a fiery red light would flare up. What signs, what life from this haughty and headstrong sea!

In winter a canvas was drawn over their heads. They were given thick woolen clothing, but they remained barefoot. A harsh spray of water blew across the bow. It was gray and gloomy. This is when the sea wore its old, malevolent face. When it began to blow more strongly, they removed the canvas and the drops beat into their hard faces. They rowed as hard and far as they could.

The galley slave traveled through dreams.

He would begin to think. To recognize things.

He looked at these faces being driven over alien seas. Volunteers, mindless enthusiasts, and human dregs driven to sea by who knew what ridiculous need. They got paid, they weren't shackled, and they weren't beaten, but day after day their life was no better than that of the galley slaves. Turks who'd been captured in the Aegean Islands or in battles somewhere in Croatia. They had the most endurance, they were self-contained and persistent. Strong men with endless will. A strange inner power kept them upright. Farmhands paying off their debts by rowing. And finally our galley slave's fellows, the convicts, criminals, and lepers, the social dregs of the galley. They were flogged, they performed the most difficult work, and underwent the worst humiliations. They kept their mouths shut. It was they who, devoid of faith or hope, fell most often. He looked at these criminal faces. These quiet people still had blood flowing through their veins. He had seen it. They digested food. It stank. Sometimes they swore and cried. They weren't people, and yet they cut humanlike figures. One day the galley slave surprised himself with this thought: you couldn't tell that they were criminals, that they had killed and plundered. Crimes don't imprint themselves on one's face. What sticks to the face are sinful, stupid habits. That was the sort of face that *comiti* and Venetian merchants had. It was the sort of face that people who saw spirits and felt the evil in themselves had.

He was stunned at the thought: Maybe that's the kind of face I have?

The galley slave sailed for what seemed like ages. He saw the seasons, he watched the changing colors of the sea, he watched the criminals and the life on ship. No, this couldn't be real. All these foreign countries, all these foreigners with swarthy faces and their bright-colored clothes, coasts rocky or green, welcoming or forbidding, cities with strange towers, with people of a different faith, with heretics, you could even say. Who belonged at the stake. But here they lived, carting their wares to the harbor and carrying them on board. Tibetan and Indian scents, that red powder that spills out of bags; carpets, scarlet and other brightly colored silks woven with gold; muslin, mirrors, ointments for the eyes and ears; damask, pearls—all the riches of the world cycled through their ship, all these miraculous products were freighted by them. And with them came good-for-nothing, treacherous Mohammedan merchants, everything so outlandish and unfamiliar and new and dreamlike.

The sequence of dreams broke for just a single moment. It happened in a Spanish port. Some Inquisition men arrived with papers and orders and a detachment of soldiers. They spent a long time on the ship negotiating, with a lot of loud swearing coming from the back cabins. Then they dragged off a German mercenary, a sailor. He had propounded a false faith to prostitutes and idlers and a tavern owner in town. It turned out the tavern owner was an informant. The crazy German would pound his table, drunk, preach his pure gospel, and rail against the greedy and sinful clergy. In Spain, in the middle of Spain, the idiot. The galley slave watched all this and listened to his heart pounding inside and he waited for them to come for him. His confession couldn't have been forgotten yet. They probably knew about him here, too. They probably had countless conspiracies and covenants and societies and heresies and sects and fires and burning hearts here, too. That day he thought it was all over. It has to be all over sometime, and probably sooner rather than later. But nothing happened. They dragged off the sailor, this is true. He howled like a madman, this is true. The crew rebelled—they could drag any of us off like that! But it was him they dragged off. The galley slave stayed between his sea and his sky. In his dreams.

The dreams parted for just that long, then they resumed their course. He watched and he saw sea monsters, storms, moonlight, the bustle of port towns, markets, and fairs; walnuts as fat as a man's head, ivory and eels.

No, this couldn't be real.

20.

They're probably dreams. Where will the bells toll, where will a city go mad? Mornings and nights. How slowly the shoreline approaches.

One night strange beasts leaped out of the water. They sailed over the surface of the sea and it was beautiful to watch them in the glow of moonlight. The galley slaves dropped their oars and called out in amazement. The *aguzzino* tried with his whip to get them back into rhythm, for a galley that loses momentum can sit motionless for a long time, but it was no use. Even his assistants refused. Everyone gaped at the animals leaping up from the water's glittering surface. They rose abruptly, like an arrow or a cannonball they flew through the air, and then, exhausted, they dropped back in with a splash. In its blindness, one of them charged straight at the ship. It looked like the monster might fly into it, but then it lost speed and dropped back down. But it didn't drop into the water—nothing splashed and sucked it into its safe embrace. It dropped onto skin and a moving human body. A man working an oar howled in terror when the beast flew onto his back, latching onto him instantly with its thousand limbs. It wrapped slippery around his body and lashed into his flesh and sucked the skin together and ripped it to shreds. Something like an arm reached over his face, turning his cheeks red instantly and making him horrible to look at. The galley slave had never experienced as much revulsion and fear as in this hell. Blood sprayed over the slimy, formless beast, which was nothing but legs and arms ripping the skin apart as though it were silk. Then it devoured the man alive.

Johan Ot stayed by the poor wretch all that night. He washed the blood off his face and put a plug in his mouth, one that was normally used when galley slaves were tortured, to keep them from screaming too much when the powers that be would flay them.

The plug proved useful now too. The poor devil shouldn't be allowed to rouse anyone out of their all too needed sleep. Toward morning the victim came to and looked around uncomprehendingly. With one hand he pointed to the plug in his mouth and Johan Ot pulled it out for him. Skittishly, the man felt his face, then abruptly yanked his hand away, it stung so much. He looked at his body, torn and tattered as it was, and gave a crazed laugh: I'm alive, though, aren't I? He looked up thankfully at the face above him and said with evident satisfaction:

"While that other fellow's being eaten by worms."

"Who's being eaten by worms?" Johan Ot asked. "Crabs and fish eat people sometimes, but not worms."

"Worms, it's worms that are eating him," the bloodied man said with relish. "The town councilman and sergeant, in fact a thief, swindler, and seducer. One evening I came back from a trip and saw him coming out of my wife's room. He was adjusting his trousers and there was sweat on his forehead. The next night he was found in his garden with his belly stabbed through, as dead as they come. They found a cobbler's awl beside him. Whose awl is this? they asked. The master's, the cobbler's, my apprentice answered. He stabbed him, they said. But it wasn't my awl. I proved that to them. It belonged to another cobbler. Still, they said it was me who stabbed him in his paunchy gut. They couldn't exactly say how or when. So, just to be on the safe side, they gave me five years in the galleys."

He's a killer, Johan Ot thought. This one's a killer for sure.

"There are more awls," the homicidal cobbler said through bubbles of blood. "There are at least two more. One for my wife and one for my apprentice."

An infernal den, Johan Ot thought. What an infernal den of criminals this galley is.

One night damp hands, warm and soft, caressed him. Half-asleep, he submitted to their tender caresses, which sent a warm and pleasant shiver through his body. Gradually the caresses grew more passionate, more insistent and forceful, and turned into an embrace. Something began to squeeze him so hard it took his breath away. Then he heard rapid breathing and gurgling right next to his ear. He shook his head. A bared, hairy chest was pressing down on him, and bloodshot eyes, a face distorted by pleasure and lust. Ot bolted upright, causing a dull thud as the hairy weight rolled off and onto the floor. It stayed there, sobbing, late into the night.

This was a man who had once demolished a royal tollbooth bare-handed and beaten all its men. This was a man who had rebelled against the authorities and their demands for tribute. This man had got his galley too. Now, awake or asleep he wanted the closeness of a warm, female body—a warm human body—a touch, warm breath on his face, a response. So now he was sobbing and moaning in a hull full of sleeping galley slaves.

Near the Moorish coast in the sun's harsh glare they caught sight of a high cliff far out at sea. The captain paced back and forth: that cliff was not supposed to be there. He took out his wagoners and looked through them, and he asked seamen who had sailed that direction. That cliff was not supposed to be there. They sailed toward it for a long time, but the cliff got no closer. What was it?

Toward evening it suddenly disappeared. No one could believe his eyes. The old sailors said it was the devil setting traps out on the sea.

On Cyprus or some other island a crowd came out toward the ship, accompanied by much boisterous shouting. The *comiti* and merchants were dragging a strange monster out through the city gate and onto the dock. It had a woman's face, but a light growth of whiskers on its upper lip. It wore a dress whose fabric clung to its tiny breasts. It snarled and growled as they dragged it on board, struggling against them with all its might. The drunken merchants and *comiti* kept reaching under its skirts and roaring with laughter. The crew howled in delight while it snarled and looked around furiously. They dragged the monster down to the captain's cabin. With its powerful hands it clung onto the railing, digging its long fingernails into the wood. On the days that followed they could hear growls coming from below, an animal-like purring, and the captain's laughter. Once he came out, all scratched and smiling.

Everyone on board laughed and winked at each other.

When they shoved off, it disappeared.

Here everything is possible and everything is natural, Johan Ot thought. In the lands he had left behind, this creature would end up in a bag at the bottom of some lake. And probably the captain, too.

One night he was on a blue lake surrounded by tall mountains. He saw happy peasant women and peddlers on an island in the middle of the lake, selling their wares. A familiar, gentle music emanated from the church. When Ot started awake and heard the wind howling, he had a lump in his throat so big that it hurt when he spat it out.

Shadows flitted around the ship in some Italian port. The crew had scattered among the taverns, while the oarsmen slept. Our galley slave sat at the prow, looking at the roofs and walls of the town and listening to its intoxicating bustle. One of the shadows crept up onto the ship and signaled back to the others: come on up, it's empty. They seized the front man and gave him a good beating. Galley slaves knew how to deliver a worse thrashing than *aguzzino* or *mozzi*. Now, for once, they had a chance to beat and kick a whimpering and prostrate body on the floor.

One mild, quiet morning, two of the chained men started to fight. All five of the men chained to the bench had to participate against their will. The scuffle drew them together into a bundle of bodies and chains and iron. The ship wavered and came to a stop. All of the men rose to their feet. They shouted and egged on the two savage galley slaves who were tearing into each other like mad dogs. Everything got knotted and twisted up between and under the benches, with much shouting and strangling and punching. Until the weaker managed to pull the chains over the oar and around the other's neck in one skillful motion. He was able to keep his opponent clamped down. It would have ended like this if the other three slaves hadn't tried to free themselves. As they moved, dragging the chains every which way, the winning combatant got caught and clamped to the wooden floor. Then the *comito* came running and started lashing wildly at the bunch of them. At first he used his whip and his feet on the entire crowd, lashing and kicking at their broad backs, and then he went at the two fighters themselves. He thrashed and thrashed until they unclenched their teeth and their fingers and one of them practically suffocated and afterward took a long time catching his breath, his head on his knees.

The first fighter had been a Turkish soldier, maybe even a bey or something, with wives coming out his ears. The other was a swindler and thief. The swindler had nearly finished the Turk off, had given him a good drubbing.

It was the same for everyone in that infernal den. No one cared who anyone else was, where he was from, or why he was here. Here everyone denounced and strangled and stabbed everyone else.

In this little piece of hell, out on the surface of the sea, the galley slave nursed an ailing merchant. He gave him cold compresses for his forehead. The merchant looked glassy-eyed, wolflike. He gurgled in his fever and emitted a stinking sweat. The galley slave spent long hours breathing into him. Giving him life.

They removed his chains.

In some Spanish harbor a group of Moriscos charged the boat. They were fleeing the Inquisition and clung to the edge of the galley. The crew beat them on the hands and heads with oars and whips and chains until they dropped into the water. One of them persisted. He swam after the ship. They pulled him out of the water and he explained that the Inquisition had charged them with witchcraft. Their land and wealth had been confiscated and they'd been beaten and driven overland onto boats and over the sea. They had trudged for months through the rocky Spanish countryside. No one had protected them. They were continually attacked by armed robbers. The cleverest among them, if they were lucky, had made it across the sea.

But a savage tribe of fire worshippers lived over there. Death was waiting there, too. The man offered himself as a slave. He scrubbed the deck and emptied pots of human excrement. The crew had fun with this, too. They would kick him and laugh. Formerly he had been a landowner. Formerly he had been the one who kicked and laughed. The crew had a lot of fun.

Beyond Corsica they were pursued by another ship, probably pirates. During the battle nobody unlocked the galley slaves' chains. They would go to the bottom with the galley. Food for fishes and crabs. They rowed as hard and far as they could.

In a port in France they discovered a Venetian galley. It had been emptied, plundered, battered. The crew beaten by the French. Their flag had been dragged through the sea, and then the Marseilles-built vessel was backed into port. It had been a terrible humiliation. Then the French took everything from them—they cut down the masts, led the galley slaves away, and kept the ship as collateral. It would stay there until Venice paid its debts and duties. The captain told this story without any shame or even a trace of a blush on his sunken checks. Instead of commending himself to the beasts of the sea, he'd let himself be cordially dismembered by this little zoo.

Some merchants boarded in Dalmatia. He overheard a conversation on deck. The newcomers laughed at the story of the Western Sea. They said they had crossed it on Portuguese ships. There was no Western Sea of Darkness, where earth and sky met in a wild embrace. There were no vanishing islands, no abyss that swallowed ships and people among cries of despair. Instead, there were new lands on the far side of that sea.

The galley slave didn't believe them.

Neither did the others.

One night the stars came out. He stood at the stern and saw a huge beast lurking behind the ship. It was working its jaws and roaring as it followed slowly. He shouted back and called out, but no one responded. Then the animal submerged into the depths.

It had probably just been a dream. All of this was probably just dreams.

The rats went on a rampage on board. They just went wild, crawling out on deck, turning and spinning around crazily, biting each other and biting the oarsmen's legs. The oarsmen hit at them with their bare hands while the seamen ran for the swords and hacked at them. One of them crawled up under the bench and he could see white foam oozing out of its little maw.

A few days later one of the sailors started tossing and turning in his sleep. Then he got up and started roaming the deck all evening and into the night. The galley slave looked at him and thought: this one is homesick. The next morning the sailor was gone. Vanished. They searched the whole ship and found him under a coil of rope. His face was all black. The ship went wild with invisible fear. The sickness is here. No one obeyed orders anymore, nobody touched anyone, nobody wanted to eat. They stayed out at sea and waited for the next one to be stricken. The captain remained calm and inspired a certain confidence. Two men wrapped the dead sailor in wet canvas and pushed him into the water.

Each person had a different plan. Some wanted to put in to port, others wanted to head out to the open sea, where the wind might blow the plague germs off of them.

They prayed.

They cursed.

They trembled.

They pleaded with the evil spirits of the sea to have mercy on them.

Who knows who helped them, but there was no next victim.

That was a miracle.

But the fear remained. Now it was clear: once the ship got to port, all of them would scatter.

On a Greek island a fanatical looking fellow came on board. He sailed with them to some Spanish harbor. He kept to himself and spoke little, clutching a fat black book under his arm the whole time. Soon it came out: the fellow's a Jesuit. A *comito* who knew how to read flipped quickly through the book. It was about the necessity of killing rulers. Written by Jesuits. When the man disembarked, the news spread: the guy was going to murder some German Protestant prince. Where was he from and where was he going? Where had the plot been hatched and why were they sending him such a long way around? The conspirators were covering their tracks. After the assassination, once they began turning the screws on him, nobody would know where he came from or why it had been done. It would be pure chaos. Black blood would spray from the prince's wound. Church bells would ring. A whole city would go mad.

New galley slaves were being led across the cobblestones of the harbor. The convicts yanked at their chains and stumbled onto the ship of their last days. He felt something tighten around his heart, something squeezed at his throat when he saw these men from his homeland. He thought he might ask them for news. One of them had fought with an estate sheriff over fishing in a stream. Now he would row. But he was stupid and loutish. They got nothing out of him—no news, nothing.

How slowly the shoreline approaches, how monotonously the oars splash their rhythm. Day after day the harbor with its red roofs and the green horizon of the mountains remain as far off as ever. Mornings and nights. Out at sea or in port. How slowly the shoreline approaches.

21.

The fire of rebellion in some distant land reflected on the sea's placid surface, in the moon's silver glint. Simon the Gull. When death is near, everyone gulps at the air with equal zeal.

There was a strange ghost that roamed the ship. A squat old man with strands of gray hair over his forehead, wearing the stiff canvas clothing of a galley slave. With his right arm and a left stump rounded off just below the elbow he would haul rags around the ship, clean up the excrement from under men who'd shat themselves, either from exertion or out of fear of the *aguzzino*'s whip, bring water and food, tie ropes to the galley slaves' clothes and drop them into the sea to wash. In winter he would stoke the oven that they set up on deck and bandage wounded arms and legs. Every day of a galley slave's life was tied to Simon the Gull. The first day that Ot had sat down to row, others had whispered to him: that guy's been through a lot.

Simon the Gull knew cures for the stomach ailments that eternally plagued the ship; he knew how to tie a line on a mainsail as opposed to a headsail; he knew how to hold a chisel in one hand when repitching the boat; he could tie both a boom hitch and a Portuguese knot with one hand; he knew all the dangers of the sea he had crossed countless times, from Egypt to Spain; he knew the coast of Morocco, which for five hundred miles was sown with the wrecks of countless ships. Without Simon the Gull there would have been no ship and no galley slaves on it. The first day that Johan Ot sat down to row, others had whispered: that guy refuses to leave the galley.

Simon the Gull was a part of the ship, like a rope or a plank, like an oar or a cabin, its irreplaceable passenger, who had outlived all its previous slaves and *comiti* and *aguzzini*. He was the ship's skill and its wisdom, its history, and he was a living reminder to all galley slaves.

For on the first day when the new convicts boarded the galley, they met Simon the Gull. Simon the Gull can tell you, the captain had said in his first and only official speech, whether what I'm about to say is true or not. You will row for the messes you've made on dry land, he said, but God has granted you the good fortune to row on a galley where you will not be abused, where only the stubborn and lazy will meet with the whip or have a dry throat and scorched tongue. Simon the Gull can tell you if it isn't a fact that galleys today are something completely different from what they were in the past. In the past they would cut off your leg instead of unchaining you, then they would throw you, legless, to the beasts down below waiting for their food. In the past a galley slave saw nothing but the backs of other galley slaves. In the past he rowed until he croaked. Today things are different, and especially on our galley. That's what you're here for, to row off your messes, and for nothing else.

But Simon the Gull didn't say much. Silently he would haul wet rags around the deck, silently he would distribute wet clothes. In the east's blue infinity he would stand at the prow and gaze at the oncoming waves. At anchor he would watch with empty eyes the bustle of the crowd below him. Did he feel drawn to it? Did any longing tear at his heart?

Several questions bored into Ot day after day. What wisdom—or what need—tied Simon to the galley? How did he hold up under the endless diligence of performing his duties? Why did he prefer to end his days here, on a searing deck or in the silken glow of a moonlit night? What evil deed gnawed and drilled at him so incessantly?

Had he killed someone? Been a crook? Raped a woman? No, those men were different. They waited for dry land and a chance to escape. They waited for the day when they could take up their awl or their razor again. Simon the Gull was not one of them. No scream in the dead of night echoed in his ears, no twisted face at a desolate crossroads furrowed his brow, nothing criminal had imprinted itself on his face.

He was far worse off than that.

One morning when Simon the Gull put a pitcher of water in his hands, Johan Ot hissed:

"Do you really mean to croak on this galley?"

Simon the Gull flinched and drew back. His eyes pierced Ot through and through. Then he reached his stump to his forehead, as though he intended to wipe off the sweat, or as though trying to remember something.

From then on Johan Ot felt Simon the Gull's vacant eyes on him day after day. Evenings, when he set the oar aside for a moment; mornings, as a new day of eternity dawned; and at noon, when time stopped, that vacant gaze followed him constantly, agitated, preoccupied.

That fellow's been through a lot, Johan Ot said to himself. I have to get to the bottom of him.

The second time he spoke to Simon the Gull, it was as he was getting ready to sleep. They collided between benches. Ot didn't step aside.

"You damned galley rat," he insisted. "Do you really mean to shove off here?"

Something broke inside Simon the Gull, something made him implode, and a strange hatred filled his vacant eyes. He looked back at his interlocutor fiercely and then, suddenly, he slapped his wet rag that stank of human shit across Ot's face. That put our galley slave off balance. He had meant to start a conversation in good galley-slave language, he had meant to elicit some words from this old ghost, but instead it had become enraged and attacked, forcing Ot to grab Simon the Gull by the stump and shove him down into the benches. Before he had a chance to get away, a searing pain lashed Ot around the waist—the *aguzzino's* whip wrapped around his waist and then his back, causing him to drop to the deck, where he was then stomped on by boots, on his belly, his head, everywhere.

That night Simon the Gull came to see him. He washed his stinging abrasions with water and soothed his bruises with his damp hands. That night Simon the Gull finally spoke up.

That night the fire of rebellion in some distant land, the shaking of chains in some dank cell, the cries of crazed birds in some bluer sky reflected on the sea's quiet surface, in the moon's silver glint.

THE GALLEY-SLAVE NARRATIVE OF SIMON THE GULL

OR

HOW THE OPPRESSED BECAME THE OPPRESSOR

He came to the galley as one among that infinite legion of Protestants who were forever taking their places on the rowing benches alongside criminals and violent madmen. Among that sorry legion of rebels of all callings and classes and from all the lands of Europe where speedy trials had put an end to thought and action based on the unmediated gospels. It had been so long ago, and the memory of the processions marching down to the sea had grown so pale, that it was like a faded inscription on some ancient tablet.

He had been an Anabaptist, a reformer, a passionate adherent of that new concept, a changer of people and the world, a rebel against

God and the authorities. He had been a leader of credulous people who had gathered around him in throngs. He would organize meetings and use the arm that was now a stump to point to the licentiousness of the clergy, their blasphemous profligacy, their theft, their scheming, and their lies. His movement met with success, the idea spread, and his passionate followers swore unflagging allegiance. He got thrown into jail. He survived it and, when he got back out, he resumed his work even more passionately than before. He was beaten, but he didn't submit. His followers helped him. Until the day when a delegation and a detachment of soldiers arrived in that town by a distant green river. Now things took a different turn. Whoever didn't profess the true faith—the authorities' faith—within a certain period of time was deemed beyond hope. At best, the heretic would be exiled. At worst, sent to the galleys. Depending on his level of responsibility. Responsibility was to be measured in terms of ardor. Ardor was to be determined and attested to by informants.

Many of them defected. Simon held out. Then the delegation ordered his church blown up with gunpowder. The explosion reached into the sky with its flames. The night glowed. And that same night a gallows was erected. And that same night someone set fire to the house where the soldiers were staying. Now it was all or nothing. Some of the followers were captured. Each of them pointed a finger at him. Only Simon and a predicant were left. All the others deserted him. Simon refused to submit. He and the predicant hid in the countryside and tried to persuade citizens still on the fence to stand fast. But they were denounced and captured. An attempt was made to convert them in their cell. Days and nights in the dark, without food. Simon withstood everything. Then he found himself among the legion marching in chains to the sea. The legion of the steadfast. The rebellious. The stubborn. On the galley they threw him in with the worst criminals. Into the wild animal cage. And indeed the galleys were much worse back then. A beating like the one Johan Ot had taken would have ended with him at the bottom of the sea. But even there Simon refused to rest. He started converting the murderers and rapists. He would assemble them and incite them. One day he rose up before the *comito*. I can't go on, he said, not with this food and no rest. They beat him like an animal. He held out. He returned to his oar. He didn't end up at the bottom of the sea. The captain was determined to break him. First he would break and beat Simon, then he would ease him back into the wild animal pit. But only once he had made the prisoner yield, once Simon started to beg. But they didn't break him. Only the sea could break him. The sea knows what to do with people. During a storm Simon's arm got caught in the *scaloccio*—the enormous oar that he rowed with four others—the two pieces of wood squeezed together, and when a wave seized the oar so hard that they lost control of it, it crushed Simon's skin and bone. The captain still wanted to see Simon cry and beg and plead. That hot afternoon they bound him and tied him tight to a mast. His blood served as bait, and crazed birds came darting and diving around him. Huge, starved seagulls from the coast of Africa started perching on his head. He had endured everything—but those crazed shrieks, those grotesque voices, that insane seagull speech that God was visiting on his pride—that he could not stand. He cursed. He shouted. Finally he begged. Finally he wept and begged for death. Let them throw him in the sea, let them kill him on the deck. But he couldn't endure those birds and their insane speech any longer. The crew took him down, but they didn't kill him. The captain wanted to see him crawl. Through human shit. Day after day amid the human shit that dribbled out of the sick guts of the galley slaves. That's where the captain wanted to have Simon, in plain sight. For himself, and for the sake of all the others Simon had rebelled against, for the authorities' sake and for the sake of the order that Simon refused to recognize. At first it was hard. At first he couldn't do it. So they dragged him back up, for the seagulls. After that he had nothing left.

After that he became Simon the Gull. But the captain wanted even more. Simon would work for him. He would spy on the other galley slaves and the crew. Listen to what they said and report back to him. And that's what he did. Then Simon wanted to kill himself, but he couldn't do it. He couldn't do anything anymore. Every last bit of strength had seeped out in that insane dance of the birds, the last trace of his will to rebel was gone with the wind. Here he was at the bottom. At a Moorish port the captain allowed him to leave the ship. All night he wandered around, but he didn't even have the strength to flee. He returned to the ship. They gave him a whip. He lashed with it at the galley slaves' broad backs. Until he drew blood, until they passed out. Then he couldn't do that anymore either. The muscles of his arm, which had grown accustomed to the oar, began to sag. They atrophied. All that was left was a rag. He could hold a rag in his hand. All that was left was the galley. He had no one to go back to. The galley was inside him. There was no former life for him to resume. The galley was everywhere. He would be Simon the Gull forever. The day-to-day source of the captain's power and authority. A living reminder. Simon the Gull will tell you. Simon the Gull will tell you if it's true or not. Simon the Gull had seen fires, tempests, and shipwrecks. A battle with pirates where a ship went down to the bottom with all of its galley slaves still chained to their places. A burial as silent as the tomb itself. Before the battle they had fastened a plug in the mouth of every galley slave, so they wouldn't cry out in pain if they were injured. And no one did cry out, not even later, when the ship went down. Nobody managed to unchain them, and down they went, slowly but surely, their faces distorted and their pupils dilated in horror. Some of them tried to commit suicide beforehand by banging their heads against the sharp edge of their benches. Or by pulling their chains taut around their necks. Simon watched the pirate ship collide with theirs and break all the oars in an instant. And in that instant the oar handles broke the limbs and backs of eighty galley slaves. It began at the stern and rattled its way to the bow. Simon moved with the captain and officers from one galley to the next. From one cesspool to the next. From one set of groans to the next. They were always the same. They all stank the same and were all equally bloody.

Simon the Gull no longer had any route of his own. No dry land and no anchorage. Every oar-stroke was a new move to shore and away from it, at the same time.

That night Johan Ot said:

"I will never, ever be Johan the Gull."

He watched the hunched figure shrug its shoulders and get up. As Simon the Gull stood there, the old man's eyes were totally vacant. His lips formed a smile. Why, oh why had he told his story? Why did he bother to tell it to anyone? Were all these men haunted, destroyed, killed by the age-old longing of galley slaves—to return to port? Or to fly up and join the seagulls in their freedom? Or to fly up amid the nighttime stars just when things are at their worst, up among the stars, up into the sky, so that they'd never find you on this galley or anywhere ever again?

That night Johan Ot had an insight. On the day when Simon the Gull ceased to be a galley slave, he had lost his freedom. That day the galley itself became Simon's high seas and dry land both. And Ot realized the following: that deep inside every galley slave who remained a galley slave were the roots, the kernel of his freedom. No one could drive it out of him. No whip, no merciless sea.

It didn't kill him. The story didn't finish him off. The story kept him upright. Hold out, hold out this once, and then I'll vanquish all death, he thought. Ot no longer tried to do himself in through hard work and the thought of the sea, of the traces of madness frothing behind the ship. From harbor to high sea, from infinity to anchorage. He submerged himself completely in his dry land, which had to be somewhere. The man who lived for his awl, the Turk with his wives waiting for him, the slave who had killed and the one who had stolen—together with them Ot breathed and lived for the day when he would no longer be contained by this rocking heap of wood, which the waves of the wayward sea battered however they wished. He thought of escape. On some dark night, at some dark port. They had taken Ot's chains off after he healed the merchant. Since then he'd rowed as a volunteer rows. But the men who signed onto the galley due to debts or who knows what other stupidity were no less galley slaves than the convicts. There was just one difference. No chain wrapped around their waist and legs like a snake, and the thought of escape was more immediate and real.

After the incident with the rat that spewed white foam, after the incident with the infected sailor, it was obvious there were plenty of men consumed by the thought of leaving that damned hunk of wood behind for good. For now they were prey not just to storms and *aguzzini* with their truncheons and whips, not just to pirate ships and dangerous reefs—now fear gnawed and ate at them from within, consuming them slowly and surely. All of them knew that if plague broke out on board, that was the end. Then they would all go to the devil. Because no port would take in a ship like that. There was no escaping that kind of ship, no way out at all. None of them would survive.

Ot's plan matured.

One morning, when they were sailing through the islands of Greece, which enticed them from all sides with their green trees and stone nests of houses—one morning an Italian volunteer nodded to Ot.

"What would you give to be there?" he asked, and he pointed at the island, where the wind was bowing the trees so low that the mariners could feel the roots clutching the earth even from this far away.

"Everything," Ot said. "Everything."

"Everything?" the swarthy Italian asked.

"Absolutely everything," Ot said.

"Then that's good," the Italian said. "We're keeping you in mind."

A shiver of excitement went down Johan Ot's back. He'd rowed mindlessly all day, and he still hadn't been able to tear his eyes away from the gap in the hull where the oar went through. Trees. And houses. And paths leading between them. To walk on those stones. Just to walk. To sit down. To feel the eternal firmness of earth.

The plan got underway. Something was going to happen.

That afternoon, at the shift change, the head *comito* called Ot to come see him. Standing straight he reached right to the ceiling in his dark, stinking cabin.

"You know why you're on the galley," the *comito* said affably. "You're a poisoner and there's no hope for you. You know that you're going to stay here as long as we want, probably till your dying day."

The galley slave understood.

They needed a Simon the Gull. Another one. There weren't enough of them. That's what this was about.

"We've taken your chains off," the *comito* said. "You're better off now. You row in shorter shifts. But we know what it's like to have nothing more to look forward to for the rest of your life."

The galley slave drew into himself. Keep your mouth shut. Don't answer.

The *comito* sat down on his dirty bunk.

"It's up to us," he said, "it's entirely up to us to decide how you're going to live. You could live well. Or you could go through quite a bit. Ask Simon the Gull about it."

The *comito* stopped talking and looked at Ot. He pierced him with his eyes, pinning him to the wall of the murky cabin.

"After all, it's entirely at our discretion," the *comito* said after a while. "We could turn a blind eye in some port somewhere. We could, you know, let you go."

That's the bargain, Ot thought. A dishonest bargain. They've never let anyone go.

"Wouldn't you like to go home," the *comito* smiled. "You don't want to stay here forever. Like Simon the Gull. See, he doesn't want to leave the galley."

Was it back then, the galley slave thought, was it back then when they unchained me that they came up with this idea? Or not until now, when they suspect something's actually going on? Now that they've got wind of something?

"Something's brewing," the *comito* said. "And you know what it is."

The galley slave clenched his teeth.

"No," he said. "I don't know anything."

"Oh, really? Not a thing?" the *comito* asked affably. "So nobody's afraid of the sickness? And nobody's planning an escape?"

"No," the slave said.

"Listen, poisoner," the *comito* said, getting up. "I'm going to ask you one more time if something's brewing and if anybody has hinted to you about something or not."

"No," the slave said. "Nobody's said anything."

The *comito*'s eyes glazed over.

"So there's nothing?" he exclaimed again and shoved Ot in the chest. "So there's nothing?" He opened the door and kicked Ot through. Outside he grabbed him and shoved him up against the railing. "So there's nothing?" the *comito* shouted, banging Ot's head against the wood. Then he quit his yelling and bent down to Ot's ear, so that the galley slave could feel the man's damp, vinous breath as he whispered quietly, distinctly, and calmly:

"What would you give to be there," he recited. "What would you give to be there? You'd give everything," he then shouted. "You'd give everything, absolutely everything, you filthy, mangy poisoner. You'd give everything," he bellowed, the spit spraying from his mouth.

"The Italian," Johan Ot thought. "It was that damned Italian the Gull."

He wasn't beaten. He wasn't hoisted up for the seagulls to peck at. They just deprived him of water. His tongue, his only food, moved through his parched mouth like a piece of dry wood.

But he didn't give in.

He didn't become Johan the Gull.

He got his chain back around his waist and feet.

Despair as vast as the sea latched onto his heart.

In the end, he thought, in the end it's the same here for everyone. All of the men on board ship, with chains or without them, with a whistle in their mouth and a whip in hand or with a plug wedged between their teeth and an oar in their bloody hands—all of us are together and we're all inside the same hunk of wood.

The sea with its winds and waves and spirits doesn't give a damn about the insignificant differences between us.

When death is near, everyone gulps at the air with equal zeal.

Shorelines came and went. Oars splashed senselessly at the water and drove the galley from one place to the next. The sun kept burning and the stars kept shining. Ot saw his hopelessness and the sunburned backs of the galley slaves, he saw the dance of muscles under skin, muscles that endured and endured despite the churning of the waves. He saw foreign lands, Spanish, French, Portuguese, Mohammedan, and other unknown harbors, their walls and towers, and at night the lights in their taverns. He saw the endless surface of the sea that flooded his pupils and roared in the gray mass of his thoughts and he hated the scent of the sea and its salt spray. He saw strange monsters out in the water and in people, storms and the glare of the sun, the snares that the devil set, the edge of the Western Sea, men with boundless freedom in their muscles and chests.

This is how the stocky galley slave with the grim mask of the sea and the wind on his face looked at his cracked hands and his cracked dreams.

Strange thoughts whose beginnings he was unaware of and which he could never think through to the end, thoughts woven in his head but which in the midst of his never-ending mindlessness, his fruitless, automatic activity, he never completed.

Among criminals who were each other's bane and each other's hope, between the canyons of the roiling sea, he decided over and over again: they will not break me. I may go mad, I may end up among the fish or the stars or the seagulls, but they will not break me.

Fear washed away to who knew where, along with the sea spray. Ot was no longer afraid.

Now, for the first time, he no longer trembled at the thought of the knife and all the other sharp objects waiting to be applied to his skin. For the first time no one was tracking him, noting his dangerous connections and secret covenants both here and in the beyond.

He thought: What are thoughts made of? Who shapes them? How does this shaper turn a man's thoughts either good or bad?

He thought: What is the Western Sea like? And the abysses that swallow up people and ships? What sort of monsters lurk in them? What currents and streams vanish and eddy there?

He thought: What hides in the deep? How does the spirit below move the sea? Who sends the beast that comes leaping out of the water and eats an oarsman alive, ripping his skin like silk?

He thought: What are dreams made of? Is this oar, this ship, these sunburned backs around me, this silence, these cries, that sun at the roof of the sky, these Moorish lands, these black people, church bells, towers, market-goers, traders, laborers in the harbors, are all of these things a dream?

There is no doubt that the universal derangement that shunted our galley slave back and forth, that all the accumulated muddle of netherworld and reality had gradually but inevitably frazzled his brain tissue. Strange things were happening inside there. All too often processions of pilgrims or the kindly faces of people from Ot's village would appear in the middle of the sea. All too often the light would refract and a sharp edge would cut into a thought, a memory, a deed.

The boundaries between assumption and reason.

The boundaries between dream and truth.

The boundaries between sea and sky, the boundary of the horizon. All boundaries were broken.

22.

Equinox. Madness grinds in his jaws. The sea knows what it wants. Shrimp nest in the soft parts of the body, fish eggs fill your insides. A tiny, silent menagerie. A dead man screams while a live one keeps quiet.

Precisely on the day when they said *equinox*, the galley slave put his hand to his brow and face and felt cold sweat under his fingers. The sun was reaching down toward the Western Sea and would soon be inside it. On the other side of the sky Ot saw a dark wall. It rose up out of the sea and reached to the sky. It was sharp and solid and black and vertical. The sea here was peaceful, but Ot knew—this was going to be bad. He stood at the prow. At first he couldn't move. At first he called out, loudly. He ought to have gone below and to aft, but the sight of the approaching wall of air had him chained to the spot. It grew and broadened and kept coming. Very quickly, in fact. Behind him Ot heard curses, shouts, and men hurriedly working—they were lowering the mainsail, drawing in the oars, and unchaining the oarsmen. Men bumped into one another on deck, looking powerlessly at the approaching mass and mixture of sea and sky.

Something kept Ot at the prow. Sultry air was steaming everywhere and the cold sweat kept beading on his forehead. The sea was motionless. Fishes and birds and sails on the horizon—everything had vanished.

They were all alone and waiting for the wall to slam into them.

Across the deck the sun was still dazzling, but the area around the ship was growing dark in spite of that.

When the sharp gusts started, Ot came to and crept back into the safe huddle of frightened bodies. A black cloud separated from the wall then and rushed straight for the galley. The distorted features of men and sea monsters were visible in it, moving through its enormous space in outsized forms and huge, pliant layers, flowing into each other and exchanging forms, figures, shapes.

Their movements and transformations drained away all the muscular tension of the people on deck. Torpor spread through their limbs and the marrow in their spines softened. They were enchanted by the stupendous phenomenon that had overcome them. They were powerless.

Some of them prayed.

Others stared straight ahead.

Some waved their arms in the air and clutched at their hair.

Others tied themselves with ropes to the masts.

Then, in an instant, the sun vanished, a prickly, satanic squall blew over them, and they were in darkness.

The wall struck, and the galley slave thought that this was what it must be like deep in the Western Sea.

Because water and sky had united.

Somewhere wood creaked, and then every human voice was lost in a violent drumming. Monsters had stirred earth, water, and sky into a frenzy.

Jagged pinpricks filled Ot's eyes and when he looked at that world, when he looked at that other world, at first all he saw was a horrible glare. Everything white and sharp and glowing. Out of the dark, mad abyss straight into this dazzling light. He lay on the deck like some dead animal, like some exhausted and ailing pack animal that only chance had left breathing. The others walked past and over him.

His mouth was dry and stinging and when he moved, he felt all his limbs ache.

But what did that matter—the main thing was he was alive, alive, he had come back from that insane other world alive.

How many more times would he?

This moment wasn't as joyous and simple as the galley slave initially thought, laughing and talking to himself, mumbling into his knees out on the expanse of the sea.

The mindless abyss had battered the ship as much as a ship could be battered. Half of the foremast jutted up like the remains of a tree trunk after a forest fire, and everywhere there were splinters and rags, everything was broken and scattered to the far ends of the world and the sky.

Several oarsmen had been carried off, along with one of the merchants and a *comito*.

But that wasn't the worst of it. Worst of all was that the men simply didn't know where they were. Where their hunk of wood was floating in the vast watery plain. For all they knew, they had been sucked in and then spewed out on the other side of the world.

That was the worst of it.

Now Ot wanted something to eat and drink. They pointed him to the sea and the fish in it. Now he'd had enough, now he wanted off the ship. And only now did the galley slave realize that this place they'd been blown to was the devil's domain for certain.

Now he was irrevocably there and he felt the periphery of his vision fill with another powerfully glinting darkness. The glowing mass fixed to the vault of the sky up above. The immeasurable surface extending to all the ends of the earth. A silence the likes of which he'd never heard in his life. The overpowering silence and the empty space around him took his breath away. There was no motion to drive the glowing sphere into the Western Sea, where it belonged, where it would sizzle loudly as it sank into the dark depths. There was no bird with its noisy nesting place nearby, there was no breeze, there was nothing. For all these reasons, the galley slave had no doubt: the devil had a hand in all of this. With a gentle pressure he was tightening the ring around Ot's heart as it continued to beat, barely audible, in his weakened chest. How many days had passed since the moment when the abyss had retreated, nobody knew. There was the sun at the top of the sky and the sea all around beneath their feet, there was a hand that covered a mouth and suppressed a scream; a hand that teeth bit into so hard that they drew blood; and there was the murky, calm, and dense water all around. The air refracted, the silence crackled, the eyes bulged out of their faces, and the teeth from their gums.

The air refracted.

The water refracted in the silence.

It was quiet.

Not even the gentlest breeze.

Things were hopeless.

The sea knows what it wants.

The galley slave summoned the devil. His eyes glazed, his face feverish, his body cool, he ran around the galley and summoned the devil. He descended into the dark belly of the ship, into the hull, reached into a pitch barrel, and smeared the black stuff over his face and into his mouth till he lost his breath.

He offered it to the others: have a little pitch, eat up, it's good. He looked one man in the eyes and said: give me your heart and I'll set it on fire. That will save us. I'll raise your burning heart on the mast.

He told another: I'm Magic Jack. Tomorrow I'm calling in a favor. Our conspiracy, our network is functioning. We'll get water, we'll get food, we'll get some cool place to sleep.

Then he began skipping around as he tried to rip his own heart from his chest.

The crew looked on, but when Ot tried to light a fire on deck as he recited some strange words, their cups ran over.

They beat him up.

He whimpered and moaned so much that it reached even into the cruel sea's soul. He had wounds on his skin and a fire in his body. For a long time his watery eyes stared up at the great glowing eye above, that ever-present sphere. Ot's pupils alone followed its steady movement into the Western Sea. At the moment when it dipped into the water and began to sink, the galley slave got up.

Now it's going to sink down to the other side of the world and sky.

God, he said quietly, it's all over with me. I don't know exactly what happened. Maybe I did make off with some gold monstrances from your temple in the darkness of night while bonfires burned on the hilltops. Maybe I really did abandon my family, maybe I wandered the world, maybe I skulked around with secret societies. I don't know if it was really like that, because the Karolina of Styria tightened its grip around my mind and held me by my heart, and I lost all my memories. But now I remember and can see the green of my home again. So I'll give you the monstrances back, and yield to you all my sinful days and nights. I'll give you everything, if you just give me a little breeze, a little air, a little water.

He thought an answer would come, a sign, a breeze or some such.

But there was nothing.

Just the sun, which continued to burn without respite. The men lay all over the deck and now no one paid any attention to the mad galley slave stumbling over their bodies and roaming and running all over the galley. He spoke of a mountain where St. Lorenz lived, and a stream with Jožef, and a lake where the Virgin dwelled, and the Western Sea with its chasms and huge beasts waiting for him, and poison in his beggar's bag, and the Spanish boot, and the empty town.

But one of them still had his wits.

He knew it was over and that it would only get worse and worse. A new agony drew him to his feet, and then his cracked, waterless mouth bit into the last remaining biscuit.

He got up and with a powerful lurch of the upper portion of his body he slammed his head into the sharp edge of the bench.

There was a dull thud, and then it all poured out.

The soft contents oozed through the gap of his broken skull.

Everything that was inside our galley slave's body rose up into his throat and toward his head. If only he could vomit himself out.

Then he was seized with convulsions.

There was no water. The galley slave sniffed over the surface of the wood for water and bit into it. The air glowed hot, as did the inside of his mouth. It stung, it burned, with embers circulating up in the sky, over the sea, through his limbs, his gut, his chest, his head.

Madness ground at his jaw.

The sailors, all hunched up, huddled in the corners.

But somebody was walking. Hale and hardy. He stood by the railing and watched for dry land to appear.

That one is a criminal, they said. That one will survive. That one has smooth, taut skin, that one is healthy. The devil himself is helping that one, that one will do fine. That one has spring water, someone said. That one has a supply.

It turned out that a number of them were hiding water. Everyone who was thirsty leaped, searched, rifled, and rampaged up one side of the ship and down the other, ripped out planks, smashed furniture, scattered ropes, slashed the canvas. Not the captain or the merchants or the *comiti* could stop the galley slaves' rampage. They lay in their beds, listening to the madness on their crazy ship. They waited for their own ends to come. The galley slaves smashed everything until they found a small cask, barely tapped, that was full of some viscous substance. All mixed up and masticated. There was barely a slobber's worth of fluid in it, but it was wet. Our galley slave snarled and whimpered. He didn't know how it happened, but he was holding onto the hardy young kid, the healthy little sailor by the neck, and he snarled, fumed, and grunted as a white rabid rage fogged his eyes and a blue fury colored his face, and then he bit into him, bit into the soft, supple, taut, juicy flesh, healthy flesh, full of circulating life essence, water, nutrients. Ot's haggard hands thrashed until the soft thing below gave way and sank, melted. Whatever his fists and teeth couldn't accomplish, his nails did, their sharp spear points digging into the soft surface until rivulets of warm blood welled up. The boy lay on the floor, inhaling his own bloody saliva. The galley menagerie stood around, grunting at the kid. His eyes turned inward as wild fear caused the sailor to collapse on himself.

It wasn't a blow that finished him off.

He was done in by a cry as clear and sharp as a knife.

Land ho. Behind them stretched a dark line of dry land.

Behind them stretched a dark line of dry land, and the little sailor's soul shed his body gently and passed over the sea. It will be fine, finding its way to some shore, but the body—the body will be eaten by beasts. Tentacles with countless suckers will tear the skin from that body, fish will nose into the wounds to rip the skin off its bones, shrimp will nest in the soft parts, and fish eggs will fill up the abdominal cavity. A whole menagerie of tiny, silent sea creatures will overcome that poor Christian body.

This is why our galley slave remained silent. He looked down and saw and sensed all of this and felt slightly deranged. Because now he could hear Carniolan bells ringing. They came from below, from the dark depths, and as they echoed he could hear the little sailor's screams being strangled by their deep darkness from top to bottom.

It was as though the dead man were screaming while the living man was silent.

It was of course the cry that had driven the little sailor's soul out of his body and out over the expanse of the sea toward distant shores, but the galley slave had undeniably made his contribution. No wonder—some madness was circulating through his body, storms were toying with his soul and running riot through his innards. Wasn't he again in the grasp of dark forces? Wasn't there some devil present yet again?

The galley slave had vast expanses in his chest. The whole lunatic, confused world, all of its rational and irrational dimensions were careening through his scar-covered body. And just think: he had survived every death.

Now he was silent.

He could feel the sharp teeth plunging into the lacerated skin. He could feel the rapid movements of the piscine multitudes jostling for pieces of the dead man's flesh, and he watched that silent struggle. Each one ready to eat the others, all of them eating flesh, and in perfect silence at that. Even the tentacles, with their suckers drawing blood so that they filled and swelled, performed their work steadily, peacefully, silently, without any gulping or gurgling. And the thought jabbed into the shell of Ot's skull: Look at them gobble. Look at them and know: some day this will be you at the bottom of the sea.

Now he saw the land.

Who knows which coast it was this time, which heap of rocks and clumps of trees and bustling harbor activity. At last a cool wind had blown over the sea. The galley slave could feel the cool breeze (from where? the green groves of home?) soothe his tightened jaw, his skull's corroded shell. He could feel the madness pushing farther and farther out, retreating in large circles, its claws melting as it latched onto and devoured less and less. Nothing more than a tiny grating sound came up from the bottom of the sea. That was the shrimp chomping on the little sailor's bones.

At this point his memory gave way.

The galley slave was pretty much spent. A little tiny bit of memory was still left, a little bit came back here while a little bit slipped away there. But the business of past and present kept getting more and more bound together. They kept splitting apart and then coming together closer than ever, the inexorable grinding of nature had crushed thought and senses both, leaving before Ot's eyes a snarl of everything hazy and unintelligible in his life. There's just one thing I don't understand, he said, the strange thing is that though the confusion just keeps growing, and despite all the chaos, I'm still alive.

And so this business approaches its end. The galley slave made some promises. He asked God for some things and the devil for others. Certain things he did himself, while certain other things were done to him. In any event, a cool breeze was blowing now, and partly by rowing, partly by sail, their Marsiliano pressed toward the shore.

What happens now?

Will there be some new mess, some new derangement, or will we at last find out the final destiny of this wanderer? Will he finally shed his blood and breathe his last on the far seas?

Instead of the clarity you would think has to come sooner or later, the forces of nature and spirit drive us into ever deeper riddles, a more and more tangled world and web of dreams and reality.

So there's no putting off the question: are we actually following the right person here, the right fate? Or did some threads possibly get tangled somewhere and whisk the real story off to who knows where?

Where is the devout man who rowed his little galley and entreated God?

Where is the lunatic who sought to make pacts with diabolic and sorcerous forces?

Where is the mysterious stranger who listened to the drumming speech of the earth and beheld burning hearts out in a forest meadow?

Where is the fugitive who cowered in ravines and ran from guards?

Where is the beggar and vagabond, staring dumbfounded at toothless Anton's *Mene mene tekel upharsin*?

Where is the member of the conspiratorial society called Magic Jack, exposed by the sharp eyes and insight of the municipal judges?

And where, after all, is the Western Sea, and where are its depths, where are the things that happen in daytime and nighttime, the ringing of church bells out over the great expanse of the sea?

Where are dreams, and where is the truth?

It's time for the shore, for terra firma and words of clarity.

23.

Misunderstandings. What was on the handcart? Is this the beginning of some ending or other that we can expect to see creep out of a swamp somewhere? A youth, the pox-ridden little sailor. Lifeward, homeward. The galley slave gazes yearningly at other shores like some Fair Vida, some Lady of Shalott.

When he woke up and looked around him, he saw that everything was a little dark and reddish. That was the sunrise. He could feel the strength within his weakened body begin to come back to him, and he scented a powerful, salty stench. It smelled of piss, of men, of sweat, of swamp gas, of spit, vinegar, and rot, of food scraps and flies that were nestled on a heap of bones in the middle of the room. Their contented buzzing was clearly audible, the buzzing of big flies eating scraps and crawling over each other in a thick swarm. So he had eaten and slept and rested. But where?

But where?

Something thundered over cobblestones down below, a deafening sound that forced its way in among the buildings, and out the window he could see a man dressed in a smock that reached to the ground, with a peculiar sort of head covering, with a whip in hand, pulling a shaft followed by an enormous cart that was loaded to the top with empty baskets. Was that a naked male body lying athwart them up on top? The more Ot's eyes adjusted to everything, the less his mind understood. Here he was, standing in the middle of this room alone—again—with no idea which way to move, which way to step. Then he moved and went to the door. He opened it and through the dark gap that yawned there saw the outline of some stairs, a stone stairway, smooth and washed, leading down somewhere. Sounds of movement came from below. Ot headed down carefully, feeling his way, and then he saw a big tavern table with food flung about on it, overturned bottles, wine stains, a jumble of plates and bones and knives and meat and bread, a dirty floor and dogs lazily nosing around. A few men, a few women lying here and there around the sides, dozing over the table or squinting at the coming day. Candles were burning in niches in the wall and it probably wasn't quite clear to the drunken company that day had arrived—the beginning, life. They were fuzzy about something that our galley slave knew: that night was over and day had begun, wherever this was.

Over there was the captain, and the flush-faced Venetian merchants from the ship. Here they were, tired, calm and collected, as though taking a stroll aft on the galley's gallery.

One of the women had her dirty skirt rolled up, exposing her white, white thighs. She looked at Ot exhausted, with sad eyes, a jug in hand.

I've got to get out, the galley slave thought. Out, out, to see what, where, and how.

He stepped over drunken bodies to get to the door, which was not all that simple, since someone was always shifting or snarling and the dirty mutts kept getting underfoot. The woman with the white thighs lazily followed Ot's progress. He stared back. When he got near the door, he saw something flash in her eyes. That light in those tired eyes, the sudden recognition revealed by the light , the sudden movement of her rounded body as it drew up on its elbows, exposing her white thighs even more—all of this stopped Ot for a moment. She nudged the fat man sleeping beside her, causing him to grumble and jump and look around the room in alarm. She said something to him in a strange, gurgling language and pointed at Johan Ot, who stood in the doorway hesitating, wavering between the door and the room: should he heed her gurgling or should he leave it all and get out?

He decided to get out. But the instant he took hold of the ring on the door, a harsh shout stopped him. The shout was followed by some masculine gurgling and feminine squealing, which was clearly directed at him. When he turned around, he saw the fat man standing on his wavering legs, staring daggers at him. The man waved his hand and pointed a finger: come here. The galley slave was still wavering, but then the other started to approach him, and somebody else with nothing less than an actual dagger in his hand appeared by the door. This meant that Ot was expected to obey the command of the fat man's finger. So he went over to the fat man and then the other bent down and gurgled something in Ot's face for a long time. The galley slave understood none of it. He went over to the captain, who turned away. As did the merchant from the ship. They don't recognize him. They'd never seen him before. Ot was understanding less and less of what was going on.

The woman finally offered him some wine and pointed him to a seat. Now it was obvious that here was where Ot belonged. Why, he had no idea.

He sat there and sluiced himself with the wine, which was stale and warm. He watched the others wake up in various parts of the room, rubbing their eyes and pulling themselves together. Yawning, they stared at the newcomer. They gathered around him. With one hand the fat man was working on a big piece of meat he had taken from a sideboard and doused with red wine, so that each bite dribbled through his beard, while the other hand squeezed those white thighs. He had stopped paying attention to Johan Ot. So Ot got up again and tried to find his way back to the door. He was brought to a halt all at once by the bodies and menacing looks in his way. There was nothing to be done about it. So Ot sat, with hour after hour passing. Interest in the newcomer gradually abated. They had their hands full with their food and drink and feeling the women up.

Outside it was unusually quiet. When was it that wheels had thundered over the cobblestones? And was that really a male corpse on that cart?

The galley slave thought: I have to get back to the ship before it sails.

He tried to get this across to these drunk and debauched people. He pointed and waved and made faces. Ship, sea, sails, oars. The captain and merchant left for the upper rooms when they noticed his efforts. He tried to follow them, but was stopped again. He went from one of the revelers to the other and tried enunciating into their complacent faces. At first nobody listened to him, nobody saw him. Then he could feel a heated gaze following his efforts. That woman could understand him. She was looking at him with growing alarm as her eyes grew wider and wider. There was terror settling inside those sockets. Then she shrieked and explained to the fat man what she had understood, what Ot's movements had told her. The fat man grumbled and began to speak.

Now Ot could sense that there was hatred mounting in here. The other men backed away from him. They tore the jug out of his hands and threw it out the door, where it smashed on the pavement. Two of them ordered him: up. They led him up the stairs, put him back in that room, and bolted the door behind him.

Toward evening they came back, accompanied by a young man who asked questions. A picture was now painted before the galley slave's eyes: he was under suspicion. Boats had brought sickness, they thought. Which meant his boat too, probably. The whole crew was in quarantine. But his captain and that merchant had managed to sneak out and visit this tavern of conspirators, and by a strange coincidence Ot had come with them.

The rat under his bench flashed through his memory. White, milky froth had oozed from its maw. One man had died, but the others survived to go on sailing the seas and put in at various harbors. The sickness had bided its time. Now it would show its teeth.

Another flash: the rats coming out from everywhere that night and biting each other. The men beat at them with their bare hands or hacked at them with swords. Yes, one of the rats died under his bench and white froth oozed from its maw. And then, one day, one of the sailors started tossing in his sleep. Then he got up and roamed the deck all night. The galley slave had thought: this one wants to go home. The next morning the sailor was gone. They searched the whole ship and found him under a heap of ropes. His face was black and white foam dribbled out of his mouth. And he stank so badly they had to hold their noses.

One of a number of nighttime incidents.

Ot knew: every incident has to have its consequences.

He tried to explain to them. He wasn't sick. He had been in many ports, but the sickness had not touched him. One of the sailors had died on their ship, and they had wrapped him in wet rags and thrown him to the sea creatures. The sickness ended there. Ot was going back home to his ship. But they understood nothing. He had a home of his own somewhere. He didn't have to die in this stench with white drool in his beard, black in the face. They didn't listen to him. The town had its laws: quarantine. That's where he would finally die. Nobody came out of there alive.

Quarantine.

Quarantine. It was a building with thick walls. A warehouse in the harbor. They dragged him there down streets that were thick with the smell of burning fuel—perhaps blackened corpses? Human pulp? He struggled and bit and flung himself on the ground. They threw him inside. Mariners and travelers from all the ends of the earth cowered in the corners. Men in their prime, grandfathers, children, women. Each one had dragged a heap of straw into his own corner. The sick and the healthy. Were there any actual sick among them? There was a stench hovering in the air.

This place will do them all in.

Had he escaped all possible deaths, had he sailed the far seas just to shed his life here, in this filthy hall, in some unknown harbor?

He felt driven into new storms, into endless new madness, into new traps of universal chaos, driven always toward the edge, the edge of death, the edge of life. Why shouldn't the bastard experience sickness, why shouldn't the galleyman, dragged from death's reach by strange forces in the past, now witness a dark layer of black death creep up his legs, why shouldn't germs and evil spirits rampage and explode in his blood and turn it gradually into a white sludge for him to vomit out with everything else he carries inside? Why shouldn't he crawl into some corner of a quarantined tomb and drop his soul there, in this distant country, alone and unremembered? Why shouldn't demons drag his soul then through winds and seas and boundless deserts to wander mad in search of its home?

But lo and behold: he was not destroyed.

Here is the gist of the galley slave's most recent experiences, in summary: he didn't perish at all.

From here he'll once again find his way to the beginning, to his homeland, his way to the beginning and his way to the end of this edifying tale.

He walked around looking at the people huddling by the walls: a wife separated from her husband, a mother from her child, a son from his father. Ot walked and spoke and babbled: Death will get you if you're afraid. If you have heart and if you get some help from the ebb and flow of nature, you'll survive.

And he'll survive. All our questions are superfluous. His legs won't turn black and his blood won't turn to sludge.

Not the sea, not storms, not judges, not people, and not plague will be able to break this sinewy body, this face wearing its dark mask of oceans, this soul devoid of ideas or concepts.

Ot moved catlike through space. He touched everything. He ate and drank and swallowed the thick, stinking contaminated air. He listened to air pass through his windpipes and he felt the living pulse of his healthy body.

Everything had been visited upon him. Was there any misfortune he hadn't been served up, any type or form of suffering and torment? What evil remains to be inflicted on him? To be thrown overboard for sea creatures to eat? He'll swim to the nearest shore. To be pushed into an abyss? He'll get caught on some branch budding out of the cliff. To be strangled, have his throat cut, or his heart ripped out of his body? He'll keep breathing and lick his wounds.

A boy was gasping and wheezing in a corner. His handsome face was distorted by the blistery skin that was creeping toward his eyes from all sides. He pulled some rotten, fermented straw up over himself and wriggled under it. All the signs were there: the boy was a goner. The mangy wretch was so quiet and so pathetic, yet wheezed so in the face of death! With no mercy in his heart, our galley slave watched the boy suffocate as he forlornly, hesitantly bade farewell to this world.

Was there perhaps some breath still propelling life through this crumpled ghost?

Ot wondered this, but he didn't care.

Then the handsome, blistered youth unclenched his teeth and a quiet, though sharp and clear curse came through them. At this, the earth swayed beneath the galley slave's feet. His cruel and hardened soul was suddenly upended by a gust, off balance, the room opening up onto all the corners of the earth, thought coursing through his chest and blood pulsing through his body. Outside, the bells of all nearby churches started ringing. That homely curse smelled of earth and stalls, of low-slung smoky huts, of leather and linen and clean clothes. A fresh breeze blew through the room: this was a down-home curse, a word full of familiar things, his beloved homestead.

Ot leaped toward that face, embraced the blisters and breathed words, life, and health into it—not for him, not for the boy—just for himself, for some connection, for some news. For a sign, for a message from the world of a distant memory, for contact, a shout. Amid those blisters, in that blackened face, the boy's eyes were darting, full of surprise, full of mute speech, although all that came through the spittle on his lips was meaningless babble. Now the galley slave decided in favor of life. He would save this wretch, drive the blisters from his face and the sickness out of his blood.

That's what he would do.

All through the following days and nights he boiled water on the fire that was kept stoked in the middle of the room, and poured it into the opening between the blisters. He fought for the food that was brought and, without touching it himself, pushed pieces of it through the youth's spittle and moans, into his mouth.

All through the following days and nights Ot kneaded the ailing body and cleansed it of infection. He cleared all the sour, stinking hay away and made the youth lie on the dry floor.

We're going home, he breathed into the boy. Home, do you hear? And through the following days and nights life began to reassert itself through all the mucous gasping. The blisters retreated from the boy's face and his limbs moved in a way that indicated that his healthy humors were being replenished.

Home.

Through the following days and nights, through hours of waiting and watching with red eyes and a hint of terror down his spine, Ot saw uncannily familiar features emerge from under the vanishing blisters on the youth's face.

Was this a dream? he wondered. A dream or some new, horrible trick? This boy, these familiar features, this face, these wounds healing on his face and body. Wasn't this the face of the young sailor Ot had beaten on the high seas until his fists sank softly into the red-glowing flesh? Hadn't the soul fled this face when the call of land rang out and finished him off? Weren't shrimp nesting in these wounds? Wasn't the kid lying on the seabed now, with fish and sea monsters swarming about? Weren't algae and other plants slowly and gently enshrouding the little sailor's face?

I'll bring us both back to life, Ot said, I'll resurrect us both from the death that we're living, he said, no more mange and scabies, he said. Tomorrow, he said, first thing we'll go look at the new, steep, tapering waves reaching our ship from afar, from the horizon with its bright peaks.

Over the following days and nights the youth began to speak. The fewer blisters there were on his face, the fewer germs of sickness in his blood, the more nonsense and heartfelt talk there was.

Nonsensical, heartfelt talk. Scant thanks indeed for saving his life. It turned out the pustular youth really was from the land where limpid streams raced, green forests rustled, and winds bowed the grass in springtime with flowers budding here and there, where snowcapped peaks shone in dazzling sunlight. He really was from the place where the galley slave had lived one of his lives, where a linden tree blossomed in front of each house, where grain ripened through hot summers, where the sunset faded behind the next mountain, where death was holy, friendly, and pure when it came.

That's where I'll die, he said. That's where we need to go.

A fire blazed in the middle of the stone cell. The guards threw all the hay in a heap, pulling it out from under the filthy bodies and scattering the mangy inmates with whips. The dying want straw. They cover themselves with it as the end approaches. Now it was burning. By the wall in a corner, in an unknown port, in quarantine, in death's burning anteroom, the taciturn galley slave listened to the youth's story. At a depth that could almost have been that of the seabed, in the midst of that tomb in which no one expired, glowing and crackling between the walls—was this indeed the young sailor's face? Didn't a path lead from here straight into the embrace of darkness? Both of their faces were illuminated as the glow of the burning morgue reached across them. The young babbler. He had been in an army unit, wandering around Bosnia with some regiment from Carniola, breaking up homesteads, carrying a harquebus over his shoulder, catching the dust of white roads in his teeth, and warming himself by the campfire on endless nights. He, too, had looked many deaths in the face. He, too, had completed his stations of the cross. He'd been captured by Turks, who sold him to the Venetians. He had been on the galley and now here, with him, in quarantine, facing the final end.

Not that, the galley slave said. Not a word about that. Talk about home, your homestead, places where the relentless glare of the sun doesn't burn and frazzle. Home, your house, the linden, the fields, the meadow, talk about those things, you mangy scab-face, that's what I woke you up for, for some news, the good word, the truth spoken clearly.

The youth went quiet. It was bright and red now, as though it were broad daylight in that pit. Acrid smoke drew through large openings in the walls. It carried the stench away, the thick smell of sickness out through those holes. Now they were throwing the last bits of rags and straw onto the fire. This was a blaze for the living. Was the quarantine coming to a close? Whoever didn't go onto the fire, whoever didn't cover himself with straw, whoever didn't have milky froth oozing out his mouth, whoever didn't have black arms and legs was going to live, was healthy. Nobody died. The sickness went back underground. It would erupt somewhere else.

This is why the fire blazed so cheerfully.

The smell of burned, dead, sick, damp straw had become hopelessly thick and the two of them were coughing and tearing. They heard the waves crashing against the shore and they heard the scratching of a gentle rain that calmed them. A new stench accompanied the rain. It pressed to the ground and into their room. The galley slave saw his opening: no one was watching them. Everywhere there were clouds of acrid smoke blocking the view to the next pallet. He grabbed the kid and pulled him to his feet. He was wobbly on his weak legs, but able to move. They crept along the wall—down below was the sea. It dashed dangerously against the rocks and roared and called: come on. The youth stopped and went slack. Come on, the galley slave beckoned.

You're going to push me, the youth said. You're going to push me into the sea again.

Who knows, perhaps he would have pushed him, perhaps he would have jumped himself, perhaps they would have leaped over the cliff together, smashing into the rocks down below? Leaving their limbs scattered this way and that, their blood and other pliable substances for the raucous birds, the squawking black creatures to snatch. Always they circled the quarantine in huge swarms, waiting and waiting. In vain. Yes, the black birds would have snatched up their scattered remains in an instant, and then would have attacked the trunks of their corpses with sharp beaks.

The galley slave stood at the edge of the wall and looked down, while the youth covered his eyes and scabs with his hands. No, this was no escape. This was no attempt to flee from quarantine, because down below there were rocks, beyond them was the sea, to the left was a wall and to the right was a wall. Soaked birds were walking close by. They stood beside the escapees calmly and waited. The galley slave looked down—the sea—he looked through it, beyond it, and behind it and saw that this is where the ground went down all the way to the sky beyond, everything was tilted toward the horizon, toward the place where all his shadows lived.

Toward the shadows? Toward them?

And home from there?

From inside, from the vault, from the opening that thick smoke was still crowding through, into the rain and the air, they heard shouts. The cries came out through the smoke and the stench, but with a clear resonance, sharp and loud.

The youth ran inside to see. When he came back, he didn't see anything at first. When he came back with the happy news, excited, at first all he saw was the bare wall and empty space from which the galley slave must have leaped onto the rocks, and he saw the black birds circling through that empty space in the spray of the waves as they rushed up the cliff and then drew back into themselves, into the deep. This is what the boy saw at first when he ran back, panting, coughing, black in the face, his bright eyes scouring the empty walls.

Then, right next to him, right at his feet, he heard a sharp cough and noticed a figure sitting, hunched over, hands clasped around its knees, cradling its head in its arms, its back bent. This back which had borne the burden of every storm, shipwreck, and fire, which had been lashed by the bailiff's whip and carved by the butcher's knife, a back that had taken blows without breaking, now this back, when the galley slave stood up and slowly straightened it, was bent.

Yes, now he was just like some old man.

He looked at the sea for a long time, staring like some Fair Vida, some Lady of Shalott, and then quietly, but clearly, distinctly, he said: "It's over, isn't it? The quarantine is over." The boy nodded encouragingly. So they walked through the smoke, past the fires, past the enfeebled bodies on the ground, slowly walked to the door and out onto the street.

With the sickness? Did they take that rot and decay that had killed no one here along with them to their next destination?

24.

*Air thick with humidity. Infectious air. Everything shoving and crawling
its way from the sea to the interior. Is this where the end begins? Rats.
Roadblocks. Fetal position. Something burns and nips in his guts.*

The air was so thick with humidity that it stifled the crackling of the
fire at the edge of the road and caused its reflection to twist and refract through the night. Dark figures were sitting around in the wan
light or pacing in boredom. The dim glow reached several fathoms
up into the sky, where the low vault pushed it back down. Ot and
the boy were so close that they could hear individual words and the
clatter of the night guards' weapons and could see a figure in a long,
black cloak walking among the men. Then a sound thundered into
their ditch by the road, which was overgrown with brush on all sides.
Something clattered and creaked up above them, someone with his
giddyap was driving the clip-clop of horse hooves down the road, and
the wooden rumble of a cart behind them. The sound grew louder,
and as it rattled right past them, they saw three men sitting up above.
One held the reins in his hands, while the other two were armed, each
with a knobby, bludgeonlike musket leaning against his shoulder.

When the rumbling got to within about twenty paces from the fire, the figures there jumped to their feet. A harsh shout stopped the creaking and clattering. There was some movement and readjustment done on the cart, and then all three of them jumped down. The driver approached and began a shouted exchange with the soldiers. Then the soldiers held out a long, fat stick in his direction. The driver hoisted one end onto his shoulder and dragged it back to the cart. There, with the help of both his armed men, he tied a bundle onto it. Then all three of them took hold of the lower end of the pole, leaving the other end to sway with the bundle above, as though some fat fish were swinging from it, fighting to get free. With much loud shouting they carried the pole before them to the fire. Then they stopped, still at a considerable distance. The figure in the long cloak disentangled itself from the light and raised its arms in the air. Slowly they set their load down, and the figure with the upraised hands, which had thick, woolen gloves on them, took hold of the bundle and carried it off to the rear, where a smaller fire smoldered and smoked in a dank effort to provide heat. A large cloud billowed from there, and the smell of juniper and vinegar assaulted their nostrils. On this went, with a second bundle and then a third, until all of the cargo was transferred to the other side. The soldiers continued chatting around the fire the whole time. Then things got stuck. On the cart a puppy began to squeal and howl plaintively. To all appearances, one of the men from the cart wanted to take it to the fire, but he was refused abruptly and vociferously, this response flaring up from several of the soldiers all at once. Impossible. There was no end to the arguing. The one with the puppy persisted and the others persisted as well. Finally the three from the cart withdrew and talked for a short while. There was no choice. In the glow of the fire they saw an arm brandish a sword in the background, producing a rasp and a dull thud on the ground and flashing briefly, thus putting an end to the negotiations about the dog. Next they tied some other objects and items of clothing onto the pole, one after the other, and then they themselves crossed in a wide arc over to the small fire in the rear of the camp. The figure in the black cloak appeared out of that suffocating cloud. With a smoldering branch producing a black cloud of smoke in one hand and an earthen pot in the other, he approached the cart and the horses himself and got down to business. He enshrouded all of it in a gigantic cloud of smoke, and now that same powerful, acrid smell of juniper and vinegar so completely flooded the ditch where Ot and the boy were hiding that they couldn't hold out any longer.

Carefully they crawled out and made their way through the underbrush down the hillside. They left the voices behind them, and once they were deep into the valley they saw a narrow cone of faintly glowing light up in the sky behind them.

Despairing, the boy sought out Ot's face through the darkness. How many hours, how many days, how many weeks had they been on the road? How many times had they tried? How many times had they attempted in every way possible to break through the cordon that closed off the country on all sides with fires, military roadblocks, armed peasants, and crazed bailiffs who shot first and asked questions later; with plague commissars and the stench of vinegar and juniper steam? Traveling merchants, beggars, vagabonds of all sorts, fugitive galley slaves—especially fugitive galley slaves—and sailors from ports where the plague was raging—all were desperate to get to the interior, into the safe refuge of this armed and closed country, each carrying the germs of the frightful sickness that would soon break out once more, without warning. How many stories were there of a single traveler wiping out an entire village or a town? He would sleep at the inn, and when they found him the next morning, blackened and pustular, it was already all over. And so they were enforcing countless exacting and cruel safety measures to shut off the country.

Our two fugitives were roaming from one fire to the next, fleeing from soldiers and guards and trying to get through on overgrown mountain paths.

When was the day and when the night where in some far-off port they had gazed into some other fire and some other, bluer sky? After they left quarantine they had wandered through that deranged town, which everyone was escaping. Its inhabitants and any chance visitors were fleeing to all the ends of the earth and taking the germs of the sickness with them to every point of the compass. The disease had submerged, desisted, and now lurked in blood and veins, the better to erupt some other day in some other place and continue its rampage. That night when everything collapsed and the town lifted its state of siege, Ot and the boy had broken into an empty house and drunk all its wine. The kid vanished that night, and when he came back, he was exhausted but smiling. Such a beauty, he exclaimed, such a black pearl, and now I've given her a little, blistery Moor of her own. But there was no time for laughter, because when they left the house, they had to stop at the first corner. Out in a square armed sailors were assembling galley slaves that had scattered like birds in the sudden chaos. From all sides they were pushing and driving them onto ships. So Ot and the kid ran and hid in an empty house. That morning they were petrified with fear. There was a banging on the door downstairs, and when they went to the window, they saw Simon the Gull with a group of armed men. The posse was charging from one house door to the next, like dolphins. Simon the Gull was sniffing out fugitive galley slaves. Their door banged and banged, while the fugitives stood rigid with fear by the window and waited for it to crash open. It didn't. Its large wooden bolt held out. Simon the Gull and his men gave up. They moved on down the street, and even now, even from here, even from here in this gorge his hunched figure still shone in their eyes, his stump waving and pointing out doors for his drovers to bang on. The fugitives went on hiding in that house, each day waiting for Simon the Gull to sniff his way back and pound on the door. But it got quieter and quieter down below. Within a few days all they could hear from the square was a few isolated voices, and then it fell completely silent. The town was empty. Everyone had fled. Down in the harbor there were still a few ships. Among a crowd of refugees they managed to press aboard some new hunk of wood where absolute chaos reigned, where no one was in command, and where all signs pointed to the ship's never being able to sail. Among the frightened crush of bodies there were some sailors and some fugitive galley slaves; eventually they banded together and it seemed that the ship would set out from its unhappy harbor after all. But the ship would have to sail in all directions at once, since each passenger was heading for his own shore.

Finally they pushed off, but the passage was short, only as far as the next town. Here again everyone was scattering. Here again there were soldiers rounding up fugitive galley slaves. In the harbor Ot and the kid looked for a vessel heading to their homeland. At one point they actually made a deal. They would row, and in exchange for their work they would be put ashore wherever they wanted. But it fell through, because the captain lifted Ot's canvas shirt and saw the marks on his waist left by the chains sliding over his torso for so long. It looked as though the fugitives were going to meet their end in a foreign land. But finally they had a little luck. Some suspicious-looking and -sounding Venetian merchants with a suspicious cargo were taking any rabble aboard who were willing to work.

They had made it. They were back.

They huddled in their gorge and watched, powerless, the dim glowing cone of the fire up by the road.

Johan Ot could feel the kid's eyes probing his face fearfully. We can't get through anywhere, Ot thought. After everything we've been through, here we are, stuck in this valley. And he had sworn to get this young sailor home. A miracle had lifted the boy's face from the depths of the sea, from that teeming, silent swarm of beasts of prey, and put it before him. It had gotten them onto a ship and over the sea. It had got Ot into this ravine. It would pull him out of it again.

On the other side of the gorge they felt their way through the forest to the top of a hill. They could feel they were at the top, though they couldn't see anything below them. A mass of humid air covered the earth everywhere and the stars were invisible. They couldn't even see the fire on the far side of the valley.

They pushed blindly onward along the ridge.

When they stopped, tired and out of breath, they could feel some morning light begin to penetrate the thick air, and on the hillside to the left of them they could make out the dark shadows of even surfaces. They were walls. Houses.

They sat down in the damp grass and waited.

There was no rooster cry, no barking of dogs, no voices, no signs of life.

The day rose, but still nothing moved or made any noise down below.

"Wait here," Ot said and headed down toward the houses. The kid stayed behind and when Ot glanced back he saw a look of despair on the boy's face. The thought practically bristled from the boy: He's going to leave me. I'm not going to leave him, Ot thought. I'm going to save him. For that blow, for that shout that carried the young sailor's soul over the sea.

There was no life at all in the village. The courtyard of the first house had a big heap of charred rags and objects lying in it. Items of clothing lay everywhere. Something had happened here. They were burning contaminated rags. The door moaned when Ot shoved it open. Emptiness groaned from inside. The people had fled from here. Pots and shards lay on the floor. As if somebody had left the room in a hurry, taking only the most essential things. Ot found a piece of smoked meat in the tiny, dingy, ill-lit room. He looked at its red-dish, smoky matter for a long time, then made a sudden decision and tucked it under his shirt. In another house he found a skin of wine and a string of garlic. A warm peasant jacket, a knife, a leather belt. He wrapped all of it up in a thick blanket and threw the bundle over his shoulder. The kid was shivering in the morning dampness when Ot returned.

He draped the blanket around the boy's shoulders and offered him some wine. The kid drank it in big gulps. Before they attacked the meat, they each bit into a big clove of garlic, eating some of it and smearing the rest over their faces and hands.

"We've got to find herbs and a lot of wine," Ot said. "But first we have to get past the roadblocks. It's going to get worse here soon."

All morning they rested above the abandoned village. Ot went down one more time and collected everything that was usable or ed-ible. There wasn't much of the latter, but there were enough warm clothes for both of them. They built a big fire and used it to thor-oughly smoke the peasant clothes, which were stiff with sweat and smelled of the barn. One more time they smeared themselves with garlic, which they crushed and mixed with wine. When they took off, toward evening, the air was still stuffy and humid and swarms of flies and other vermin of unknown shapes darted around their heads.

"Watch out for them," Johan Ot said. "Flies, rats, grasshoppers, mosquitoes, fleas, all kind of vermin. They crawl through infected shit and drag sick air behind them."

They waved branches continually to chase off the pests, of which there were more and more. Slowly it grew dark. They climbed a nar-row, steep path toward a rocky cliff that hung over their heads like some heavy cupboard that might rumble down the hill any minute and take all things living and dead with it. As the forest grew thinner, the brush grew thicker, lower, and harder to walk through, with sharp stinging nettles. It reached toward them on the path from all sides with its snakelike creepers. They were almost directly beneath the cupboard when their next footstep felt the absence of firm ground. They sensed a huge hole at their feet. All they could see was its edge and the darkness beneath. The path resumed somewhere under the cupboard.

In a helpless rage Johan Ot raised his arms over his head. The boy kept feeling ahead on the right. Suddenly some stones crumbled under his feet and he slid over the edge shouting a curse. He managed to hold on, with all his strength. He propped himself up on his elbows, but his feet were scrabbling over stones that collapsed and rolled into the darkness. Ot ran over, grabbed onto the boy, and pulled him up. There they swayed uncertainly.

Then, at once, they seized hold of one another other and lurched into the brush alongside the path.

"Bastards," Johan Ot swore. "That's another path they've demolished. There's no damned way through anywhere."

They had no choice but to go back.

Dispirited, they headed back down the path. This night was moonless, starless too. It was dark and they sighed in relief when they made out the first trees. Now they advanced through the sparse forest from tree trunk to tree trunk. The kid was losing his will.

"I can't," he said. "I can't go any farther. It's pointless, and anyway, I'm still covered in blisters. Where do I think I'm going? Here or at home, I'll die all the same."

Ot came to a stop. He grabbed the boy and shoved him farther into the darkness. He pressed the wineskin to the kid's mouth until the warm, stale wine started gurgling down the boy's throat. Then he drank some himself, tossed the skin over his shoulder, and took his companion by the arm.

"Walk," Ot barked.

The kid followed obediently.

"Our only chance of getting through is at night," Ot said a while later. "At night they'll be sleeping by some fire."

They came to the end of the pathless slope and stepped onto a sodden road. It was several paces wide and led along the ridge of the hill. They saw the fire ahead and a stone's throw off to the side of it the second one. Here between the two of them. Somewhere here they had to find a way through.

For a while they advanced down the road, and then they dropped into the brush alongside it as they had so many times before. Once again they were so close to the fire that they could hear voices. Beyond the thin brush alongside the road a broad meadow opened up. At the bottom of it there was forest, and if they got through it, they would be on the other side.

"We're going to run for it," said Ot. "Understand? You're going to run so hard your lungs burst. Don't stop till I say so."

The second fire wasn't visible now, concealed by a slight rise on the right.

They crouched and listened intently. Only bits of voices came through the night. Nothing was happening by the fire to suggest that the guards were particularly alert.

"Now," Ot said, and the two of them raced out into the meadow. With huge strides Ot bounded over an empty space that had no visible bottom; he fell and stifled his groan of pain, then got up and ran on, hunched over. He sensed he would make it, that there was nothing in the world that could stop him now. A few more leaps and he dove into the brush at the edge of the dark forest. He couldn't hear the kid. Ot waited a while longer, then he decided to head into the woods.

At that instant there was a terrible explosion behind him. In fact, somebody had called out first, and then somebody else groaned, and then came the explosion and the flash of light, shattering the darkness and silence into a thousand pieces. It seemed as though the entire meadow was illuminated and that men were running from all sides toward the center. Ot hesitated for just a moment. Then he turned and raced back up.

He had reached about halfway when he heard gasping and somebody calling out. He felt his way in the direction of the sounds and presently caught sight of two dark figures—or, more precisely, a tangle of two figures that had merged into one and were struggling and groaning on the ground. Ot grabbed the uppermost one by the collar and pulled, pulling with so much force that the figure groaned as its collar cut into its throat. With both hands Ot shoved the shape that had been sitting astride the kid down the hillside, so that it tumbled and finally vanished.

The young sailor had stared at the sky and the struggle around him with such darkness in his eyes, his arms lifeless at his sides, that it looked like he might never move again. As though he were lying on the deck of the galley on a hot afternoon, with the blazing sun over and inside his head. Johan Ot grabbed the ragged body and pulled it to its feet. Follow me, he said, follow me. But the other didn't move at all. Ot grabbed the kid by the waist and dragged him up the hillside. The guard, down below, who had already recovered from his surprise, had begun shouting at the top of his voice, and now all the other voices started rolling back down, toward the edge of the forest. They'll be looking for us down there now, Johan Ot said. We have to keep going back up.

Once the fugitives had been slogging down the muddy road for a while, it seemed as though all the voices down below had disappeared in the darkness. To the right, where the fire was, Ot could hear the neighing of horses. The soldiers would be covering the road, too. He dragged the boy's faint and frightened body, paralyzed by nothing more than fear, off the road and into the woods. They headed straight up a narrow path through thorny bushes. At this point the kid came to his senses and his legs began moving again, as he recovered from some sort of stupor. They didn't stop until they reached the top, just under the cupboard.

There were no pursuers behind them.

They stayed there till morning without any wine. They still had some meat and some garlic left over. But worse was the gnawing question: where to now? They had tried everywhere to find a gap in the wall of guards, sabotaged paths, fires, and dark forests. The kid said nothing. He held tight to his knees, huddling there, and didn't look up. They could have made it to safety tonight. Ot had been on the other side, so to speak. But the boy's last drop of strength had clearly dried up. He hadn't run across that meadow, he confessed contritely that night. His legs had suddenly given out, so he'd dropped down to the ground. He could barely move.

So he crawled on the ground and suddenly this figure loomed up before him. But apparently the boy's snakelike movements scared the guard. He was just then buttoning his trousers and nearby there was a terrible, pestilent stench that very nearly did the boy in all by itself. But when the man saw that the creature in the grass was quite help-less, he bent down and grabbed him. The soldier called for help, fired a shot, and that was the end of their escape for the night.

"Listen," Johan Ot said. "Whoever's afraid, whoever hesitates will be struck by the sickness."

He lifted the boy to his feet once again.

"You've got to," he said. "You've got to walk."

He pushed a small piece of garlic into the boy's mouth, which the youth ground listlessly between his jaws.

Ot lifted the boy up again, and he shoved him again, and again they headed back down the same path.

As they approached the road through the trees, they heard numerous voices coming from the place where the fire had been the night before, where the roadblock must have been. Something was happening there. Johan Ot ran downhill and stopped in the brush. A minute later he came running back, out of breath, and pulled the kid along with him.

"Come on," he snapped. "It's our chance."

They headed straight down onto the road and walked briskly toward the roadblock. The closer they got, the louder the noise became.

A grim crowd of poorly dressed people stood there, with bags and packages under their arms, with bundles over their shoulders, with cows and several pack horses jostling between them. A hundred or so stocky peasant men and women, some children and some dogs getting caught underfoot. Smoldering agitation moved through the crowd, with shouts reaching across the open space in front of them, threatening gestures, women's pleas, children crying. Ot and the boy pushed their way into the crowd and up to the muskets. About twenty paces down the road a silent detachment of soldiers was lined up. Out of that motionless iron wall the huge mouths of musket barrels gaped at the crowd, and the soldiers' swords were unfastened, hanging ready at their sides. There were about fifteen of them in the front row, with a swarm of men and weapons behind them. Something was moving in that group behind the iron wall. They were drawing carts together and building a barricade.

The people wanted to get through. The people wanted through at all costs. What are these men doing here, why are they blocking the road? You should be in Bosnia pointing those guns at some Turks!

Were the soldiers going to let them perish among the vagrants, sailors, galley slaves, and other riff-raff that had been pushing up into the highlands from the ports?

Beads of cold sweat formed on the boy's forehead. Johan Ot was pacing around nervously. If they were discovered, if these people discovered fugitive slaves under their peasant's clothes, then there would be no escape. This crowd was dangerous, and an angry mob would be even worse than the soldiers. Worst of all was a frightened mob. Johan Ot had experience with mobs. This one was both angry and frightened. But the fugitives had to stay. This mob was going to get through the roadblock, one way or another.

A few peasants with swords in hand now pushed their way to the front. They were going to free up the road with bloodshed, if need be. Better they be struck down here than submit to the whims of the filthy plague, with its black buboes, pus, and then that horrible, desolate way of kicking off, with everyone running away from you.

The fugitives pushed their way forward, as the front line leaned its backs into the frenzied press of bodies behind it, which billowed and surged ahead. Ot looked into the face of a young soldier in the iron wall, whose eyes danced restlessly over the peasant swords and whose jaw trembled slightly. They're afraid too. Hearts are beating loud and fast in the iron wall too.

"Halt," someone called out from the rear of the soldiers. A young, swarthy-faced officer with a droopy mustache raised his arms and stepped out in front. "Halt."

The crowd wavered. The command passed through the dense group of bodies like a razor, causing it to flutter and droop.

"Just one more step forward," the officer shouted, "and there will be blood."

The mustache stepped all the way forward until he was directly in front of the crowd's first line of men, facing the sharp blades of the armed peasants. Everyone went silent, so that the officer's calm, quiet voice could be heard distinctly.

"We're here to stop you," he said. "And we've stopped plenty others who've had far better weapons in hand."

"Those peashooters," and he pointed a finger back to his men. "Those peashooters make a hole in a body just about the size of your noggin," he said, pointing a finger at the forehead of the peasant standing closest to him.

"Listen to me," he went on. "We have orders signed by Archduke Leopold. These orders are explicit. First, to allow the mail through according to a specific procedure. Second, to allow individuals through who have a *fides*, a medical certificate stating that no one has croaked from the plague in his area over the past six weeks. Third, to allow individuals through who volunteer to spend six weeks in quarantine. We have a shack that holds twenty people and that shack is full. Fourth, in the village below us—and I know this for a fact—whole legions of rats have been dying for the past ten days. In other words, to sum up: for the time being, you may not pass."

Toward the rear of the crowd there was movement and shouting, and this commotion pushed their front line forward. It looked like the brave young officer was not going to be able to stand and lecture them for much longer, and that soon blood would come gushing from his handsome skull.

"For the time being," he howled and the crowd fell silent again. "For the time being, I said. We have set up a new quarantine shack. The lumber has been cut and the Capuchin monks who will tend it are already on the way. In the meantime I want you to set up a camp here. Don't allow any newcomers to join you. We will give you exact medical instructions. Then we'll admit you to quarantine one by one."

"No need," somebody called from the rear. "By then we'll all be lying dead and black."

This realization passed through the crowd like lightning. In its belly, somewhere in its center, it went wild. Anger and fear spilled over into instant madness. The belly of the crowd went wild and roared. As if on command, all of the peasants then shouted so violently that the officer involuntarily stepped back a pace, and that step of his released an avalanche. Objects—walking sticks, stones—came flying from the rear toward the front line of soldiers. Some of his men came running to rescue the officer from the mess he was in, but he was already getting hit by the various projectiles and was covered with blood in an instant. Blunderbusses on tripods then exploded like little cannons. The front row of the crowd wavered. Huge red flowers bloomed. Before the deranged crowd knew it, and before it could push forward, there were explosions all around. Now a chaotic, mad dance ensued. The ones up front pushed to the rear, the belly went wild once more and pushed toward the periphery, and the rear scattered like frightened birds. The women screamed, crazed dogs went running with their tails between their legs into the woods, and the iron wall moved several steps forward, bare swords in hand. Terrified by the iron wall advancing on them and by the wailing and by the bloody wounds all around, the peasants in the front row—or what was left of them— began to turn their weapons against their own people. Against the ones who were mindlessly pushing and shoving forward.

Johan Ot dragged the kid out of this hellish scene of human destruction. Through the crush of bodies and arms shoving in all directions, stocky peasant arms that had lost all control of what they were doing, through the lowing of cows and neighing of horses trying to back out of this latest tangle, past jaws petrified in fear and rage and eyes glistening in madness, through the narrow gaps opened by this dancing madhouse, Ot dragged the youth out. He shuddered when he saw the kid's face. The boy was just as petrified as the peasants: his arms flailing in all directions, and even at

Ot; his eyes not recognizing his benefactor; his jaw trembling and his mouth dribbling white spittle—no, froth—out of its corners and onto his chin. Behind them there was another terrible explosion, but they were out of the crowd now, on the periphery, among the others who had seen their chance to escape and were running over the meadow or into the woods. But anyone who tried to take advantage of the confusion to slip past the barricade sorely miscalculated. Soldiers from the neighboring guard post had come to help and were positioned in firing lines along the edge of the forest that Ot and the boy had tried to get through the night before.

The two fugitives dragged themselves uphill, back toward their overhang and the cupboard above it. When they entered the forest, they could still hear the unbearable screams, curses, and gunfire from the ferocious battle below. No, this was no ordinary fight, this was a mindless riot. For on one side was the plague with its legions of mad rats, and at the other gaped the black barrels of muskets and the glinting blades of swords.

They stopped at the point where the thorny underbrush began and with it the path to the cupboard. It was so quiet here that the silence of this air, saturated with humidity, seemed to be squeezing their temples.

"We're not going up," Ot said. "We'll die of hunger and thirst up there."

So they went back down through the sparse forest, then walked along the ridge and presently saw beneath them the houses of that abandoned village. Now things were different there. From a long way off they could see the big white crosses that someone had painted with lime on the walls, the windows, the doors.

The plague.

The boy gasped for air and sat down.

Without a moment's hesitation, Johan Ot headed down the hillside.

"Whether you die of hunger or the sickness, it's the same shit," he said.

But down below that white cross stopped him in his footsteps. As he stared at it some fear crept from his guts up into his throat. As his eyes scanned the rags and charred remains in the courtyard, he suddenly focused on a huge rat. It lay there helplessly like some undersized pig, with its little black eyes, its legs jutting out to the side. Ot rubbed some garlic under his nose and shoved the rest in his mouth. He kicked the door open and went in.

This time too there wasn't a living or dead soul present. This time too everything was scattered and broken in haste. It wasn't until the third house that Ot found some wine and brandy. On top of the cask, in the dark, his hand felt some plant sprigs. Juniper. This cheered him up.

Loaded down and with a cheerful countenance he returned to where he'd left the kid. Things looked none too good for the boy now. He was sobbing.

"We'll never, ever get past the roadblock. We'll be trapped here, in agony, without any help."

"Keep your mouth shut," Johan Ot shouted, and now he gave the reins to his anger. He dropped the load he was carrying and kicked at the whimpering heap on the ground so that it came unclasped, rolled over, and started beating the ground with its fists.

"I can't go on," the kid moaned. "I'm carrying the sickness. I'm not healthy. In quarantine it clotted in my blood. I can feel it getting ready to strike, inside me."

Something was mounting inside Ot again. A deck was swaying beneath his feet and the hot glare of the sun was pecking at his temples. He clenched his fists and bit into his lip.

But didn't hit the boy again. He let him alone. Let him have his cry. Ot got down to work. He dragged some brush into a heap and lit a fire. He let it burn down and begin to smolder. He shook some of the juniper onto it and broke some green pine branches. Then he poured wine onto the coals, so that the vinegary mixture crackled and stank. He grabbed the kid by the scruff of the neck and shoved his head into the smoke.

"Breathe," he said. "Swallow the smoke."

The boy coughed and choked. His eyes bulged out of their sockets from the strain. Then Ot let go of him and exposed himself to the steam. He pulled some salt from his pocket and rubbed it over the youth's face. He shoved some garlic in the kid's mouth and offered him wine to drink.

"No," the boy waved him away weakly. "No wine from that pestilent village with its white crosses. Stinking rat wine. Rats with white crosses on their backs are crawling everywhere. Everywhere."

"My god," Ot wheezed. "The boy is delirious. Delirious with fear. His eyes are darting all over in fear, terror is making them spin in their sockets. He's going to die like a rat, he'll croak from fear if I don't drag him across the border."

Ot covered the kid with a blanket and moved him closer to the fire. The boy fell asleep instantly. Ot sat down beside him and felt a leaden fatigue weighing on his eyelids. For a moment he succumbed, then he started in his sudden sleep and lifted his head. The fire was still smoldering and a gentle breeze was bending the tops of the trees up above. I have to get across, he thought, I've got to get across. He got up and put more wood on the fire. Then he headed into the forest, walking briskly. Soon he came upon the muddy road and without hesitating followed it toward the fire that shone in the distance like a lamp.

When he got close, he saw figures leaning over and carrying bodies to a huge ditch that had smoke coming out of it. This is what it's like after a battle or the plague, Ot thought.

The peasants were burying their dead. The soldiers kept watch over them from a safe distance. Some women remained at the edge of the ditch, singing their grief in long, mournful refrains. Ot could also hear crying and the murmur of an encampment coming from the forest above the road. They hadn't pushed through. Now they had to follow the officer's instructions. But where was that brave soldier now, Ot wondered, in which tent is blood burbling from his lips?

Several horses were shuffling at the side of the road, just as Ot had expected. He approached them quietly and stroked the first one on the head. The animals didn't seem alarmed at all. This horse looked at him with its dull eyes, as stupid as stone. It let itself be untethered. It had a bit in its mouth and a wooden saddle on its back. Its cargo had been removed. Ot led it into the darkness and the animal placidly followed. Nobody shouted. They had too much crying to do and too much work with their corpses.

Once he was far enough away, Ot mounted.

"There," he said aloud. "Now I'm a horse thief on top of everything else. I'll probably end up hanged, a petty little thieving crook."

The next day was dawning when he returned. The kid was sitting by the extinguished fire, shaking. He didn't even look up at Ot. His eyes were still dancing feverishly. Ot bound up everything they had in a blanket and slung it over the horse's back. The boy complied willingly as Ot hoisted him up into the crudely fashioned but comfortable saddle. Ot took hold of the reins and led the draft animal with the delirious youth on its back out of their encampment.

In a wide arc they skirted the highland with its countless roadblocks and sabotaged paths. In broad daylight they rode down a muddy trail through a ravine. They overtook a filthy tramp who looked at them and laughed.

"Your friend's not healthy," he said.

Ot said nothing in reply.

When they rounded the bend, he heard the tramp call out and laugh: "There's a welcoming party waiting for you in the village."

Johan Ot would have liked to dismount, walk back, and shake the tramp's hand. This was what he had wanted to hear. There was a roadblock up ahead.

At the first diverging path Ot reined the horse in and jumped off into the mud. He picked up the reins and led the horse into the forest. He pulled the kid off the horse and let him sway with all his weight on his shaky legs.

"Sit down," Ot said. "Rest. Tonight you're going to need to be strong for a while."

The kid sat down obediently. Ot stuffed some garlic in his mouth.

"Chew it," he said. "Grind it up."

Toward evening he noticed that the boy's eyes had calmed down and were shining now in his blistery face. As if some new realization had stopped their feverish dance.

"Damn," the kid said. "Why are my guts burning so much. They just burn and burn and burn."

"Hold on," Johan Ot said. "Hold on just a while longer."

He waited until it got good and dark. He threw off all their gear, keeping only a little wine and shaking some of the juniper berries and garlic into his pocket. Then he helped the kid get back onto the horse. The boy had some of his strength back. He would be able to cooperate. Then Ot leaped up onto the horse behind the other's back. The draft saddle was spacious enough for two. Slowly the horse plunked down the road. Ot nudged it on and it struck him that the horse could probably gallop if it had to.

A fire was crackling at the edge of the village. Fat branches popped, as if someone were banging metal against a hollow wall.

They were noticed as soon as they drew close.

Two shadows stood up in the light of the fire and Johan Ot could see them both unfasten the swords at their sides. Doesn't matter, he thought. A routine precaution.

"What's your hurry, damn it," the one standing closest growled. Johan Ot drove the horse a few paces farther on before stopping. He could see the guard's face with perfect clarity. It was covered with a red beard. The man was rubbing his eyes, trying to see in the dark. He had been staring into the flames all this time. That's good, Ot thought. He can't see the boy. All he sees is the darkness.

"Papers?" the red beard snapped in the sleepy, out-of-sorts way that all guards have.

"Sure," Ot said.

"Let me see," the other gurgled and spat.

"You can read a *fides* at ten paces?" Ot asked in a calm, masterful voice.

The other grumbled and came closer, still rubbing his eyes. He doesn't expect a thing, Ot realized. He has no idea what sort of dirty trick is in store for him.

The red beard approached the horse. When he drew even with its head, Ot slammed his foot into the man's chest so hard that the guard didn't even have a chance to groan, and just collapsed into himself. Ot then kicked his horse in the sides with all his might. The sluggish beast whinnied and gamboled and then lurched in pain and despair into its clumsy dray-horse trot. Ot caught sight of the other soldier, who was holding his sword with both hands, and then he heard death whistle over his head with its metallic acuity. The shouting was behind them already and Ot must have been in the middle of the village by the time he noticed the shadows running toward him. But then suddenly they were out of the village, suddenly the horse was mucking down the muddy road, leaving only the shouts knocking around in Ot's head: get him, get him. They rounded a bend and the forest swallowed them. Ot stopped the horse and jumped down into the mud. He grabbed the kid with both hands and jerked him like a sack out of the saddle, and the boy fell into the muck like a bundle of rags. Ot got him onto his feet, put one arm around his waist, and with the other slapped the horse's fat hindquarters and then gave it another swift jab in the belly.

That old nag won't be stopping anytime soon, Ot thought. He dragged the kid, who was wavering on his weak legs, in among the trees, deep into the forest. They must have been a long way from the road when Ot finally heard the sound of their galloping pursuers.

He went on dragging that bag of flesh and bones along behind him, endlessly. I can't, the kid gasped repeatedly, but Ot absolutely refused to give up. You're safe now, he breathed, you're safe, understand? We got through, there's no sickness here. I may have killed you once, but twice now I've given you your life back. Twice, do you hear? This is the second time I've pulled you out of the shit.

At this point even Johan Ot had begun to rave and fuss a bit.

Toward morning the side of a huge barn collided with him. There were no white crosses here, but even so, it was deserted. Ot dragged the youth inside and let him down on the hay in the middle of the large empty space. Ot flopped down beside him. In the middle of the night some gagging and spitting jolted him into a half-sleeping state. The kid was leaning against the wall. He's puking, Johan Ot thought. Too much wine, too much excitement for him. Then he heard his own loud gasping and groaning echo off the walls of the great chamber.

What is this groaning, he thought, what is this whining?

Ot woke up around noon, with light slicing into his eyes. His eyelids were as heavy as lead again, and it felt as though his body had been thoroughly battered and beaten. He raised himself up on his elbows and had a look around the large empty space. It was humid inside and a thick wet substance was trickling down the walls.

The kid lay right beside him. His back was touching Ot, but the boy's head was curled partway toward his knees. He was rolled up in a ball, his arms squeezed to his belly. Ot moved away and gave him a kick in the rear: get up, it's day already. But the huddled body only twitched slightly at the blow and then returned to its original position. Ot took hold of the boy under his arms and pulled. He felt something oozing and sticky under his fingers. The youth's body had stiffened in its fetal position and reacted to the pressure of Ot's hand like any other inelastic substance.

Ot jumped to his feet, stepped over the boy, and using both hands rolled him over on his back. The kid's eyes were covered with pus. Instead of a mouth there was a decaying, soggy cavity covered with some slimy substance. Around his ears, on his neck, on his belly—everywhere—there were elongated, dark cherry-colored boils. Even the familiar blisters on his face had burst and were oozing a slimy pus.

The galley slave stood up straight and looked at his own hands. The stuff he had sunk them into in the taciturn boy's underarms was dripping down his fingers.

"Impossible," he whispered. "Impossible. Did I drag you across just so you could die on me here?"

But the other made no answer. He was irrevocably dead now.

The plague had broken through the roadblocks.

25.

The low vault of an empty sky.

At first it seemed as though the grass was growing so high that its wet tassels reached almost to the tile roof. But it wasn't the grass, because when Ot parted it and approached the black wall, he saw that it had sunk halfway into the ground. He went around to the door. An iron gate hung there, only attached by its hinge at the bottom. It looked like this wrought iron was about to crash inside and bury everything beneath it. The interior was dark with humidity. Mold crept over the walls, and when Ot looked close up, when his eyes drilled through the murk, he saw that there were some extremely tiny animals crawling there and that all of this vermin was slithering and hissing in its endless reproduction, on its march of conquest. Saint Sebastian lay on the floor. He lay on his belly, so that his red-painted cheeks and pierced limbs weren't visible. Next to the piece of wood that had once been an arm, there were some rags. Yes, that had once been his banner. The other beggar was still on his feet. His color had faded completely, he was all gray and gnarled, but his arm still pointed to that swelling on his leg. It was obvious he wouldn't be able to hold out much longer. But the statue of Saint Roch was wedged between the altar and the wall, and that kept him upright. As soon as the wood rotted, or even sooner when the iron gate collapsed, he would be worse off than Sebastian. A few splinters and some damp, decaying wood would be all that was left.

The chapel with its dark red tile roof, its damp and blackened walls, had sunk halfway into the ground. Swampland, humidity, and time. They would swallow it up.

Ot waded into the wet grass and came unstuck from that sunken piece of the world. Now the air was not just humid, it was saturated with some thick substance. He felt a tightness in his chest and several times he lapped at the void, at pure oxygen, which his mouth could never find enough of. He felt he needed wind, a cool, fresh breeze that would drive this pestilent stiffness somewhere else, up into the sky or into the ground or anywhere, that would thin the slime in his veins, in his blood, all through his body.

He glanced back at the chapel again. Those two are finished, he said to himself. And I recognize all of this. I've walked all around here before. All my paths meet here. All the threads come together. All things are fulfilled.

He knew that he was about to step onto the narrow, grassy approach to a bridge. To the left the swamp with its warm vapors and its current through the motionless overgrowth of reeds and grasses, to the right the thick undergrowth, dead and stinking nettles, and the sun up above, persistently glowing through the thick mixture of air and watery tissue, and finally the sparse shrubs on higher land. He knew all this and he wasn't in the least surprised when the stroke of a bell slogged through the clotted air and the black hats of thatched roofs suddenly appeared. He walked down the narrow path between the fences and stopped at a courtyard where an old man was rummaging outside a wooden shack as he talked loudly with someone inside the house. A female voice from within answered him steadily, calling out. The old man noticed Ot and stepped back a pace.

"Don't come in," he said. "Don't come any closer."

Ot stopped at the fence.

"A little wine," he said. "Just a swallow of boiled wine."

"We don't have any," the old man snapped. "We don't have anything."

The old man's eyes glinted with a strange kind of fear.

"I don't have the plague," Ot said.

The old man crossed himself and cast his eyes heavenward. "Nobody knows when he has it," he said.

Ot laughed.

"He's afraid of me," he said, "and I've come so far."

He knew that from here the path led to the tavern and his eyes sought out a particular house and a particular sturdy fellow sinking the blade of his ax into blocks of wood. The house was empty, with boards nailed over the front door. They're running away, he thought. They're running away from their fear.

In the evening he knocked on the tavern door. It echoed emptily inside and nobody answered. Ot kicked at the wood, causing the siding to give way and squeak. Upstairs a window opened and somebody holding a candle looked out, his pale face awash in the glow of the candlelight.

"No vacancies," he called out. "No vacancies tonight."

"How about in the barn?" Ot asked.

"Get going," the voice in the window said calmly. "If you don't want me to punch you in the chest," it added.

Ot walked around the house and crawled under an eave. He collapsed into a Z and fell asleep without a further thought.

He could feel somebody watching him and when he opened his eyes, there before him, indeed, was the innkeeper's angry face. The man stood at a safe distance, holding a club in his hands.

"You bum," he said. "What did I tell you last night, you panhandler?"

Johan Ot smiled and then slowly got up and stretched. The other looked at him, incredulous. Ot grew serious and calmly replied:

"Listen, innkeeper, I know you've used that club to put a lot of people six feet under. But all of them were asleep."

He took one step closer.

"Don't come near me," the innkeeper shouted, backing off. "Don't come near me, you filthy animal."

Ot had to laugh again.

"If I show you what I've got under my arms," he said, "will you talk to me then?"

The innkeeper turned white.

"I'll kill you," he shouted. "I'll kill you."

Johan Ot began to roll up his sleeves.

"How are you going to kill me," he asked, "without touching me, without me spitting on you, without me breathing all over you?"

"If you were sick," the innkeeper's voice softened uncertainly, "you'd have sores and pus all over."

Ot scratched his head. "So you say I've got the plague," he said, "even though it's not visible anywhere. You know, when you can see it, it's already too late."

The innkeeper shifted from one foot to the other, as though thinking it all over intently.

"What do you want?" he said presently.

"Well," Ot said, "now we're getting somewhere. You're going to get me a bottle of wine, some bread, some juniper, and some garlic, and set it out in the courtyard. That's all. It won't cost you much."

The innkeeper turned and went into his house. He could be heard arguing with somebody inside, then he came back out with everything Ot had demanded.

"There," he said. "Now get out of here."

Ot collected the items and stuffed them in his shirt and pockets. Now that the innkeeper could see that the newcomer really didn't have any other intentions, he relaxed and started talking.

"Is there any plague where you've come from?"

Ot had a good laugh. "Just a tiny bit," he said.

The innkeeper grinned with him. "Sure," he said. "That's a concept the plague doesn't understand—'just a tiny bit.' It's either all or nothing. You're oddly good-natured for a tramp. I'd even hazard a guess you've been through a lot worse. Maybe escaped from a galley, or some other horrible way to die . . ."

"It won't get you anything to turn me in," Ot said. "These days even the worst galley slave isn't worth a jug of water. But if you're of a mind to report me, remember this: a galley slave's arm is long, longer even than the arm of the law."

"No, no," the innkeeper shook his head fervently. "I don't ask any questions. People's affairs are none of my business. Making them my business would just be bad business. But one thing," he added after a pause. "Just one more thing. I've seen your dark face somewhere before."

And I've seen yours, Johan Ot said, turning around, and with a dismissive wave of his hand he left the innkeeper standing there.

Out in front there was a big cross with the crucified Christ on it and the Mother of God underneath. Far in the background the outlines of house roofs were visible. The Maid of Heaven was wearing a blue cloak, with what looked like a hood over her head and a gentle look on her face, but she seemed tiny beneath her huge suffering son, who had his bloody hands stretched out from east to west. With her gentle expression she looked down at a sleeping figure beneath her and a horse that the godless fellow had tied right to the cross. Johan Ot poked at the sleeping man's heels. The man started in his sleep and immediately had a dagger in hand, and was on his feet.

"Goddamn it," he said. "Is every miserable hick beggar going to start poking at me now?"

Johan Ot sat down at the man's feet, took a swallow of wine, and then offered it to him. Amazingly, this was the first person he hadn't frightened away, the first not to draw away from him. Still, he didn't accept Ot's wine.

"Thanks," the man said. "I drink my own." He went to his horse and upended a skin there to drink from.

"Really," he said, "it's the best protection."

"That and garlic," Ot said. The other shook his head.

"No," he said. "Wormwood, anise, valerian."

"To each his own," Ot said.

"To each his own," the man with the horse said.

It occurred to Ot that he might actually be able to talk with this traveler roaming the terrified countryside, the same as him. Maybe pick up some useful tip. At least the traveler didn't have that idiotic, terrified look in his eyes.

"Has it already started on the other side?" Ot asked. The fellow took another swig from his skin.

"Not yet," he said. "But if I were you, I wouldn't be in a hurry to get there. Those people have gone just a bit crazy with fear."

He told Ot that the locals, who in ordinary times had hearts of gold, had a strange custom. During the last plague, thirty years ago, something had come over them, and they decided to dig a big pit—a grave, in fact—in front of the church. They vowed to use it to bury the first person who left the church during Mass. It turned out that a young girl had a sick mother at home. She ran outside and they buried her mercilessly. Alive. Elsewhere a young man returning from his girl's house at night was also caught and buried alive. Now the fear had grabbed them again and it could well happen that somebody else was going to bite the dust like that, in one of those villages. The people were convinced that this burial rite had already helped them once. Sure, they'd been stricken with grief over the poor girl, but what else could they do?

"So there you go," the fellow said. "Best not to be on your own in these parts."

He waited to see what kind of effect his words would have. Johan Ot reached to his forehead and wiped off the patches of moisture collecting all over his skin. When he said nothing in reply, the traveler climbed up on his horse.

"But I must admit," he said, "that so far they've managed to fend off the plague. There's order there. That's due to strict laws and steadfast faith. If only they could manage without the live burials . . ."

Johan Ot waved a hand dismissively and gritted his teeth.

"They won't bury me," he said. "Not me."

Or burn me, or hang me, or starve me, he added after the other offered his "God forbid" and swayed off on horseback toward the inn. Not now, not anymore.

After that, things veered quite suddenly and unexpectedly from this peaceable scene of homecoming toward their conclusion.

All afternoon Ot hid out in a copse above the village. When it got dark he went down to a certain house. A timid silence reigned all around. There wasn't the sound of a single dog or a single human voice. The door was nailed shut and so were the windows. Ot tried to rip a board off, but the wood moaned and squeaked so nastily from the rusty nails that he dropped that plan. He climbed up a tree to get onto the roof, which was in shambles. Huge black holes yawned in the straw. He let himself down carefully, but something gave way under his hands and he crashed down until he felt a huge cloud of dust descending on him and then rising back up. The interior of the house had been completely trashed. They must have made an awful noise in here, he thought. The house had been looted down to the last nail. Only the damp walls remained and black dirt on the floor. Ot took off his thick peasant jacket, spread it on the floor, and sat down. He leaned with his back against the wall.

In the middle of the night he heard movement outside. Somebody was prowling around the walls. Then from right up close, behind his back, a voice spoke.

"Look," the voice testified, insistent yet subdued. "Somebody let himself in through the roof. Somebody is inside the bewitched house."

Ot was on his feet in an instant. He pressed up against the wall and held his breath. A board on the window groaned. Then another was yanked off, and somebody stuck his head inside. It turned this way and that through the opening and Johan Ot felt an enormous urge to punch the nosy, rotating melon right in the temple. Then it vanished.

"There's nobody there," it said outside.

"But I saw someone, I saw them," the other kept insisting.

"There's nothing," said the one who had just been offering his neck to blade and club. "There's nothing now. Tomorrow we'll report it to the judge. The bewitched house is not to be trifled with. Some dangerous creature could sneak back inside."

They left after they nailed the window shut again. Ot rested for a while and at first daylight he decided to leave. But how? He tried jumping up to grab a sheaf of straw and pull himself out. The door and windows were nailed shut. Damn it, he said. Don't tell me I've climbed into jail in my own house? He stood in the middle of the room and hesitated. The morning sunlight streamed in white cones through the holes in the roof. He figured they must have nailed the window shut with the same nails they'd pulled out, since they probably didn't have tools with them. They would have used some stone to hammer them back in. Ot slipped the blade of his knife into a crack and pulled. The boards groaned. He hit at them with his fist until his skin flushed red and then the wood finally gave way. He threw his jacket and bottle out the window and wedged himself into the opening. For a moment it seemed he was stuck. He shook and thrashed wearily. If they catch me like this, he thought, trapped in the window of this ramshackle building, barely upright . . . At this thought he shuddered so violently that he slipped right through the hole like a fish and rolled into the wet grass.

And so he returned, and things veered suddenly, unexpectedly toward their conclusion.

For when he came into town, everything had been abandoned and everything had gone mad. Until then the sickness had walked behind him or with him, but now it was a step ahead of him.

Neither roadblocks nor pesthouses, neither plague commissars nor fervent prayers, not even the live burial of young maidens could hold it back. Not even Sebastian and Roch, who at this point were alone in the last gasps of their battle with its poisonous vapors down in the lonesome, dark chapel.

There was no guard at the city gate, there were no more security measures. In a single moment everything had collapsed. A sort of procession was creeping out of the town toward a grassy meadow. Its members moved unbelievably slowly, wailing their endless lament intended to reach up to heaven and perhaps move someone there to pity, but which instead dissipated in the rubbery, oily atmosphere full of pestilent matter. Carts filled to the top with all kinds of junk proceeded past the lamenters. Some people scrambled to get inside, others to get out. Some ran out on the streets, while others locked themselves in their houses. The soldiers had lost their authority and the guards threw their weapons on the ground.

Now it was each man for himself.

The town had gone mad.

Panic had conquered it. Chaos would obliterate it.

A crowd of merrymakers broke into a tavern. They rolled barrels out from the cellar and tapped into them. They would go out happy and drunk.

Johan Ot insinuated himself into this merriest and wildest of company. And that's where he found out.

It had broken out that night.

The rumors all conflicted. Some claimed there were already dozens of dead, while others claimed that the dying had only just begun. The sickness had broken out in a pesthouse, a quarantine. No, a cat had crawled into some nun's bed a few days ago. When they opened her cell, she had turned black. No, a trader had stayed overnight at the inn and then left. Then an official from the provincial capital gave up the ghost in the same bed. The plague had crept into the fur coat of some Croatian soldier. Merchants had brought it. It came overnight. Just yesterday nobody expected it, just yesterday order and good will still ruled in the town. Just yesterday the market was full of life, the court was in session, and the stores and workshops were open. But last night they had found a corpse with black spots. The plague had lurked in dirty water. It had come borne by pestilent air.

That morning the authorities had tried to conceal the truth and reassert control. But there was nothing they could do. In an instant the realization spread from one person to the next and an indescribable panic seized the populace.

God's punishment didn't permit itself even the least respite. It didn't rest for even the briefest moment once it had presented its papers: I'm here.

Loners locked themselves inside their shacks. Once everything was over, their stinking, disintegrating remains would be found there.

Merrymakers crowded into the taverns. With women and wine. All the barriers were down. All inequality vanished. No one harassed anyone else. Everyone was stuck here, all facing the same fate.

Friend abandoned friend, wife abandoned husband, daughter abandoned parents. In a single day the taverns filled to the rafters. Nobody knew where these unknown comedians and musicians came from, nor all the whores and galley slaves. They had simply been sucked into this mad vortex from all sides.

Abandoned children wandered the streets. Capuchin monks nailed plague houses shut.

Lunatics with their spells and flagellant processions reappeared. Robbers and beggars too. Witches offered their brews. Poisoners offered their poisons.

Wild shouting, chaotic singing, and horrible blasphemy.

In a single moment everything came apart. Chaos and universal delirium whirled together.

Johan Ot had arrived at just the right moment. At his beginning and his end. Things were lurching so suddenly and so quickly toward their inevitable end, into the final abyss.

The chaos and madness lasted for two days. On the morning of the third day bands of soldiers pressed in through the city gates, followed by Capuchins, plague commissars, officials, volunteers, and convicts—these last having been offered the job as an opportunity to demonstrate that they had been reformed. The big white crosses that they painted and that began to appear on the doors and windows of certain houses were the first sign that someone was trying to take matters in hand. Clouds of smoke began billowing through the streets. The officials saturated the infected houses with juniper smoke, then gave them a thorough airing out. Fires were lit. Heaps of fuel for bonfires grew in courtyards and right outside the front doors of houses. Rags, furniture, clothing—everything found its way onto the heaps. Bailiffs locked up houses and nailed boards all over them. Several houses by the river were emptied out and used as quarantines. Apothecaries were found and forced to begin grinding and brewing their powders and potions. Barbers were assembled and forced into the baths, where they handled the sick and bled them of their pestilent blood. The most suspicious among those infected were isolated and the convicts brought food to them in baskets hanging from long poles.

It looked as though the authorities were going to be able to stanch the chaos, even if they were unable to apprehend the original culprit who had brought the plague into their midst. They launched exacting, thorough investigations. The epicenter had to be found and destroyed. The plague had to breed somewhere, it had needed to start someplace, and that would be the source of all this evil.

The investigation pointed to a tavern by the city gate, where the more affluent merchants gathered. They would conclude their deals there and wash them down in the company of young strumpets, of whom there was no shortage in these difficult times (or in better times, for that matter). The officials applied the screws to the innkeeper and anyone who hadn't yet fled. News spread quickly. The sickness had indeed been brought by merchants who had used forged documents to squeeze past the roadblocks. One of them was found lying lifeless in bed, with black boils and nasty abscesses. The innkeeper had wanted to suppress the whole business. The dead man had been dumped into the river at night, his clothes and bedding secretly incinerated, and the ashes buried in the ground. Naïvely, the innkeeper and his accomplices thought that would be the end of it. But it was already too late. It had already erupted. The accused could all have fled in the resulting chaos, but it didn't occur to any of them that anyone would start an investigation in this madhouse. The criminals were apprehended while drinking and debauching themselves. They literally had to drag the merchant in question—who, together with the innkeeper, would answer for the crime—off and out of a whore.

At the very first hearing, even before having any proper pressure applied to him, the man made such unusual statements that the whole case became clear. The fellow had the devil within him. He comported himself aggressively and shamelessly, denying his guilt vociferously and claiming that God always, but always visited his punishment upon the proper people.

The news instantly made its way through the whole town. That same evening the talk at all the inn tables was of the envoy of the devil who had come to sow mad plague seeds among them. Who had testified that the plague only ever struck down the feeble-minded and the iniquitous. That same evening, groups of drunken and infuriated townspeople rioted through the streets and demanded the merchant's head. The comedians and musicians had already composed scathing ditties about the merchant who carried the plague in a beggar's bag from one town to the next. With the assistance of Satan, of course.

And what was most surprising of all, what confirmed the suspicions raised during the very first hearing: the plague now went underground. Not completely, of course, but instead of the ten victims it had taken down the first day, on the day after the evildoer was arrested, only five people died. Based on all the vast experience and all the knowledge that the plague commissars had amassed, there should have been more victims. This was the best proof that they were on the trail of the source of the misfortune. That they had seized the serpent by the throat. All that was left was to crush its head.

In the morning a crowd of happy townsfolk gathered outside the city hall, where a summary court was going to pronounce its verdict, and the defendant, without any doubt, would be led through the streets to the gallows, the river, or the stake. Barricaded houses had opened back up, and alongside healthy citizens there were those already shaking with fever, as well as peasants, soldiers, officials, Capuchins, and other men, women, and children—everyone jostling one another to get a look at the fiend who had brought the seeds of evil into their town as he met his just end, and the dark misfortune of which he was the agent was ended as well. Only the most cautious townspeople remained in their houses and watched the merrymaking in the streets and on the square from behind half-open shutters. In vain did the head plague commissar issue a decree commanding all citizens to remain indoors, because today a criminal and envoy of the devil was going to be justly punished—put to death, of course. In vain did the Capuchins and the physicians in their beaked masks try to convince the people that the slaughter was not yet over, that Satan's messenger had sown and scattered his seeds, and that the plague would continue to rampage. Nothing had any effect. Everyone rushed out into the open. The air smelled of the wine and juniper smoke that the Capuchins were waving overhead, as well as of garlic and other piquant scents. But mostly of wine. A majority of the townsfolk were dangerously drunk and the soldiers had lost their taste for trying to subdue them.

In the meantime, a surprising piece of news swept through the crowd. It even reached into the tavern where Johan Ot was swigging wine. That night, express couriers had brought new evidence related to the investigation of the criminal merchant. The condemned man didn't deny a thing. He even went through all the accusations and confirmed them, one by one: yes, he had been whelped in a Satanic nest. His grandmother had been fried alive. But the fiends inhabiting the brood she had whelped lived on. Why, she had plucked the eyes out of Christ on the cross and gone blind. She had forced mothers to murder their own children. She had given people potions that caused their skin to peel off. Together with other witches, she had killed a peasant. Now everything was as clear as day. Now there was no longer the least hint of doubt.

The guards who brought—or rather, shoved—the accused through the tall, arched doorway of the city hall were dressed in long cloaks, leather gloves reached up their arms, and their faces were concealed behind enormous masks. Only their eyes and red mouths were visible through small openings. At a safe distance behind them came the judges with all the insignia of their rank, followed by the commanders of the interventionist forces and the plague commissars. The first circle was completed by Capuchins carrying smoking juniper branches, and the second circle by soldiers with lances and truncheons in hand. They swung these at the good, honest folk before them and beat the nearest ones on the head, so that for the duration of the procession there was always an empty space around the diabolical evildoer.

The people roared with enthusiasm and rage when the company moved from the courtyard out the door of city hall. Each one was squeezing a cross or a small icon of Saint Sebastian in hand, as well as Saint Roch or Saint Rosalia, a statuette or tiny image of the Immaculate Virgin, and, at the very least, a stone, a piece of wood, or some other hard object that they could fling in the face of that criminal beast.

The guards shoved the miscreant onto a wagon drawn by an old, limping nag. One of the justices climbed to the top of a wall and held a piece of paper high in the air. He began to read. In all the uncontrollable shouting, not a word of it could be heard.

Then the procession moved on.

Johan Ot sat in the half-empty tavern. He was full to the brim with wine and his head kept slipping into the lap of an ample woman who stroked his head now and then, but for the most part stared vacantly at all the commotion outside. In a corner a few musicians who had finally been given a break were also nodding off. The tavern had been demolished. Chairs were broken and wine trickled across the floor past broken jugs and pieces of meat and was splashed over the walls and windows. All signs pointed to this being the end of the merrymaking, because as soon as the noose cinched taut around that merchant's neck, order would be reestablished, and the galley slaves, whores, decommissioned old soldiers, and musicians would be swept away with the rubble.

Outside, the start of the day's great event was announced by the shouts and drunken booing of those who preferred not to gather around in front of city hall and instead just headed outside with mug in hand so they could wait for the miscreant to pass by the taverns and then head straight back inside to celebrate his death. Their shouts merged with the rage of the approaching crowd, which was producing a hellish din as it marched downhill. Drumming, shouts, hymns, prayers, and curses—everything mixed and blended together, sounding as though a great tidal wave was approaching. Johan Ot got up and steadied himself on his table. He picked up his mug, knocked back a big swallow, and staggered to the door on his shaky legs. Just then the wave hit the building and everything shook. There was movement outside the door, and somebody inside shouted, "He's here, he's here," and indeed, there he was. High above all the heads outside there swayed a young face that was a bit flushed from drink and a bit bloody from a cut that trickled from its forehead down to its cheek. As the condemned approached, the people around Johan Ot pressed crosses and holy icons to their lips. The din had well and truly arrived now, and Ot got shoved aside and ground up against the wall. The fellow up above was shouting at the yelping, enraged crowd: "You're all going to die in the filth of your own cruelty and stupidity!"—or, anyway, that, more or less, was what Johan Ot could make out from among the words of the snarling beast on the cart, who must indeed have had some devil under his skin to be struggling so madly, so hopelessly, alone.

But at the same moment Ot had a flash of recognition. It coursed through him so violently that his whole body shook, as though seized by a spasm. He felt nauseated by this sudden clarity and all of his drunkenness passed in a trice. He had to hold onto the wall. A razor-sharp thought ploughed through his innards.

Adam, the thought billowed and flared, as though a sizzling ember were passing from his guts to his chest and out through his mouth. That's Adam.

Ot shoved aside some drunk who stood in his way and dashed after the howling mob that was already receding. He got close enough that he could see Adam's face again, contorted in constant shouting.

Ot pushed into the wall of bodies wherever he could. Adam, he shouted, you fool, why did you confess, you damned fool, you don't believe, you've never believed, Adam, wait, you goddamned madman, what did you blab to them?

But the wall was solid. Ot couldn't get through and even his voice got lost in all the frightful din. The merchant had so enraged the crowd with his shouting that he had only the soldiers and Capuchins to thank for the fact that the crowd wasn't smashing him against the cobblestones right there and ripping the skin off his body.

Johan Ot assaulted the wall of bodies once more. He bit and pummeled his way toward the cart. He had the impression that the condemned man's eyes fixed on him for a moment. Ot felt their gazes meet, but the merchant didn't recognize him. Adam looked at and through Ot with a glassy stare.

Then the crowd engulfed the cart. The wave passed over Ot. He was left standing as if his way were barred by a wall of bricks, rather than of men. I never had a chance, he thought, I never even had a chance to tell him that I was spawned in a witch's nest too, that there's a devil in me, too.

The crowd surrounding Satan's envoy had now reached the bottom of the street. Ot saw their hands reaching up. Somebody had managed to grab Adam. They were going to spread him all over the ground after all.

But he wasn't lynched. The authorities still held the reins. They succeeded in seeing the entire process through to its conclusion in a lawful and dignified way. They hanged Adam, then they sewed the body up in a bag and sank it to the bottom of the river.

This, however, was the last lawful act that the city authorities performed with the help of the interventionist units. Because that night the plague struck as never before.

The people caroused in the taverns and out in the streets. The devil's brood had been extirpated—or, actually, just one limb of the devil's brood (the innkeeper was let off with a jail sentence of several years for non-compliance with health and hygienic measures)—its sorcerous seed washed away, the epicenter of the sickness demolished, the serpent's head crushed.

But late that night, at the height of the revelry, there was a disturbance. Capuchin monks and physicians wearing beaked masks began cropping up everywhere. They used long hooks to drag swollen, blackened, stinking corpses out of houses. At first just here and there; at first it appeared these were just the last few cases, the last gasps of the killer as she swung her black fist a few final times on her way out. But soon it turned out that this night was proving worse than the previous ones. A few men began spewing in a street here, a few others collapsed in a tavern there. No, this was no mere drunken vomiting. This was the plague.

Now the town went entirely insane. A drunken crowd surged against the city gate: out, let us out, we're all going to die here. The gate was locked and there were guards armed with mounted harquebuses on the ramparts. There were a few explosions and then the crowd surged toward city hall. Stones clattered against its façade. But no one was there to say whether the gate would be opened or kept shut to keep the pestilent killer from raging through the countryside. Because there were few people still alive inside city hall. The judges, plague commissars, court bailiffs, scribes, prosecutors, and hangmen—everyone who had gathered for the good, old, customary trial banquet had been dragged off one by one by the Capuchins and crows' beaks with their huge iron hooks. Dead. Whoever was left had barricaded themselves in a separate room with a guard posted outside.

Someone still ruled, someone was still issuing orders to the soldiers, someone was still trying to keep order, but the crowd couldn't find out who it was. More and more sick people mingled with the healthy ones. They would babble and stagger, hug the walls, and try to crawl off into hidden corners, harried by a terrible fear. Some of them vomited, while others fouled the air with their diarrhea. They would clutch their bellies and scream that it was ripping their guts to shreds.

They died on the streets and in back rooms.

Toward morning the crowds had dispersed, retreating into the houses, barns and shacks.

With their long iron hooks the Capuchins and the crows' beaks dragged the dead into huge plague ditches with smoke rising out of them, as though hellfire were raging below.

A terrible stench pervaded the air.

That night the city counted nearly thirty dead.

The taverns were a scene of recklessness, immorality, delirium, and crime.

Nobody knew from what cave the countless criminals, prostitutes, beggars, fire-jumpers, poisoners, gypsies, strange disfigured faces, and cripples had crawled—the sort of people that honest folk would give a wide berth to in healthy times—if they didn't light a fire under their feet, that is. But now this swarm had risen up and skittered to this scene of human misery, its final end. The authorities had tried to take matters back in hand by ordering the arrest of some old witch and trying to put together a new trial, but nobody cared about that anymore. For how many years they had been putting these vermin away in towers of justice, committing them to the galleys, cutting off their noses and ears, for how many years they had been hanging and burning them—and behold, now all this human filth had risen up out of the swamplands and slithered into these insane taverns, mixing with honest townfolk. Yes, suddenly they were all equals. No one was pointing a finger at anyone now.

They all swilled wine and swallowed the herbs that old potion makers had brought with them: pine sap, juniper berries, garlic, chicory, germander, lemon rind, rue, and lilac berries. They downed brandy and oil and wormwood wine. On and on they drank, shamelessly reaching for women, shoving masks over their faces and throwing their money around. No one was anyone's debtor. No one was anyone's anything. They were all here together facing the end, and the plague's cold embrace.

No one remembered the merchant who'd had the noose tightened around his neck that day and then been dropped underwater. Some Capuchin who had abandoned his duties began raving and telling everyone that the plague's envoy had in fact been God's envoy—God's, he shouted, not Satan's, but nobody listened. Johan Ot saw the man's inflamed eyes, with mucous oozing out of them, and he knew: this one's a goner.

Of himself Ot knew this: I never exist and I won't this time, either. He sat in the middle of all the mad merrymaking with a jug of wine in front of him and he listened to the bitter pain that was glowing in his guts and reaching up toward his chest. There its cold grip clasped his heart. He had Adam's face, swollen from drink, always before his eyes, and that trickle of blood coming from somewhere under his hair. His shouts and his hopeless lone fight with the drunken, terrified, antagonized mob. Its noise surged through Ot's skull incessantly until it finally subsided. In the sudden silence he gaped at the jug before him, while that monstrous jumble of heads continued to billow before his eyes. It was completely quiet, that crowd, emitting no sounds, just gently wafting and rocking. The dangerous crowd washed before Ot like the silent and dangerous waters of the Western Sea.

In that silence he got up and passed through all the contorted faces and masks, past the hands that reached up with fingers outstretched in front of him.

Outside the evening was dense with stale air. Ot lifted his jug to his lips and his eyes scanned the low vault of the empty sky. He felt faint and leaned against a wall. How weakly his legs were holding him upright. His muscles were giving out, like they were turning into

fat and would collapse at any second. A strange fear latched onto
Ot, and he felt his chest constrict. When, he thought, when was the
last time I felt afraid? He wandered around the building and a dark
shadow drew a wide arc around him. Out back in the courtyard the
barn door stood wide open. Inside there was light. Ot went toward
its glow. The remains of a fire were gently shimmering and dying.
Weakly he scooped up an armful of straw and threw it onto the embers, so that it flared up and illuminated the big, empty, silent space.
He reached into his pocket and threw a fistful of juniper into the
flames as well. It smoked, its acrid scent spreading through the barn.
Ot sat down on the ground, leaning his back against the wall, and
he put a big clove of garlic in his mouth, chasing it with nearly half
his jug of wine, which he downed in big gulps. Those other embers
in his guts and chest weren't letting up, they refused to be quenched
in the cascade of warm wine slush that he poured onto them. They
burned and burned. And while it burned inside, down below, a sharp,
caustic pain was spreading through his head. It pushed outward, and
Ot could feel it jab at his eyes, causing his eyeballs to bulge out of his
skull. He leaned over toward the fire. He picked out a piece of dead,
blackened wood. Slowly he turned toward the wall and with an unsteady hand he painstakingly drew the following sign:

S	A	T	A	N
A	D	A	M	A
T	A	B	A	T
A	M	A	D	A
N	A	T	A	S

He took a deep breath and leaned his head on the wall beside the inscription. He felt overcome with weakness, and he tried helplessly to expel the fire from his guts, from the soft tissue moving and slithering inside. Then in his skull he once more felt the sharp grip of the pain that was trying to detonate everything around him. He vomited on himself: he spat up all his vinous, pus-ridden, mucilaginous innards. He tried to wipe off the slobber that crept down his chin, but his raglike arm refused to obey him.

His body was disintegrating, and when he lay down on the floor, his stinging eyes could see on the ceiling, through the flickering shadows, big stains and damp spots creeping together and apart, contorting into fuzzy, indistinct shapes. They crept and moved in the silence. The terrible silence throbbing in his head and this space.

Then he heard voices. They came closer and then in through the doorway. All at once they were thundering beneath the rafters of that cavernous space. Discussing something or other in ordinary words. He wanted to say something, but he couldn't open his mouth. Then he saw them.

There were two of them standing tall by the fire, their shapes reaching almost up to the ceiling. One of them was wearing a long, waxed cloak, his head covered with a hood. He had a small bag hanging around his neck which almost certainly contained the sanctified host. His right hand held a long, white stick that was curled at one end, while he was using his left to rub some ointment or other on his face. The other figure was wearing a mask over his cloak, with a big, beaklike nose on it. In the place where his eyes should have been, there were glass goggles that reflected the flame. Juniper, the first one said. The wretch was trying to save himself. The priest pushed the hood off his head and bent down to the ground, toward his eyes. Johan Ot looked into that toothless mouth that kept moving and talking, just as another once had, a long time ago, next to the same wan face. As if that damned beggar Anton with his vile breath were leaning over him once more.

The Capuchin stood back up and shrugged his shoulders. Did you bring the mint balm? the one with the beak and the glass goggles asked. Yes, his companion answered, and the lemon and wormwood too. He was silent for a moment, and then he gave a subdued laugh and added: Well, sure, and some wine.

The beaked one put on his leather gloves and brought a long iron hook in through the doorway. He hooked it onto Johan Ot's trouser leg and pulled. Look, the Capuchin said, look at the scars he has around his waist. The other bent down. A galley slave, he said. That's from the chains.

Again he could feel the beaked one pull on the hook. His head thudded onto the floor.

I'll get out of this, he thought. I'm going to get out of this.

Tomorrow I'll be sober and these damn dreams will be gone for good.

In 2010, the Slovenian Book Agency took a bold step toward solving the problem of how few literary works are now translated into English, initiating a program to provide financial support for a series dedicated to Slovenian literature at Dalkey Archive Press. Partially evolving from a relationship that Dalkey Archive and the Vilenica International Literary Festival had developed a few years previously, this program will go on to ensure that both classic and contemporary works from Slovenian are brought into English, while allowing the Press to undertake marketing efforts far exceeding what publishers can normally provide for works in translation.

Slovenia has always held a great reverence for literature, with the Slovenian national identity being forged through its fiction and poetry long before the foundation of the contemporary Republic: "It is precisely literature that has in some profound, subtle sense safeguarded the Slovenian community from the imperialistic appetites of stronger and more expansive nations in the region," writes critic Andrej Inkret. Never insular, Slovenian writing has long been in dialogue with the great movements of world literature, from the romantic to the experimental, seeing the literary not as distinct from the world, but as an integral means of perceiving and even amending it.

DRAGO JANČAR was born in 1948 in Maribor, Slovenia, and is one of the best-known Slovenian writers at home and abroad. After studying law, he worked as a journalist, an editor, and a freelance writer, and traveled to both the U.S. and Germany. In 1993, he received the highest Slovenian literary award, the Prešeren Prize, for his lifetime achievement, and in 2009 he was awarded the Premio Hemingway. His novels include *Northern Lights* and *Mocking Desire*. He lives in Ljubljana.

MICHAEL BIGGINS's other translations of Slovenian literature include the novels *Northern Lights* and *Mocking Desire* by Drago Jančar, Boris Pahor's *Necropolis*, Vladimir Bartol's *Alamut*, and several collections of poetry by Tomaž Šalamun. He teaches Russian and Slovenian languages and curates the Slavic and Baltic library collections at the University of Washington in Seattle.

Collected Stories.
The Journalist.
My Life in CIA.
Singular Pleasures.
The Sinking of the Odradek
  Stadium.
Tlooth.
20 Lines a Day.
JOSEPH MCELROY,
  Night Soul and Other Stories.
THOMAS MCGONIGLE,
  Going to Patchogue.
ROBERT L. MCLAUGHLIN, ED., Innovations:
  An Anthology of
  Modern & Contemporary Fiction.
ABDELWAHAB MEDDEB, Talismano.
GERHARD MEIER, Isle of the Dead.
HERMAN MELVILLE, The Confidence-Man.
AMANDA MICHALOPOULOU, I'd Like.
STEVEN MILLHAUSER,
  The Barnum Museum.
  In the Penny Arcade.
RALPH J. MILLS, JR.,
  Essays on Poetry.
MOMUS, The Book of Jokes.
CHRISTINE MONTALBETTI, Western.
OLIVE MOORE, Spleen.
NICHOLAS MOSLEY, Accident.
  Assassins.
  Catastrophe Practice.
  Children of Darkness and Light.
  Experience and Religion.
  God's Hazard.
  The Hesperides Tree.
  Hopeful Monsters.
  Imago Bird.
  Impossible Object.
  Inventing God.
  Judith.
  Look at the Dark.
  Natalie Natalia.
  Paradoxes of Peace.
  Serpent.
  Time at War.
  The Uses of Slime Mould:
  Essays of Four Decades.
WARREN MOTTE,
  Fables of the Novel: French Fiction
  since 1990.
  Fiction Now: The French Novel in
  the 21st Century.
  Oulipo: A Primer of Potential
  Literature.
GERALD MURNANE, Barley Patch.
YVES NAVARRE, Our Share of Time.
  Sweet Tooth.
DOROTHY NELSON, In Night's City.
  Tar and Feathers.
ESHKOL NEVO, Homesick.
WILFRIDO D. NOLLEDO, But for the Lovers.
FLANN O'BRIEN,
  At Swim-Two-Birds.
  At War.
  The Best of Myles.
  The Dalkey Archive.
  Further Cuttings.
  The Hard Life.
  The Poor Mouth.
  The Third Policeman.
CLAUDE OLLIER, The Mise-en-Scène.
  Wert and the Life Without End.
PATRIK OUŘEDNÍK, Europeana.

The Opportune Moment, 1855.
BORIS PAHOR, Necropolis.
FERNANDO DEL PASO,
  News from the Empire.
  Palinuro of Mexico.
ROBERT PINGET, The Inquisitory.
  Mahu or The Material.
  Trio.
A. G. PORTA, The No World Concerto.
MANUEL PUIG,
  Betrayed by Rita Hayworth.
  The Buenos Aires Affair.
  Heartbreak Tango.
RAYMOND QUENEAU, The Last Days.
  Odile.
  Pierrot Mon Ami.
  Saint Glinglin.
ANN QUIN, Berg.
  Passages.
  Three.
  Tripticks.
ISHMAEL REED,
  The Free-Lance Pallbearers.
  The Last Days of Louisiana Red.
  Ishmael Reed: The Plays.
  Juice!
  Reckless Eyeballing.
  The Terrible Threes.
  The Terrible Twos.
  Yellow Back Radio Broke-Down.
JOÃO UBALDO RIBEIRO, House of the
  Fortunate Buddhas.
JEAN RICARDOU, Place Names.
RAINER MARIA RILKE, The Notebooks of
  Malte Laurids Brigge.
JULIÁN RÍOS, The House of Ulysses.
  Larva: A Midsummer Night's Babel.
  Poundemonium.
  Procession of Shadows.
AUGUSTO ROA BASTOS, I the Supreme.
DANIËL ROBBERECHTS,
  Arriving in Avignon.
JEAN ROLIN, The Explosion of the
  Radiator Hose.
OLIVIER ROLIN, Hotel Crystal.
ALIX CLEO ROUBAUD, Alix's Journal.
JACQUES ROUBAUD, The Form of a
  City Changes Faster, Alas, Than
  the Human Heart.
  The Great Fire of London.
  Hortense in Exile.
  Hortense Is Abducted.
  The Loop.
  Mathématique:
  The Plurality of Worlds of Lewis.
  The Princess Hoppy.
  Some Thing Black.
LEON S. ROUDIEZ, French Fiction Revisited.
RAYMOND ROUSSEL, Impressions of Africa.
VEDRANA RUDAN, Night.
STIG SÆTERBAKKEN, Siamese.
LYDIE SALVAYRE, The Company of Ghosts.
  Everyday Life.
  The Lecture.
  Portrait of the Writer as a
  Domesticated Animal.
  The Power of Flies.
LUIS RAFAEL SÁNCHEZ,
  Macho Camacho's Beat.
SEVERO SARDUY, Cobra & Maitreya.
NATHALIE SARRAUTE,
  Do You Hear Them?

SELECTED DALKEY ARCHIVE PAPERBACKS

Martereau.
The Planetarium.
Arno Schmidt, *Collected Novellas.*
Collected Stories.
Nobodaddy's Children.
Two Novels.
Asaf Schurr, *Motti.*
Christine Schutt, *Nightwork.*
Gail Scott, *My Paris.*
Damion Searls, *What We Were Doing*
and Where We Were Going.
June Akers Seese,
Is This What Other Women Feel Too?
What Waiting Really Means.
Bernard Share, *Inish.*
Transit.
Aurelie Sheehan,
Jack Kerouac Is Pregnant.
Viktor Shklovsky, *Bowstring.*
Knight's Move.
A Sentimental Journey:
Memoirs 1917–1922.
Energy of Delusion: A Book on Plot.
Literature and Cinematography.
Theory of Prose.
Third Factory.
Zoo, or Letters Not about Love.
Claude Simon, *The Invitation.*
Pierre Siniac, *The Collaborators.*
Kjersti A. Skomsvold, *The Faster I Walk,*
the Smaller I Am.
Josef Škvorecký, *The Engineer of*
Human Souls.
Gilbert Sorrentino,
Aberration of Starlight.
Blue Pastoral.
Crystal Vision.
Imaginative Qualities of Actual
Things.
Mulligan Stew.
Pack of Lies.
Red the Fiend.
The Sky Changes.
Something Said.
Splendide-Hôtel.
Steelwork.
Under the Shadow.
W. M. Spackman,
The Complete Fiction.
Andrzej Stasiuk, *Dukla.*
Fado.
Gertrude Stein,
Lucy Church Amiably.
The Making of Americans.
A Novel of Thank You.
Lars Svendsen, *A Philosophy of Evil.*
Piotr Szewc, *Annihilation.*
Gonçalo M. Tavares, *Jerusalem.*
Joseph Walser's Machine.
Learning to Pray in the Age of
Technique.
Lucian Dan Teodorovici,
Our Circus Presents . . .
Nikanor Teratologen, *Assisted Living.*
Stefan Themerson, *Hobson's Island.*
The Mystery of the Sardine.
Tom Harris.
John Toomey, *Sleepwalker.*
Jean-Philippe Toussaint,
The Bathroom.
Camera.
Monsieur.

Running Away.
Self-Portrait Abroad.
Television.
The Truth about Marie.
Dumitru Tsepeneag,
Hotel Europa.
The Necessary Marriage.
Pigeon Post.
Vain Art of the Fugue.
Esther Tusquets, *Stranded.*
Dubravka Ugresic,
Lend Me Your Character.
Thank You for Not Reading.
Mati Unt, *Brecht at Night.*
Diary of a Blood Donor.
Things in the Night.
Álvaro Uribe and Olivia Sears, eds.,
Best of Contemporary Mexican
Fiction.
Eloy Urroz, *Friction.*
The Obstacles.
Luisa Valenzuela, *Dark Desires and*
the Others.
He Who Searches.
Marja-Liisa Vartio,
The Parson's Widow.
Paul Verhaeghen, *Omega Minor.*
Aglaja Veteranyi, *Why the Child Is*
Cooking in the Polenta.
Boris Vian, *Heartsnatcher.*
Llorenç Villalonga, *The Dolls' Room.*
Ornela Vorpsi, *The Country Where No*
One Ever Dies.
Austryn Wainhouse, *Hedyphagetica.*
Paul West,
Words for a Deaf Daughter & Gala.
Curtis White,
America's Magic Mountain.
The Idea of Home.
Memories of My Father Watching TV.
Monstrous Possibility: An Invitation
to Literary Politics.
Requiem.
Diane Williams, *Excitability:*
Selected Stories.
Romancer Erector.
Douglas Woolf, *Wall to Wall.*
Ya! & John-Juan.
Jay Wright, *Polynomials and Pollen.*
The Presentable Art of Reading
Absence.
Philip Wylie, *Generation of Vipers.*
Marguerite Young, *Angel in the Forest.*
Miss MacIntosh, My Darling.
REYoung, *Unbabbling.*
Vlado Žabot, *The Succubus.*
Zoran Živković, *Hidden Camera.*
Louis Zukofsky, *Collected Fiction.*
Vitomil Zupan, *Minuet for Guitar.*
Scott Zwiren, *God Head.*

FOR A FULL LIST OF PUBLICATIONS, VISIT:
www.dalkeyarchive.com